CROWN OF CINDERS

THE IMDALIND SERIES, BOOK EIGHT

REBECCA ETHINGTON

IMDALIND PRESS

Published by Market Street Books LLC

Copyediting by C&D Editing
Production Management by Market Street Books

ISBN (print) 978-0-9964632-7-0
ISBN (e-book) 978-0-9964632-6-3
Printed in USA
This Edition, November 2016

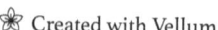 Created with Vellum

THE IMDALIND SERIES

BOOK ONE: *Kiss of Fire*
BOOK TWO: *Eyes of Ember*
BOOK THREE: *Scorched Treachery*
BOOK FOUR: *Soul of Flame*
BOOK FIVE: *Burnt Devotion*
BOOK SIX: *Brand of Betrayal*
BOOK SEVEN: *Dawn of Ash*
BOOK EIGHT: *Crown of Cinders*
BOOK NINE: *Ilyan*

This book is currently undergoing an expansion and edit. You will be able to upload a beautiful revision upon re-release.

Sign up for my newsletter and get alerted right when the updates go live!

For more information about what is happening and why, please visit my blog!

CONTENTS

1. Sain	1
2. Joclyn	19
3. Sain	48
4. Joclyn	63
5. Ryland	86
6. Joclyn	105
7. Sain	122
8. Jaromir	143
9. Dramin	157
10. Jaromir	174
11. Joclyn	196
12. Joclyn	218
13. Sain	234
14. Ovailia	251
15. Ovailia	264
16. Ryland	280
17. Wyn	289
18. Joclyn	306
19. Joclyn	320
20. Joclyn	329
21. Sain	344
22. Ovailia	356
23. Joclyn	369
24. Sain	391
25. Wyn	409
26. Ryland	423
27. Joclyn	436
28. Ilyan	444
29. Joclyn	449
30. Wyn	476
31. Ryland	492

32. Ovailia   517
33. Joclyn   530

Also by Rebecca Ethington   551
About the Author   553
Acknowledgments   555
Joclyn and Ilyan's Story is Now Complete   557

You gave this book a name.
So, I created a world.
May you get lost in its pages.

Love you, always.

1

SAIN

"I HAVE A JOB FOR YOU. Do it well, and I won't kill you. Fail and your life will end in a much more painful way than poor Edmund finally found."

The man Ovailia had spared cowered on the ground below me as I spoke, blood still dripping from my fingers, forming little pools of red by my feet. It was the red the man couldn't look away from.

The red matched the fluid seeping from the corpse behind me.

"Stand."

He didn't hesitate. He moved quickly, his eyes still on the pools of blood, unwilling to look at me.

"I want you to go and tell everyone what you saw here. Tell everyone of what Sain, the first of the Drak, really is. Can you do that?"

"Y-ye-yes ..."

Ovailia laughed as the man stuttered and wet himself in fear.

I smiled, my lips pulling away from my teeth as my eyes gleamed.

"Good. Then, when you are done, come back to me, and I'll have another little job for you. You have a new master now. Do you understand?"

A nod and then the man tore from the room, stumbling over his own feet in his attempt to escape me.

"Do you think he will do it?" Ovailia asked, coming so close behind me I could feel my magic roar in an attempt to reach her.

"Yes, I do. Now is when things really start to get interesting." Pulling Ovailia to me, I let my magic swell, moving it to reach her, realizing it wasn't her it wanted.

It wasn't her it craved.

It was sight. It was the world that was yet to be.

"Now is when everything gets real." With two strong hands against her collarbone, I pushed her away from me, watching her stumble on her heels in an attempt to find her balance.

I didn't care.

Allowing my magic to swell into sight, I saw the whispers of what was to come, shadows of what was about to happen. What needed to happen. I couldn't let that man go.

"Wait," I said to the man who was now down the hall, still trying to make his escape. My magic stretched out to him, wrapping around him and pulling him right back into the room.

I could hear his panicked screams due to the movement, could hear Ovailia's disgruntled complaints from being thrown around. But all I saw was black, the fear and anger of my two companions fading into the screams of another sort.

Of sight.

"See what I have done!" My own voice echoed inside my mind as the images solidified.

I watched the crowd of horrified Trpaslíks appear in the hall of council, a large stone room that hadn't been used in decades if not centuries. They looked at the corpse of the man I had destroyed, anger and fear clear on their face. One man yelled then another then another, and the sight began to shift to the same room. This time, it was full of bloodied bodies and bowed heads, Edmund's loyalists cleared from the wheat like the chaff they were.

Useless garbage.

My heart rate accelerated at the sight of that, at the knowledge of what had happened—what could have happened if I had sent Damek out into the hordes with news of my accomplishments.

A revolt.

I had to stomp it.

The sight began to shift again, fire moving within the hall of Imdalind as a child laughed and cried in the background. It was a clear image, but one I waved away. I didn't need to see

3

more. I already understood the path my sight wished me to take. I already understood what it wanted me to see.

The fire-drenched hallway faded to the dim room before me as the black left my eyes, some prophecy half-formed on my lips before I pushed it away, too.

Ovailia stood before me, still irate at my hasty banishment, her arms folded over her waist like a stubborn child.

"What is it?" she snapped, her head high as she watched me, making it clear she hadn't missed a moment of the sight. Knowing her, she had even tried to tap into it.

Luckily, the Black Water had been removed from her spine. I didn't need her knowing too much about what I was planning, about what was coming.

"Something wonderful," I said with a smile, taunting her as I stepped toward Edmund's last remaining guard, leaving bloody footprints behind me.

The silence of the room pressed against my chest as the sight's magic still reverberated inside me, loud and abrasive, the same image of the ignited hallway breaking through.

Just a flash of fire and smoke, and my heart stopped.

While I didn't know what I was seeing, I knew someone else who might.

Someone who shouldn't see any of this.

Edmund's dead eyes looked at me as my heart picked up, a sudden fear gripping me, the disgusting emotion far too real.

I hoped I wasn't too late.

I needed to stop her from seeing any of this.

Stop her from knowing what had happened.

I needed to put a block around my sight, a block around everything concerning me.

A Zámek.

The same magic had cursed Wyn. The same magic had been taught to Timothy by me in an attempt to kill her centuries before. This time, I would use it the way it was meant to be—to block a Drak's sight, to stop them from peeking into someone's life, into their fate.

Only powerful magic could cause such a wall. Although it would also block me from seeing into her fate, causing me to go into any upcoming battle blind, it was a risk I would have to take.

I needed to keep this from her. They couldn't know what had happened until the perfect moment.

Body tensing in hesitation, I closed my eyes, knowing how much exertion this was going to take.

A Zámek was not done often, if at all. And I already knew it would weaken my ability, weaken my sight. But for this, it was a risk I would have to take.

Heart pounding, eyes shut, I let my magic swell within me, all of my power pulling into me, against my heart that held it, against my lungs that breathed it.

Swelling inside of me, strong and powerful, it began to shake, the energy condensing in a wave of power and sound that moved into my bones, rattled my skull. I could already feel the shield beginning to form, hard as steel, as dark as

5

death. It was heavy enough to keep out even the most powerful magic of sight, to keep the future and past contained within me so that only I could see.

"What are you doing?" Ovailia snapped from beside me, her voice oddly distanced over the rumbling static that was filling my mind. "Sain, what do you see?"

Ignoring her, I focused on the power that seemed moments from exploding out of me. The rumbling grew worse until I was convinced the vibrating I felt moving inside me was visible from the outside. I half-expected Ovailia to scream in worry, but there was nothing except silence, nothing except my strained breathing as the iron-clad shield began to move away from me, stretching past the caves and over the fields that surrounded us, butting right up against the large shield Edmund had placed over them all.

Heaving with the effort, I kept myself upright, determined not to show the weakness the Zámek had on me, knowing I could easily pass out from the effort.

Timothy had almost killed himself, and he had spent a month putting it in place.

"Sain?" she asked again as I opened my eyes to glare at her. "What's going on? What are you doing?"

"I am securing your future," I said with a smile, the hidden meaning humorous to me.

Ovailia narrowed her eyes before looking away, obviously not happy with the response yet unwilling to pursue it any further.

I had more exhilarating things to deal with.

"You," I snarled, aware that I wasn't certain of his name, although it wasn't something I would remedy. A man without a name was more valuable than a man who clung to a weak identity.

"Y ... yes?" He lifted his head slowly, his body shaking as he pulled himself back to his feet, his head bowed in humility.

It wasn't respect he was showing, however; it was fear. His focus was still fixed on the drying blood that coated my skin, that dripped from my disheveled beard, on the bright red footprints trailing behind me, on the body of his former master, and on Edmund's guards who littered the room in a garden of death.

It was the remains of Edmund that he stared at the most, however. The air was saturated with the scent of his charred body. You couldn't ignore it was there.

You couldn't ignore what had happened.

"*Yes?*" I repeated the response with a hiss, my eyebrows lifting.

Even if the warning in my voice hadn't startled him, I was sure that did.

"Yes, master," he amended quickly, his body shaking in fear, the anxiety making it difficult for him to stand. He continually shifted his feet, his hands flexing and grabbing at the air as if it would somehow support him.

"Do it," I whispered, taking another step toward him, leaving another damp and sticky bloody print behind me. "Bow."

He didn't hesitate to fall to the ground, his hands and arms tucked underneath him as he quivered in a pathetic show of reverence. He looked like nothing more than the disgusting gelatin the mortals would eat.

This would not do.

"No, you idiot. I said bow, not cower."

He shivered, the wobbling mass vibrating before me as my magic rushed from me and wrapped around him, infecting him, controlling him, contorting him into a form more acceptable for someone of my stature.

He screamed out in fear and pain as I contorted him, his arms twisting into unnatural positions before I tucked them underneath his torso, twisting him into the perfect form.

"Lovely," I whispered, stepping toward him as his screams faded to pained whimpers. "That is a bow."

"Yes, master," he repeated once more, his voice stronger, as if the quivering would protect him from what was coming.

"I have changed my mind," I began as I walked closer still, more bloody footprints appearing in his line of sight. "I have seen what is coming, and I have a new job for you."

He jerked a bit, obviously confused and needing some kind of eye contact to verify what I had said.

My magic flared once in warning, jerking him back to the position I had placed him in, a small whimper of pain seeping from his throat.

"I no longer wish for you to tell them what has happened here. I wish for them to see it. I *want* them to see." Flashes of the sight I'd had filled me, the screams and blood echoing inside my mind.

Turning toward Ovailia, I couldn't stop the smile, knowing her part in all of this made it all the sweeter. She watched me intently, still not pulling herself away from the remains of her father.

"Tell them all," I continued, the dried blood on my face pulling and cracking as I smiled toward the quivering mass below me. "Trpaslíks and Chosen are to gather in the old council hall. Tell them their *master* has an announcement to make, nothing more."

I stood, waiting, focused on the pathetic man, on the quiver in his spine.

He said nothing. He did nothing except shiver.

I could feel my temper rise from being ignored, my magic heating and rising from the insubordination.

"Can you do that?" The words hissed past my teeth, and he shivered more, his head wobbling in what I assumed was a nod.

It didn't matter. It wasn't good enough. I did not have to put up with this type of behavior anymore. Never again. I wasn't going to let him get away with it.

"I don't appreciate being left waiting," I snapped, and his back jerked as my magic wound around him once more, lifting him into the air with a jolt before slamming him against the far wall. Pictures rattled with the impact, a flurry of dust and tiny rocks falling from the ceiling as I jerked them free from the crevices they had been hiding in for thousands of years.

Ovailia shrieked in surprise behind me, but I didn't turn, my focus remaining on the whimpering man whose bloodshot eyes were wide as I controlled him in the one way I knew how—with fear.

"I gave you a command, and I expect it to be carried out with perfect precision. Tell no one of what you have seen. Instead, instruct them in what their king has asked."

King.

My heart was light with the use of the word on my own tongue. My smile so wide that the man before me shuddered, nodding his head furiously in obedience, the words of acceptance and understanding lost in the buzzing that now filled my ears.

After I dropped the man from the wall with one twitch of my magic, he scuttled away, desperate to do what had been demanded, desperate to comply before it was his own flesh that was burned. I, however, remained frozen in place, my eyes trained on the rough stone of the wall, on the streaks of faded blood Damek had left behind, on the word that was echoing on repeat.

King.

"What did you see, Sain?" Ovailia asked from behind me. I didn't even look at her. "What are you planning?"

King.

"I plan nothing," I snapped, still not looking at her, the word continuing to repeat within me. "It is the magic of the earth that lays my path. I am simply wise enough to follow."

Years of plotting, of manipulating, of using everyone around me ... After years of carefully setting the stage, I had finally accomplished what I had set out to do.

I was king once again after being stripped of my ruling power so many centuries before. And soon, everyone would know. Soon, everyone would bow to me as they had before, as they had for centuries.

I was one of the first.

I deserved nothing less.

And I had regained it.

Now, all that was left was to destroy the last remaining people who could take away this role. The last people who could challenge me: Joclyn, Ilyan, Wyn, perhaps even Ryland if he ever conquered the madness Edmund had given him.

Four people were all that were left in my way. And I would make them pay, for fighting me, for their parents' mistake of removing me from the role I had been born to fill.

I had come from the mud. The earth had created me. I was the only one suited to rule them, the only one who could.

"King," I said aloud, pulling my focus away from the wall and to the twisted charred corpse that Ovailia stood beside, her back straight and lips pursed as though she were guarding him.

Foolish girl, guarding the man she had killed.

Sending an irritated glance at the woman in question, I walked right past her, bee-lining for the body of the former. I almost expected her to step between me and my prey, but she remained still, her arms folded, lips pursed, and one long finger tapping against her forearm like a metronome.

"Is that what you wanted?" she asked, her voice filled with the same false sugar she had never quite mastered.

My face twisted into a scowl at the deceptive quality in it.

"To be king?"

Nostrils flaring in an effort to control my temper, I turned toward her. Ice ran down my spine as anger shook inside me due to her ignorance while she stood frozen over the body of her father, the smell of smoke surrounding us.

"I was king, Ovailia. I was the leader of these people. I should have never been removed from that role." I scowled, but she didn't so much as flinch at the anger.

"With the first four holders of magic, you mean?" She remained still, that finger still tapping, her eyes widening in some kind of disbelief.

My anger erupted at her ignorance. A loud laugh broke past the chill in the room as my magic surged, bright and powerful. Long, winding ribbons of yellow and gold trailed from me, dancing through the air before falling to the ground and wrapping around the remains of Edmund. Smoke and ash filled the air as I shifted him, his dead weight sagging and rolling around as I removed the bathrobe he still wore. The white cotton was stained with his blood, singed from the same flames that had devoured him.

"The four were the true rulers of these people. We were the kings and queens of this land." I chuckled at the memory, the sound haunting as the bathrobe came free from the charred remains. The body fell to the ground in a plume of black ash that fell over us like snow.

Disgust filled Ovailia's face as I felt her magic trill across the air, a shield keeping the ashes of her father off her.

I, however, let them fall. I let them cover me as I snagged the robe gently from the air, the fabric wet and crusty as the blood began to dry.

"You mean my grandmother." It was a statement, a forgotten connection hitting me full in the face.

Her grandmother.

The same power of the first that I had worked to destroy was flowing through her veins, as it was Ilyan's. The addition of Edmund's Chosen blood made them powerhouses that had hindered my accomplishments for far too long. Powerhouses were too big of a liability.

"Yes, your grandmother," I mused, holding the robe gently in my hands as I took a step toward her, ash falling from my hair and shoulders with the movement. "How unfortunate."

"And why is that unfortunate?" she snapped, her voice strong, though I could sense the tiniest shake behind it.

"No reason," I said with a smile, the icy look making her flinch for the first time.

Oh, well. I supposed I would have to add her to my list. Not that I hadn't already intended to kill her after I had gotten my use of her. Now, it would have to be a bit sooner than expected.

Ilyan, Joclyn, Wyn, Ryland, and Ovailia. Thank all that I had already disposed of Edmund's little puppet Míra in the pile of corpses, leaving Ilyan to set her aflame. The child had still borne Edmund's Štít, which would not have died with his death.

The last of his magic, now I had to dispose of the last remains.

"All the other four are dead now," I hissed, moving the robe from my arms and letting the blood drip across the air as I threw it over my shoulders, the damp fabric heavy. "I am the only one left, the only one fit to sit in this role."

"The role of the blood-soaked king?"

"Yes." My smile grew, the title fitting. "With a robe of blood and a crown of cinders, I leave death in my wake."

"And hell before." Ovailia stepped toward me, the tap of her heels against the ash sounding like bells. "You are the devil this world needs."

A flash of the sight I'd had in the cathedral in Prague caused me to flinch: the white room, the voice of the woman. It blinded me, the pressure of her voice splitting my head.

Pushing the imagery and memory aside, I attempted to ignore the sudden *boom* of my heart that had exploded in my chest.

"No, darling," I growled, pressing down on the sudden and despicable emotion, letting my anger and power smother it. "I *am* hell. It is the devil who searches for me."

I expected her to flinch from the confession, flinch from the smile I fixed her with, but she persisted, her trademark glare in place as she casually brushed her hair behind her ear, her lithe fingers delicate in the motion.

Beautiful.

Intoxicating.

Lustful.

I swallowed, feeling my magic swell with the motion, trying to push itself beyond my skin to reach out to hers, to find hers.

I held it back, not wanting to feel the sweet need of her magic, not wanting to lose control. Not with her, not now.

I had a feeling, with the smile she now had, she knew exactly what she was doing.

"Maybe *I* am the devil."

"Then I will destroy you, Ovailia. Just like all the others."

It was a threat, but she smiled, her breasts heaving as she moved closer, as though she couldn't keep herself away from the danger that was dripping from my skin.

"Try."

I hadn't expected the word. I hadn't expected the weight behind it. My perfectly planned rebuttal stalled on my tongue, my magic tangling with hers in a heightened lust the threat gave me.

I swallowed, and she smiled, obviously sensing the control she had over me.

Perhaps she was the devil.

I would have to turn her skin as red as her father's. And soon.

The imagery of that simple thought was beautiful.

"You killed them, too." She already knew the answer. Not that it was that difficult to piece together after everything she had seen. Of course, she wasn't completely right, and I wouldn't let her know that.

Yes, I had killed two of them, but the third, that repulsive Vilỳ, had been dealt with by Edmund before I could. Imprisoning him, using him to infect himself and to infect his son, that idiotic boy who had released it, leaving him to infect my own daughter.

That little piece of information was too important to get out. If Ovailia knew how much power flowed within my dratted child, I was convinced I would lose her allegiance. She was too valuable of a weapon to lose.

I needed her ... for now.

"You killed them all," she whispered, moving closer as the flutter of her words moved over my skin.

"I did," I admitted openly.

Her smile grew as mine did, the room silent and still as we faced each other.

The pulse of my magic was becoming unsteady. I needed to put a stop to it.

"I killed your grandmother," I whispered back, my voice soft, while the words were hostile. "I stopped her heart. I devoured her magic like I did to your darling daddy."

Her eyes clouded over as she flinched at my verbal assault, stepping back as I stepped closer, a wicked grin now stretching my lips, letting my teeth gleam in the dimly lit room.

Her chest heaved from either the proximity or with the words; I wasn't sure which. She could either kiss me or attack me. I would gladly accept either.

"Are you sure you want to be the devil?" I prodded, taking yet another step toward her, expecting her to step away again.

She held her ground, her blue eyes hardening into the emotionless steel that was so common for her.

"I have already killed many who thought they could rule the hell that I am."

Her lips pulled into a tight line, her nostrils flaring as she attempted to control her breathing, to control her anger. The rage of her magic was strong as it flew through the air, obviously moments away from attacking. I wished she would.

The imagery of her blood flowing over my hands to join her father's was as delicious as it was frightening.

I couldn't kill her yet, though. This emotional warfare would have to suffice for now.

"Will you be the devil, or will you help me harness hell?" My chest swelled, my heart pounding delicately from the excitement of the game I had entangled her in. The trap was so perfectly placed that, no matter which step she took, she would be trapped.

She knew it, too, judging by the hatred that started to creep into the beautiful blue of her eyes.

It made me want to kiss her more.

To kill her as I did.

Love, lust, and death traveled hand in hand.

"Do you serve me?"

"I do serve you, Sain," she whispered, her voice strong, yet I could hear the work it took to disguise the shake behind it.

"Don't forget that, my beautiful creature." I wrapped my hand around her waist, pulling her to me, my hand strong as I let my magic press against her skin.

The anger in her eyes dissipated with the contact.

My own desire for her death faded right alongside.

She melted into me, lust taking control and firmly securing my control over her. This game of cat and mouse had begun.

Or rather, a game of heaven and hell.

It would be a matter of time before she showed me the devil she truly was.

It was then I would destroy her.

2

JOCLYN

"Twins?" I couldn't get the sound of disbelief out of my voice. The loud scoff was clear, echoing in the alley where we had all congregated. The damp walls and shadows attempted to swallow it whole, but the disbelief was that loud.

"Twins? Really? Congrats! I'm planning your baby shower, Jos," Wyn said, jumping up and down like a spastic teen. "I've always wanted a niece ... or two. I could show them the world and entertain them for hours with the hole in my hand." She pulled the glove off, wiggling her finger through the open space the Soul's Blade had left behind after her impalement, a mad grin on her face. "They'll love it," she said as she looked at me through the large, circular hole.

"Shut up, Wyn," I snapped, attempting to throw her arm off me, beating away the bright red blush I was cursed with simultaneously. "And put your glove back on while you're at it," I added, knowing she loved to show that off every chance she got. I wished it didn't make my stomach turn. Leave it to her to find pure joy in random mutilation.

Ilyan's lips twitched into what I knew was a hidden smile. Meanwhile, Wyn dissolved into a fit of giggles, leaning over a large fern that was nestled up against the tall stone wall of the alley Ilyan had pulled us all into. I could hear Risha reprimand her, but I tuned them out. I was already the shade of a tomato. I didn't need to make that any worse.

"What do you mean *the kids* are twins?" I asked again, the scoff now resorting to a squeak of embarrassment. At least Ilyan did better to disguise his smile this time.

"I mean that Jaromir is claiming Míra is his twin, and she is saying the same thing," Ilyan said.

Wyn's giggles finally subsided, and Risha looked up from the distraction, thoroughly annoyed. Ryland, on the other hand, looked as red as I did and possibly like he had forgotten how to breathe.

I stepped closer to Ilyan. "And we know they are telling the truth because ..." I prompted.

"Seeing as they both have identical stories about upbringing and are currently reminiscing about a St. Bernard named Bruno, I would think the consensus is that they are not lying. Have you ever heard him speak of a sister, Ryland?" Ilyan asked his brother, hoping for backup.

"No." Ry's curls bounced with a shake of his head. "Then again, he wouldn't talk about his family. He always closed up like a clam when family was mentioned."

"So we have no way of knowing other than what we are witnessing right now," Ilyan spoke clinically, like he was a doctor delivering unfortunate news about a growth on the bottom of my foot.

I do not sound like a doctor, and you do not have a growth on your foot. Ilyan's voice filled my mind without a trace of amusement. He looked at me with a lifted brow, his bright blue eyes a bit wider than normal.

His reaction was out of place enough that I knew something was up, something more than what he was telling me.

"All you need is a lab coat," I prodded, waiting for the knot in his expression to calm from the joke. His scowl, however, increased.

What is going on, Ilyan? I asked, the warning lights in my mind going off as I pressed my magic into his, expecting the onslaught of thoughts and emotions, but I only came face to face with a buzzing, the fear and panic that had gripped him blending together into violent noise.

Nothing serious, he replied. The anxiety in his voice didn't exactly spell relief.

I tensed further, fixing him with a sidelong glance as Wyn pulled at my attention.

"The peanut gallery is going to have a field day with this, Jos," Wyn began as she threw her arm around me, careful not to make any skin-to-skin contact, the unspoken rule since we had somehow imploded part of the cathedral.

I knew the move was meant to calm me—what with the subject matter and all—but the tension of Ilyan's secrecy was increasing. The weight of Wyn's arm on my shoulders wasn't helping with that. I already felt a need to attack her. At least in jest.

"The king and his crazy bride having twins."

Okay, maybe merely for the sake of attacking her.

"I am not crazy," I grumbled, the jab about twins not affecting me for once. Of course, I hated being reminded of the whole mess that Sain had left for me. It wasn't exactly *fun* being thought of as disturbed by the people you were somehow supposed to lead.

"Well, not in the way any of them seem to believe, anyway." Wyn's giggles returned with triumph as she jumped from me to Risha and Ryland. Bouncing between us like a ten year old, she threw her arms around them like some goony best friend, arms over both their shoulders. She pushed them apart, oblivious of the magnetic dance those two were always practicing, even though she wasn't. She never missed anything. I wished she wouldn't bring this one up quite so much.

Was I happy for Ryland? Yes.

It didn't mean I wanted to deduce the number of children they would have or dissect the nature of their bonding ceremony. The whole thing made me a tad uncomfortable.

Shaking my head like Bruno the St. Bernard, I pushed the thoughts from my mind, squishing my face together in an attempt to get myself—and everyone else, for that matter—back on track.

"Is no one else concerned with the ridiculousness of these claims?" I stepped forward, the sound of rocks crunching against stones echoing oddly around the enclosed space.

"You mean about the twins?" Wyn began. With one look, I shut her up, and the playful best friend vanished, replaced by the cold-hearted assassin in less than a second. "You mean that the girl we pulled out of a pile of dead corpses Sain created just so happens to be the twin sister to the boy you and Ilyan saved when Edmund's damn rats were flying around the city, destroying everyone and poisoning my boyfriend slash fiancé slash baby's daddy slash love of my life?"

"Yeah, that." Now it was my turn to restrain the giggles. Who knew Wyn could talk so fast?

"Nope," she continued, dropping her arms from Ryland and Risha, both of which had looked uncomfortable and now grateful for the escape. "Weirder things have happened, like having Edmund's son's best friend slash the Silnỳ also being Sain's daughter slash the one everyone was looking for, for like, five hundred years or something."

"Why is everything slashed?" Ryland chuckled from behind her, running his hand through his curls in obvious confusion. "I, for one, think my former best friend slash sister-in-law has a point."

Wyn snickered at the response, smashing her fist into his in triumph. "Bones."

"Why is it former?" I questioned, exasperated, and pursed my lips, grateful when Ilyan wrapped his arm around my waist before I could do anything more juvenile. I could already feel my magic prickle in irritation. A foot stomp wasn't that far away.

"If we could get back to the children."

"I think the children have already taken over the conversation, Ilyan," Risha snarled, folding her arms over her waist as she attempted to help Ilyan take control of the conversation.

Unfortunately, she had picked the wrong way to do this.

"Harsh, Risha." The playful joy was gone from Wyn. "I'm several hundred years older than you, and I don't think you want to be referring to your queen or your boyfriend as kids."

If I had been drinking, I was convinced the liquid would have covered Risha in a glorious shower. As it was, I coughed, all air sucked from my lungs in a very un-queenly fashion.

Ryland turned a brighter shade of red than I had, his jaw snapping open and shut.

"We have much bigger problems," Ilyan interrupted, his voice a powerful bolt of energy as he spoke in Czech. It crashed off the stone in the tiny alleyway, the infirmary that Jaromir and Míra were closeted up in echoing the sound. "Whether those children are twins or not."

"Problems?" The single word left my chest in a gasp as the weight of Ilyan's emotions finally left the buzzing hive of panic and pressed against my mind in a rush, the intensity painful.

Ilyan! I spat into his mind, fixing him with a look of concern I knew wouldn't go unnoticed by those around us. *What is it?*

Sadness crossed his eyes before the memory flashed into mine. One of the healers had told him about what he had found inside the girl's chest, about what they thought it was, unable to tell for certain.

Even with that little bit of information, I already knew.

The reality was ice and fear, winding up my spine.

"No," I gasped, my mind running the gambit of what this could mean. The same worries and concerns I could feel in Ilyan echoed inside me.

"Huh?" All sign of humor was gone from Wyn now. Her face twisted up as she looked between us. "Can we please not use the whole internal mind jabber right now? Your faces are kind of freaking me out."

I turned toward her, not wanting to break the news that would affect her more than it had me. Edmund had done the same to her brother, after all.

Ilyan nodded once before stepping into the center of the small circle, his long braid falling down the center of his back. The long, golden ribbon he wore extended to his toes. My own wound throughout the intricate braid he had given me this morning. I wished the braid I had placed in his hair could match. Thank goodness Ilyan was a patient teacher. I would get there.

"They have found something near her heart, similar to where Edmund placed his Štít within Cail." Ilyan's voice was even and powerful as he addressed the four of us. I could feel his power ripple off him, the energy from him seeping into me.

"Edmund put a Štít in a child?" Wyn said with a snap, her magic moving amidst the confined space, drowning me. "Again?"

I gasped at the intensity, at the anger that had weaved its way around it, steeling my magic in preparation for who knew what. I was also aware I couldn't take her on if it came to that.

The whole "explode on contact" thing was going to be irritating after a while.

"No, Wyn, Edmund put a Štít in a weapon." Ryland's voice was a death knell as he stared into the darkness of the alley somewhere over my head, his eyes so shaded my heart skipped a beat. A jolt of electricity moved within me as my mind went to the exact same place as his. To the same place that little girl had come from: the hell that Edmund had put inside our minds. "It wasn't a coincidence," Ryland continued, his voice pinched as he narrowed his eyes on the alley behind us, as if the overgrown passage between the hospital and outer wall had offended him. "Father sent her here. I've seen this before," His voice was still a hollow shell, although he was in control of himself far more than I had seen him lately when concerning his father.

"So have I," Wyn admitted, all signs of the goofball teenager gone now. "It was one of the first things we did before I killed the Drak—put a Štít in one of the younger ones ... took control."

I shuddered and fought the need to step behind Ilyan. Instead, I straightened my spine and gritted my teeth in anxious worry. It was something unmissed by Ilyan who turned toward me, a small smile playing on his lips while his eyes danced with pride. The same emotion circled into each of us before the concern came back ten-fold.

"That's more than a problem, Ilyan." Risha's eyes were hard as she came to stand beside Ryland, her shoulder pressing against his in what I was convinced was a comforting move. His eyes calmed at the contact. "That's a freaking explosion."

"She hasn't exploded yet." Ilyan sighed, turning to each of us, his eyes hard with the volatile anger that was so normal for him as of late. "Besides, I'm not sure she can."

"What do you mean?" Ryland asked, the darkness fading from his eyes.

"It appears to be a Štít, and it is in the same place as Edmund placed it inside of Cail. It is the right size, but it's a shell, a hollow void. There is nothing there."

Everyone looked at Ilyan in confusion. His jaw was a tight line as his mind moved around mine, a million questions flooding me as he tried to process and understand what that meant.

"A hollow Štít?" Wyn asked, writhing her hands one over the other, her eyes narrowed in pain. "As in, there is no magic in it? He sure likes to poke holes in things."

"Not that we can tell." It was then that he looked at me, his eyes sad and apologetic, the hidden remainder of his thoughts moving through me.

"No," I gasped, understanding what was needed of me.

His apology grew deeper.

Unwanted panic rose up in my chest, bitter as bile. I gritted my teeth as I turned from him, staring into the darkness as Ryland had done before, the same chill of my past running over me.

Haunting me.

I knew it was an overreaction. I had faced Edmund head to head. I had prepared myself to kill him.

And I would.

But feeling his magic inside of me ... "I'd rather gouge my eyes out than feel his magic again," I said aloud, the grumble of irritation strong.

You know his magic better than anyone, můj kamarád. Even me. You can see what I might have missed.

"That seems kind of excessive." Wyn leaned against the wall I was staring at in an attempt to break my death stare. "Your eyes are far too beautiful for gouging. Take it from someone who has a gouging injury, they hurt. I wouldn't recommend it. Besides, I have no idea if this gouging is justified because you are doing it again."

"Doing what?" I snapped, trying to ignore the shivers of my magic that were vibrating inside me, the hunger to destroy the man in question clear.

At least the residual panic at the thought of feeling his magic was leaving. I hated when those past scars made themselves known.

"Secret mind swapping. Again. Pass the Kool-Aid, why don't you? Then at least everyone can join in."

When I pulled my focus away from the nothing, her small, smug face came into view, her eyebrows lifted in playful prodding.

"He wants me to see if I can find Edmund's magic inside of her." I filled in the gaps with a snap, still too frustrated to give into her oddities.

"Well, then." All the joy was sucked out of Wyn's voice now, the playfulness gone again. "Gouge away. Although, I wouldn't suggest using a Soul's Blade. Those things sting." She waved her hand absently before moving away, her short, auburn hair bouncing in the shadows.

At least Wyn understood how horrifying a proposition Ilyan had put in front of me.

I know you can do this. Ilyan's hand was soft against my back as he came up behind me, the weight of his palm strong.

I know I can, too. It doesn't mean I want to. As I leaned into him, he turned us back toward the others, the three of them standing in the shadows with differing looks of confusion and anger covering their faces.

"I cannot feel anything within the void, but that does not mean it is empty. We have all seen Edmund do worse," Ilyan announced, pulling me closer to him. "I need Joclyn and Ryland to meet with the children to see what information they can glean, what Joclyn can find."

"Pass the eye-gouger," Ryland grumbled, the same darkness taking over his eyes again. "Not that I have anything against this plan, but do you really think it's wise, Ilyan? You know what Edmund's magic does to me."

"To both of us," I added with a grumble.

"And the plot thickens," Wyn said with a smile, throwing her arm around Ryland and pushing the very shocked Risha out of the way. "I think I need to be there, too, Ilyan. You know, for moral support."

"As far as I see it, Wynifred, you are still on probation, so don't push your luck." Ilyan's voice was a snap, but Wyn didn't seem to mind.

She waved him off, her eyes smiling as she turned toward Risha, who was obviously not amused with her antics.

"I rescue the king from a deadly corpse army, and this is my thanks? I might be as despised as Sain made Joclyn out to be. No offense."

"None taken," I said.

"Wynifred," Risha began, her voice hard as she attempted to hold the same power Ilyan held over my somewhat out of control best friend.

Wyn looked at her as though she were a weird teacher's pet.

"It's time you listened to your leader."

"Why? Is he going to assimilate me or something? Because I am pretty sure he knows that won't work."

It was all but impossible to hold back a snicker, especially with Ilyan's hidden laugh echoing inside my head.

His fingers pressed into my back. *I have told Risha before not to play with fire ...*

Maybe she has to get burned first, I replied, watching Wyn and Risha engage in some sort of epic staring contest, only to have my focus pulled away by familiar broad shoulders.

"Joclyn." Ryland's voice was a reverberation that pulled me past the dark and right to him, the emerging cat-fight forgotten. His rugby muscles twitched as his lips pulled into a half-smile. "You ready for this?"

I stiffened. "Can you ever be ready for something like this?"

I tried very hard to ignore the way my spine had instantly stiffened. It wasn't something Ilyan was going to ignore.

Ilyan stepped beside me, towering over his brother and me as he pulled me against him again. "Just keep those pretty eyes where they belong, and I think we will all be happy."

"Agreed," Ryland responded far too quickly. Luckily, Ilyan chose to ignore it.

"I need you to investigate the Štít. See if it is, indeed, a Štít and whose magic is controlling it."

I nodded once at Ilyan's request. It seemed simple enough, though I already knew it wouldn't be.

"Ryland knows Jaromir well enough that he should be able to put them at ease. Find out as much as you can … *See* if you can."

"So, as much info as possible," Ryland recapped, tapping his fingers against his hip bone as he mentally counted. "Keep the kids calm, check for magic, and Joclyn can do her Drak mumbo-jumbo."

"It's not mumbo-jumbo, Ry," I interjected.

He opted not to hear me.

"Oh! And not killing each other," he continued, the afterthought sitting in my gut like a stone. "Definitely cannot kill each other."

"That would be preferable." Ilyan's fingers tightened against my waist.

Don't worry, Ilyan.

"I promise not to kill you," Ry said directly to me, his face twisted in an odd humor.

"I promise not to lose control and make friends with rats." I couldn't help it. Try as I might to get the words out with a straight face, I didn't quite make it. The sound of my laugh pulled the focus from the bickering old ladies, and Ryland's own chuckle followed behind.

Ilyan looked concerned, his face contorted in a frown as he pulled the memory out of my head, his concern and sadness attempting to drown me.

"Perhaps Wyn was right," Ilyan said. "Maybe this is a bad idea."

Everything will be fine, I reassured him, the tiniest bit of self-doubt still trying to move into a paralyzing fear. However, I wouldn't let it. Even Ilyan's sudden worry wasn't enough to let me second-guess myself. *If anything happens, I can probably subdue him* and *put on a puppet show for the kids before you get there.*

"A puppet show, huh?" Ilyan taunted, the worry fading away and making room for the smothering pride I was so used to from him. "Like *Punch and Judy*?"

I was lucky to get the reference, especially with the way looking at him was making my head spin, my stomach swirling pleasantly.

"Yes, but without all the violence."

My lips extended into a wide smile as I lifted myself onto my tiptoes. His eyes danced as I pressed my lips to his, his arm winding around my back to pull me against him. He held me there as he deepened the kiss, tugging the long ribbon in my hair to lift my chin toward him.

"Excuse me," Ryland snapped, my stomach tying itself up into immediate knots. "I'm standing right here."

I had obviously forgotten.

Ilyan, on the other hand, had not.

He chuckled darkly, one hand still wound around my waist as he gazed down at me, his eyes soft, fingers a gentle caress against the side of my face. I, on the other hand, looked like I was about to be bowled over by a herd of wild buffalo. My heart definitely felt like that was imminent with the way it was thundering.

"I am aware, brother," Ilyan said, pushing some of the strands of hair that had come free from the braid behind my ear, his eyes locked with mine. "I felt like you needed a small reminder that you won't, in fact, kill Joclyn over small triggers. You are stronger than the crap he infected you with, both of you."

Ryland's jaw dropped in shock. I almost expected him to explode in frustration. Hell, I almost wanted to from being used in that way, but it had been a *really* good kiss.

The shock began to fade away as Ryland laughed.

Wyn bounced over to us at the sound, Risha sulking behind. Wyn was obviously ready to absorb whatever drama she had missed. However, Ryland kept laughing, Ilyan joining him while I stood sandwiched between them in confusion.

"Thank you, brother," Ryland said around his laugh, his hand soft against my shoulder as he pried me away from

Ilyan; the man in question chuckling as his brother pulled me out of the alley.

"We'll be back," he said with a wave of his hand.

I stumbled backward after him, my focus drifting between Wyn and Ilyan, both of whom were looking at me with varying levels of confusion and enjoyment.

I should be mad at you, I growled into Ilyan's mind.

The widening smile on his face was the last thing I saw as the alley swallowed them, the stone wall and large wooden door of the hospital sliding before me like a stage prop.

But you aren't, mi lasko. You love me too much.

Hearing those tender words inside my mind set off a warm soap bubble of joy inside me. It rattled my bones in a pleasant way that made me long to wrap myself up in it.

I do, Ilyan. I love you.

As I love you, my darling. His magic flooded me with his words, so dear, so warm and pure that I missed Ryland releasing me from his grip.

I came back to my senses as he waved his big hand in front of me.

"Sorry to interrupt the love fest, but we do actually have a job." Ryland stepped away from me, moving toward the door with a light step. If it weren't for the way his fists kept clenching and unclenching—one of his tells—I would say he was looking forward to this.

"What love fest?" I tried very hard to keep the guilt out of my voice as I followed him up the stairs, my worn sneakers squeaking against the stone.

Ryland turned, a sly smile on his face before he turned away. His shoulders tensed as he pushed the door open. "It's painted on your face, Jos. It's either you and Ilyan ogling each other, or you're dreaming of a hamburger."

"Ew."

"What do you mean, *ew*? Sometimes, I wonder what you've done with my best friend." Laden with truth and loss, his words hung between us as we began to move across the long, darkened room.

The tall windows that lined the space were covered with curtains so thick they kept the red light away. I could almost convince myself we had stepped back into reality.

Just my best friend and I, off on some epic adventure.

With that and the bright white lanterns that hung from the ceiling, everything in here looked almost normal, like a regular hospital ... if that hospital were in eighteenth-century France.

The old metal-framed beds sat at regular intervals. The healing Chosen were curled up in white linens, moaning and groaning, not an IV bag or EKG machine to be seen. Just glass bottles of oddly colored medicines and bowls of assorted dried plants.

Despite the archaic nature, it was all so normal.

"You used to love hamburgers."

Except for that, I could almost believe it.

"I used to not be a Drak, either." I sighed, trying my hardest not to look at the people in the beds we passed. "Between your brothers, my brother, and my pain in the behind father—"

"Everything changed." Ryland stopped in place as he finished my sentence, his eyes focused on the children ahead of us. Something more than fear and loss was etched in his eyes.

They sat, Míra tucked into one of the many iron beds, Jaromir sitting against the footboard, jabbering and laughing as if they weren't locked up in a healing ward stuffed in the middle of a war.

Watching them, I waited for Ry to move, but he stayed still, frozen in a world I wasn't convinced I belonged in anymore.

"Ry?" I asked after a minute, my heart rate beginning to pick up in fear. Everything about him seemed normal, but that didn't mean he wasn't going to turn on me and attack.

Ilyan, sensing my worry, pressed his magic into me via our connection, the warmth flooding me in an attempt to settle my fear. But there wasn't any fear, only worry about what Ryland was going to do. My brain made battle plans about how to restrain him without hurting too many of the people around us.

"You're a queen," Ryland said to break the silence, my heart tensed at once.

As if I needed a reminder that I didn't fit.

The words were so simple it should have been calming, but he was still frozen in dread, his eyes gazing into nothing. Even his magic had disappeared from my radar.

I hated when he did that. It was a nice parlor trick his father had left him with.

"We've been over this, Ry." I was still hesitant to say much, my magic prickling more in preparation.

"No, I mean, you are a queen." He finally pulled out of his stupor, spinning to face me. The gaunt nothing had left his face, and a brilliant eager light had taken its place. Still, I couldn't relax, even though Ilyan had seemed to. Whatever he was viewing through my eyes had put him at ease.

It would be nice if he would share some of that calm, but he was silent.

"Yes."

"Little girls love queens. They love princesses."

Everything fell into place as Ryland wrapped his hands around my shoulders, shaking me slightly in his excitement.

I could feel the confusion slip from my scowl. Either that or it was the brain damage from being jostled around.

"So, I should be a queen? Like, in a theme park where little girls line up in pretty dresses and get signatures and pictures?"

Ryland nodded, obviously proud of his deduction.

Ugh.

"I should have worn one of my council dresses." It was a grumble of irritation that Ryland chuckled at. He knew my hatred for dresses better than anyone.

I wasn't sure I would get into a dress, anyway, but I knew that frayed jeans and blood-stained sneakers weren't going to cut it. Ryland, however, didn't seem to care. He smiled eagerly and stepped away, jogging toward the kids in his excitement.

"Jaromir!" he yelled, jerking awake several of the Chosen. Jaromir turned, his face breaking out into the biggest smile I had ever seen, causing the mark on his cheek to squish together.

With a rush, he ran from the bed to tackle-hug Ryland around the waist.

"I heard you have news for me," Ryland said.

"The best news!" the kid erupted, grabbing Ryland's hand and dragging him toward the girl who still sat on the bed, blonde hair braided down her back, face wilting in what I assumed was fear. "This is my sister."

"Hello, Míra," Ryland whispered, his big, meaty hand wrapping around the girl's tiny one, his magic surging from the contact. I was confident he was laying the foundation for what I needed to do. "It's so nice to meet you. Welcome to our home. We are so glad you are safe."

"So am I. It was so scary out there," the little girl squeaked, her response hesitant and worrisome.

I could tell she was attempting to look brave, to look innocent. The shake in her voice was perfect, the way her shoulders pulled into her ears carefully done.

It was almost overdone, a perfect replica of another deceptive man I was related to.

That might be why I saw right through her.

I saw through the wide eyes and looked into the darkness

that haunted her. I looked past the innocence in her voice and heard the malicious voice that had haunted my dreams for so long. I heard the wickedness that had hunted me in shadows.

I would love to say I heard it because of what Ilyan had said, because I knew there was a Štít inside of her, but one look to Ryland and I knew I wasn't alone.

I wasn't the only one who had heard it. I saw his back stiffen, freezing him in place, his hand still wrapped around the little girl's as his muscles knit together. I could almost hear his mind buzzing with anxiety, my own spiking in fear of what seemed like an imminent attack.

So, you hear it as well? Ilyan whispered into my mind, the words lost amongst the panic I was fighting.

Before my magic could awaken into a flood, however, Ryland shivered, his curls bouncing as a ripple moved down his spine like a dog shedding water.

"Well," Ryland continued, his voice shaking with exertion, fighting the demons exhausting him, "you are safe here." He smiled warmly, although I could see the panic in his eyes.

The little girl looked at him with her wide, dark eyes picking up on the change. I was certain she couldn't piece the reasoning together as to why he had reacted that way. At least, I hoped she couldn't.

If Ryland was right, and Edmund had sent her, we were all in a bit of trouble.

"I brought a surprise," Ryland continued without missing a beat, turning away from the children to face me. "I present Queen Joclyn."

The girl's eyes widened, her awe obvious. Her brother, meanwhile, looked concerned and somewhat fearful of my presence.

She sat as awestruck as a little girl in a theme park. Ryland had announced me, and the spotlight shone right on my face. At least my braid was pristine. She didn't even seem to notice the holes in my dirty jeans.

"*Queen?*"

"Hello, Míra. I am very pleased to meet you," I told her, trying to ignore the way my stomach swam.

Leave it to a child to make me feel more like a queen than all the councils and pretty dresses combined.

Ilyan chuckled at my complaint as I kept the smile plastered on my face.

I didn't extend my hand as Ilyan had instructed me months ago. Instead, I kept them politely by my sides.

The girl looked a bit affronted at first, something that vanished when Ryland and Jaromir bowed a bit toward me. The legitimacy of my claim unquestioned, her eyes widened.

"Hello." Her voice was barely above a squeak, the awe wiping away all sign of the darkness I had heard behind her voice before. "Are you really the queen?"

"Yes." I chuckled, my smile widening, the girl's eagerness at meeting me infectious. "I am. Queen of the Skříteks. That's the magical people charged with protection," I answered at the confused look she gave me, which seemed a little forced.

"So, you can protect me?"

"Yes, we can," I answered, careful to stay standing. Even though I wanted to sit beside her, I knew I wasn't there yet. I still needed to gain her trust. "We protect everyone in here from the dangers outside. We even protect Ryland, and he helps to protect us. Although, I'll tell you a secret."

Her eyes enlarged as she leaned toward me. Even Jaromir tried to get closer, which was saying something because he had always been pretty much terrified of me.

Trust gained, I sat down on the bed next to her, leaning toward her in an obvious show of secrecy, one I could tell they wanted in on. Magic reverberated over them pleasantly as I watched for any sign of danger, of that magic I hoped I would not find.

One mischievous look at Ryland, and I giggled. The poor boy looked concerned about whatever I was going to lay on them. I had a library of secrets about him, after all.

"I could never beat him in a Nerf gun battle." I jerked my head toward Ry, the two children looking confused before they dissolved into a fit of giggles.

Jaromir leaned even closer to me. "I love Nerf guns," he whispered, playing into the vein of secrecy with perfect accuracy.

"So do I." I leaned in even closer, aware of the burly man who was standing not too far away, magic bristling. "We should get some and gang up on him sometime. I think we could take him together."

"I heard that!" Ryland interrupted loudly, the false frustration clear.

The kids, however, missed it, erupting into loud fits of

41

giggles that I gladly joined in on, knowing at once what I had to do.

"It's a plan," I whispered to Jaromir, leaning into them in joint conspiracy, something they both lapped up.

"How about you, Míra?"

With the focus drifting to the girl, she nodded her head once as a wide, pure smile donned her face.

I extended my hand toward her, palm flat, ready for a handshake. She looked at it in awe.

A queen's hand.

Purposefully, I hadn't shaken her hand when I had met her, and now I was offering it to her ... like an equal.

She looked at it, hesitating, that same darkness penetrating her eyes.

Tension coiled in my body, the same sensation I felt seeping from Ryland. I was convinced by the silence that surrounded us that he wasn't even breathing.

"Want to be part of my team?" I asked.

The darkness grew as she looked at me, her jaw tightening, taking away the innocence of the child and replacing it with the madness of a different king.

Ilyan!

I said nothing more before she placed her hand in mine. My magic reacted at once to hers, pushing me into sight.

A gasp so loud it echoed in my ears seeped past my teeth. My eyes turned black as the ember burn filled my vision before pulling me into her reality, into her past, into her future ... and right into Edmund's palm.

The taste of blood filled my mouth as, within my sight, Míra fought child after child in cruel battles, adults circling around her, money changing hands as she felled child after child. Sweetmeats were handed to her from would be masters as she killed more, as she conquered more.

She was happy, stuffing her face with the candies, but then the image shifted, moving in a shadowed tent and Míra as she lay, crying in a disheveled bunk, hundreds of identical cots surrounding her. The Chosen that Edmund had created, many dirty and misshapen, writhed and cried as they fought impossible illnesses. They wallowed in dark and filth, left on their own as they recovered from the bites that had infected them thanks to Edmund's Vilỳs.

The darkness around the bunks overwhelmed me, the smell of feces and the hollow sounds of inescapable death smothering the air. I gasped underneath the pressure, desperate for fresh air, only for the scene to change to the bright sun of a stadium, to the cool chill of the winter that was on the other side of the barrier. Sounds of cheers replaced the cries. The same money-hungry men filled a stadium, and in the center, smeared with blood and mud, Míra fought with hatred clear on her face as she ended the life of a boy her age with a well-placed kick.

Heart stampeding in my chest, I watched her approach Edmund, watched him place the Štít. Then with his magic infecting her, he left Míra to train, to hurt my father, to rip the spine from someone's back, the amount of blood that seeped from the wound covering everything.

Evil filled the girl before me, an evil so deep I could feel my magic bristle with a need to snuff it out.

"Ilyan, I need you to come with me."

The panic in me increased with those three words, spoken by the girl whose hand I still held, her face shifting into view as the sight changed.

Míra yelled at him as explosions sounded around her, rattling the cave as she screamed at him to follow. She screamed again before running down a hall deep within Imdalind, opening a door as everything continued to shake around her.

"I know where he is," Míra gasped out as she burst into the room. "You have to hurry."

She stood in a room I had seen a million times before, the door closing with a thud, leaving her standing in the large open stone space that Ilyan always died in.

Over and over again.

This time, it was different.

Míra stood, facing someone I hadn't expected. Not in this moment.

Ovailia.

"Are you sure he didn't follow you?" She asked with that acidic voice of hers.

My heart picked up into a panic at the sight of her there, horror drowning me as the scene began to shift, changing and mutating as everything stuttered and shifted. Ovailia stood in the middle of the room as Míra shifted;

disappearing, only to be replaced by Ilyan, only to have everything shift again and both Míra and Ilyan stood before her.

The two of them continued to dance around the sight as everything flickered, the screams of all the players rotating as everything continued flash and change.

Ovailia screaming.

Míra crying.

Ilyan dead.

Míra dead.

Míra was there one minute and gone the next. Ilyan was there, standing by Míra, then he was spread out in blood soaked horror the same as before.

"Watch!" Ilyan yelled outside of the sight, the one word breaking through as everything stuttered.

My heart clenched as he fell to the ground, blood spurting out of a wound in his neck before it rewound to him standing, Míra behind him, her eyes nervously watching him and Ovailia.

"Death!" Ovailia screamed, the word out of place as the child vanished again, Ilyan spluttering through an injury.

Again and again, it shifted. The images rolled around as I tried to make sense of them.

I had seen this vision a million times, manipulated by my father as he changed the murderer, changed the death. This time, however, everything felt more real.

With my heart stampeding, the shifting room faded into a

snow-clad forest, fading again into an unfamiliar alley. Words and images ran over each other as everything altered, a heavy wave of red flowing over the image, drowning it all in blood.

Míra fought Sain, desperately trying to defeat him before she fell to the ground, bleeding from her chest and her mouth.

Blood covered the child as Sain threw her in with the bodies he had destroyed, assuming her for dead. But he was wrong, as we were.

For, as the sight shifted again, she was now running down a hallway within the cathedral, Jaromir at her side. Then a door opened as Thom came into view, a single shot of magic speeding toward him from her hand.

A scream ripped from my throat. The sound emerged in the real world as the sight's ember burn drowned the blood, fading into black as reality greeted me home.

My heavy breathing was the solitary sound in my ears as the ember left my eyes, leaving me staring at the child, everything painfully tight inside of me.

"You're the Drak," she gasped, all pretense of innocence gone now. The child was smothered with the evil and hatred I had sensed in her before.

"And you're Cail's replacement. You are here to kill Thom."

Ryland stiffened behind me, but I stayed still, my hand a vice around hers.

My magic held her in place as I searched within her, looking for any sign of Edmund's magic, feeling the Štít for any sign of the dratted man.

"Wrong." She smiled, deep and dark. "I am here to kill you all." Her magic surged from the hollow space within her, the strength elevating with the hope of attack.

Smothering it, I let my magic wind around hers, freezing it in place as I searched for some sign of the man I despised almost as much as my own father, searching for some sign of Edmund's control.

His rancid magic was there, wrapped deeply within her, but it was a faint residue, almost like a weaker memory of what the man currently was. No, what he *had been*.

That couldn't be right.

Her magic surged again in an attempt to break past my barrier, but I overpowered it, taking control before she could get any farther, locking her in place.

Her eyes clouded with fear at the restraint, my smile spreading as hers died, drowning in the shadow of my fire.

The doors far behind us slammed open as Ilyan, Risha, and Wyn ran into the hall. The girl's fear increased, her hand shaking in mine as Jaromir began to cry in confusion; Ryland's gentle hold around him was neither comforting or wanted.

"I have bad news, little girl. You are all alone here. Besides, if what I saw is true, you will save us all."

3

SAIN

LOUD BUZZING, like a hive of angry bees, bled past the heavy walls of the tiny room I had closeted myself in. Thousands of Trpaslíks' voices drifted from the old hall in shades of worry, concern, and excitement. The emotions mixed together in a dangerous harmony as beautiful as the sweet and salty fragrance of blood that flowed up from the twisted corpse at my feet in low, smoky tones. The scent of charred flesh followed like a delicate afterthought. It was a perfume that could have been made by a French master in the dark ages. Seamlessly blended, impeccably intoxicating.

A smile, long and terrifying, stretched my lips, pulling at the sticky hairs of my beard uncomfortably as I looked over the tangle of flesh, at the blackened skin and bone, the crimson blood. The same color that covered my arms in cracked patches, the same color that blossomed over the robe I still wore like a talisman over my shoulders. Watercolor roses against white and black. The bloodstains were as intricate as the embroidery you would find on a king's cloak.

And that was exactly what this was.

The cloak for the blood-soaked king.

And soon, everyone would know.

Eyes wide to the pitch dark of the room I stood in, long greasy strands falling over my face, I stared, my heart pounding against bones in eager anticipation of what was about to happen.

I closed my eyes, needing to see it again. The weakened strains of my sight pulsed over me in the usual prompt, the powerful ebbs and flows of the ability weaker than normal, thanks in part to the Zámek I had placed around us. Regardless, they moved through me like a wave of steam, rumbling within my blood until I let it take me, let it pull my mind right back to the same sight I'd had before.

Instead, it was black.

Black silence that was broken with a voice that clenched my heart like a vice.

"Be prepared, for fire will come, and fire will be needed. Water will do."

That woman who had haunted me for so long, who had infected my sights for the past few months. It was her voice in the dark, her voice that controlled me before my sight pulled me back to that horrifying night at the cathedral.

The eagerness of my heart turned to stone filled fear as the words of the prophecy filled my mind. I waited, scared of what more would come, but it was merely silence, silence broken by the ember glow as my sight left, my magic retreating back into me, leaving me standing once again in the dark storeroom. The sound of the gathering crowds buzzing in my ears.

Tension knitted itself into my muscles, a misplaced doubt winding inside of me. A doubt I needn't have. Pure Drak magic led to truth. It showed what was to be; and I had already seen what I needed to know.

"I need answers, not riddles, woman. You can't hide from me forever." I said, the same promise I always made to the faceless entity who haunted my sights angry on my lips.

My irritation twisted through me, making me more dangerous than I would be otherwise.

At least I had an outlet beyond the door.

As if on cue, the door opened, the murmurs of the crowd bathing the silence as Ovailia slipped her way in, light and sounds dissipating as the door closed behind her.

"They are primed and ready," Ovailia said without hesitation. "Half are expecting the war to start. And half are expecting Edmund to present Ilyan's head on a pike."

"That man ...? Damek, was it? He did his job?" My questions were coarse in the dark, the residual stress from the sight leaving and desire taking its place. Even the tension in my shoulders left, slipping down my back and dripping into the thick pools of blood and ash I stood in.

"Yes." She smiled, her eyes gleaming in the dark as she stepped closer, stopping right before her father's corpse, as though she were somehow afraid to disturb him. "No one has any idea what is coming."

"This should be fun." The hiss of my voice slithered across the dark as my magic flared, the penetrating green orb filling the tiny space with ominous shadows.

Ovailia looked at them as though they were emeralds, eagerness clear in her eyes as she fixed me with a dark and menacing smile. "It will be a true bloodbath, as you saw."

"As I want."

I could feel her magic in the air, winding around her, winding around me, taunting in the dark, trying to lure me in.

I ignored it. Now was not the time for me to give her what she wanted. To give in to the weakness I was positive she knew I had.

"As *we* want," she corrected.

With those few words, my blood turned to fire and ice. Pride and anger swirled together as my eyes narrowed, the danger and warning clear in my eyes.

I knew she saw it. I could tell by the way she sighed, lifting her hands to her hips, an ugly disparaging look twisting her features.

"I didn't know there was a *we* in this," I said with steel, the warning clear as I stepped toward her, ignoring the corpse that sat between us.

With one firm foot on his shoulder, I stepped onto his body, a crack echoing in the dark as I balanced on bones and skin.

This time, she grimaced. This time, the sharp inhale between her teeth was based on an emotion I hadn't thought it possible for her to hold.

The defiance faded from her face as her eyes widened, her jaw tensing and teeth clenched together.

"Oh, I'm sorry," I gasped, false sympathy dripping from my tongue so heavily it aggravated her more. "Do you not like this?"

She said nothing, just watched me, her eyes narrowing dangerously.

"Do you want me to stop?" I asked, laughing this time.

Still, she glowered at me, her eyes hard with anger as she began to chew on her cheek.

I dug my heels in, twisting my body to and fro as I mutilated the already broken shards of a man, pushing the beautiful woman before me to her limit.

Still, she stood.

Still, she glowered.

My dance continued until it became clear she wasn't going to participate in my little game.

It angered me. I could feel my temper rising alongside my magic, the powerful torrent ready to attack, almost desperate for it.

Even with the battle waiting for me on the other side of the door, a little warm up wouldn't be too terrible.

"Do you want me to stop?" I broke each word up into syllables, staccato sounds that stabbed into the dark like daggers.

Ovailia narrowed her eyes further, the tension in her jaw leaving as her long, graceful fingers pushed the hair behind her ear again. The tiniest of wicked smiles then played around the corners of her lips.

"No." She took a step forward, planting her heel firmly beside my own foot before she lifted herself onto her father's body, joining me on the corpse that, in a way, would become a frightening cornerstone for my reign.

"Good," I hissed, wrapping my hand around her waist before pulling her into me. I let our magic dance together, knowing the connection was dangerous. "Since I killed him, I can do what I want with him. He is mine, as all those people are mine. As the future is mine.

"There is no us," I continued, pushing her farther into me. "There is no we."

"Not *yet*." She smiled, and my eyes narrowed.

I dug the tips of my fingers into her side as my magic flared. My temper was rising so quickly I could barely contain my magic, contain my anger. I knew she felt the warning pricks of my power. I knew she felt the pain.

But she didn't show it.

She stood against me, her hand soft on my forearm as she fixed me with the same dangerous smile.

"Careful, Ovailia. Remember what I said about a devil."

Her smile faded at my words, the power she thought she had over me fading into a question. She stepped away, pulling her heel out of Edmund's back with an odd squelching noise before it tapped against the stone of the floor, the click like the bang of a gun, signaling the change.

"Everyone is in the hall," she continued as though the last few minutes had never happened. "We've scoured all of Imdalind and pulled all the Trpaslík guards from the camp.

The qualified Chosen are here. The others are locked in their tents as you requested. Damek and I have already barred the doors, although I am not positive we can hold this much magic behind them if they were to revolt."

"Let me worry about that."

The fear in Ovailia's eyes relaxed as I stepped off the corpse of her father, the tension in her shoulders loosening. She whimpered as I moved closer, her eyes soft as my fingers trailed over her skin in a move that she perceived as intimacy. She was foolish enough to have missed the control I had taken, to have missed the protective shield I had placed around her.

"Well, then"—her smile grew as her magic swelled, her beautiful frame taking another step toward me—"we are ready."

"Wonderful." Even past the mask of emotions I always hid behind, I couldn't stop this smile from releasing. I couldn't stop the greed from coloring my eyes.

Ovailia watched it spread as she let her hand drift up to my shoulder, her own brand of lust intensifying, seeping into the air and mixing with the flavor of death in a luscious aroma.

"Wonderful," I repeated as I breathed it in, letting the sweet smell of victory fill me. The last tendrils of Edmund's magic burned inside me. "Go and introduce your father, Ovailia."

Ovailia said nothing as she vanished from sight, smiling demurely. The soft click of her ever-present heels following my good little pet to her task.

"Now we get to play." My heart rumbled as I turned,

addressing the lifeless corpse as if it were an old friend patiently waiting for his turn. "Up you go."

Edmund's magic was destroyed, Míra and the Štít gone. There was no longer any magic in this vessel. Otherwise, I would have controlled him as I had with the bodies within Prague. Instead, I let my magic seep inside him, strong as it filled the icy cold of rotting flesh, moving him like a puppet on a string.

Ticking throughout him like the pulse of a metronome, my magic brought his body to life, shifting and jerking with a steady beat. He moved as though he were under a strobe, his arms and torso shuddering in a haunting stop-motion that jerked and pulsed. Loud cracks broke through the air as his bones began to shatter, unable to hold the weight of the decaying man. They pushed their way past the charred and blackened remains of his flesh, glistening white and shining brightly against the grit of black ash.

I moved him to a standing position, his legs twisted beneath him, head lolling on his shoulders like a newborn. Dead white eyes stared into nothing as the singed ends of his always perfectly cared for hair fell over his gaunt face in the limp curls that were so similar to his sons'.

"Hello, old friend," I cooed as I twisted his head to one side, his mouth agape as a dry and cracked tongue protruded from behind yellow teeth. The blade that still protruded from his chest was more obvious now. "Ready for some fun?"

"Trpaslíks!" Ovailia's voice boomed from beyond the door, heralding what was coming, causing the beat of my heart to increase. "Our master, our king has gathered us here for wonderful news!"

The jovial crowd answered in a cheer, a shout.

Before Ovailia could continue, I closed my eyes then stretched my magic past the wall to see the horde gathered there, to see their eager faces, to see Ovailia who was alive in her element as she led them toward the destruction I had planned for them.

Ovailia continued as I opened my eyes to view the corpse who wobbled before me, the room beyond fading to green.

"I suppose you need to look nice for your fans ..."

Removing the robe from my shoulders, I threw it over his. My magic twitched inside of him as the door swung open, and Ovailia's voice echoed loudly inside of me.

"I give you my father!"

Magic surging, I prodded him forward, toward the eager throngs that were waiting to see him.

Ash fell from his body with each step, chunks of what was once flesh littering behind him as the movements jostled his fragile remains. They fell like a train behind him, like a cloak of coronation; except, this one was in the death and failure of his reign.

With broken steps, he left the dark confines of the alcove and shuffled into the light, into the large hall and the joy and excitement Ovailia had resonated.

The cheers continued before the screams started. Anger and panic took control as I turned Edmund's body, his dead eyes looking into the crowd, the large jagged shard of the Soul's Blade clearly protruding from his heart.

The crowd deteriorated into a panic as many turned to rush the door. Many more rushed Ovailia or the podium, coming face to face with a powerful shield. Any attack they sent that way faded to smoke.

The attacks, the fear—everything poured into me with an energy I devoured with a lustful hunger. I let it energize me, fill me. Wonderment broke through my chest in a deep, menacing boom that increased the thrum of my heart. The sound increased, magnified by the room I stood in, drifting over the crowd as they began to hush, increasing the fear of this unknown who was stepping out from the shadows.

The depth of my laugh flourished as the shock of seeing me standing before them began to sink in. Unbroken, unwavering, no longer the sniveling imp they had watched cower behind their master for centuries.

That creature had gone. All that was left was an unknown hell, the devil in me just dying to get out.

Fear dripped in the air, infecting the magical people who were now my pawns with a virus they wouldn't be able to shed anytime soon.

"Good evening." I spoke as casually as I could, fully aware that the menace of my laugh had attached itself to the two words. "I thank you all for accepting my invitation, for following the commands of your king."

The multitude stared at me in confusion and shock, their eyes wide as they looked from one to another, trying to understand what was going on.

"You called ...?"

"What happened to Edmund ...?"

"What is going on?"

The nefarious smile crept over my face, baring my teeth to the light as I stripped the blood-soaked robes from Edmund's shoulders once again, letting the damp cloth glisten as I furled it through the air like a banner.

Screams cut the startled silence as the blade glistened from his chest, the naked body of their master left disrobed.

I gave them no explanation. I said nothing more. In silence, I simply stepped toward the broken man, his blood shrouding me as I wrapped my hand around the blade that still protruded from his chest, the uneven rock strangely hot.

"Don't worry," I said, smile expanding as I glanced back out toward the captive audience. "He's already dead. I killed him. I defeated him. As we will Ilyan in a victory that I will lead you to."

Their cries of protest and fear echoed in my ears as my focus drifted back to Ovailia who stared at me, the same stiff jaw in place, her hands like rocks against her thighs.

"To victory," I repeated to Ovailia, my focus on hers as I pulled the blade, cutting into ribs, lungs, and flesh, ripping Edmund open from breast plate to hip bone.

The already rotting and burned organs spilled out of him in a cascade of gray and red. A shower of the darkest crimson covered my legs, sliding over the stone as it flooded the faces of those who stood closest, the fear escalating as every question he had was answered.

A breath of silence filled the hall before the screaming began again, panic ruling them.

It was then, with the blood of their master over their face and his milky eyes staring vacantly into them, that they attacked.

Streams of color flashed across the air, hitting against the same shield as before. The gray stone of the cave was illuminated by the flash of anger as attack after attack flew through the air.

Then, with one look at Ovailia, hair sagging in front of my face in madness, I dropped the shield, letting the attacks fly right toward me, brilliant colors inches from taking my life.

They never hit me.

Instead, a spark of ability pressed me into the world underneath our own, letting me escape them in a seamless stutter. Reappearing with a tiny pop at the back of the large hall, the sound unheard over the eruption of violence that had taken over the space.

Hundreds of attacks still sped right toward where I had been, the air alight with color, each missing their mark and embedding themselves in the body of their former master.

Screams rent the air at the sudden shift of events. Trpaslík women ran to the aid of the man who had been mutilated by dozens of spells. More ran toward the door, the untrained Chosen cowering and whimpering against the walls in mad attempts to escape the fray.

Then everything stopped.

Frozen.

Silent.

Men stopped attacking. Women stopped crying. Chosen froze in pathetic cowers. And I alone stood in the back of the hall, laughing as my power infested them, freezing them in place. The sounds of fear were snuffed from the air as I placed each of them in a cage of my magic. No matter how much they fought, it wouldn't allow them to move.

"Well, now," I said, my steps heavy as I walked past them, weaving my way through the sea of large, frightened eyes as they watched me, the one thing that moved in a sea of stone. "That was quite the fit you all threw. Mind you, I don't necessarily blame you. I can image your surprise. You thought me a pathetic weasel. And now I bring you the body of your tyrant. Now I hold you all with a power that even Edmund could not master."

Fear dripped heavily in the air with each word, the emotion dangling in their eyes, clear in the labor of their breaths. It pressed against my soul, and I breathed it in with a sigh, letting it fill me, letting it fuel me.

Stepping onto the raised platform in silence, Ovailia stepped back with one sharp look from me, the warning obvious.

This was *my* show.

Two steps and I was to him.

Edmund's body was already ripped apart, blackened, burned limbs thrown into the dark behind him with the force of the attack. Nevertheless, it was his skull I wanted. It was the head that still looked out at them all with a slack jaw and wide-eyed horror.

The skull that so many of them could not look away from.

With a wide smile, I scanned the crowd as I placed my foot over the skull of the once powerful king, watching the fear line their eyes as, with one swift movement, I crushed the man who had once crushed them.

"You can choose one master, and I suggest you choose wisely. If we wish to destroy Ilyan and take Imdalind for our own, we do not need someone who cannot see the dangers we are surrounded by. What we need is someone who can see the truth of what lies ahead, see all possibilities in our path. And I can see all."

The words were perfectly placed, soothing little reminders of what I was and what I was capable of. They did not go unnoticed.

Those same eyes that looked so frightened of me before now looked between themselves in confusion and awe.

"I suggest," I began, my voice a low warning as I began to pace before them, "that you consider your options carefully. You do not want to see what I can truly do. A little freezing trick is nothing compared to the true power of a Drak."

I stood still in the center of the platform, my smile wide as I faced them, letting the fear mount as my magic did. The powerful force went unfelt as it wound through each of them, moving into them, infecting them.

Preparing them.

And then I released them.

"If you fight for me, then do it. Kill those who still bow to Edmund. Destroy those unworthy to stand in my presence."

The sounds of anger, fear, and battle erupted again as the horde before me reanimated, bodies falling, spells firing.

Attacks sped toward me once again, simply to be deflected with a single thought. Beams of color and flame followed, falling to the ground like sand. One after another, they came until the war that was opening up before me began to shift, the line of good and evil fading.

And Trpaslík turned against Trpaslík.

My words had not gone unnoticed.

One by one, those who battled before me began to turn on each other. The war was no longer about who could destroy me, but on choosing which side to stand on. Choosing which side of the line you would claim as your own.

Laughing, I watched as the battle strengthened, body after body falling to the ground. Explosions sounded around me as the battle intensified, as they began to rip each other apart.

"Careful," I whispered to myself, turning away from them with a grin. "You might get hurt if you don't choose wisely."

Kicking the shards of bone off the stone floor, I stepped away, grateful when Ovailia followed me, her own laugh clear in the scream-filled air.

4

JOCLYN

"ARE you hoping to find something to kill?" I teased, increasing my gait in an attempt to keep up with Wyn. Knowing I had to be quiet. Being loud while we were outside the cathedral was not smart.

Wyn, however, seemed to be trying to make as much noise as possible. Even her footfalls were deafening.

"I'm not saying it would be a bad thing." Her voice was a heavy mumble as she finally came to a stop.

Pulling a weathered and wrinkled map out of her back pocket, she consulted it, peering through the hole in her palm like it was some kind of periscope.

"If you want to use it like that, you should get a magnifying glass inserted." I tried to ignore the way my stomach flipped and flopped at the imagery. Then I turned away, letting my magic flow over the darkened streets we were stopped in.

I supposed, if we were going to be loud and obnoxious, I

should at least make certain we were as safe and guarded as possible.

"Don't think that it hasn't crossed my mind," she said with a wink, pressing the mangled hand flat in the air. "But I worry it would mess up my magic, and it has such a pretty little circular array right now."

I would grant her that. Whatever that blade had done to her hand had not only made it impossible for me to heal, but her magic flew around in new and, should we say, unique ways.

"Just conjure glass into it, and you're all set," I said absently, my focus two streets away on a Vilỳ that was picking through garbage.

Luckily, looking at Wyn's map, our target was in the opposite direction. As long as I could keep her quiet, we would be good.

"I think that's the best thing you have said all day," Wyn hissed in an eager whisper, balling up the map then shoving it into the back pocket of her filthy jeans. Not like mine were much better. We were in desperate need of a washing machine. "Of course, then I couldn't torment Jaromir and his angry, little counterpart. It's so fun to make them squirm."

I figured I would let that one slide and followed her into an alley ahead of us. Wyn was not a very big fan of Míra. Not that I blamed her. I had seen her killing Thom, after all. And while that was something I probably shouldn't have shared with Wyn, I did also see her in the caves with Ilyan. I saw her with him, and he was still alive.

I knew there was something more to it. There had to be, considering the moment I had seen that one distorted sight with Ilyan and Míra in the cave, everything else had kind of turned off. The images from within Imdalind had become shadowed and broken or, even worse, nonexistent.

Everyone except Wyn had agreed it was worth keeping her alive. At least for now. It didn't help that, after two weeks of waiting for the girl to slip up and go bat-shit crazy, Wyn's trust level had reached an already extended breaking point.

"If I can't torment them, then what's the point?"

You would think the girl who had committed genocide and was somehow able to regain forgiveness would be a little more understanding.

"Not having a creepy hole in your hand?" I knew she wasn't going to accept that.

In fact, she dismissed it with one irritated glance, sprinting away from me, darting behind a towering building and into one of the many dark alleys that littered the city.

Rolling my eyes, I started running, trying my best to keep quiet, only to have my foot land squarely in a crimson-tinted puddle I preferred not to imagine the origins of.

Liquid splashed up my leg, soaking through my already worn and frayed jeans. I shivered at the cold, wishing there were a way to wash them.

Perhaps I could convince Wyn to take a detour to a clothing store. Why was it always my pants?

"Great," I grumbled more to myself than to the renegade I was chasing.

Shaking my leg like a dog during an enjoyable belly rub, I attempted to get as much of the liquid off as I could. However, it stayed put, staining me. The color was made that much more disgusting by the deep red light the city was bathed in, the looming shadows of the building drowning everything in purple and gray.

Purple and gray. The imagery seeped into me as my head began to spin, sight's familiar swirl attempting to pull me down.

It wasn't safe for me to let it take me completely, not here. Not when we were so exposed, not when night was so close.

Keeping control, I continued forward, letting the vision play over my reality in a shadow, the faded scenes running over each other.

A flash of light.

The explosion I had been encompassed in before.

The blood-filled rain.

Nothing here was new, something that normally would have irritated me. But, after the darkness and Míra's twisted sight, I wasn't going to dispel any of this as a recap.

Dramin had taught me that much, yet he was still being far too secretive about telling me more. Besides, you couldn't stop a battle; you could only face the war. And the more information I had for that, the greater my chance of survival.

No, of everyone's survival.

Stopping in the middle of the filthy street, I stared into the smoke-filled room of Imdalind I had seen a million times. I stared into the shifting atmosphere, the familiar blood and screams gone, replaced by the whimpers of a child.

The smoke began to dissipate as my heart rate accelerated, hoping I would see something this time.

I could hear Mira's screams, but all I saw was fire. Nothing else was clear as an adult woman began to laugh, her voice oddly youthful as the smell of burned flesh hit me. The aroma was strangely familiar, as if I had smelled it somewhere before. But even the pile of death that Sain had forced us to dig into and dispose of had not carried the same power, the same familiar undertone.

This was something different.

"Water flows." My own voice said within the sight, the imagery leaving as I stared down the darkening street once more, heart galloping in my chest at a painful, unsustainable rate.

Joclyn? Ilyan's voice ripped through me the second I rejoined reality, his fear making it obvious I had blocked him from the vision again.

I'm fine, I said, my internal monologue strained with emotional exertion. *I thought I might see something within Imdalind and Edmunds camp, but there was nothing. Again.* I was sure he could hear my disappointment, so I quickly added, *We are safe, although Wyn might be planning on killing Mira.* I hoped he would leave it alone.

That explains why your heart is moving like a motorbike. His panic seeped into me, his magic following close behind. The powerful warmth filled me as my heart rate began to slow. *We need to do something about those two.*

Míra and Wyn? I don't think anything can be done until Thom is alive and well, and Edmund is declared dead.

Speaking of that ... Ilyan prompted, and my mind followed his perfectly as I took one step forward, turning into the alley where Wyn had already begun digging through one of the five large dumpsters there, making far too much noise for what was considered safe.

She's still looking. We are at a clinic in the eighth district.

I had no sooner given Ilyan an update than Wyn threw a large box behind her, the glass-filled thing hitting against the stone wall behind her.

Maybe she was trying to get us killed.

I cringed, stretching my magic out into the city. At least I could feel if someone was coming before they got here. Even if she rang a gong, we should still be okay.

I looked around me at that, my magic strangely aware of the surly best friend who was still doing who knew what in the alley before me.

Stay safe, můj kamarád. I would be most upset if you did not return to me in one piece. His voice was deep and sultry, his love a profound joy against my heart.

Sighing deeply at the comfort it gave me, I felt the stress of the unknown drift away.

I didn't respond. I knew I didn't need to. He was right there inside my mind, inside my heart. His love grew in response.

Pressing my hand against the gritty stone of the building Wyn had dodged around, I propelled myself forward, out of the pink light of sunset and into the black pitch of the alley. My eyes adjusted, my magic flaring simultaneously as the shadow of Wyn digging inside the dumpster became clear, the ghostly whispers of sight following right behind.

"Stabilize your foot, or you're going to fall."

Wyn looked up from her digging, her nose wrinkled in irritation before she did, in fact, stabilize her foot and go back to digging.

"It's freaky, you know," she said in obvious irritation, her focus back on the dumpster she was excavating, reading tiny vials and boxes before throwing them behind her into the dark alley. "That you can see everything."

"If you think that's freaky, you should *try* seeing everything." I was well aware my retort didn't make it above grumbly teenager status. "Then again, it is better than being stuck scavenging with someone who will reek of three-month-old cabbage and fish bones."

"I guess I should be thanking you, then." This time, the game was clear in her voice, the smile sparkling in her eyes as she shot me a sidelong glance.

"You should," I taunted, playing along. "You should also be a bit quieter if you want to live."

"Nah." She didn't even look at me as she threw yet another box behind her. "I've got my friend and some super-powered magic. We can take them."

"But then you would owe me more once I save your ass," I teased, leaning against the wall in feigned boredom, really hoping she would take my advice and shut up. I wasn't in the mood for a fight, even if I could take them all. "Being alive and not stinking is quite the tall order, especially for a queen."

"I'm sorry. *You* would be saving *me*?"

I chose to ignore that.

"I accept gratitude in the form of allegiance, sword swearing, and of course, jewelry. Bowing will no longer suffice."

The hint of a devious smile broadened over Wyn's face, a small trickle of a laugh escaping as she jumped down from the dumpster to face me, a sagging bit of cloth clutched in her fist.

"I'm fresh out of jewelry, your majesty." She seemed mournful, but there was something behind her eyes that set off alarms in my head.

What was she planning?

"It is most unfortunate. Would a hoodie suffice?" She lifted her hand then, the movement sending a wave of rot toward me.

Nose crinkling, I stepped away, horror filling me. "No!"

"What do you mean, '*no*,' Jos?" Wyn whispered, careful to keep her voice low as she took a step toward me with what I was convinced had been a hoodie at some point held out toward me eagerly. "You love hoodies."

"I love hoodies made of fabric, soft cotton ... not rot and bug feces." It was all I could do to keep the panic out of my voice. It wouldn't take much for her to force that thing onto me, and Wyn was now matching me step for step in my effort to get away. And she was enjoying it, given the way her smile broadened.

"Get that vile thing away from me!" That time, my reaction was too loud, something we both noticed right away.

Each of us froze in place, waiting for the ugly hissing of the Vilỳs or some disgruntled Trpaslík to come around the corner after us, brought right to us by the sound.

Hoodie forgotten as Wyn extended it between us, we waited.

My magic flared as I stretched it around the streets, through the sky, looking for any sign that someone had heard. That someone was coming.

There was nothing. Not even a whisper, which was something that frightened me even more. This city was never this safe, not with noise that loud. The security of nothing was clear.

So, where were they?

"Boxes are okay, but screeching is not?" I asked, the reason for her audible battle becoming clear, the look in her eyes cementing it in place.

She wanted the battle.

I shouldn't be surprised. It was a Trpaslík thing, one she was extraordinarily good at controlling. But with Thom still down for the count and us being unable to spar thanks to imminent explosions, she had been a bit cooped up.

I should have seen this coming.

"Wyn," I groaned, "can we please not kill anyone this trip?"

"You say that like it's the worst thing in the world."

"Last I checked, murder was pretty high up on the *Worst Things in the World* list," I spat, my magic flaring violently as the revolting thing Wyn still held spontaneously combusted from within her hand, the dark alley igniting in brilliant orange light as my magic engulfed it. "Whoops."

"Jos!" Wyn hissed, jumping away from the flames as she dropped the hoodie to the ground. "No fair. You burned my sacred offering to the queen of the Skříteks."

"Is that what you were trying to pass it off as?"

"Some queen you are."

I knew it was meant in jest. She was still smiling like it was. But I reacted the wrong way. The words cut me a bit too raw.

"Well, it does seem to be the consensus."

"Eh," Wyn said with a shrug before turning back to the looming pile of trash. "Don't listen to 'em. They are the idiots for listening to a deranged old man who tried to kill you ... and me ... oh, and that whole pile of corpses—"

"That he brought back to life."

"Don't give me nightmares." Wyn leaned against the trash can, a hand on her hip. "I mean, I used to kill people for a living and that ..." Wyn paused, her eyes wide, before she forced a shiver, the exaggerated motion shaking her.

"What, you mean you don't have them every night?" I tried to joke, but it had too much truth behind it. And, instead, it came out as an odd squeak that Wyn did not miss.

"We all do ... about everything. I think that happens when you live underneath a sky the color of blood. It infects you somehow, like cabin fever. We should be happy we haven't all gone crazy."

I shot her a look at that, one eyebrow hiking up into the wisps of my hair, my brow pinching together as I tried to laugh, something she didn't try to restrain.

"I did say *all*. Not *all* of us have gone crazy," Wyn mused, a deep sigh coloring the words as she pulled out another box, inspecting the label with a squint. "But all the ones who follow Sain have. Seriously, how can you look at that crazy and still follow it around? Gah!"

"Maybe he cursed them all to see me as a giant, moth-eating lizard."

"And him a romance novel model. Crazy nut-bags, the lot of them."

"Romance models or Sain's sheep?" I asked, entertained by the image of both.

"Both. You'll see once you kill Edmund, free us all from the dome of doom, predict the future, and save the world. They'll all come to their senses and see how dumb they are being. Not all in that order, of course," she added as a desperate afterthought, wagging her finger in my face in warning as she winked.

"Oh, well, if I don't have to go in order, then it seems *much* more manageable!" I couldn't help the eye roll, something Wyn laughed at.

"You wait. You'll do it. The 'sight said so' and all that jazz." Wyn turned away from me, back to the dumpster and the task at hand, still not very quiet about it.

Trying to ignore the rhythmic clanking of glass and cardboard, I turned away, keeping my magic trained on the city in case someone decided to hear this racket and come running.

The red tint of Prague was fading into a bruise as the night stretched over it, a cloak that dragged over the city and dipped into the alleys in a deep purple that swallowed everything in a dangerous pitch.

We were running out of time, we couldn't stay out here much longer. The shades of sunset we were bathed in were especially beautiful if you could ignore the danger the dark held.

"It's almost sunset," I began, walking back toward the pile of old office supplies she was wading through. "Do you think you can wrap it up in about five minutes?"

I hated asking the question, and I could see her shoulders tense up from where I stood. Her muscles were defined underneath the threadbare band shirt she wore. Jefferson Starship's faces were all faded and distorted from years of washing and wearing.

"Well, you know, if finding this crap wasn't so difficult, I would have found it months ago ..."

"Point taken. You could always tell me what you are looking for." I prodded gently, hoping not to enrage her with the question I had asked multiple times before. We had been out looking for the mystery medicine before, and her answer was always the same.

"Why? So you could go off and find it before me? No, thank

you. If I tell you, you could go using your sight and finding it for me. I have to do this myself."

I was met with the low dejection of an already impending defeat, a buzzing sadness that infected me and chased all of my fears away.

Wyn stood before me, broken and folded like a paper doll, every fear and vulnerability inside of her encompassing the alley like butter, in plain view for me to see, to understand.

And I did.

"I wanted to be the one to save him, Jos. Save him before the girl kills him. I have to do something, and lately, I haven't been able to do anything other than put everyone's lives at risk and destroy Ilyan's precious cathedral and disobey orders—"

"You saved me from my father."

"True." The paper she was made up of straightened a bit, the snide, confident girl who had plowed her way into my life becoming more visible. "Sain's an idiot, though. He's probably going to kill himself soon if he's not careful. Accidental maiming on a coat of armor or something."

I laughed at the imagery that was far too good to pass up.

"Let me do this, 'kay?" she pleaded, the desperation in her showing.

I nodded, understanding that part far too well.

Sometimes, you've gotta do stuff on your own, just to prove to yourself that you can.

"I know, Wyn." I stepped toward her, hoping she would see the truth in my eyes.

Wyn met my eyes, vials wrapped inside her grubby fingers as she stood there, her mind working and winding in the air between us.

I could almost feel the tension and fear that was seeping off her.

I guessed trust was harder to rebuild than I had always assumed it to be. It didn't mean it wasn't worth the effort, though.

"It's for Thom," she finally whispered, her voice so soft I had to take a step closer in order to hear her. "Dramin read in one of those books that you gave him about ephindredem... or something. I have it written down. It's supposed to jump-start the heart."

I stared at her, knowing exactly what she was talking about. I replayed at least four movie scenes in which some sort of Miraculous adrenaline recoveries were featured, and my stomach twisted at the memory. I would help her find it, though I wasn't going to help her administer it. She was on her own for that one. I drew the line at giant needles.

"That's actually not a bad idea," I said.

Wyn's face lit up before she bounded away from me, back to the piles of trash from the clinic we were next to.

Well, if she was going to do it herself, I should at least be glad she was using her brain.

"Not too much longer, though," I told her, careful to keep my voice low. "It's getting dark."

She didn't even seem to hear me, or she pretended not to. I would be dragging her out by her prized T-shirt.

Be careful. No one wants to deal with Wyn after one of her T-shirts gets ripped.

I smiled at the sudden addition of Ilyan's voice. He seemed as stressed as Wyn.

True. But don't worry. I'd sooner hit her over the head with a club, I responded, leaning against the damp wall of the alley while Wyn searched. *She is a one-woman show. I guess it's good I make a fine lookout.*

You make a fine everything, můj kamarád.

I giggled, whether I wanted to or not, something not missed by either Ilyan or Wyn.

Ilyan's sweet emotion filled me as the comforting warmth of his magic did, a gift to go alongside the compliment.

Are you meaning to drown me in sugar?

Anything to keep my mind off the disgusting behavior of these people.

The warmth of his magic left at once, the same stress I felt with the first whisper of our connection coming on strong.

I frowned, not liking the way everything was upsetting him, both of us really.

The infection my darling father had left behind was spreading out of control.

The natives are restless. I ... I froze, my words ending as a flare of unfamiliar magic pressed against my back. It was a strain of evil I had felt many times before, running along the stone of the walls and asphalt of the road as someone drew closer.

One of Edmund's guards and another Trpaslík on watch. Looking for us. For the noise, no doubt.

I knew she had been too loud.

Joclyn? Ilyan asked, fear leaching from him, and for good reason. He could undoubtedly feel it, too.

Now you can be worried.

Nah, I know you can take them, mi lasko. Let Wyn have some fun.

Why does everyone think killing is fun? I asked, my heart moving into a tense storm as I closed my eyes. A clearer image of the two Trpaslíks walking down the main road toward us flooded my mind, their heads bowed in low conversation.

Between Wyn and me, they didn't stand a chance.

"Wyn," I hissed, moving toward her before they came any closer.

Wyn looked up with a smirk of enjoyment as she read the map of what was coming. Her own magic sensed the evil approaching.

I might be the only queen in history who didn't like a good fight.

You are also the only queen in history fighting has been required of, so that is not a good analogy.

Whatever.

We will talk about this later, Ilyan. Right now, I apparently have to supervise Wyn. At least I know she can handle it.

She can more than handle it, můj kamarád. She can destroy it. Ilyan's laugh faded away as Wyn bounded right up to me, the wide grin on her face spanning from ear to ear.

"There are two, one for each of us. Are we playing kill or capture?" she asked, pressing her fingers together like an old-school villain. Well, old-school for me, anyway.

"Kill and run. I'd rather not attract any more."

"Point taken," Wyn said, popping her knuckles. "As long as I can play a bit."

Rolling my eyes, I stood in silence with her, the sound of their steps beginning to echo in the alley around us. The low tones of their quick Czech conversation rumbled over the stone in such a way that I was having trouble parsing certain words, no matter how extensive my knowledge of Czech had become as of late.

The closer they moved, the clearer their voices became. The reason for their hushed conversation became clear as I heard something that made me second-guess the impending attack.

"Do you think it will work? Do you think we will be able to dethrone him?"

"It better. After what he did to Edmund, that dirty Drak deserves to die. He deserves a fate worse than the burning he gave him."

Edmund.

Dirty Drak ... Sain.

Burning.

Something about that didn't make sense. Sain doing something to Edmund and burning? I must not have heard him right.

I moved as close as I dared, my ear toward the street as I listened, staring at Wyn who looked back at me with a mirror of confusion.

We couldn't kill them, not now. Something had happened, and we needed to know what. From the way my sight was squirming and burning inside of me, I already had an idea.

These two had the piece I was missing.

"The first one to capture wins," Wyn whispered, her voice low as the power of her magic swelled, the two devils only steps away. "We just need one, after all."

"Did you hear that?" The deep gruff of the Trpaslíks voice had barely cleared the air before Wyn stepped out from the shadows of the alley, her hands sparking in warning.

"Good evening, gentlemen." She might have been greeting a new client with the honey in her voice. "Lovely night for a stroll, isn't it?" She popped her hip out, pursed her lips, and flipped the short bob of her hair seductively. The motions were so practiced I knew at once what her game was, and I knew it would work, too. It was far too Charlie's Angels not to.

"Wynifred! The dirty traitor! Stand down and be killed, girl."

Well, okay, it would have worked if it weren't for that.

"Don't go spouting out labels like that," I said, trying to

keep my voice as calm as Wyn's as I walked out beside her. *Try* was the operative word there. I was certain I was shaking far too much. "My friend here has been plagued by the exact same ailment and the pain it causes ... Besides, it's rude."

"So rude," Wyn added, careful not to touch me as I moved dangerously close to her. Our magic, which was already on high alert, sparked from the close proximity. "You'd think your master would have given you better manners."

I waited, convinced the anger-fueled tirade Edmund's men usually met us with would fill the dark. Instead, there was silence mixed with shock, eagerness, and just the right amount of fear. Although, I was positive the fear was more from me. I had exploded most of them outside of Rioseco. Consequently, perhaps the fear wasn't quite so one-sided.

"Hello ...? She insulted Edmund." Wyn sighed, upset at the lack of banter. "Where is the growling, the grumbles?"

"Lost along with their confidence," I said, smiling as the first attack went free, a bright purple line of magic that flew from my hand and right into the man before me.

His scream was loud as it hit him in the chest, sending him flying through the air to land about thirty feet away.

His partner looked between the two of us, looked into the reality of the massacre he had walked into, and turned to run.

Two steps in, and Wyn's magic wrapped around him in a visible line of fire, the heat so potent he couldn't move past it no matter how many times he flung his body against it. He screamed in pain with every impact, collapsing within his prison in a gasping heap of singed flesh, fear filling his eyes as he looked for a way to escape.

"Can we not maim people we are hoping to get help from?"

"Information, not help. And I wasn't maiming." Wyn's focus didn't leave the panicking creature she had captured. "Besides, didn't you shoot someone through the air? Who's not maiming now?"

I thought my eyebrows disappeared into the flyaway bangs of my dark hair.

Wyn sighed, the roll of her eyes making it clear I wouldn't let her get away with killing the man. "Fine. No *maiming*. I already won, anyway."

"Only because I attacked instead of restraining," I grumbled, taking a few steps toward my target. "I didn't expect you to restrain."

"Well, I can play with him later."

I couldn't help the disgusted wrinkle that moved over my face at that.

"So it's a win-win."

"Yeah, yeah," I grumbled, turning toward the darkened street where the man had landed, expecting to see his twisted, contorted shape, but nothing was there. There was merely the darkening pitch of the street, the damp road, and the hint of a bloodstain reflecting what little light was left from the day.

"What in the ...?" My magic flared as my fear did, power stretching from me as I searched for the man I had attacked, searched for the somewhat familiar magical footprint.

He couldn't have gone far.

"So, you!" Wyn's voice boomed from behind me. "You wanna come back with me? I have some really great questions for ya."

"Wyn?" I asked as I whipped around, nervous panic filling me as my magic flared. The disappearance of the man's magical sign ignited into panic as it reemerged, this time right behind me.

It took me a moment to realize what I was seeing was not, in fact, reality, but the whispers of a future.

"Wyn!" I screamed as the repeated shadow of the present flashed after its apparition, the man's magic already flaring and ready for attack.

She reacted to my scream, dodging out of the way as her own ability warned her of what was coming. The sudden movement freed her prisoner from his cage, and the man fell as another ribbon of color sped toward Wyn, intent on attack.

"I told you I would kill you!" the Trpaslík screamed as he attacked again. Mine came a second behind, hitting him square in the chest as Wyn's attack intersected in a weird array, the hole in her hand sending the color wide.

The two beams of color converged into one, the brilliant light seeping into his skin like an infection. It swept over him, sending him to the ground in a twitching heap.

Wyn once again captured her prisoner, her cage stronger as the flames licked around him, the heat and pressure a brilliance in the alley.

Knowing she could handle herself, I stepped toward the now lifeless man who was misshapen on the ground, his eyes wide and vacant as he stared into nothing, his whole body quivering as our magic devoured him. I guess that was what happened when you met both Wyn and me—a quick death.

"We really need to be more careful," I said to myself, unable to look away from the flesh below me that was beginning to bubble and boil.

"He didn't explode," Wyn stated, obviously absentminded as she restrained her prisoner.

"Yet." I said the word to myself, pulling away from the haunting way the Trpaslíks body moved.

"*Now* are you going to talk to me?" Wyn snapped, a revelry in the attack still winding inside her. I guessed she really was winning. An attack and a capture.

I laughed to myself, turning back to Wyn and her prisoner.

The Trpaslíks face was turned up in a wicked smile as he met her dead-on.

"You say *talk* like I have another option," the Trpaslík mocked, the jeering I had expected from earlier clear and vibrant. "I would rather talk than go back to what that blasted man has done." The man's obstinance faded to something closer to disgust, a disappointment I never thought I would see on a Trpaslík coloring him.

"What blasted man?" I asked, the snippet of conversation from before pushing against my heart. My magic flared so powerfully I was surprised it didn't pull me into sight.

Joclyn? Ilyan asked in obvious concern.

I ignored him. I couldn't answer. I couldn't think beyond the pieces that were slowly pulling together in my head.

The Trpaslík smiled from behind the fire, his eyes focused on me, the sneer returning with a dangerous light. "You know?" he queried to himself, "I think I'll keep it all: the answers, the truth, and most of all ... my freedom from the hell Sain has created."

With that, he walked into Wyn's cage, destroying his own life before we had the chance to stop him. Wyn screamed in disbelief, and my jaw went slack in confusion, not wanting to believe the possibilities that had made themselves clear.

5

RYLAND

"I HEARD THEM OVER THERE, MÍRA!" Risha's voice rolled over the rubble of the cathedral like the morning fog of the mountains near my old home.

It was a lone voice, a single haunting apparition that echoed and moved as if it had come from the smoke itself. But I knew better. I knew she was somewhere out there, behind the fog, hunkered down in the dark with her teammate, trying to find a way to capture our flag.

Trying to get past us.

We wouldn't let them.

Taking one sidelong glance at Jaromir, I nodded once in the direction of our flag, an old Hawaiian shirt we had tucked underneath a large slab of concrete. Perhaps, by sending him to guard it while the girls attempted to defeat me, I would be able to take them out. Then we might have a chance.

We had won two out of the last three games, and the girls

were being ruthless this time. They obviously didn't want to lose again.

It was getting late. The sun had already set, which meant they were running out of time to claim a win.

Jaromir smiled at the silent request, his eyes full of understanding as he scuttled away from me amidst the ruins of the once beautiful cathedral. What little was visible of the formerly pristine mosaic tile was smashed to bits.

The sound of shifting debris was a distorted resonance in the open space. It rippled against the fog and drifted into the purple sky far above us where the crimson stars danced to the noise.

Noise I already knew was too loud.

If they didn't know for certain where we were before, they did now.

My heart beat more heavily. I had endured endless battles and terrifying realities, but somehow, playing capture the flag with two unrelenting girls was more terrifying.

The sound of Jaromir's footsteps faded as the smoke folded around him, swallowing him whole.

I stood alone, my hands at the ready, magic buzzing within the heavy pulse of my blood, the panicked energy making my fear worse.

Silence stretched, so still that, standing there, I could hear the movement of the fog. The whispered rush of fog and smoke that moved through my hair, whispered in my ears.

Shifting my feet, I turned to look behind me, my heart beating with a painful throb as rocks tumbled away from the small rise I stood on, falling end over end with a clack of sound.

"You're supposed to be quiet," Risha said from behind me, her voice a seductive murmur as the familiar warmth of her magic ran over me with the strength of a hurricane.

The fog around us moved from the intensity of her power, a deep desire for her rippling alongside.

My magic longed for hers, as I did. It pulsed with the contact, turning to ice the second the spell took hold, wrapping around me and freezing me in place.

Immobile, I could feel myself teetering back and forth, unable to hold my balance on the pile of rubble. It was something that was not missed by Risha, who smiled wickedly, stepping around me and upsetting the stones underneath me further.

"Don't, Reesh," I pleaded, grateful I could still speak.

"Don't what?" she teased.

A giggle echoed from somewhere behind her, making it clear that Míra was watching the scene from somewhere in the fog, the density clearing a bit as the magic began to wear off.

"Save me, Jaromir!" I yelled desperately, all hope lost when both Risha and Míra laughed harder, this time joined by a little boy's giggle that I knew too well.

"No!" I yelled, as Risha's smile hit its maximum, her hand moving forward and pressing against my chest, the tiniest pressure sending me backward.

Falling, I landed hard against stone and wood, my immobile

figure rolling down the tiny hill like Jack must have done with that darn pail.

I wished I had a pail. Then I could use it as a helmet. I could feel every jagged edge of rock against the soft tissue in my arms and back. Wood and stone hit my face and head with the strength of a battering ram. And while I rolled, I hissed and gasped in an attempt to break free from the bind Risha had placed over me as her malicious laugh echoed throughout the fog. She was quite pleased with herself.

"We've won, Míra!" Risha said, running right up to me and placing her foot square on my rib cage, posing beside me like a big game hunter with a new kill. "I have defeated him, and it was glorious!"

Míra's dark, little laugh resonated over the rubble and fog as she ran up to us like a bullet, her arms stretched out like a plane, the frayed floral shirt clutched securely in her fist.

"We win! We win!" she said, skipping and jumping, her hair waving away the smoke behind her.

Even oddly construed here on the ground, a smile seeped across my face. It was such an odd occasion to get anything more than a sneer and a glare out of that little girl.

"Very funny," I grumbled, still trying to shift underneath the lock that Risha had pinned me with, still unable to move more than an inch.

Perfect. I was a lion down for the kill, pranced around by Míra. And to make matters worse, Jaromir joined her dancing and prancing, screaming "We win" right alongside his sister.

"Hey!" I yelled, my voice distorted, my cheek smashed

uncomfortably against a large bit of stone. "You're on my team, Jaromir!"

"Not anymore!" The boy laughed with his sister as they danced and played, stone and wood crunching around me in an odd orchestra.

"Jaromir knows whose side is the winning one, Ryland," Risha teased as she stepped down from my sore and bruised torso, releasing the magic with the softest touch of her fingers against my face.

My stomach swooped and spun at the contact.

"He defected?" I was aghast, my eyes wide as I sat up to face the treacherous child.

He didn't even seem affected by the strength of my glare. He laughed harder, his face squishing oddly due to the large kiss on his cheek as he continued dancing behind his sister's long, blonde curls.

"Yeah, he didn't want to lose, I guess," Risha said, sitting down beside me and trying her best to find a clean bit of rubble to avoid soiling her long skinny jeans.

I wanted to tell her it was hopeless yet couldn't bring myself to do it.

"You sent him away, right toward Míra, and we didn't even have to bribe him."

"Ah ..." Realization dawned on me more quickly than it normally did. "It was a rookie mistake."

"They are a tad bit loyal to each other." Risha lifted her thumb and forefinger, as if to display the depth of that loyalty. Instead, she framed the children who were still dancing and playing and laughing.

"Let's hope that loyalty can switch in other ways before it's too late." I tensed. I had spoken out of turn, and I knew it. Risha did, too.

Her back straightened as much as mine had. It was a very clear rule that we didn't discuss everything within earshot of the twins. Although I was confident they were both preoccupied enough that neither heard, I could never be certain with them. They didn't miss much.

If I had thought Jaromir was attentive, it was nothing compared to Míra.

"Patience, Ry," Risha sighed, her focus still on the kids. "I think we are closer than we were a few days ago. She hasn't tried to kill you in the last few days, so that's a step in the right direction."

"Well, it's a good thing I can fight back. Otherwise, I might be short an arm by now. Maybe I deserved it. I am dangerous." I laughed, and Risha did, too. It wasn't much of a joke, not with the way Míra looked at me. You would think I had one eye and three heads or something.

Or maybe you look like me.

The voice came without warning, the unwanted depth rippling inside me like a stab wound, and I recoiled. I hadn't heard the haunted voice blossom from inside of me for days. Almost a week, in fact. I hadn't put words to it, but the hope was there that I was free of it forever. Yet, here he was again, shattering my desire and infecting my mind with a poison that burned within me like acid.

"Ignore it," Risha said without looking at me, extending her hand to wrap around mine, the silent vow of support as wanted as the way her touch made my insides tango.

"I wish I could," I said more to myself than to her. After all, the voice was right; it was the reason Míra was afraid of me. It was also the reason I was here.

I carried the image of my father, and she had lived under his rule for months. From what Joclyn's prescience had shown her, Míra had lived through the same hell as I had. She had lived with the same violence and threats. She had lived through the same brainwashing nightmare.

No one in this camp would understand that. No one in this camp would know how to face that.

No matter how my eyes and curls terrified her, I was the only one who could understand what she had gone through and help her overcome it.

I guessed the dark, broken piece of my subconscious was good for something besides the crazies.

"You can, and you will," Risha reassured me, her thumb gentle as she ran it over my knuckles. It took everything in me to restrain the shiver that moved up my spine at the touch, my stomach flopping around like a dead fish. "I know you can," she repeated, her voice soft.

We sat on the rock and rubble, her hand wrapped around mine. I stared at the green in her eyes, at the small amount of freckles that moved over her nose, at her lips and the way they gently arched …

"Are you guys going to kiss?" Jaromir asked from in front of us, bouncing around on his heels a few feet away.

I jumped, and Risha jerked back to reality as I did. Everything around me spun as my heart rate began to slow down, reality catching up with me. I was already missing the dream.

Was it a dream? I couldn't be sure. But I was definitely having trouble breathing.

"Jaromir!" Risha shrieked, pulling her hand away as she shifted her weight. "I didn't see you there!"

Jaromir smiled bigger, his teeth flashing as he ran toward us, placing himself between us as heavy and thick as peanut butter.

"I've been here the whole time, Risha. We were playing a game... right here in the cathedral ..."

"A game that I was betrayed in!" I yelled, wrapping my arm around his shoulders and ruffling his hair.

He yelped in protest, but I didn't let go. This one, he deserved.

"You're a dirty little traitor!"

"I did nothing of the sort!" he shrieked, jumping away from us and back over to Míra who glowered at the outburst. The wicked child I had grown used to took over her features.

"Traitor," I grumbled under my breath, exaggerating my irritation to comical proportions.

Jaromir attempted to look guilty for half a second before breaking out in laughter.

Míra, however, looked between us, her arms wrapped

around her torso as unmistakable terror crossed over her face.

Fear.

Fear that I hadn't seen since that day two weeks ago when we had pulled her out from amongst the dead.

"I wasn't a traitor, Ryland." Jaromir giggled, pulling my focus from his haunted sister. "I was a spy. Those are infinitely cooler."

Now it was my turn to laugh, although Míra didn't seem to get the joke. Her fright increased, her eyes darting around as if she were looking for a way to escape.

"A spy!" I yelled, trying to keep the joke going while my spine tingled with the sudden change of tension that was affecting the air around us. "That's just as bad!"

"No, it isn't, especially when you have magic." Jaromir laughed again, waving his hands before him. A few stones lifted into the air, dancing amidst the last of the fog before falling back down to the ground with a ripple of sound. "Then you can do anything you want."

Risha sat next to me as stiffly as a board.

At least I wasn't the only one to notice Míra's erratic behavior.

"So, you can change sides whenever you want? Be a bad guy or a good guy at will?" I asked, knowing I was moving into dangerous territory. "And that's okay?"

"Well, maybe not a bad guy ... but I would change sides not to be bad. Definitely," Jaromir said confidently, sinking down onto the rubble with his legs crisscrossed.

I leaned toward him, rocks crunching beneath me at the shift in weight. "So, are you saying my side was the bad side in our game?"

"No!" Jaromir interjected loudly, forcing out a laugh.

Míra jerked, the same look of fear running over her face.

"You aren't bad, Ryland. But Míra was on the other team, and she's family."

"Edmund is *my* family." A statement. One simple, horrifying statement that sent a ripple around us, causing Jaromir's jaw to go slack, his eyes wide, while Míra stiffened like a jolt of electricity moved through her, different waves of horror taking control. "Should I defect to his side?"

"No!" Jaromir jumped to his feet, a new wave of defiance taking me by surprise.

I had never seen him so against my father. Before, he had been interested. Before, he had wanted me to train him like my father had me. Now, he looked as scared of him as his sister did, as scared as if Edmund himself were standing behind me, threatening each of them with death. I didn't think I was that far off with the way Míra had begun shaking, her jaw so taut I could see the muscles in her neck.

"Edmund is evil!" Jaromir continued, the strength of his shout rippling over the ruins, threatening to bring the rest of the cathedral down around us. Thank goodness the magic Ilyan had put on it so we could still use it as an arena held, though I could hear the stones groan under the weight. "You aren't evil, Ryland. And neither is Míra."

"I agree, Jaromir," Risha said with a smile, leaning forward to ruffle the boy's always out of control hair. "I don't think Ry's bad. And I know Míra isn't."

I smiled, expecting the fear to slip off her face and the calm child to take its place. However, her anger grew, erupting inside of her in hatred deeper than we had seen before.

"No," she said, the single word a slap as she rushed toward her brother, rocks shifting beneath her. "I *am* bad. He made me that way."

"No," I started, my heart aching with the truth behind her words, the familiarity hitting me deep. "He didn't—"

"Ko, nuchín tě xadít!" she interrupted, the loudness of it feeling like a slap.

"Sho shceš adych uděbal?" Jaromir responded, his voice low and under his breath, so low I almost didn't hear him.

I didn't understand what they were saying in the first place. The secret language of twins, something I had heard about on several occasions, but had not witnessed until a few weeks ago when Míra had come into my life.

It was endlessly irritating, but we had chosen to put up with it for now. We needed her to trust us. She only trusted Jaromir right now, and she needed that. Taking away their secrets was simply going to strengthen her distrust of us.

"Meneshte ho botkni che mě, Jaromir!" Míra screamed, the reaction exactly opposite from what I had been hoping for.

My muscles tensed in my neck, my heart rate increasing at the sudden outburst.

"Míra," I scolded, knowing I was sounding a little too much like a TV dad, "you don't need to yell ..."

The words left my mind with one stern look from the girl in question, sparks zapping around her body in a very clear warning. My magic surged in preparation for restraint, not wanting today to end this way, not after all the progress we had made.

"You need to calm down, Míra," Risha interrupted, towering over her as she stood, not letting the child's magic deter her. "I don't want to have to take you back to the hall yet."

Míra flinched, Risha's choice of words affecting her.

The sparks of warning had stopped, but the hatred and anger didn't leave her eyes, her rigid posture straightening more.

"Zíš, sho to je, víte, sho pochředuji. Neshbosydňují." Míra's eyes were dead as she spoke directly to Jaromir, the anger lessening into a desperate plea, one that he didn't miss.

As though he had been slapped, Jaromir straightened, some hushed exchange breaking between them before he turned back to me, his eyes as hard as hers now.

"Ale meschi, adi ván donohl." His voice was as numb as the expression on his face, the mysterious fight they were engaged in coming to a head.

"Dubeche nuchet, dokub schete, ady všismi žít." Míra looked at us as she spoke, her eyes still as hard.

We understood nothing, yet her warning was clear.

"I know there is some good in you, Míra," Jaromir whispered, his focus on his hands before lifting them to hers, his eyes filling with tears. "I know you don't have to do that. I know you will find a way."

I jerked as much as Míra did, her eyes shocked before reverting back to anger. Glancing between Risha and me, she feared what we had heard, what we had understood, which wasn't much.

He had spoken in clean Czech, yet it was still no more than gibberish with nothing to connect it to.

"I know there is good in you, too, Míra," Risha added, leaning toward the kids and stretching her hand toward the girl in what she probably thought was a sign of friendship.

However, Míra stared at it, her lips sneering in disgust before she stepped behind her brother again, using him as some kind of barricade.

"Then you don't know me," she hissed, the bright eyes that should have been full of so much joy and youthfulness cold and dead.

"I know you," I interrupted, my heart building into a painful staccato as I made the connection, as I truly understood what she was saying. Even the monster in my mind understood. The deep rumble of his laughter rolled within my subconscious, lifting my heart rate further. "I know where you came from. And I know what my father would ask of you. I know you and the hell you are stuck in better than you think."

"You don't have a clue. You could never know what he would want of me. What I have to do," she snapped, the preteen angst ripping amidst the air between us.

So much for the afterschool special.

"I do because my father made me kill my mother."

Míra stiffened, Jaromir following suit as their eyes narrowed. Míra's motions were slow as she turned to face me, nose wrinkled in a look that was haunting, something that turned the fear and familiarity I had sensed before up to an eleven.

"He asked me to kill someone," I continued without waiting for a response, "and I did, not knowing there was someone else I could go to. Not knowing there was a good side."

The stress and tension in our little group were higher than they had ever been. None more so than from Risha, whom I was certain was crying.

I ignored it, not really liking it when people cried for me.

"There isn't a good side, Ryland," Míra whispered, the hatred dripping from her face and leaving me staring at the true little girl for the first time. "Not with this. Everyone gets hurt. Everyone is going to die. I can't stop it. No matter what, it happens."

"That can't be true—" Risha began, her words cut off with one sharp look from the little girl before us.

"It is, Risha. Everyone is going to die."

My heart stopped beating. The world spun around me as what she said sunk in, as the truth behind it sunk in.

Jaromir looked between us, his nose wrinkled as he clenched his jaw, a different kind of fear taking over him. I didn't think words more haunting had ever been spoken by a child, ever spoken by a little girl with so much sadness, fear, and hatred in her eyes.

Like a geometric video game, her words began to fit

together. Ts and Ls and sticks all fell into place. I could hear the tiny game music in my head, the steady tempo increasing as the beat of my heart did. The sounds moved at a rapid pace in a countdown that I already knew I couldn't outrun.

"My father trained you." The statement was molasses in my mouth, but Míra didn't look away. "He trained me, too. But that doesn't mean he owns us."

But I do.

I own your mind.

I own your will.

As I do the girl's.

And she's right; she's going to kill you all.

Watch and see.

You deserve it.

I let the hatred in my demons fuel me as I stared at Míra.

Jaromir looked between us in panic, the fear on his face deepening due to what I had so openly confessed.

Risha gripped my hand as she leaned closer, her actions making it clear she knew what I was doing. It was making me uncomfortable.

I knew she was trying to get me to stop, but I couldn't. I was like a freight train hurtling toward the cliff, the destination on the other side of the cavern clear.

"He doesn't own us," I repeated, my focus on the girl in question. "We don't have to give him that power."

Her hatred deepened, but this time, it was toward me.

"It doesn't work that way, Ryland. You don't know what you are saying."

"I do, Míra. I—"

"No, you don't!" she exploded, her rage rippling over her as her fists hit against her thighs. "You don't know!"

"Wíš sho; řechmi nu," Jaromir tried to calm her, his voice weak.

Míra glared at him, the look increasing the just-been-punched look the boy had.

"Mebleť che po tosho! None of you know what you are talking about!" She turned toward us, the anger clear as she clenched her jaw before, with the slightest of pops, she vanished into thin air, pulling herself into a stutter as she left our side.

The already tense bands of muscle in my shoulders and arms tightened, my heart seemingly forgetting how to beat as I stared into the space she had been.

A stutter.

A darn near perfect one from what I could tell, performed by a child. It shouldn't have been possible, not even with the Štít inside of her. I had watched Cail for years. Even he hadn't been able to stutter. He hadn't been able to do anything without the permission of Edmund.

He had been his slave.

As this girl should be if the Štít was Edmund's as Jos had seen.

"Míra!" Jaromir screamed, freaking out as he turned around, looking for his sister. "What did you do to her?" He rounded on us, anger burrowing through him so fast I was worried he would turn on us, too.

"We didn't do anything," Risha gasped, clenching my shoulder as she stood up, her eyes scanning the hills of rubble in a desperate need to find her. "She shouldn't have done that."

"She shouldn't be able to," I pointed out, forgetting Jaromir's panic as I, too, stood up, looking over the piles of rubble for some sign of her.

What had we done? We needed to find her before she did something.

As I stood, another small pop sounded, the girl reappearing in the same spot she had left moments before.

"It's a stutter," she said, proud of herself. "I bet you can't do that."

I couldn't, but that wasn't the reason I was staring at her with such fear. It wasn't the reason my heart had turned into a thunder of noise and my muscles had tensed into cords of iron. It wasn't the reason Risha's fingers were sparking in preparation for the battle she was convinced was seconds away.

"How did you do that?" I asked, my voice dead against the panic.

"It's a stutter, dummy," she repeated, irritated I hadn't followed the obviousness of her statement. "I knew you couldn't do it."

"I can't, but how can you ...?"

She opened her mouth to answer then stopped, the malicious intent on her face fading away.

"Did Edmund let you have full control?" I asked.

"Once I got here, everything changed," she hissed, that same powerful pride taking over her again. "He knows I'm here. He knows what I am supposed to do. I can't stop it. I'm not a good person, Ryland. I can never be."

"No," Risha gasped, putting it all together a second before I did.

Regardless that what she was saying was horrifying, the mysterious job one that I knew at once we needed to stop, it was what she had done that was the real danger.

It was what it meant that made her dangerous.

"The hollow Štít ... It's not hollow because he took it away. It's hollow because there is nothing on the other side." I spoke to myself, the same realization clear on Risha's face as her chest heaved in panic.

"What are you talking about?" Míra asked from beside us, obviously confused. "My Štít isn't hollow. It's cursed."

I could see how she would think that, but it didn't fit.

We ignored her, our eyes wide as things fell into place.

"He would have to be ..."

Dead.

I put the word into place in silence, the reality not one Míra should know. Not yet. Not with whatever certain death and expectation she was facing. She was such a loose wire that I didn't want to give her hope, only to have her erupt. At the same time, I didn't want to leave her in the dark for long.

If this were true, it could be the difference between her loyalties, from pulling her away from whatever job she had to do.

"Get them back to the hall. Don't take your eyes off them. I need to talk to Ilyan. I'll be back," I said to Risha, not waiting for her nod of understanding before I took off into the air, my magic lifting me higher as I soared away from them and toward the main courtyard.

The whining and bickering hordes Ilyan had been trapped in for days would have to wait. I needed to find him.

6

JOCLYN

"Never do that again!" Wyn's voice was a snap in my ear, accentuated by the not so playful swap against my backside as she fell to her knees, gasping and heaving in a desperate attempt to catch air.

"Ryland said the same thing two weeks ago." I laughed, magic pulling me toward Ilyan, desperate to be near him now that we were back in the cathedral.

"I can see why," Wyn gasped. "That was awful. No wonder no one other than you and Ilyan has even tried that. I mean, do you have a death wish?"

"No death wish, just not a lot of time."

As I pulled her back to her feet, she gasped, her eyes wide in obvious panic that I was about to do it again.

"Take a chill, Wyn. I'm not going to do it again. And it was a stutter, not a colonoscopy."

"A what? Is that some kind of party mortals have? Because it sounds awful."

"Never mind." This time, I did roll my eyes as I dragged her behind me. We weaved past the illuminated tents that littered the courtyard. The canvas domes glowed in the darkness in glittering jewel tones of red, blue, yellow and green.

It was magical if you could ignore the dark shapes that wandered amongst them, darting around the camp in shadows, whispering in groups, and cowering in the dark like some demon was ready to strike.

"This way." Gripping Wyn's gloved hand, I pulled her after me, letting the strong tug of Ilyan's magic guide me. "He's this way."

"Lead the way, Your Majesty," Wyn taunted. "In a nice, gentle walk if you please."

Ignoring her, I pulled her behind me, darting around a large, red dome. The familiar red light emanated from it until it intersected with the blue tent next door, casting ribbons of blue and red and purple around us like a rainbow.

The beauty was lost, however, as I took one more step and the whispers hit against my chest like the sharp point of a nail, the lingering shadows staring at me unabashedly, hands held over mouths as they hissed and speculated on realities they could never understand. Some didn't even bother to hide their questions or comments. They let them run freely, loudly, and aggressively. The words bounced off the canvas and alerted everyone to my very presence. Anyone who had already retired to their tents became attentive, emerging from the canvas at the prospect of drama.

"I don't know why he chose her."

"She probably broke the original prophecy, too. Broke them all. Now we don't know ..."

"You saw all that fire ... and that girl ... so much blood."

"She probably wipes the blood on her face and turns into a dragon. Eats goats raw," Wyn interjected from beside me, adding her own flavor to the growing horde. Her loud scoff was not missed by any of them.

An old woman's eyes grew wide before she darted back into her tent, hisses seeping through the canvas after her.

"They are going to believe that, you know," I snapped under my breath.

Wyn smiled more widely, proud of herself. "That's the point —to make them so ridiculous they won't know what to believe."

I wasn't convinced that was actually helping, but whatever. Wyn was my greatest ally, and I was glad to have her.

"You and I know the truth, and that's all that matters."

"That is blood on her hands! I wonder if she killed someone else."

I wiped them against my pants, my heart dropping to my knees as the whispers increased, alerting me to what I had done.

Wyn, however, laughed and said loudly, "Don't let them see the goat blood, Jos. I don't want to share my dinner with anyone."

That time, I laughed, the sound an opposition to the fear

that leeched around us, wiping it all away and leaving everyone looking confused.

"Their fears are unfounded," Wyn said with a slight laugh from where she stood beside me like a bodyguard, her oppressive frame enough to scare off anyone who might try something. "Someday, they will see the truth."

If I were going to have a bodyguard, I would choose Wyn, even with her crazy reputation. She would sooner kill someone than let them tear me down. I wasn't always positive that was a good thing.

"And what truth is that?" Darting between a green and gray tent, I came face to face with a bright-eyed child who promptly screamed and ducked inside. "That I eat children for breakfast? Because that one seems to have gotten out."

"No," Wyn groaned as she pulled me away from the tent and toward the tall blond man who was looking at me as warily and worriedly as he always did as of late. If it weren't for the intense love in his eyes, I would say he was half-dead already. "That Sain is a bloodsucking leech who was crossed with a dinosaur. Leechasaurus rex." She waved her arms around like a gimpy Tyrannosaur, her tongue darting out in some weird hissing-slurping concoction.

"Do we need to get Wyn admitted somewhere?" Ilyan asked in deeply accented English as he walked toward us before wrapping his arm around my waist and pulling me close. "She seems to have pulled the last strand of sanity away."

"If I've lost sanity, it's thanks to you two," Wyn teased, the twisted dinosaur impersonation fading away. "Wars and imprisonment and death and all that crap. I think, after all this is said and done, I deserve a vacation."

"Only if I can go with you," I provided, my mind focused on the imagery Ilyan was obsessed with: the white sandy beaches of our Tôuha.

I relaxed, the still whispering crowds surrounding us not seeming to matter so much anymore. My magic flared at the thought of the vision, binding strongly with Ilyan's as it tried to pull us into the sub-consciousness together. It was a pleasant feeling, but one I couldn't really act on right now, especially right here in the middle of a crowd.

"It's the south of France," Ilyan corrected my mistake aloud, making it clear he was as tuned into me as I was to him. "I like this idea, Wynifred. After this war is done, we can all go to the south of France."

"Deal." Wyn stuck her hand out like some kind of property broker. Ilyan took it without hesitation, the stress on his brow fading away. "And thanks for the mind reading interpretation. I hate feeling lost in you guys' half-muted telephone call."

"Anything to help," Ilyan said in quick Czech, his smile fading away as yet another disagreement broke out a few tents away from where we stood.

Angry voices rose above the dark, shattering the calm silence of the night like a bass drum.

I jumped at the sound, looking toward them and knowing we should intervene.

This one is on them, Ilyan growled inside my mind, pulling me against him as he led us all away from the fight, away from the tents and into the dark shadows that surrounded the courtyard. "We have worse things to address than juvenile issues."

"Seriously, that may be the smartest thing you have said all week," Wyn whispered in the dark, her own irritation with the constant bickering clear. "It's so obvious you guys have never had kids. You are like helicopter parents with an army grade whirligig, always zooming in, ready to fix everything."

"Whirligig?" I asked, slack-jawed.

She ignored me.

"Let them fight; let them bicker; let them repeat whatever lies they have. When the band breaks up, it won't matter, anyway. Only one thing matters. And unfortunately, he doesn't bring good news."

"Sain." His name was a snarl, my magic flaring in irritation as it attempted to pull me into a sight. I let it flare, willing to let it take me, but nothing happened, nothing more than the memory of the man stuck in Wyn's cage and the words he had said before he had taken his own life.

"Why do I have a feeling this is not the normal tirade?" Ilyan asked as he turned to me, his accent deepening with irritation. "What happened with those two men you saw?" He looked at me quizzically, one eyebrow disappearing into the flyaway strands of blond hair that had broken free from the messy braid I had given him.

"It's not," I groaned, my heart booming. "I am not sure Edmund is in control anymore."

That got his attention. His magic pushed into me with such force I gasped, the scene replaying itself inside my mind as Ilyan watched everything unfold.

Once.

Twice.

He pulled the memory of the scuffle in the alley out of me, looking at it like it were his own. His thoughts were rushed with panic as he dissected everything as we had, the reality terrifying if not glaringly obvious.

"No. It can't be." With a gasp, he detached his mind from mine, leaving me staring into the dark of the courtyard again, the bright pops of color somewhat disorienting as everything spun.

"I hated when you do that," I barked All powerful or not, every time he dug inside my brain, it left me one gasp away from covering all of our shoes with vomit.

"You think it's true?" Wyn took a step closer, lowering her voice as her eyes darted around to make certain we were alone. But the dark was encompassing, and with the way the people around the tents paid us no mind, I wasn't confident they could see us, let alone hear us.

They can't, Ilyan provided, tightening his hands around my waist.

"Given what the Trpaslík said," Ilyan continued aloud, "I can't say for certain, but it sure seems that way. But, knowing Edmund and Sain, we can't rule this out as a well-conceived trick."

"Wouldn't be the first time," Wyn grumbled. "I hope it is that. I have plans far better than burning to end that man's life."

"I thought *I* was supposed to kill Edmund?" I asked,

confused by Wyn's random confession, but also by the situation in general. "There was this big prophecy—"

"I changed my mind. Besides, every day that prophecy seems less and less like a reality you will ever have to face," Wyn said, feigning some kind of sobriety. "Congratulations, you aren't going to die!" She smiled brightly at me, but it wasn't a look I could return.

A wash of despair I hadn't expected moved over me, a pain and a sadness I didn't understand pressing against my heart.

I jerked at the emotions, trying to figure out where they were coming from, simply to be pulled out of the fear that brought and into the reality that was attached to it.

"Ilyan," I gasped as I turned toward him, the words quickly replacing themselves as his pain became mine. The memories of the happy father he had known moved through us like a movie reel.

I placed my hand on his arm, my touch gentle as I tried to gauge his mood from the oddly crippling weight moving over me.

Wyn froze in place as she put her own Lincoln logs together in her mind, her mouth forming a wide O of understanding.

My father had killed his father.

The irony of that statement was strangely cruel.

Perhaps we can laugh at it another time, Ilyan's voice filled me, the pain in his mind infecting the words. He didn't need to say more.

I wrapped my arms around him, letting my magic fill him

from tip to tip as I warmed him, fully aware that this was a pain that couldn't be smothered. Evil dad or not, as the memories that I was currently being filled with proved, he hadn't been all bad.

"I'm sorry, Ilyan," I whispered. "I didn't realize."

"If it makes you feel any better, it hurt when I killed my da— when I killed Timothy," Wyn said, running her fingers over the faded marks on her arm as she shuffled her feet uncomfortably. "I didn't expect to feel anything, either. Jerk that he was. But then ... I mean ... I guess there were good times, too."

"Thank you, Wynifred." Ilyan looked up at her at that, his eyes wide as his jaw set in what could easily be confused as anger.

Wyn didn't even flinch. She pursed her lips together and shrugged as if Ilyan had done nothing more than reject an offering of cake.

"Have you seen anything more besides what you two witnessed in the alley, mi lasko?"

"You know my visions have been changing, and everything outside the dome seems to be broken. I can't access any of it. If Sain did something like this, then that could be why." I swallowed, my hand still strong on his back even as he looked up at the stars hanging high in the lavender sky.

"Was my father there?" Ilyan very rarely referred to Edmund as his father, and given the situation, I shouldn't be surprised. Still, it caught me off guard, his grief intense.

"Not—"

"Wait," Ilyan cut me off, his hair fanning around his face as he turned toward me, the stars forgotten as his eyes filled with an odd, maniacal energy that I hadn't seen for some time. "Has Edmund been in any of your sights since the ending began to change?"

I blinked, my mind running over his question as sight after sight ran across my recall, the answer becoming apparent.

"No."

"And the funeral?"

"I don't think I want to hear any more," Wyn groaned and walked back toward the Technicolor courtyard.

Ilyan and I stayed still, our hearts pounding as our eyes locked, more pieces of this complicated web falling into place.

"Has the funeral changed?" Ilyan asked again, his heart clenching as mine did. That painful reality was one neither of us wanted to face.

"No, It's the same. It still does that crazy backward thing that Dramin and I can't figure out. But it's the same."

"Is Sain in any of the sights since the change?" The excitement he had exhibited before faded as he asked the question even he knew the answer to. We had talked about my sights enough. Heck, he had peeked into one no more than an hour before.

"Yes."

"So, it's true." The same pain ran over his face at the admittance, his shoulders slumping a bit. "Even if he is still alive, Sain has—"

"Guys?" Wyn interrupted as she rejoined us, her focus on the cluster of tents right before us. Her eyes were wide with fear, as if she expected some demon to appear and gobble us up. "Ryland's coming."

She had barely spoken the words when Ryland pushed his way between the too-close canvas, his curls sagging under glistening sweat. The entire effect made him look like a lost dog who had fallen into a pool of muddy water on accident and was still bewildered by what had happened.

"Ry?" I asked, confused, as Wyn remained frozen between us.

I didn't know what had spooked Wyn so much. She could sense magic, not moods, and yet something had infected her. She looked like she could vomit, run away, or both.

"Finally. I've been looking for you," Ryland gasped out as he continued his sprint toward us, his shirt so soaked I expected him to remove it.

My stomach jerked uncomfortably at the memory attached to that thought, the imagery of Ryland removing his shirt too close for comfort.

Ilyan cleared his throat beside me, pulling me against him as a frown came upon his face.

I cringed, my stomach falling to my toes in embarrassment.

Ilyan's thoughts weren't on mine, though. They were on what we had been discussing. They were on his father as his eyes focused on his baby brother.

Ilyan hadn't been Edmund's solitary son.

I was a fool for not having remembered that. I had practically grown up in their house.

Well, in the kitchen, anyway.

I recoiled, the flash of a familiar face haunting my memory. Luckily, no one noticed. Everyone was far too focused on what was before them.

"We have a problem." Ryland panted, his voice broken as he ran his hand through his hair, tiny droplets of sweat flying away from him.

"Unless it involves our father coming back from the dead to avenge us, I would say we have more important things to handle right now, little brother."

Wow, Ilyan, subtle much?

I guessed he had already moved past guilt and into anger.

"No, I ..." Ryland began before stopping short, his jaw swinging so low I was worried it would hit the ground like some old cartoon character. "Come back from the *dead*? You already know?"

"Well, Joclyn heard ..." Ilyan began, stuck in autopilot before Ryland's words caught up with him, smacking him in the face. "What do you know, Ryland?"

"Our father is dead."

I stared at Ryland, my eyes wide as I attempted to remind myself how to breathe. For all I knew, I had been smacked in the chest.

"You know? But how?"

"I am really lost," Ryland said, running his hand through his hair as he looked from person to person as if something on our faces would piece it together. His bewilderment grew.

"Don't be daft, Ry," Wyn scolded. Her sympathy had already been used up for the year, it seemed. Or maybe she no longer had any. It was hard to tell. "Jos and I overheard some Trpaslík henchmen talking about it—"

"And I just realized why Míra's Štít is empty," Ry interrupted her, his voice still raspy from attempting to catch his breath. "It's not connected to anything. The other side ... It's gone. His magic is in her, and she has full control."

If there were a time and a place for a staring match, this would be it.

None of us moved. We stood, frozen in the dark, staring at each other, the glowing orbs of the tents seeming like ominous enemies waiting to attack.

"Where is she?" Ilyan asked, the king coming out like a lion.

"I had Risha take her and Jaromir back to the hall with the healers. She can stutter."

Ilyan jerked at the word. He probably would have run right to her if I hadn't held him in place.

"So I am unsure what good it will do," Ryland continued. "But I gave them orders not to let them out of their sight."

My heart was once again trying to pound its way past my rib cage. I thought overhearing about my father's witch burning was one thing, but even I could tell Ryland was spooked.

The accidentally-falling-into-a-pool-of-mud look was suddenly making sense.

"So it's true, then." Ilyan's voice was little more than a growl. Even Wyn was on edge. I could taste her magic in the air. "Sain has killed our father."

"Is that what you heard?" Ry's voice caught, his eyes wide as he stared at Wyn and me, His glare was so intense that, if I weren't standing right there, Ilyan's arm still wrapped around me, I might have thought I was seeing this through the eyes of sight. "That Sain killed him?"

"And apparently took control of his camps." Wyn scoffed. Disgusted, she popped her hip out, wrinkling her nose as if the filth-covered man were standing right before her. "King Sain. I think there was a reason that role expired centuries ago. Is it sad that I kind of want Edmund to still be alive? I mean, I've kind of been wanting to kill him for a couple hundred years now ... It would suck to lose out on that honor at the last minute. And all because of a dirty Drak."

"Whoa, that's harsh, Wyn." Ryland was on the defensive, his shoulders squaring as he moved toward me as though he were preparing to fight for my honor.

As if I needed it.

"I'm not sure how to take that, Wyn, so I am just going to assume you are talking about your swim in the dumpster earlier and the fact that my father doesn't like to bathe. Given that, I am not sure who is the 'dirty' one."

Ryland snickered as Wyn's jaw dropped, the upset forgotten as that mischievous light tickled her eyes, a rebuttal moments away.

"That's enough," Ilyan snapped as he ceased his pacing to

rejoin us, the humor in his voice barely masked. "Wyn, let's not accidentally insult my wife."

"Who says it was an accident?" she managed to sneak in.

Ryland snickered, but the side glance Ilyan fixed her with shut her right up. She locked her lips with an imaginary zipper, a smug victory remaining clear in her eyes.

"We have bigger issues than bathing and garbage bins," Ilyan finished lamely, extending his hand toward mine in an invitation that needed no explanation. "We have no way of knowing for certain if Edmund is dead, but if he is, we need to prepare as best we can for Sain's control, especially when eighty percent of our people favor him. We need to find out who stands with us and who is against us. I would rather prepare for a rebellion before Sain's zealots act on it. We need to keep this information from them as long as possible."

"And how do you suggest we do that?" I asked, not liking where this was going.

"A council," Ilyan said, a powerful smile running over his face, his magic pressing against all of it with exhilaration for what was coming. "A very well-placed council."

Everyone looked at each other. With the way Wyn's eyebrows were flying away, I would guess they were as lost as I was.

There was no denying the power in Ilyan's face, however. He knew exactly where we were going. And we were all eager to let him lead us there.

"Ryland, I need you and Risha to help guard the kids. Take

turns if you must. It won't help if the girl can stutter, but I have a feeling she won't leave Jaromir behind. And Joclyn's the only one who can take someone with her without risking life and limb. I'll want you at the council, so leave Risha there to watch over them so you can attend council in the morning."

Both Wyn and Ryland turned a delicate shade of green at the memory of the "trauma" I had put them through. Go figure.

"Joclyn and I are going to go to Dramin. We need to track the sight, dig deeper and see if we can find any concrete answers or clarify what is coming. Dramin knows the most about Drak and Sain—"

"And I will dance naked amongst the trees ..." Wyn began, her snide retort for being excluded from the to-dos blocked with one sharp look from Ilyan.

"No, Wyn, you are in charge. I need you to supervise the masses and prepare them for a council tomorrow morning."

"Tomorrow morning?" Wyn interjected, aghast.

Ilyan ignored her.

"I need you to make sure everyone is in attendance."

"Wait," Wyn gasped, further shock widening her face. "You are putting *me* in charge?"

"As long as you keep your clothes on, yes." Ilyan didn't seem too happy about this. His lips were a tight line, and he wouldn't even look at her. He still hadn't forgiven her for destroying his chapel, not that I blamed him.

"No prob, boss. I won't let you down."

"Well," Ilyan sighed, his eyes closing as he dragged his hand through his hair again, "desperate times call for desperate measures."

"Burn."

7

SAIN

RUNNING BENEATH THE STARS, the sparkling specks choked by smoke, I could already see the flames. I could see them lick the sky, light the night on fire with the light of a sun. It was as it had been in sight, the dratted imagery coming before, not soon enough to stop it.

Not soon enough to save the people who were trapped in the large, white tent.

At any other time, I wouldn't care who lived and died. I wouldn't care who was sentenced to a fiery death. I had killed enough. I had created enough death. I had enough blood on my hands.

But these were not on my hands. They were not deaths I had created, not deaths I had wanted. I needed their allegiance, not their deaths. I needed to win a war with warriors, not graves.

I still needed them.

I needed them alive ... for now.

"Did you see anyone leave the tent after the fire?" I asked Damek who ran beside me, his breath coming in ragged shards as he tried to keep up with me.

Damek had shown up after the sight had left me, pulling me out of bed and back into the madness that was ripping everything apart.

"Nothing out of the usual, my king." He heaved, his eyes still on the brilliant light before us.

The heat of the fire saturated the air, even from hundreds of yards away.

"Did you see *them*?"

He knew who I was talking about, and he swallowed, a quick side glance cast my way before he looked forward, trying his best to keep his back straight.

If it were anyone else, I would assume this behavior to mean he was working with them, but I had covered his back with Black Water a few days ago, leaving him with nine long scars and me with a perfect window into his life, into his allegiance.

He wasn't working with them.

"No, my king," Damek finally said, the bend in his back making it clear he was still feeling the residual pain from the water. "But I am still of the opinion they are not working alone. From what I have heard ..."

Stopping in place, I wound my magic across the air as I stopped Damek's forward progression. His words ceased as I pulled him back, sending him through the air with a yelp and bringing him to stand right before me.

The crackle of the fire snapped over the hot air as we stood so close to the fire that the screams of those dying, the screams of those trying to help, were clearly heard.

"I have told you before, Damek, that you can only kill a snake by cutting off its head." I stepped closer to him, placing my hand on his shoulder, my long, unkempt thumbnail pressing against the skin there as I ran the thumb of my other hand over the length of his knife.

His shoulders pulled up to his ears, the fear obvious despite his eyes never leaving mine, my hand still heavy on his shoulder.

It had been two weeks since I had killed his former master, and already, his bravery and allegiance were shifting. After two more weeks, he would be quite the formidable servant, even without a Štít.

I was unsure even Edmund could have accomplished such a feat.

"Step on a devil's tail and just upset him more," he continued for me, my magic relaxing against him as he stumbled back, trying to find his feet.

"Yes." My response was a hiss, the sound made louder by a flare-up of the fire, the blast lighting the field as brightly as the sun.

The screams increased with the explosion, the sound of a tent collapsing following behind.

Damek flinched, his eyes wide as they turned toward the now crippled tent. I didn't even look, something Damek didn't miss as his eyes returned to me, the fear in him intensifying.

"I need you to find them, Damek. All three right now." I stepped closer to him as ash began to fall around us, the tiny bits of fluff drifting across the scorched air like snow. "Find them. Bring me information. I want it before the fire has turned to embers."

Boring my eyes into him, I let a smile curl my lips back over my teeth, a look that leached into him with the tiniest of flinches.

"Yes, my king," he whispered, bowing his head with one last glance before he ran back into the night.

"Where is Damek going in such a hurry?" Ovailia asked as she emerged from the cloud of ash and smoke Damek had disappeared into. "To get a pail of water?"

Even in flames and smoke, she was perfect. I had torn from the room, grabbing only my blood-soaked cape. She had dressed to the nines, complete with bright fire-red heels and skintight jeans.

I swallowed, gritting my teeth, keeping my magic restrained tightly against me unless she attempted something.

"I sent him to find the three bastards," I growled, turning back toward the flames, away from her.

"The usurpers." She spat the word with as much malice as I felt. "Do you think it was them?"

"Sight has shown me them standing in these flames, Ovailia. Do you really wish to question my ability?"

With one sidelong glance, I put her in her place. Her jaw tightened as she scowled at me, her steps slowing enough that I easily outstripped her.

"Why don't you get a pail of water, Ovailia, if you think it would help?" I didn't turn back to see her reaction, and I didn't give her any other instruction. I continued forward, picking up my pace to a run as I caught up to the horde of people.

Hundreds were running around, pulling Chosen from the tents, attempting to heal them. They stood, ash covering their heads and shoulders, magic stretching in an attempt to extinguish the flames.

It was when someone really did run forward with a pail of water, throwing the tiny amount of water on the wall of smoke and flame that I knew what we were facing.

It wasn't fire set with heat and tinder. It was magic, ignited with ability, shielded by a strength I hadn't seen for a while.

It wasn't fire meant to kill; it was fire meant to test the ability of those in the camp.

No, meant to test me.

Unsurprising, given with what the usurpers had been doing since I had marched the remains of Edmund onto that stage. Testing me. Testing my ability. Finding the cracks in a Drak.

Fools. There were none. I had been born from the mud. I was the perfection of power. It was a matter of time before they found that out.

They might have escaped the genocide I had staged in the hall, but they wouldn't live long. All I needed to do was find the perfect way to attack, to teach them a lesson.

"Ovailia!" I called, standing still as screams and smoke and flame engulfed the air around me.

The heat of the flames licked my skin, igniting the strength of the magic within it. It permeated the air, the magic that controlled it hidden under the heat. I felt it in waves of anger and malice that matched my own, beating amid me in knots that tensed my jaw.

"Yes," Ovailia spoke from behind me, out of arm's reach, as if that would save her from my wrath.

"Come here."

There was a moment of hesitation, the sound of screams and fire still echoing before the crunch of her heels against dirt and ash echoed over it. Her steps brought her right before me.

She stood with her hands firmly on her hips, her hair billowing behind her. Eyes flashing dangerously as she gazed at me, her disgust at being seen in such a state a dire warning that I let roll off my back with the tiniest of smiles.

I did love her when she was like that: defiant, angry, powerful.

This was beautiful.

This was the femininity that I desired.

"Do you feel it?" I asked her, prodding at her ability as I took a step closer, letting my magic free from where I had captured it, letting it run around her, taunt her.

She felt it at once, her hands tensing against her hips as her eyes narrowed. "Feel what?"

She wasn't amused.

My smile deepened. I loved playing with my food.

127

"The power in the flames, the strength of the magic that has created them."

Her eyes widened at that, the unexpected answer slapping her in the face.

Taking two quick steps toward her, I pulled her into me. Her magic continued to swirl through the air as she caught sight of what I and a handful of others had realized.

"Pekelný," she gasped, exhilarated horror echoing back at me. "Fire bred from hell."

"It seemed fitting that a devil would bring fire for me." I kept my voice low as I leaned into her, my magic running wild in its attempt to connect with hers. Doing my best to control it, to keep it close enough to Ovailia that her better judgment was compromised, I pressed my lips against her neck. I trailed them over her skin before coming to a rest on the hollow of her ear.

"I want you to put it out." The words were seductive, but she reacted as if they were poison, trying to pull away from me in shock, only to find my arm wrapped around her waist like an iron bar.

"You can't be serious, Sain," she retorted after recognizing her prison. "No one can put out pekelný."

"I can," I whispered, pulling away enough that she could see the power and warning in my eyes. I wanted her to feel it under her skin as my magic ran over her like silk. "But I don't want them to know that just yet."

Her eyes widened in further shock before the façade she always wore slipped back into place. The disgruntled mask crumpled her features until she was nothing more than an old woman with a hatred for all things living.

"Do you think it's them?"

I didn't respond to her query.

I turned her in my arms toward the wall of fire that we were now surrounded by. "Put out the fire, Ovailia."

"Sain ..."

"I know you can," I continued before she had a chance to rebut. "Show me how powerful you are. Remind all of these people that you are more than your father's pawn."

I felt her stiffen underneath my grip, her breathing picking up as, with wide eyes, she stared at the flames.

"You are more powerful than anyone here," I told her, letting my magic run over her skin, letting it soothe her as it attempted to move into her.

As she inhaled sharply, her magic rose up to meet mine. The warmth and strength of her power were a drug against me. Even with the power I held, the strength and anger that moved inside me, all I wanted was to kiss her, to take her and forget that the flames burned before us.

The heat of the flames was weaker than the heat that her magic sent into my blood.

Dangerous.

"I think it's time you remind them of that."

Pressing my lips against her neck with the deepest longing, I felt her pulse beneath my kiss. I savored the stuttered beat of her excitement before I pulled away, ripping my magic from her.

Backing away, she lifted her hands, the pressure of her power filling the air. Her hair swirled amidst the vortex of heated air as she stood alone, feet before the flames.

Moments from the fire attempting to devour her, moments from my Míraculous rescue.

I couldn't let them all think her powerful, but I couldn't destroy the flames on my own, either.

Laughing, I folded my arms over my chest, feeling her magic swell as mine began to spin. The streams of gray and black were a beautiful contrast against the flames as they spread from her hands. They sped through the air and slammed against the wall of fire with a reverberation that shook the ground beneath us all, ripping through the sky with a howl akin to an animal. An animal inches from death.

The screams of fear increased as the fire fought back against the attack, a wall of smoke flooding us, filling the air until it was hard to breathe.

I smiled at the magical battle before me, laughing at the war, only to have the laugh echo back to me.

The heavy wave of smoke shifted beneath me, choking me as the power in it became an infection, an infection that sparked against my sight. My head began to spin as my magic consumed me, pulling my mind into a different smoke-filled space.

Unable to pull myself out of the sight, I was surrounded by billows of gray and white so thick I could scarcely see past them. I couldn't be here. I needed to save Ovailia from the flames before they devoured her. I needed to save them all, to show them all what their new leader was capable of.

Yet, the magic had trapped me within it, the urgency great. It had been decades since I had been pulled into a sight of such importance, and *now* it chose to take me.

I needed to get out of here. Time was not on my side.

"Is there any news?" a deep, gruff voice I recognized filtered past the smoke, the very words beginning to clear it. The heavy shroud dissipated and left me standing in the center of a smoke-filled room where three Trpaslíks sat around a table.

"You," I barked, knowing the word would go unheard to those in the sight before me.

It was them, the same three men who had haunted my sight for the past few weeks, who had attacked the quiet silence that I had expected as king and challenged my crown at every turn.

Every turn that I met them at, that I had defeated them at.

Too bad no one living knew the very basics of dealing with a Drak.

Perhaps I should give them a hint. You couldn't defeat them, because you could not hide anything from them.

Through the distorted darkness they were surrounded by, the figures that sat around the table were clear and crisp beyond what was normal, the precise imagery too clean to be of this world. This was coming.

Perfect. I could use this premonition to find them. I could use it as my opportunity to destroy them.

Alojz, the man who had spoken, pulled the elongated pipe he was known for from his mouth with an embellished sigh, a billow of lavender smoke wafting around his head like a crown before dissipating into the already pungent space. "I am tired of waiting," he growled, the last of the smoke from his pipe floating into the air. "The Chosens' camps are on fire, and he still hasn't shown."

I tensed, my heart beat ramping up violently at what the old man had said.

This was not coming. This was now.

I could find them.

The older Trpaslík leaned across the table, his eyes wide as he looked at his two companions. The small tilt in his lip was partially hidden beneath his carefully trimmed beard, something that I had yet to adopt with my own scruffy mane, choosing to let the wild look I had adopted frighten my people, instead.

The mad, blood-soaked king.

"We are still waiting for word, Alojz," Georg said before leaning back in his chair, the wood creaking beneath him. "Perhaps the fire has devoured him."

A snicker ran over the three men at the suggestion.

Alojz returned the pipe to his mouth with an elongated sigh, obviously unpleased with the response.

"We must have hope," Bronislav said with a sigh, the portly Trpaslík looking very elderly beneath the yards of graying beard. "I worked for centuries to develop that attack. This was not what I had wished to use it on."

The attack, the fire that I could still smell in my nostrils. I needed to get back there before all was lost, yet I couldn't pull myself from this sight. This was exactly where I needed to be.

This was what I had been waiting to hear.

"Nothing will work unless we can find a guide to know how his sight works," Alojz said, his voice muffled from the stem of the pipe he had placed firmly between his teeth. "Everything we have done has given us inconclusive results."

"What was the reaction to yesterday's assault?" Georg asked, the change of conversation abrasive, especially coming from the usually quiet Trpaslík. His voice had barely risen above a whisper. If it weren't for the rattle of the long curls of his beard, I might not have even known it had come from him.

My prescience swirled a bit as my head spun, the smell of the smoke that surrounded me in reality smothering me, making it hard to breathe. The anxious excitement over what I was watching did not help much.

They had always spoken of upcoming attacks, of attempts to dethrone me. And while I had always assumed it was something more, I had never had any proof.

Now I knew.

With this dark query, their true plan had been ripped wide open for me to see, revealed by the very sight they were so cleverly attempting to decode. It was a grand plot yet one that reeked of deadly derisiveness. It would never work.

Now that I knew, I would crush them.

"It was a twenty-minute delay, followed by the execution of two innocents. He was grasping at straws. Although, there is a rumor that he burned the victims," Bronislav's voice wafted beyond the smoke toward me.

"What do you mean *burned*?" George whispered, his eyes wide in fear.

I couldn't stop the nefarious laugh. I was glad they couldn't hear it. They really had no idea what they were up against.

It made me eager for what was to come. I would definitely *burn* Georg first.

"With that water he drinks," Bronislav began, a fear behind his voice that I hadn't expected. "He burns to see—"

"So he's looking for us," Alojz interjected, his own voice shaking. "How do you hide from a being who can see everything?"

How, indeed? I asked myself with a smirk, partly disappointed that they had come to such a conclusion before I'd had a chance to *show* them what was to come.

"We have every spell and shield around us right now, Alojz," Georg interjected, his beard shaking rampantly from his chin. "As far as we know, he won't be able to see us. No one will willingly break. They all want him gone."

My laugh boomed so loudly I could have sworn some of them jumped, their jerks so large even the table shifted under the weight.

"Simple shields won't stop me," I hissed to myself, partially aware that anyone around me in reality would be able to hear what I was saying. "I can see everything, and none of you will get away."

"Are you telling me that all of this has been useless?" Alojz's knuckles were white from where he gripped his pipe, the rest of his body remaining calm. That tiny, little thing made his frustration of the failure as clear as my shock.

"No, not at all. We haven't been at this long," Georg pleaded, his calm barely able to appease his companion's tempers. "I am positive Bronislav's fire will work. Then we will know what we are up against. We will know how to defeat him. I wouldn't want to act drastically when we don't know—"

"I think we know enough." Bronislav's brow furrowed in anger as he glowered at the elderly Trpaslík before him.

Georg did not recoil as the younger man had obviously expected. Instead, he stood still, his eyes narrowed in silent defiance. The glare he was known for shone clear within the smoke.

The two men were locked in a staring battle, the dim flickering light of the single lamp between them not even pulling their focus. With each flicker of the light, the darkness that surrounded them became clear. A dark that swallowed the remnants of what had undoubtedly once been a bed chamber surrounded us, the shadows of furniture loomed around them like monsters.

Monsters not unlike the Trpaslíks that were moments away from a well placed fist fight.

"There is no point in waiting," Alojz continued in an attempt to cut a pointless battle off. "There is a match scheduled for next week—the first since Edmund's murder.

I am convinced it is all done in show, a foolish attempt for the filthy Drak to prove himself our ruler, to take his place where our master once sat. To defile the thrown!"

They all growled at that, their voices full of the volatile disgust I had become used to.

"What better opportunity to prove his inadequacy than to destroy him in the very pits that are meant to prove his worth?" Alojz continued. "What better place to demonstrate what he really is? We can dethrone the murderer and squash the Chosen back to the slaves they were bred to be. It is the perfect opportunity, one we shouldn't pass up."

It was a glorious speech; I would give him that. And it was one the other two conspirators revered. Their eyes were wide with excited bloodlust as they signaled their agreement.

My own greed grew as they began to snicker. Bronislav produced a rolled piece of parchment from the smoke-filled air that surrounded him. Georg shifted uncomfortably as the parchment was unrolled.

My heart rate accelerated as the familiar schematics of Edmund's war pits were revealed before me, the ancient lines marked with what looked like red crayon, lines of differing depth and motions crisscrossing over one another.

I didn't have to be privy to their code to know what I was looking at.

Their final attack was laid out step by step in intricate detail.

It was beautiful and brilliant. In fact, if it weren't for their general underestimation of my ability, it might work.

The new information swelled into a pleasurable warmth in my chest before the vision began to shift and change. A heat moved past me as the room was devoured by the smoke once again, a plume overpowering me, only to be replaced by the red burn of my sight.

Tensing, I expected to open my eyes to Ovailia's charred body, to the entirety of the tent village in flames. However, it was smoke.

The long, wispy tendrils of graying clouds flew past, leaving me above the red-tinted world of Prague, hovering above the dilapidated buildings and blood-soaked streets.

Everything tightened. A fear I hadn't expected sprung forth as the worry of returning back to reality left me. Who cared if Ovailia burned to death? Who cared if I lost all the Chosen? What I was seeing wasn't supposed to be visible to me, not with the Zámek in place.

I could still feel the magic inside of me. I knew it was strong. But the city ... Was she strong enough to break past the barrier without me knowing?

Was I strong enough to see her reality, even if she couldn't see mine?

The latter seemed more probable. Joclyn might be capable, but even she didn't possess an ability of that caliber.

Pushing the fear of Joclyn's ability away, I gritted my teeth and let my sight take me down into the middle of the city, into the cathedral that had been home until a few weeks ago.

Tents of every color filled the courtyard, sitting haphazardly,

Skřiteks and Chosen whispering and fighting amongst the temporary housing.

Perfect.

I had hoped the little seeds I had planted would take hold, and it appeared they had done more than that. Weeds were ripping everything apart, ravishing Ilyan's perfect little garden.

My sight continued to move beyond them right into the heart of Ilyan's sanctuary, right into the burned and battered cathedral that was ready to come down and the two children who sat in the middle of the rubble.

Jaromir and Míra.

Míra.

She shouldn't be there with him. She should have never made it inside of Ilyan's compound. I had seen her die. I had seen her burn with all the others I had hidden her amongst. I had watched Ilyan kill her, unknowing that a child was stowed away within the dozens of corpses.

"No!" I gasped, the single word a shout as the reality of what I was seeing hit me. "I can't be wrong. I am *never* wrong."

"And yet, Wyn is alive, as well," the haunting voice of the woman from the white sight hit me full in the chest as the children talked and laughed amongst the rubble, throwing rocks at each other in some kind of game.

"Not for long. Wyn will die just as this one will," I growled as the child-like laugh of the voice ripped into me. "Just as you will."

Gritting my teeth, I pushed the anger from me, banishing

the taunts from my mind, knowing how much more of an issue this truly was.

She had been sent to do that which no one else had been able, and by the looks of it, she was still intent on that task. Her resolve was driven by a magic that was still lodged deep inside of her heart, a magic that would not have died, although I had shed the blood of its master. The magic was now a threat to me in more ways than the tiny child could ever have realized.

Edmund wasn't dead yet.

They sat amongst the dirt and ash of the rubble-strewn hall, marble and stone piled around them in heaps of gray, a smile on her face and not a speck of char on her skin.

"I like it here," Míra whispered.

The smile on Jaromir's face broadened like she had confessed some dirty little secret.

"Good," he whispered, his voice a grating squeak that twisted inside of me. "Then you should stay."

I tensed as Míra did. Her shoulders pulled up to her ears as her eyes hardened. A heavy glance was thrown at the boy with the weight of iron bars. He flinched as my heart rate accelerated, the true meaning of that smile not lost on us.

"You know I can't, Jaromir." The calm of her voice was gone. The hard edge was so reminiscent of Edmund's that my sight pulled away in recoil, ready to show me the ghost of the man standing beside her. Nothing was there except the two children.

However, the two children were quickly fading as my vision

did, their voices overlapping each other as the two visions blended together. My sight muddled everything together as it faded into the red ember glow of nothing.

"I have to go, Jaromir. I have a job, and it's important."

"I say we act tomorrow. If we do as we have discussed, then even his sight cannot stop us," Alojz's voice overran the rubble of the cathedral, burning through me as the imagery of the children shifted and faded into oblivion.

I tensed as I gazed into the nothing, knowing what to expect and hating the fear it had impregnated me with.

"We have to kill him," the child and Alojz spoke together as I jerked, the movement rooted in reality as my heart rate began to pick up into a gallop.

"All I see is death with you, Sain," the same woman's voice boomed in my mind, tainting me as I jerked back to reality, to the smoldering tent, the fire long extinguished, the scent of smoke and death heavy in the air.

"It's about time you rejoined us." Ovailia stood before me, her arms folded over her waist, lips pursed, eyebrows disappearing into her hair. It was the same look I had loved so much. But now, instead of feeling my magic pulse and rise to meet hers, I felt anger. The raw white heat ran through me, making it hard to breathe as my vision shifted before me.

"The fire ..." I gasped, the simple words drowning in fury.

"Is taken care of ... unsurprisingly." She smiled, the wicked twitch at the corner of her mouth, the pride that shone through her eyes, awakening a demon within me. "You always said Edmund underappreciated me. I guess you were right."

"Taking care of one poorly placed spell hardly makes you more powerful than the crippled Chosen the flames devoured," I snapped, trying my best to keep my anger contained. The heavily shifting world before me made it hard as the edges of my vision continually faded to black.

Her eyes hardened, the purse of her lips drifting into a tight line, her jaw locking in place. "It was—"

"If you think that is success, Ovailia," I interrupted her, letting my words smack across her cheek as I stepped toward her, "then you may not be as powerful as even I assumed. But please, let me know when you have accomplished something worth mentioning."

The heat of her anger was white hot against my skin as I stripped her bare of any pride she had possessed. My anger of being surpassed in skill was paramount.

"What kind of accomplishments do you want, Sain?" she snapped, her eyes boring into me dangerously. Any other time, I would have smiled; I would have laughed; I would have taunted.

But the anger was too deep, the betrayal too fresh.

She wasn't supposed to be this powerful. I couldn't let her think it. I couldn't let her know.

"Anything that a child could not accomplish." I struck hard and deep, and her eyes narrowed at me in pain and anger, her jaw taut. "Anything that a pathetic Chosen couldn't do. Not this ... My foolish daughter could do this!"

Ovailia said nothing before turning away, her hair swinging down her bare back, revealing the scar that had been opened and reopened, both at my expense.

"You don't even wear your battle scars well. All that magic and you are still left wanting."

She didn't turn, didn't reply. Still, I could still feel the heat of her anger, her magic as strong as the intensity of the volatile flames.

It was then that the laugh finally escaped me, my humiliation escaping me in a razor sharp snap that cut across her skin. It cut across the air and put her firmly in place on a pedestal far below mine. She could never be my equal, and it was time she knew it.

"Damek!" I yelled as she retreated into the dark of night.

Thankfully, the man ran right up to me at my call, eager to get to work.

"Gather all the Chosen, injured or whole. We have work to do."

"Yes, my king," he groveled, hesitantly moving away before turning to run.

"We have a war to start," I said to myself, letting my words drift beyond the last of the flames, knowing who I had to kill first.

I supposed Ovailia wouldn't get to serve her true purpose, after all.

8

JAROMIR

"DON'T YOU DARE, MÍRA," I begged, leaning forward to stop her hand before it moved into the ring we had drawn in chalk on the floor. "That's my last marble, and I need it."

"No, you don't." Míra wrinkled her nose, wiggling a bit before narrowing her eyes at me. The threat was clear, even in the dim light of Risha's magic.

I tried not to purse my lips. I hated when she did that, being all rebellious and rude and stuff. It had been worse since she had gotten here.

Sometimes, I would swear she hated me. But she couldn't. She couldn't hate me. I was her brother; she was my best friend ... You didn't hate those people.

"You don't need it. It's your last one. I get that one, and you lose."

The anger in her voice made me flinch as I sat back against the metal frame of her hospital bed. Folding my legs beneath me and sticking out my lip, I glared at the ring of marbles we had drawn in the middle of the hospital floor after Ryland had made us leave the ruins.

"Why do you think I don't need it?" Now I was pouting. "I won't get better at this game if you don't give me a chance, and I want to master it before Ryland gets back from talking to Ilyan. He's been gone an hour. I might still have time."

"If you haven't mastered it now, you aren't going to."

Ouch, Míra. She could at least talk to me like she didn't hate me.

I didn't like the changes in her. We used to always play together before. We were a team. We would have ganged up on Risha and beaten her. But Risha was winning, too. I was left in the dust.

It wasn't fair.

"Let's play fair," Risha reminded us from where she sat on the other side of the circle. Her back was against the other row of beds, her hands full of the marbles she had already won.

Míra laughed once under her breath, as if she had both caught me in a lie and an irritation. The sound made me grumpier.

Great, now she was laughing at me.

"Ugh," I grumbled, doubting whether it was from being caught in my attempt to stay in the game or at being laughed at by my sister.

I sat back, folding my arms over my chest, sticking my bottom lip out, wiggling in place, my skin crawling to get out of there, something that irritated Míra for the first time in, like, ever.

Momma used to say we looked like a mouse crawled up our backside when she needed us to sit still. Neither of us could. We would sit and wiggle and giggle until Momma would finally get fed up and "zip up" our mouse.

Now, there wasn't a mouse. Just my sister, all zipped-up.

And me alone, wiggling in irritation.

I had been the best at magic. At least, that's what Ryland had said before Míra showed up. And now Míra was here, and I was having a hard time keeping up. I had to beat her at something!

"Chin up, skunk," Risha said as she leaned toward me. "You can win the next game."

I liked Risha, even if she did have the gross habit of ruffling my hair like a dog when she was proud of me. Even my mom had never done that. It made me feel like I was five or something, which I obviously wasn't.

Wrinkling my nose until the ugly mark on my cheek stopped pulling, I clenched my fists. My magic was hot and angry under my skin. At least I knew my magic could still do something, even if it was merely getting hot and uncomfortable.

"Go ahead, Míra," Risha prompted.

My sister looked at her like she was going to eat her. Gnaw on her bones or something. Like she had on an especially chewy steak Momma had made once. She had sat for twenty minutes, trying to get all the meat off.

The images smacked me in the face with a flash, and I laughed, a snicker seeping out before Míra slapped me with another deep glare.

"Good-bye, marble," she said with a smile before waving her hand over the circle.

The twelve marbles that were left began to wiggle and pulse under the weight of her magic. The dust on the floor lifted into the dark, refracting Risha's light into odd stripes of color. The wind she conjured moved around as she began to roll her marble toward mine. The tiny thing left a trail on the floor as it beelined right toward the yellow swirl of glass, my last piece in the game.

"No, no, no," I groaned, moving my hands to my face as I leaned forward, wishing there were a way to stop its progress. But I already knew her magic was too strong, too accurate.

Ryland had trained me well. I could do some crazy things. But "move your marble and no one else's using just wind" was so freakin' hard!

I kept moving other people's marbles or rolling mine too far. I even hit a sleeping patient in the head. I had laughed, while he hadn't found it very funny. I wouldn't, either, being woken up. I was kind of happy for getting to stay up so late.

This had never happened before Míra had shown up. So I guessed it was good, even if I kept losing marbles.

Míra laughed beside me as her marble hit against mine with enough force that it rolled outside of the circle, across the stone floor, and hit one of the many bed legs we were surrounded by.

"I win!"

"No fair." I was grumpy. I didn't like losing. And I really didn't like not getting a chance to figure something out perfectly. Both had been taken away. Grumpy. "We need to go again. I *will* win next time."

I would, too. Now that I knew what the game was, they couldn't stop me. Just wait until I got back in the game.

"No," Míra spat, her voice harder than was normal for her. "This game is boring. All your games are boring."

In a flash, she changed, the little slivers of the sister I knew disappearing behind the hateful girl I really didn't like. The one who made me wonder if she had been taken over by aliens or something.

With how she acted, it was a real possibility.

She's your sister. I knew it was true, but she had changed enough that it was freaking me out.

"I thought it was fun," I replied, hating how nervous I was to counter her.

She had yelled at me enough lately, and I was pretty irritated at losing. It was making me feel all volatile and stuff. I didn't know how to fight with magic, but I was convinced I could figure it out pretty fast with how angry I felt.

Momma used to say she was lucky. Having twins at the end of six kids was hard enough. But we were like two perfect little angels, obedient best friends. We never fought; we got along. We understood each other on some deep level.

I guessed that was over.

"It's supposed to fine-tune your magic. The precision we master here can be the difference between life or death in the real world," Risha said as she began to gather all the marbles back up, already placing them in piles, ready for the next game.

"No wonder I am so good at it. I'm pretty good at the *real world*, which is nothing like this, BTW."

I jerked. Míra had sounded exactly like our older sister, KasMíra. I hadn't thought about her since the day everything had changed. Hadn't thought of the way she would get so mad. The way she and Momma would yell.

As I glanced between the two of them in a panic, the hatred that zapped between them made my insides squirm, little electric sparks that hit against iron beds and marbles in a little thunderstorm.

"Oh, really?" Risha scoffed, not looking at Míra, her focus still on the marbles. "That doesn't surprise me, given Edmund. He probably had you training with the Trpaslíks ... They are a very violent people. And irritating."

Anger oozed from my sister like a rotten tomato in the sun, feeling putrid in my stomach.

"Guys ..." I pleaded, knowing this was heading for trouble.

Neither of them noticed or cared.

"What does that mean?" Míra spat, jumping to her feet.

I jerked and hustled after her, wondering if I would have to tackle her to the ground.

"Calm down, Míra," I hissed at her, but she breathed harder, hissing behind her teeth like she was going to spit fire.

"I'm not meaning any offense." Risha finally looked up from the now organized marbles, her voice calm, though her eyes were narrowed, full of distrust and fear. "It means that I know Edmund. I know the Trpaslíks and their culture. I am fairly certain I know what he would have you do."

"I doubt that."

"I first went to their 'pits' when I was a child. I never went back. It was disgusting. Edmund even tried to get them banned before Timothy appointed him king in his stead."

"Timothy?" Míra asked in confusion.

The calm in Risha's voice left as she began to laugh. The sound was that same mocking that Momma would give our sister.

"You need a history lesson, little girl, before you start pretending like you know everything."

It was then that Míra moved. I saw it a minute before she rushed her, and I wrapped my hand around her wrist, pulling her back toward me, hoping the small movement would be enough.

"Stop, Míra. Please," I hissed, trying my hardest not to yell.

Míra fought against me once more as I pulled her back. I got her attention this time as she turned to face me, her hair swishing through the air from the intensity.

"Why should I? She's not very nice," Míra asked, her words masked by the language that we had adopted as children. Brought on by a speech impediment, the switched consonants made everything we said hidden to even the best Czech speakers. Even Míra's speech therapist couldn't understand us, which was probably why it stayed around even after her palate was corrected.

"I'm trying to help them, Jaromir. I *want* to help. But they keep talking to me like a child," she pleaded, and my heart hurt from the response.

"You are a child, Míra." I forced the words out, careful to make sure they were masked.

"Edmund didn't treat me like a child."

"But he wasn't nice. You know Risha and Ryland and all of them are nice."

"But I can't tell them ..." Míra continued in code.

Risha looked between us before moving back to the marbles, poking them with her finger. I knew she was really paying close attention, trying to figure out what we were saying.

"He'll kill me if I don't, Jaromir." She had said it before, and even though I didn't flinch, I was shaking. Míra's wide eyes were scaring me. "He's going to kill everyone if I don't. I know I can save all of them ... You have to help me."

"They can help you, too, Míra. You have to trust them."

Míra looked from me to Risha, staring at something.

I clung to her harder. Maybe this time, she would agree with me. Maybe this time, she would tell them what was going on, and then all of this could stop.

"Risha can fix it. I know she can."

"You know I don't believe that. I can't. I have a job to do."

Now I did cringe, a big shiver that rolled over me, and my heart thundered in my chest, knowing what she was talking about.

"Please don't, Míra. Not now. Not ever." I had tried to talk her out of it since she had brought it up, and this time was going to fail as much as the other ones at the rate I was going.

Míra looked at me once before sinking back down to the floor, the bed she leaned on creaking.

"Can we at least play a real game?" she said in straight Czech, her voice like an adult, pretending the last few minutes hadn't happened. Momma used to do that, too. "Go have a battle in that ruin or something?"

Risha laughed. "Sorry, kid, but that is the last thing we are going to do."

"And why not? It's practical, and I'm sure Jaromir—"

"It's dangerous, Míra," Risha cut her off with a snap.

The two of them stared angrily, leaving me standing above them like a statue. I was starting to wonder if I could sneak out of here and find Ryland on my own.

"Besides, Ilyan has forbidden that kind of war-play."

"No wonder everything here is so boring." Míra poked at the marbles Risha had set before her, letting a stream of magic shoot into them before seeping right back into her, a purple line of light that flashed for a second then disappeared. "You don't do anything."

"We do plenty," Risha said with a sigh.

Míra looked up at Risha grumpily, her lip pulled out like it used to when she was a little kid.

"We don't kill people is all." Risha was calm. It still didn't stop the knot in my stomach from tightening right back up. I didn't think I could have sat back down next to my sister if I had tried right then. The knot was too big, and my legs weren't moving.

"Lame," Míra groaned, her word choice one she had been using since we had turned six. "I miss the pits."

Risha smiled, her eyes both delighted and frightening as she leaned toward my sister.

My focus was still drilled right into her.

"Well," Risha began, clapping her hands together, and both Míra and I jumped in turn.

My sister turned toward Risha at the sound, a movement that I wasn't convinced was voluntary.

"This may not be the death pits, but seeing as Ryland hasn't gotten back yet ..." With a smile, she pushed the marbles toward us, a pile for each. "Who is ready for another game?"

"I'm telling you that it's boring, and it's not going to help to train anyone, especially Jaromir. Especially with what's coming."

"Aren't you cute?" Risha cooed, the normal joy in her voice coming back ten-fold. She smiled wide before patting Míra on the head the same way she did me. "You're like a pit bull puppy."

Maybe she thought everyone was a dog. It looked even more like she was petting a dog from this side.

"Keep barking kid, but until you tell me *what's coming,* it's not going to get you what you want. Sit down, Jaromir."

I didn't need to be told twice.

I sunk to the floor with the speed of a bullet, plopping down and crossing my legs. I probably shouldn't have gone so fast, because now my bum hurt. It didn't matter, though. I had a game to win.

Smiling, I pulled my marbles toward me, ready to play. My mind kept buzzing with what Míra had said just now, with what she had told me before.

So much killing. Thinking of her doing it was making me uncomfortable. She had always hated that stuff. She would always hide if anyone died in movies. And now she wanted to watch.

And death pits? What were those?

Nothing made sense.

"Hey, Jaromir," Míra snapped, her hand strong as she pushed into my shoulder and popped my thoughts like a bubblegum bubble. "It's your turn. I thought you were going to win this time."

"What?" I asked stupidly, pulling myself back into reality. "Oh, yeah."

Leaning over the board, I prepared my magic, determined to knock at least three marbles off course, only to stop in place as the loud booms of Ryland's voice echoed across the dark and silent hospital.

"There you are!"

Loud shushing followed him as he ran up the rows of beds to us, several of the patients disturbed by his arrival.

Risha laughed at him, the sound so happy I laughed with her, letting it chase out all the sadness like Momma had always told me to do.

Míra looked like she was about to explode.

"We are right where we told you we would be," Risha said, continuing to laugh as more and more of the other inhabitants joined in on the chorus of hushes. They sounded like snakes. "Playing marbles. Míra is winning."

"That doesn't surprise me one bit. That girl is good!"

I was positive he meant it as a compliment, but Míra scowled more.

The smile on Ryland's face dimmed a bit, a fear I hadn't seen before shining through.

"You have no idea," Míra growled in code, and my spine tingled in fear.

I knew she was going to say something creepy again, and I doubted I wanted to know what.

"Just wait ..."

"Míra, don't!" I yelled, forgetting to code my words.

The hushing fell silent at my panic, and Míra moved so close I expected her hand to slap over my mouth.

"You don't have to—"

"Stop it, Jaromir," Míra cut me off before I said too much, her coded words ricocheting throughout the now silent hall.

"You can't convince me. I'm out of time, and I don't want them thinking I'm good. It'll only hurt them more. I'm not good."

"Míra ..." I pleaded, but she ignored me, standing to face Ryland, who towered over her like a burly prison guard.

The man I had always looked up to turned into a giant as he puffed up.

"You are a powerful kid, Míra," he rumbled from above her. "But don't push it. I like you in one piece, and I am pretty sure your brother does, too."

Míra finally flinched, the stranger deflating a bit and leaving my scared little sister behind.

"Yeah, I do," I added, shuffling to my feet and pulling her away from him. "I really do."

"Good," Ryland said, his voice kind yet the hulk remaining. "So, one piece it is! But for now, bed time. Ilyan's orders. He wants you rested before he comes and plays capture the flag with us tomorrow."

"Ilyan's coming here?" I jumped, I didn't know if I should be excited or scared. I had heard enough stories about what he could do, although the few times I had seen him had been terrifying. He was more of an angry giant than Ryland was at times.

"Yep," Ryland said, obviously proud of himself, yet he seemed almost as scared as I was for some reason. "I told him about our game, and he wants to come."

"I'm sure," Míra grumbled, plopping herself down on her bed with a loud squeak of springs and metal.

"It'll be fun!" Ryland was really pushing this, but looking at Míra's reaction had me worried.

He wasn't the person she was supposed to kill, was he? I didn't want him to die. I didn't want her to die.

I needed to convince her to ask for help. Or maybe I needed to ask it myself. I knew they could help. She needed to trust them.

"Have sweet dreams of lollipops and unicorns, not death and destruction," Risha said as she blew out the lamps between our beds, covering each of us with the rough cotton blankets that smelled faintly of smoke, blood, and an old soap my grandmother would have used.

I stared into the dark, listening to them whisper as they left, trying to figure out a way to convince my sister to trust them. My brain was already foggy with exhaustion.

"I wish that were possible," Míra mumbled from beside me.

I was pretty certain that was the most honest thing she had said since she had come here.

9

DRAMIN

"How am I expected to think straight if you refuse to remove your feet from my face?" I didn't think I could have said those words with a straight face. I tried, but the laugh still leaked out, deep chuckles I was known for echoing in the still room around us.

The sound was a welcomed accompaniment.

Joclyn looked up from where she lay at the foot of my bed, her eyes peering over the cover of a large leather-bound book that had been recovered from an old school last week.

As her eyes wrinkled in a taunting smile, I could see her intent before it came.

"Joclyn!" I yelled in an attempt to stop her action, and her laugh broke past, the bed underneath us creaking as she continually dodged my poor attempts to push her away, more little toes pushing against my shoulders and face.

"Child!"

She laughed more at my outburst.

"Why must you be so disagreeable?"

"I'm not disagreeable, Uncle," she gasped out around giggles, still trying to fight me. "I'm entertaining. Admit it."

"Avoiding required tasks ... with feet ... is not entertaining." I wouldn't admit it, and she knew it. I wasn't foolish enough to think she would admit anything, either. We had both inherited the same stubbornness. "I will send you back to bed if you don't cease this!" I yelled, knowing it was hopeless.

"No, you won't. We have *required tasks,* after all. Besides, I slept last night. You have another twenty hours to put up with me."

"I guarantee I will be rid of you before then!"

Her laugh increased, her perceived win obvious. Unfortunately for her, she had forgotten I had raised a legion of offspring.

Without warning, I stopped moving, letting her toes press against my cheek before I turned and allowed the stinky little digits right into my mouth. With her toes wiggling against my tongue, I licked them, my teeth holding her firmly in place.

She screamed, loud and playful and panicked.

"Let me go!"

I didn't know if she was laughing or disgusted. It made me laugh more.

"I'm sorry. What do you want?" I asked, knowing there was no way she could understand me with the large appendage still caught between my teeth.

"Let me go, or I'll zap you."

I knew her too well by now to dismiss that the threat, so I loosened my jaw, letting her free.

She scuttled away from me, retreating to the foot of the bed and away from any other possible foot attacks.

"That was gross, Dramin."

Ah, so she was disgusted. Perfect.

Laughing, I lifted a corner of the blanket, wiping whatever residue was left on my lips, regretting the need to swallow the now foot-flavored saliva.

"Hmmm? And I suppose your stinky, little pigs against my jaw were meant as a sign of endearment, then?"

She wrinkled her nose at my question. "Point taken." Now she was trying not to laugh, something she was losing at.

"I think I will accept victory for that, then." A smug smile in place, I grabbed the volume Joclyn had previously been looking over, scanning the words in feigned interest. Unfortunately, it took me a second too long to realize that the book was upside down.

Joclyn's giggles broke free as I turned the book right side up. I still refused to look at her over the ancient type set.

"If victory required tasting my foot fungus, then you can have it." With a flip of her hand, Joclyn leaned against the wall by my bed, staring into the darkened room, the lone lantern flickering away in the. Haunting shadows licked against the dark corners, making Thom look more corpse-like than usual.

Idly twisting and fiddling with the long, golden ribbon that was bound in her hair, she began to stretch her legs out again then thought better.

"Smart move. I will have you know, child, that it was worth the victory, foot fungus and all." Closing the book, I met her gaze, smile for smile. I leaned back, as well, grateful for the residual chuckles that moved over me, joy swelling in my chest.

Joy *was* worth it, even if it did taste faintly of rotten fish and ocean sand. After all, joy came in unseen packages at times. You never knew what you were missing unless you took chances and opened every box.

It might have been an odd box that I had opened, but the rewards were great ... if only for this moment of happiness. Dismal misery had dwelled in this room since Thom and I had been placed in here months ago, but it had lifted in the last few minutes.

Part of me wondered if he could feel it, too.

He lay there, surrounded by plants and pills, covered in bandages and salves. His skin looked grayer by the day, hair dirtier, eyes and lips fading to blue.

I doubted he would have shoved anyone's foot in his mouth, but he would most certainly have something to say about it.

That was the pain in loss—the silence that he had left behind.

We sat in that silence, the flicker of lantern light dimming as the occasional chuckle became farther apart.

"Do you ever scream really loudly, just to see if it will wake him up?" Joclyn asked out of nowhere.

"I can't say I ever have," I said. Despite the idea crossing my mind a few times, I wasn't about to admit that to her.

For all I knew, she was going to try it, anyway. He did look like he was sleeping. At least, he would if I didn't know for a fact that he slept all curled together with his butt in the air.

You walked in on him once, and you never forgot the imagery, even if it had been forty years ago.

This was a much better look for him.

"I think I'm ready to try again," Joclyn whispered.

My heart skipped a beat as she pulled us back to the conversation we had been avoiding since Ilyan had left us for some much-needed sleep a few hours ago.

I needed sleep, too. However, I wasn't quite willing to admit to her how much mortality I had regained.

Tensing, I leaned forward, my hand soft against her knee, pulling her focus back to me. Eyes glistening in the dim lamp light we sat in, I had been ready to give her a slight nod to prod her forward and support her. With that look, though, everything stopped, and my heart became a heavy weight in my chest.

"I want to use Thom," she said, her eyes alive with a frightening plan. My stomach spun as I realized what she was referring to. "He's connected to his father. He's connected to Ovailia. His sights might be able to get me past the barrier since that girl showed up and chased them all away, anyway. I need to see into Imdalind. I need to know what's going on."

"Joclyn," I stopped her, everything twisting around me in a tangle of fear and anger. Knowledge of the girl and why she was here temporarily took away my fear for what she had planned. "He's not with us. You can't."

"I've seen the burn on Ilyan's arm," she interrupted, looking away from me and back at Thom's still body. "I know how you tried to see using me. I know how Ilyan pulled me out of that hell."

"Thom is not trapped in a dream, Silnỳ." The use of the title made her flinch, but I plowed on, keeping my hand against her knee, visibly shaking, the reverberation of my heart making it hard to control. "He is sick."

"So was I. So were you. So was Míra. There was sight in all of us." Leaping from the bed, she stood, hesitant to move closer, as though she were afraid to wake him.

"There *is* sight in all of us," I corrected her with the familiar phrase all Draks were raised with, knowing it was fodder for her.

Sure enough, she turned back to me, that familiar coy smile on her face, one so similar to one of my younger daughters that it was hard to breathe. Her face was so clear in my mind. I didn't know how I had missed the similarity between Joclyn and Tearney, all except for the eyes.

"You always told me to follow my magic, brother. You always told me never to second-guess. It saved you. It knew about Sain. It brought Ryland back. And it's telling me that there is something inside of Thom that I need."

One last glance and I knew couldn't stop her. I couldn't say anything that would hinder her plans. I didn't want to. She was right.

"If I leave you with anything in this life, I am glad it's that," I mused, my heart tensing at the truth Joclyn still didn't know. "I am happy you listened."

"I do that sometimes," she teased, grabbing a stone mug almost as old as I from my bookcase before carrying it toward her brother-in-law. Her dark hair fell down her back, the golden ribbon snaking over the floor.

Sitting up farther, I threw my blankets off, dangling my legs over the side of the bed as my heart pounded and pulsed. I needed to go to her, to help her, to join her.

However, with the way she held herself, the way she looked at him, she didn't need me. She knew what she was doing, her magic guiding her.

Her hands gentle, she lifted the blanket from over his feet, folding it away to reveal the yards of bandage wrapped skin that covered him. A single stretch of unscarred flesh was visible above his ankle, skin that would be burned and scalding in minutes.

The deep sound of Thom's breathing was the solitary sound as she stood, frozen before him, the mug and her hand inches away from their mark. Inches from sight.

I tensed, forgetting how to breathe as I waited for her to connect with his Drak, to connect with his time.

Eyes focused on Thom, she poured the murky water into her palm, letting it flow over her skin like rain before it dripped onto the floor in puddles at her feet. The sound filled the room before she pressed her palm against the skin on Thom's ankle, connecting her magic, her flesh with his.

Heart pounding from the memory of the strength of those connections, longing for the return, I gasped as she did. The frantic intake of air was so loud I expected Thom to sit up from the pain. Yet he remained still, as dead and lifeless as he had been for months, not even a flinch from the magic that now infiltrated him.

"Joclyn," I gasped, knowing she couldn't hear me.

Her eyes were already wrapped in the pitch black of prescience, staring into the future with a power and regality that I had seen from the moment I had laid eyes on the panicked child in the snow.

A power beyond even what I had seen in my father, seen in any Drak, emanated from her. It shimmered in the air like a wave of smoke, washing over me in a force that sucked the air out of my chest.

I'd had hundreds of children, thousands of grandchildren. I loved them all, was proud of them all. But seeing my sister —no, seeing the queen before me—filled my heart more than any other.

"There is darkness here," she said, her voice lost in the depth of the Drak, hollow with the sight of the future.

At the sound, I jumped out of my skin with a gasp and leaned forward, desperate to hear more, not caring if I fell off the rickety old bed.

"It was created by him, and when the light comes, there will be blood. Be ready. The battle comes quickly."

I stared at the black of her eyes, trying very hard to ignore the tinge of jealousy that filled me, the desire to see again still burning a hole in my soul.

The black faded as the ache began to devour me, pulling me out of my own self-deprecation.

"What is it?" My question was little more than air whispered over the stagnant silence of the room.

"There is so much death, Dramin," she gasped, her hand falling from Thom's ankle as she collapsed to her knees. "So much blackness."

Tensing, my heart ached at the sight of her breaking before me. I wished I could find a way to comfort her. I knew of the black she referred to, the hollow confusion her sight had become since that sight with Míra. It was yet another mystery to her ability that drove us both mad.

"Is he dead?" I hated asking the question and was unsure what person I was even referring to.

Edmund.

Thom.

Sain.

Ilyan.

Me.

I knew she had seen them all. It could have been any of them. I had a feeling any of them would hurt.

She pulled her shoulders up to her neck, dropping her head as she curled into herself. Time stretched between us as the silence grew, pressing against my chest and making everything spin.

"Joclyn," I whispered, my hands shaking against the edge of the bed, attempting to lift my weight so I could get to her.

"Everything keeps shifting," she finally responded, her voice dead. "Thom's alive. Ilyan's dead. Míra's there. Wyn's not. One thing is clear." She looked at me, her meaning transparent.

My death was consistent in her sights. Only my death remained the same. It was hard not to admit I was eager for that end. It was hard not to tell her how close that end really was.

I knew of the sight she had seen with the girl, seeing her walk toward Thom. Joclyn, however, did not know what I had been told in that pure white sight about the girl, about how it would be my last duty to destroy her in order to save Thom.

I was ready. I simply hoped he lived after whatever happened to me. I hoped he found happiness and lived the life he had earned.

"And Thom?" I asked.

"He is there more than not."

My tension eased as she nodded, pulling the blanket back over his now burned foot.

"At least he has a chance."

I sighed, thinking of the memory of my last true sight, of the haunted voice, and of the little girl I was supposed to stop, whom I was supposed to kill.

Joclyn nodded in agreement, her dark hair falling around her as her focus shifted back to Thom, his breathing still a slow, steady pace.

"I thought knowing everything was a curse ..."

"Sometimes, the not knowing is worse," I finished the thought for her, knowing for the first time in my life how both sides of this morose coin felt.

I wasn't convinced I wanted either.

"And to think, you lived in such savagery for so long." I smiled to myself, the joke not lost on her as I reached toward the large mug on my nightstand. The knowledge of the burn this would give me caused my hand to shake, yet I didn't care.

"How do mortals do it?" Joclyn teased before lifting her own mug to her lips, freezing halfway through the motion. "Thom is alive more than not ..."

"Excuse me?" I was concerned that she might have broken, stuck on one point as she was.

"Dramin?" she asked, the use of my name pulling me out of the reverie.

Dread filled me at the sight of the woman who was frozen before me, her eyes staring unfocused into the contents of her mug. For a moment, I thought she was trapped in sight. But no, this was a look of someone trapped in thought.

"Joclyn?"

"The cave ... Has Thom ever been inside of Imdalind?"

Narrowing my eyes at her, I racked my brain, trying to think of a time it could have happened, but there was nothing. Ilyan had kept us too well-hidden. It had been too big of a risk to have anyone see us. "No, why?"

"They are all in the cave ..." I could barely hear her as she turned away from me, her voice a mumble. "All of them ..."

I half-expected her to shout "Eureka!" and plant a flag.

"What are you talking about?"

"Just now ... that cave ..." she continued as if she hadn't heard me, her voice broken in weird places. "Where Míra was ... Everyone was there."

Her wide, fearful eyes met mine as she set her mug back down, jumping from the bed with a jolt. Not for the first time, I wondered if I should tell her what I had seen, guilt and regret pressing against me.

"Yes, it's the same time. Nothing else has changed." Joclyn began to pace the room, her hand shaking as it ran through the long curls that had come free of her braid. The move made me smile, despite the dread not easing.

"If you don't give me some kind of clue as to what you are talking about, Joclyn, I may have to report you to your husband."

She shot me a look, a slight smile kissing the corner of her mouth as she pointed to her head, her meaning clear. She wasn't talking to me.

The knot of fear that was trying to take up residence in my gut eased a bit, while my irritation increased.

I set my mug down with a little bit more of a bang than I

had intended, and we both jumped, Joclyn turning toward me in shock.

At least I had gotten her attention.

"Other people are part of this conversation, my dear," I said, leaning back against the wall as I folded my hands over my belly. "Although, I hope you will send Ilyan my regards."

She smiled in full then, rushing back to sit on the side of the bed, hair and ribbons streaming behind her in light and dark that contrasted beautifully in the dim lamp light.

"Sorry, Uncle," she whispered, taking my hand in hers. "It's ... I just realized Thom is inside of Imdalind. He's there ... with everyone else."

"This hardly seems to be an *ah-ha* moment," I sighed, deflating a bit at the anticlimactic revelation.

"Except, the before and after hasn't changed."

My heart must have forgotten to stop beating.

"The sights of before are the same ..." she continued, "and of after ... it's that ... it's the players."

"Now I am really not following."

"There was something Sain said when we battled him in Prague. I don't think I was ever meant to kill Edmund. I think the sight you had all those years ago was about Sain, not Edmund. I can still save him, Dramin."

"Which him?" I asked.

Her eager smile faltered a bit before she glued it back in place. She jumped to her feet, rushing to the door without giving me a response. "I have to go ... The council is going to start soon, and I need to see Ilyan ..." She froze, her hand on the knob.

Mine extended toward her as a weird longing overtook me, the relief from before forgotten.

Joclyn must have felt whatever poison was in the air as I had, for she ran back to me, her arms wide. Her long, spindly limbs wrapped around my neck as she buried her face in my shoulder.

I froze at the contact, my heart bumping painfully in my chest.

She had hugged me before, but something about this was different. It sat on my chest like a lead weight, my own guilt accentuating it, making it hard to breathe.

"I love you, brother," she gasped, her voice muffled from where she was hiding, making me certain she was trying to hold back tears.

"I love you, too." The words flowed as my arms wrapped around her, pulling her against me.

One squeeze and she broke free, sitting on the edge of the bed with a broad smile, her silver eyes gleaming. "You are the best brother in the world."

I didn't know if she was teasing or being serious, not with the width of the smile on her face. Therefore, I simply chuckled, the sound filling me and lifting the last of the knots that had tightened in my chest.

"That's better than being your favorite brother." I chuckled. "Then I would have been very disappointed in my competition."

She laughed as I did before moving across the room, pausing at the door with the promise to return after the council.

Then it was just me and the invalid.

For the first time in weeks, I was seriously considering yelling his name, perhaps even throwing something heavy on his head … just to see if it would wake him.

I doubted it.

"It's you and me, kid. Until that kid Míra finds us, anyway." Grumbling, I lay back, shifting the plethora of pillows into some weird nest shape. I was confident I looked like some weird animal, but it was quite comfortable.

I didn't know how long I slept, but it was deep and comfortable, tight and warm, like being wrapped up in those same pillows. I got lost in it, lost in laughing with my soul mate, walking hand in hand with her down the long path inside the forest that we always used to visit as our escape. When the kids got to be too much, when the world got to be too loud, we would walk through that forest. Escape the noise, escape the future, and just exist in our own reality, lost in the present.

That was the hardest thing for a Drak: to exist in the present and not get lost in the future or in the past.

This was a past I wanted to get lost in, however. This was a past I missed.

"Your hair is longer, Dramin." I could feel her touch against the back of my neck, the calluses that always lived on the tips of her fingers rough yet soft.

"I've been growing it out." My voice was younger, the conversation familiar, alerting me to the memory that my mind was pulling into the dreamscape.

It was a good one and one I had relived many times before.

Even beyond the dream, I could feel the calm, feel the love stretch over me, wrap around me, more tightly and more soothing than the pillows.

"I've noticed." Her voice was soft in my ear, and I turned, my heart rate accelerating at the voice of my mate, Galiya.

Her long hair fell to her waist, pulled back in a braid that hung down her back like a rope. Her eyes sparkled as she smiled, and I wished I could touch her face. I wished I could kiss her, but not yet. That would come later.

"But the question is, my darling Dramin, why?"

Even beyond the numbing love I was surrounded by, I could feel the anxiety. I knew I was about to reveal the secret I had been keeping about the king I had seen on the street. I liked his hair.

"Because I ..."

"Kiss me quickly."

The calm of the dream was shattered, my heart beating spastically into a flood as I turned toward Galiya, her eyes no longer safe and playful, but wide and fearful.

I couldn't move. The softness of the dream had left, drowning me in panic.

Even the softness of her lips against mine couldn't break it. The kiss was too desperate, too unfamiliar, too fearful.

"Be brave," Galiya said as she pulled away, her hands on my collarbone as she looked into my eyes, tears welling in hers. "We will be together again soon."

"The child is coming. You must stop her."

Those last words did not come from my girl. They came from the air. They came from my soul. They pulled me down, the tension trapping me in the hell the dream had become.

And then it was gone.

The dream was gone.

And all that was left was screaming in the hallway, rocks rumbling above my head, and the sound of a little boy crying.

The sound of blood hitting stone.

Then the door opened.

10

JAROMIR

THE OLD MAN next to me sounded like a fog horn—well, his breathing did, anyway. Loud, raspy gasps made it sound like someone was plugging his nose.

The sound stretched over the dark like some long-fingered monster who crept between the beds, touching the hearts of the sleeping Chosen and releasing their souls into the air. Whispers of souls that floated through the morning sun now seeping past the heavy drapes, catching in the beams like glitter before they were devoured by the raspy breath, inhaled with a gasp.

Wheeze, gasp, wheeze, gasp ... He took another one.

And another.

I jerked, the image becoming too real, and turned toward where Risha stood by the door, guarding us. Even though she was ominous, it was better than the monster that was stalking me. The bed springs creaked and rubbed that dumb kiss thing on my cheek. It itched if I laid on it too long. I guessed I had.

'Course, it wouldn't bug me at all if I could sleep, which was something that was not happening.

I wished I could sleep. If I were sleeping, I could at least ignore everything, like the alien-abducted monster my sister was and Ryland's war that was way too real and creepy. I could even ignore that there was such a person as Edmund Krul. That evil man had messed up everything.

I hadn't even met him, and I hated him. He had destroyed everything: my sister, my best friends, my family, my home.

Thinking about him made me all angry and jittery, like mice were running along my spine.

Exhaling as loudly as the old man, I shifted again, rolling back toward where Míra slept. The bed springs screamed, exactly as they did every time I had rolled over tonight.

I stared at the creepy hospital hall that had been dark until a few minutes ago when the sun had started to rise, sending weird prison stripes of light over everything.

Maybe I was in a prison. A prison with monsters and unknown sisters.

Could be.

"Jaromir," Míra hissed through the dark, matching the rhythm of the monster who still crept around the beds so perfectly that I jumped, unable to control the reflex.

I knew what was coming, knew what she would ask. She had been trying to convince me all week. And after today, I was pretty convinced our time was up.

"Do you remember that time we went to Russia?"

I could barely hear her, but she was so calm, so quiet I was sure this wasn't it. The knot that was attacking my stomach calmed down. I hoped I still had time.

"When we went to visit Uncle Yagi that last time before he died?" The knot was back to the same tense ball of fear. Of all the memories she could have picked …

"Yes."

I didn't like where this was going.

Uncle Yagi had suffered from cancer, a really scary one. I don't remember what kind. It was too long ago; we were, like, five or something. He had everyone come to visit him … and then he did something, something bad. I didn't want to talk about it right now.

Especially in the dark.

Especially with the creepy way that man's breath kept echoing around us. I guessed it was good we were talking in code. I didn't even know if we were allowed to talk, I was surprised Risha hadn't told us to be quiet yet.

"Do you remember how he was when we first got there? How Mom thought he was dead?"

I *really* didn't like where this was going.

I nodded, positive she couldn't see it in the dark.

"I remember," I finally got out as I tried to swallow past the constriction in my throat. "He didn't move, and his skin was so pale. His lips were blue."

I could barely breathe, let alone talk, but I tried, anyway.

"What are you talking about, Míra?"

"I'm talking about Uncle Yagi," she hissed, the calm in her voice zapped away.

The tight ball in my stomach came back. I was worried I might throw up.

"I'm talking about how, after he died and Aunt Zora came to live with us, she was happy because Yagi was happy. And everyone else went on living. Everyone always goes on living after someone dies."

"Míra?" My heart hurt.

"Your friends will go on living, too," she continued, turning to look at me with wide eyes so white they were round saucers in the dawn, swallowing up all the light.

I gasped, wishing I could move away, wishing I could run away from her, away from her eyes that were swallowing me up.

"Ilyan, Ryland, Risha, even that Wynifred girl who doesn't like me much—they will all go on living," she whispered, leaning over the bed to get closer to me. The width of her eyes grew.

I tried to move away, but I was frozen in place, trapped between the monster that continued to breathe behind me and the girl who stared at me.

"Are you sure you can save them?"

"I told you I could. It's the only way I can," she snapped so loudly I was convinced someone had heard, but everything was quiet, everything except that monster that was probably standing right over me, breathing in my ear.

For all I knew, she had put us in a bubble or something. Ryland had talked about that once. I didn't know how to do it yet.

Knowing that no one could hear us made me feel more trapped.

"You have to help me, Jaromir."

"Help you kill that man?" I could barely get the words out. I knew this was wrong. She should know this was wrong.

"Yes. Then I can go back to Edmund, tell him it's done. I can convince him—"

"You would leave?"

"I have to, Jaromir."

"Can I come with you?"

Everything hurt. I didn't want her to leave. I didn't want any of this.

My heart pressed against my skin like it was trying to get over to her, desperate for her to stay or for me to go with her.

"I can help you defeat Edmund."

"No!" Her voice, even louder than mine, echoed around the long hall. Still, no one stirred. No one moved. The world was frozen like in some fairy tale, and we were the lone ones alive. "You can't come. He will hurt you. You need to stay here. I need to save you, too. I have to, Jaromir." Swinging her legs over the edge of the bed, she sat, letting them dangle in the dark. "Will you help me?"

I didn't dare move. I didn't dare speak. I sat stiffly, watching her feet swing, listening to the bed creak under the movement.

The creak, the breath of the man—they moved together, sucking the souls out of everyone around us. The creak became a troll that shuffled under the beds, following the demon and pulling the corpses out by their toenails.

But it was just Míra swinging her legs from where she sat.

Swinging her legs.

Swinging.

Swinging as we sat in the dark. Swinging as the question hung in the air.

Swinging as the knot in my stomach continued to expand, my mind twisting our already frightening reality into something much more terrifying.

"You want me to still save all of your friends, don't you?"

I nodded.

"Then this is what we have to do. I've tried to find another way, Jaromir. This is it. I like them, too. I want them to win. I can help them, but we need ..." Her voice caught, and for a second, I was sure she was crying, sure that the alien that had taken over her body was gone. "I need to do this. I need you to help me, and I can save everyone else here. I promise."

"Are you going to kill him?" My throat seemed too full of something.

Fear.

Or vomit.

Or both.

I could barely talk.

"Yes, Jaromir. But then everyone else is safe. He's dead already, anyway."

"He's already dead?" I asked, leaning toward her in a panic, barely catching myself before I fell out of the bed. "What are you talking about? *Who* are you talking about?"

Míra was silent. The dark was silent. The hall was silent except for the creak of her bed as she swung her legs back and forth, her eyes still trained on me.

"Who is it?" I asked again, hoping she would finally answer. My heart continued beating so fast it hurt. I didn't want to hear who it was.

"I told you. A dead man."

"You saw a dead man?"

She nodded, her lips a hard line as she leaned over the bed closer to me, her nose inches from mine, the width of her eyes growing. "I haven't seen him, but I know he's here in a bed, like all of them. Except, they keep him locked up like they are trying to keep him hidden. I'm not sure if he's alive. He just lies there, and he sleeps. His hair is in cords like the wires that ran to Uncle Yogi's chest."

I knew at once whom she was talking about, and I swallowed, the movement painful thanks to my still constricted throat.

"How did you find him?" I hadn't even seen him, though I knew where he was, who he was. I knew everything about this place, like how you weren't allowed to go over there. "That's off limits."

Her smirk killed the glow in her eyes, the last shred of familiarity in my sister vanishing. "I told you. I haven't found him, but I know he's there. I know what he looks like. An old man showed me. I need you to take me to him." She waved her hand to the side. "I need to finish this so everyone else can live."

"I can't. It's off limits."

"You have too many rules," she snapped, cutting off my rebuttal like a razor blade. "Don't leave the infirmary. Don't talk to the Skříteks without permission."

"That's so that—"

"Don't look at that blond guy if you want to live."

"Ilyan's nice. You just have to—"

"Don't eat meat."

"They just don't—"

"Don't yell at the nurses."

"You shouldn't be yelling at anyone, Míra. It's not nice."

"Take me to him." The command was loud and booming, and it moved inside of me like a wave on the beach. It swept me up and made it hard to breathe.

I couldn't ignore it. After all, I had already made my decision.

I had to save them ... all of them.

And if the "dead man" was the key to that …

He was already dead like Míra had said …wasn't he?

"How do we get past Risha?" My stomach twisted painfully, not wanting to think about what I was agreeing to. "Can you do it without hurting her?"

"I won't kill her if that's what you are asking."

"No, Míra, you can't hurt her."

"Stay here, Jaromir. Don't get in my way."

"You can't hurt her, Míra."

Míra didn't respond. She merely jumped to her feet, walking away from our tiny cluster of beds with her head held high.

"Hey there, Míra," Risha responded, the yawn in her voice making it clear she was struggling to stay awake. "It's not quite time to wake up, kiddo."

Míra was silent except for the sound of her feet against the cold floor.

My spine hurt, all pressurized with fear, and I jerked, pulling the covers around me, trying to get lost in them. Hoping I would disappear in them. I didn't want to see what was coming.

"You aren't supposed to be out of bed, Míra. You know better."

"I need to go to the bathroom." Míra was obviously lying. She didn't try to make it sound like she was being truthful at all. Her voice was dead, as dead as the aliens. As dead as the old man who was sucking souls. As dead as I was becoming.

"Míra, I need you to get back in bed," Risha responded, her voice shaking in fear. Odd. I didn't think she could get scared.

But she was.

She was terrified.

It washed over me, shaking up my spine.

The old man moved closer, his long fingers reaching forward, ready to pull my soul out of my chest.

"I have to go to the bathroom," Míra repeated, the same dead girl speaking as she stepped toward Risha.

"Get back in bed!" Risha's yell mixed with the rattle of iron and metal that echoed around the room as she hit what I was positive was a bed stand, trying to get away from the little girl who kept moving closer.

I could see it in my head, my magic pushing the images into me. I didn't want to see. I didn't want to hear.

Clamping my hands over my ears and clenching my eyes shut as tightly as I could, I curled into myself, trying not to hear Risha call out in fear, trying not to hear my sister's laugh. Trying not to see the way the room erupted in fireworks of color right above our heads.

The noise of magic and the lights had always been beautiful to me. Now, I hated them.

I wasn't dumb. I had figured out months ago that Ryland was training everyone for a war, yet I hadn't understood what that had meant until Míra had shown up with stories of fighting in pits and killing people.

Even then, it hadn't been real.

Not really.

Not until now, lying here, listening to them fight, listening to Risha beg. Then it became real. It was my mother. My mother screaming as the Vilÿs chased us. The screams as they ripped into her body. Her body as she lay over me, trying to keep me safe. Safe from the Vilÿs that killed her, that marked me. Safe from the bombs that lit up the sky every morning. It was not being able to shower and having to eat gross food.

I didn't want this.

I didn't want anything to do with this.

Not anymore.

"Stop. Stop. Stop," I whimpered amidst the noise, pressing my hands against my ears until they hurt. "Stop. Please. Stop," I said until it was silent, the words on repeat so fast I wasn't certain if I was speaking them aloud. I didn't care if I was. I just wanted it to stop. I wanted it all to stop.

I didn't want this.

"Come on," Míra hissed as she pulled the thin blankets off me before yanking my arm and trying to get me to move. "We need to go. Get out of here before someone else shows up. You show me the way, and I'll make sure no one gets in our way."

"Míra ..." I groaned, tears sliding down my cheeks as I remained curled in a ball, unable to move. "I can't do this. I can't—"

"Stop it!" she snapped, her voice sending my knees into my

chest. "Don't be a baby. You said you would help. You want to save your friends, right? This is what we have to do."

"But, Risha ..." I gasped, my heart pushing against my lungs. Everything was spinning. "You hurt her ..."

I didn't want to think about what had happened, what she had done.

"I didn't kill her." Míra looked at me like she was trying to be comforting, but her voice was dead. The smear of blood on her cheek scared me as much as her tone. "She will be fine. But we have to move."

"Do you promise?"

"We have to go, Jaromir. It's our only chance."

I stared at her from the bed, watching her eyes and wishing my sister were still there. Wishing she were alive. Wishing I were.

There was nothing.

Nothing except death.

Death in the pit that Míra always talked about. The pit where you either lived or died. The pit where everyone bled. She was there, and without knowing it, I had walked in after her.

I didn't have another choice.

Míra knew it, too, the knowledge written across her face, wide and hungry.

"Now, Jaromir. Get out of bed. We need to go."

Everything buzzed and shifted around me as I rolled out of

bed, the world shaking inside a bottle, everything spinning and moving. I couldn't focus. The noises were too loud; the dark was too bright. I couldn't breathe, but I also couldn't stop.

The monster had already caught me; except, it was Míra's tight hand around my arm.

"This way." Her words spun inside my head like everything else, sounds drowned out by a constant buzzing, by the sound of my heart as it rattled through me.

I saw Míra give the same disgusting, twisted grin before I began to walk, doing my best not to look at Risha, not to smell the blood.

I saw her, anyway.

She was crumpled on the floor, her long hair fanned out around her head like the sun's rays. Her hand looked stiff, wrapped around the bed post, as blood spread over her back, over her skin, the large red puddle pooling around her.

I still saw Risha.

"Y-y-you ..." I stuttered, barely able to get the words out with how my stomach was twisting. "You said you wouldn't kill her!"

"I didn't kill her. She will live. She just won't go anywhere for a while."

I swallowed, the motion difficult with whatever was still clogging my throat.

Everything smelled like a korun českých and when I had to clean the bathroom, the smell following us out, traveling on the wet, sticky mess that had seeped into my socks.

"Let's go, Jaromir." Míra prodded my back with her finger, a sharp point that dug into my spine as her magic erupted inside of me. Sharp, little pokes dispersed over my skin like needles.

I jerked then stumbled out the door and into the courtyard as she laughed gleefully behind me.

All signs of my sister were gone. I no longer knew who I was following.

The sound of my heart was louder out in the courtyard where the dark tents surrounded us, sending it into the black sky before the red barrier brought it back, screaming at me to stop.

I couldn't.

I walked past the tents that were strangely quiet and still.

I wondered if they were empty. I wondered where everyone was, but I couldn't think. I could barely walk in a straight line as it was.

We weaved past the tents, heading toward the large hall that held the bathrooms and beyond that ...

Every step felt heavy. The large, wet mass on my sock wasn't helping, either. It was a heavy weight that I dragged behind me, as if Risha were hanging on, begging me to stop.

Everyone wanted me to stop, but I couldn't. I had to save everyone. As Míra had said, it was the only way

I had to keep telling myself that.

Knowing it was all a lie.

The hallway rattled around us, stones and bricks shaking in what I was persuaded to believe was an explosion. I knew it was too early for the ships to drop their bombs, but I couldn't think of what else it could be.

I jerked at the noise, wishing I could turn back to Míra, make sure she was okay. But I couldn't make myself do that, either. I simply walked forward, jerking as another one came, wishing they would break through the wall.

Wishing they would free us.

Free me from what I was about to do.

Momma used to always say that, even if you didn't take the cookie, if you saw someone doing it, you were still as guilty.

This was so much worse than a cookie.

One step, two beats, three shaky breaths. Everything was too loud. My heart beat. My socks against the stone. Míra's excited breathing inches from my back. Momma's voice loud and clear inside my head, nagging about cookies and right and wrong. And how wrong Míra was.

How wrong I was to help her.

Ryland could help her, though. I knew he could. I needed to tell him what was going on so they could stop her. There wasn't enough time left to stop her, though.

I had already brought her too far.

As I stopped in place, the door Míra needed was a few feet from us. I froze, my innards twisting and turning, head spinning in fear.

I couldn't be here. How did I get here?

Míra slammed into my back as another explosion rattled the walls. She was obviously not paying very close attention to where I was going. The impact sent us both toppling forward into stone floors and walls, my still wet sock sliding on the stone.

I caught myself, turning to make sure Míra was okay, but instead, I saw one of my own bloody footprints.

Risha's blood, bright red in the dark.

"What are you doing?" Míra hissed in the dim light of the hallway, obviously intent on keeping her voice down. "We need to get there. We don't have time for this, Jaromir. We have to hurry."

"No," I gasped, my voice strangled. I sounded scared. I *was* scared. I hadn't realized how scared I was. "We can't."

"What?" For as scared as I was, Míra was angry.

I tensed, my shoulders pulling up to my ears, expecting her to hit me. I didn't look at her. I stayed hunched on the floor, staring at the footprints on the floor, listening to the *boom* of explosions overhead.

"Get up, Jaromir."

"Do you remember Momma's cookies?" I asked, focused still on the floor. "Do you remember what she said about them?" When I finally looked at her, at the anger and confusion that didn't belong on her face, at the alien who looked back at me, everything broke, my heart screaming at me to run away from this stranger.

"You mean that we couldn't eat the sweet bread ones because they were her favorite?"

"No, I mean—"

"We don't have time for this," Míra snapped as she stepped toward me. The sound of her tread was as loud as my heart beat, each drum pressing against me until I wanted to scream.

I wanted to escape. I wanted to escape into the stone and never have to look at the monster my sister had become again. I didn't want to face it.

Even I knew I couldn't run away from it.

Just like the Vilỳs, you had to face it.

"Get up, Jaromir," she sneered, and my spine curled in fear of what was coming. "We need to go."

"No." I tried to make my voice as powerful as possible, but it fell flat, the sound shaking in the panic that was growing by the second.

"We don't have time, Jaromir. You said you would help me."

"I ... I said ... n-no." I could barely get the words out of my mouth. I couldn't even get up. I couldn't look at her.

"No?" She barked, grabbing my elbow and pulling one of my arms out from under me, sending me rotating through the air before slamming into the ground.

I screamed from the impact, the sound lost in the cacophony of the planes, the hallways shaking around us. A ripple of pain moved up my spine, leaving me motionless as Míra stepped over me, her long hair falling around us like the leaves of the honeysuckle bush we used to hide in.

"You don't get to change your mind. You have to help me!"

"No." My voice was stronger now as I lay below her, helpless and afraid. That emotion was leaving, though. "I can't let you do this anymore. Just like cookies."

Míra looked like she had been slapped, surprise showing before her eyes narrowed at me.

"I removed a woman's spine, you know."

I jerked visibly, fear twisting inside of me so much that I could barely move. I gasped, trying to twist away from her.

"Edmund taught me how." She smiled, her body folding as she sat on my hips the same way she had done when we used to wrestle before dinner. "You say he is bad, and you are right. You say I am good, but I can never be. Not anymore... because he made me bad. He taught me how to cut the skin, how to sever the nerves, how to mutate the bones. And then he taught me how to put it back. He taught me how to hurt. And I did. I hurt someone whether I wanted to or not."

Tears began to drip from my eyes, falling over my cheeks as I lay there, trapped beneath her, unable to move.

"I don't want to be bad, but he made me that way. And I won't let him do that to you. Not to them. You are all too good. I have to save you. I have to save you, Jaromir. I'm the only one who can."

I remained still, crying as her own tears fell down her cheeks, her own prison clear.

"I need you to help me, Jaromir. Tell me where he is."

We stared at each other, her sitting on my hips, trapping me in place, our tears dripping together, mine down my cheeks, burning my skin before they dripped onto the stone below me.

"Please. I have to stop him."

"You can't, Míra. I can't let you kill him!" My heart hurt like I had been stabbed, knowing what was coming, but I couldn't stop.

Not now.

Not anymore.

Bright green shot from my hand, shooting into Míra's chest with a jolt that sent her flying through the air away from me. Her arms flailed like a spider before she slammed into the wall with a thud. The crack from my magic echoed down the hall, stones rattling and falling from the ceiling. Her scream chased the blast, her pain breaking into me as I scuttled after her, desperate to help, to stop ...

"Míra! I'm sorry! I didn't mean—"

A blast ricocheted through the hall, hitting me in the chest. Her magic moved into me, burning me as I flew through the air. With a snap, my body broke against the ceiling, bones cracking against stones before my stomach plummeted back down to the ground, my body following along.

"Míra!" I tried to shout her name while I lay on the floor, but all I did was cry, whimper, and groan.

I tried to pull myself to my feet, but nothing was moving. All

I did was hurt, fire moving within me, burning me. All I did was cry.

"I'm sorry ..."

"You're sorry?" She snapped as she walked toward me, blood dripping down her face, streaking her blonde hair from a cut in her scalp. "You promised me you would help, Jaromir! You lied!"

I tried to get up, tried to run away, but my body hurt. It screamed back, everything aching as I kept moving. I had to.

"You're a liar!"

"No!" I yelled as I forced myself to my feet, a scream ripping out of me. The pain was so severe I could barely see, couldn't even breathe.

I could only scream.

Scream as she attacked me again, a streak of light running toward me. Scream as I dodged like I had so many times before in a million games at the park and stick battles in the alley behind our house.

This wasn't that anymore. This was pain that never ended as vomit dripped over my chin, blood running into my eyes.

I didn't want to die this way.

I didn't want to die like Risha.

I had to run as fast as I could and find Ryland, find Ilyan. Find someone who could help. I had to stop her.

I had made such a big mistake. I had to fix it.

I had to make everything better.

"Ryland!" I yelled, hoping beyond hope he would hear me … find me before it was too late. "Ryland! Save me!"

Ignoring the pain, ignoring the way the world spun, I ran as fast as I could, weaving through the dim hallways like a dodge ball as attack after attack exploded from behind me. Flashes of color reflected against the stone as I ran, screaming.

"Please stop, Jaromir!" Míra yelled, but I couldn't stop.

I couldn't.

The flashes continued as I ran, her magic flooding the hall around me, her cries clear in my ears.

"Please, Jaromir! I don't want to hurt you!"

Red.

Purple.

Blue.

Yellow.

Black.

Black.

Black.

All that was left was black. Black and pain. Pain that encompassed my body. Pain that sent me down to the ground again, slamming against the hard stone. Smooth stone. Cold stone.

I didn't scream yet wanted to. I lay, staring into the black, my eyes wide open as I froze.

"I don't want to hurt anyone anymore!" Míra cried, her steps loud as she passed me. "I don't want to be bad anymore. It's not fair."

Her voice faded away as she did, as the black became everything.

I heard the door open. I heard her laugh. I heard an old man yell.

And then there was nothing.

Nothing except Momma, her arms always so soft and warm.

"It's not fair."

11

JOCLYN

"WE ARE ALL GOING TO DIE!"

"... You are going to lead us to the end!"

"We can't follow her!"

My skin crawled as the voices ran over each other, the anger in the ruins of the cathedral boiling my blood, banging against what was left of the walls, shifting over the rock as everything shook underneath the weight of the wrath that was drowning the room. Drowning against the four of us as we stood on a large slab of what used to be roof; the large slab perched precariously on the rubble, only slightly above the hive of angry hornets below us, each one ready to sting, ready to kill.

It was a terrifying place to be, the fear already settling deep in my gut.

"Why hasn't she been removed after she burned all of the Chosen in the hospital?" A tall Skříteks voice broke above all the others as he shoved his way to the front, jockeying for a better position, a fist fight braking out because of his forced entry.

Visibly cringing, I turned away from the once civil people, away from the pink light of dawn that was beginning to peek between the buildings. I moved my focus to Ilyan, Wyn, and Ryland, who seemed just as irritated with the state of the horde beneath us.

"You are going to let her kill us!"

My shoulders hunched as my stomach twisted painfully, the words hitting a little too close to home.

Just wait, můj kamarád. I won't stand for this for long, Ilyan's voice rolled inside of me as shame riddled me. His irritation was clear as he stood side by side with the three of us, looking like he was little more than mildly irritated.

Oh, I know, I assured him. *I'm well aware. It doesn't change the fact that they are acting like immature killer rabbits, crying because we ran out of carrots.*

Ilyan laughed at that, the chuckle loud and clear as Ry and Wyn looked between us in confusion.

I shrugged, willing to keep that joke to myself. Too bad the joy in it couldn't last.

"She's not a queen; she's a tyrant." The words hit against my back, seeping into me like poison.

Poison I was desperate to ignore.

"Guys," I mused, cringing internally, gritting my teeth as I forced the humor out, "did you hear? I'm a tyrant. I guess I better start collecting taxes now or something."

Ryland snickered at me, rolling his eyes the way he always did when I was being ridiculous. Ilyan, however, just stared at me, the joke lost due to another outburst from somewhere beneath us.

I ignored it.

"At least then we could take that vacation Ilyan was promising," Wyn teased, her smirk widening as she threw her arm around my neck, the gloved hand waving wildly around my ear. "Make them pay for it."

"If they don't kill each other," Ryland mused as another fist fight broke out, the sounds of the incessant fights beneath us making me uneasy.

I wasn't the only one.

Ryland stood, tugging at the long hem of the tunic he was wearing, obviously uncomfortable in the regal clothes that were normally reserved for Ilyan. Now Ilyan and his baby brother were practically identical in those clothes. It was odd to see them standing side by side in tunics that clung to them in odd ways, tights that defined things that would be better left undefined, and long, golden chains that, a year ago, would have made me think pimp.

Now, all I saw was a king. A king and his younger brother, his second.

All Ryland was missing was the crown.

I was glad Ilyan hadn't found a dress in wherever he had dug those up from. I might not look like royalty, but at least my holey jeans were comfortable.

"But then," Ryland continued, pulling my thoughts from

gold-trimmed fabric and back to the angry shouts beneath us, my tense mate still and volatile before me, "having them kill each other was kind of the point."

"Not *the point*, per say," Ilyan said, his narrowed eyes still focused on the crowds beneath us.

My stomach tightened further. The look on his face did not give me much confidence for what was coming.

"But, yes, some form of violence is preferable before we allow them to divide."

"Divide," Wyn scoffed, laughing as a spark of magic exploded overhead, the brightening courtyard erupting in sparks of orange. "You mean, get them all angry and see who stands up for you? And here I was thinking we were conducting some highly scientific model—"

"This *is* very scientific." Ilyan didn't even look at her, his focus still on the crowd. The strength in his face mounted, the madness in his eyes becoming clear. I was in no doubt he had meant it as a joke, but the humor was lost in his power, lost in the danger that had surrounded us, the same feeling eating at my spine. "Scientific enough that not everyone will die."

"Sounds good enough for me," Wyn responded with a shrug and a smile. "I wanted to make sure my crazy matched yours is all."

"I don't think that's possible, Wynifred. But, in this instance, we at least seem to be on the same side," Ilyan said, his voice dark as his focus pulled away from the crowd to her. "Your crazy is right on par for this. Are you ready?"

"Always am, boss," Wynifred said with a grin, cracking her

knuckles. Little sparks of fire ignited from her fingers, smoke oozing out from under the glove she was wearing as though her hand was on fire. Maybe it was. "Just tell me where to go."

"Why do I have a feeling everything just got very dangerous?" I growled, looking at Ryland who looked as worried as I did.

Another attack covered the sky, crackling against the barrier that surrounded us in electric circuits that cracked like ice crystals.

This was exactly what Sain had wanted. All those whispering rumors, all those vile lies. It was all for this, all to tear us apart before the last battle began. And I had to say, it was working.

"Or, if you'd rather, I could light them all on fire." Wyn's grin expanded, her voice a hiss over the riotous screams as she leaned into the middle of our little circle. She looked like she was orchestrating some kind of drug deal.

Or a murder.

"Who are you talking to, Wyn? Ilyan or Joclyn?" Ryland asked with a laugh.

"I could be talking to you, Ry. It doesn't matter. The threat is real. And besides, fire is pretty."

"Prettier than all of this?" I asked, taking one side look at the crowd beneath us right in time to hear an obscenity or two hurled at me. The words smacked against my heart, and I flinched before Ilyan's magic roared inside of me in irritation.

"Get the pig out of here! Give your people a queen worthy of them!"

"Ouch." That one hurt.

"So says the pigs," Wyn scoffed, fire sparking as she side-stepped.

Her need to attack them was as clear as my irritation of them, which was fine. She could attack, and I could glare.

"I believe it's time." Ilyan's magic flared as his stoic glare shifted back toward the horde, one step pulling him forward. His jaw was tight as his magic washed through me with a strength and power that left me wanting.

"She shouldn't even be here!" the voice erupted as a rock was hurled over the crowd.

The rock, unlike the magic, soared past the barrier and right at us. Magic bristled, dissolving the rock into sand before it could smack me right in the face.

"A rock?" I said, a laugh coming freely. "I think I might really be a tyrant."

"At least you are a tyrant who can dissolve rocks to sand."

"What would you like me to do, Wyn?" I sighed as another fistfight broke out beneath us.

Wyn chuckled darkly at the development.

"Rocks make wonderful fireballs."

"Well, in the interest of not lighting people on fire ..." I pushed my long braid over my shoulder, letting the golden ribbon trail over my skin and float through the air in an attempt to get to Ilyan, something it seemed to do even if wind was not present. "Shall we?"

"Yes." Ilyan's voice was a growl, his eyes on fire as his magic resounded inside of me, his focus still on the crowd beneath us. "Ryland, as my second, you stand on my left. Joclyn, as my mate, you're on my right. Wyn, stay close to her and use your best judgment in counterattacks. But please be careful not to bring anything down. I'm not sure how much this cathedral can take."

"No guarantees, Ilyan. Between asking me to keep people alive and keep the rubble intact, it might be too much," Wyn said in a sing-song, her voice deep and dark in the seductress tone I had gotten used to. She was in her element.

Ilyan ignored her. I didn't blame him, not now that more rocks were being hurled at us.

"Let's go," he said.

Ryland shuffled his feet before taking his place beside his brother.

Ilyan wrapped his arm around my waist as he pulled me beside him, my steps broken as I tried to keep up with his large gait.

Watch for larger attacks from the left side, Ilyan's voice filled me, the words sounding so focused I wasn't even sure he was talking to me. *More hostility and rocks seem to be coming from that side. I have increased the shield; it should be enough to block the stones...*

Don't worry, darling, I interrupted as I walked unsteadily beside him. *I can handle this* and *not kill anyone.*

Ilyan smiled as the unstable roof shifted beneath us. I felt the shift, the possibility of it falling causing my heart to fall to my toes. But no one else shifted. The four of us continued forward as a single powerhouse, their eyes narrowed toward the crowd gathered below our makeshift platform.

Rocks peppered the barrier before us as we drew closer, sparks of multicolored magic flashing in the air and against the barrier with each step. All the while, the people fought, yelled. Fists were thrown, words hurled, and my heart galloped against my chest, a different kind of fear attempting a hostile takeover of my soul.

Ilyan's arm slipped from my waist as he stepped ahead of us. Ryland, Wyn, and I stopped in place with a subtle flick of his wrists.

Wyn shuffled her feet in an attempt to stay still, the same fear I was feeling taking over her. Ilyan was getting dangerously close to the barrier, to the rocks that smacked into the magical wall with deep ripples, to the bright streams of magic that I was positive would give him something far worse than a bit of a stomach ache.

He continued forward, his heart a riotous force against my soul as he stepped past the barrier, leaving him unprotected except for his magic that flared to deflect each attack individually. His délka vedení královsk remained behind, twisted around mine as always, bound together as we were.

I couldn't look away from him as he stood still and angry before them, his eyes wide as my heart thumped in my ears, fear filling me.

"Umlčet!" Ilyan's voice was a roar as his magic infected the word, dispersing over the crowd in a ripple, seeping into them and numbing their magic, numbing their thoughts.

Silence spread over them as anger slipped off their faces, their shoulders slumping and eyes glossing over. As one, the anger was pulled from them as Ilyan's magic infected them into a slack jaw stupor that I knew better than to believe, no matter how disconnected and stupid they appeared.

They were trapped under his magic. They had no choice other than to listen.

"Umlčet!" Ilyan repeated just as loudly, the magic grabbing them with a firmer grip, cementing them in place and pulling their focus right to him.

"You have behaved atrociously!" Ilyan roared, his voice a dark rumble of power as he stood before them, his braid long and straight down his back, the crown bobbing on his head.

With a few words, their eyes began to widen, their jaws dropping in awe as fear began to take hold. They saw him now as a king. Despite the spell, they were under the power of this man.

"This type of behavior is not acceptable for my people." Ilyan's voice cascaded over the crowd and ricocheted off the walls like a drum. "This is not the way I expect people who hold the powers of the earth to act. You have allowed that same evil magic we have fought against for centuries to take hold amongst you. You have allowed one who once walked our halls infect you. He has planted seeds of doubt, seeds of lies, and seeds of conspiracy within each of you. By letting them take root, you have let them grow into something ugly. You have allowed the foundation of terror to take hold, to destroy you all. It is you, not Joclyn Krul, your queen, who has done this thing!"

Ilyan shook as his voice rose, his crown shivering from the movement, his hands tense as he pointed at me then at them. Sparks of magic flew from the tips of his fingers as his power rattled uncontrollably throughout him. Throughout me.

My chest heaved under the weight of his power, his emotions bolstering me with a potent influx of strength and power. Looking out at the controlled hysteria before me—at the people who, with one look, began to see the same power, the same regality in me that they saw in Ilyan—I could feel it in me. Torn and stained jeans and all, I straightened my shoulders.

"For centuries, we have met in council to hear the concerns of our people to build a path into our future that suits us all. But this farce you have created is not the way it is done. I am the king, and I expect to be treated as such. I expect my words to be heard and my requests to be met. I expect my people to present themselves with decorum, pride, and the respect that I show them—nay, that their magic affords them and that their lineage has given them."

His speech rattled amidst everyone. It echoed against the stone. It seeped into bones. It infiltrated my soul in such a way that I could feel it become a part of me, and I was not the only one.

Everyone in the room stood, staring at him with their eyes wide in surprise, their jaws slack in astonishment. No one moved. No one said anything, yet I was certain his magic had been dispelled from them already.

Well, almost everyone.

"Now who's the tyrant?" Wyn whispered into my ear with a snicker, making it clear she had heard it all before.

I waved her away, not wanting to ruin this.

She scoffed in reply, but I ignored her, my mind going blank as Ilyan turned to me, gesturing me forward.

Great. Here we go.

Are you ready? Ilyan whispered in my mind, the tension in his voice as clear as it was on his face.

I smiled. Love was dripping from him, smothering the slowly awakening crowd behind him into oblivion.

Ready? I laughed. *This is nothing compared to an angry Ovailia who really wants to kill you.*

Point taken, he said, a chuckle plainly audible in his words. *Come. Let us stand together as king and queen. Those who do not see you as such have no place in our kingdom. They have no place to stand beside us in the battle we are to face. They accept you, or we reject them. This is the time we know. This is when our battle begins.*

The crowd began to shift and move as I stepped forward, placing my fingertips against the king, standing beside him as he did me, hand over hand.

His magic moved inside of me, the connection rattling my strength as my nerves twisted underneath my skin in an eagerness to get out. The same anxious energy moved amidst the crowd, theirs in anger. The emotion rushed back into them, ready to explode. To attack, to fight, to run. It was all there on their faces. It was there, running inside of me.

And now that I stood on the other side of the barrier, the emotions felt deeper, a density that threatened to explode out of me.

All I needed was another rock to come my way, which I was certain would come in a matter of seconds.

Wyn and Ryland stepped forward as I did, the extraordinary heat of Wynifred's internal fire spanning over the cool air of the room. Glaring at the audience, Wyn folded her arms over a faded Boston T-shirt, full bodyguard status engaged.

"We stand before you as your king and as your queen. We are your rulers, and as your rulers, we command—"

"She is not fit to lead us!" a solitary voice broke over the crowd, snapping through them in a wave that discharged in tiny pockets of hatred, pockets of loyalty rising up.

Violence erupted in sparks of magic, blasts and bangs echoing amidst the ruins as more than punches were thrown.

A stream of violet headed toward us, Wyn stepping in front of me, ready to face it, only to have it be intercepted by an attack from one of the many Skříteks in the crowd. The woman rushed to stand before us in order to protect us, several others following her lead.

One after another, they came, forming a human barrier, ready to protect us, to fight for us.

"We need to protect those who stand with us!" Ilyan shouted above the noise, his magic already moving over them, ready to begin. "Get our people on this roof; immobilize the rest. We will deal with them once they are taken care of."

"Sounds boring, but you're the boss," Wyn mused, winking at me before jumping off the dilapidated slab of roof, fire following behind her as she went into action.

Stay safe, můj kamarád.

Ilyan followed Wyn's lead without a second glance, his magic spinning inside me in the same type of mad eagerness I had seen so many times before. I could feel his exhilaration for battle resonating within me, fanning my own eagerness. But they were emotions that did not reach Ryland's face.

Ry stared at me, wide-eyed, fear and panic pulling at him.

My own heart fell into the same familiarity. I could already feel it trying to eat me alive.

"Ryland?" I asked, my thoughts moving a million miles as I blocked an attack right beside us, trying to pull him out of whatever hell he had fallen into. "We have to go."

We both internally went right back to the massive hall, his house falling apart around us, to the rescue mission that had been the worst kind of failure.

I almost expected his eyes to darken and his soul to turn black.

I almost ran away.

I deflected another attack to the side as a blast almost hit my feet, shifting the rubble we stood on precariously. I screamed at the movement, falling back into Ryland who was still frozen in place, trapped in his father's head, his eyes screaming for help.

"You can do this," I whispered, putting my hand on his

forearm without thinking, ignoring the flinch that came from the contact. "You can control him, and you can help us. Ilyan brought you up as his second, after all."

"I know," Ryland whispered, his voice so quiet I could barely hear him. "Just, if I lose control—"

"You won't. And if you do, I'll ..." I stopped midsentence, my voice catching as my head spun, my magic slamming into me so hard I was positive I wasn't breathing. I was positive I had been hit.

Ilyan?

Joclyn!

There was no other magic in me but my own, no other magic than my sight that was quickly taking control.

My sight ...

Joclyn!

"Joclyn!"

I fell to the ground with a thud, Ryland's scream mixing with Ilyan's as he tried to catch me. Ry's magic softened the fall, but it didn't matter.

Ryland's voice echoed in my head, the sound bolstered by the screams and explosions that surrounded us. I could still see him before me, but it was fading, the world spinning around me.

The magic moved into me, and though I tried to fight it, I couldn't. It took control. It dragged me down. Everything was so far away. It was moving away.

"Ryland," I tried to force the words out as my magic swelled in my head, erupting underneath my skin in the worst kind of goose bumps, ice against fire. "I can't stop it. You have to protect me."

I didn't know if I had been able to get the words out. I didn't know if he had heard me. I couldn't even hear the battle anymore, yet I could see Ryland screaming at me, his curls bouncing, the magical attacks exploding over his head in pastel fireworks. I heard nothing, just the buzzing as my sight pulled at me.

Ryland faded into the black of sight, the vision swallowing me like the drain in a tub, sucking me into oblivion.

The power took control as my eyes darted to black, leaving me staring at the dark, the occasional quake of what I assumed were explosions rumbling around me.

They shook my bones, everything tense with fear. I almost expected the sight to end, to drag me back to the war. However, with one sharp inhale, a flood of color wrapped around me, a million images coming one right after another before they stopped in an alley I recognized as being in Prague. Except, the sun was too yellow, the street too clean.

The children, however, I knew at once. They were younger, but I knew their smiles and their button noses. I had never seen Jaromir without the mark on his cheek, yet I knew him without question.

"I don't like fighting," Jaromir groaned as he sunk down against the wall, folding himself into a tiny pretzel.

The world around him rattled with another blast, glass banging in frames, rocks shivering on the ground. He didn't seem to notice. He simply lay still, his back shaking with tears as Míra came up beside him, wrapping herself around him like a cage, her cheek pressed against his back.

"I don't like it, and it's getting worse." Míra's voice was a distant whisper as it moved within the sight of the past.

The sound of Jaromir's cries was haunting as they rattled with another blast.

"Promise me you'll never hurt me like Papa hurts Momma," Jaromir begged, sitting up so fast that Míra had to scuttle to avoid impact. "Promise me you'll always love me?"

"Silly, Jay-Jay. I'm your best sister. Of course I'll never do that."

The kids smiled and laughed, the sound of their promise following me as they moved away, like oil through water, colors swirling and dancing until a cave took their place.

I expected the same cave I had seen so many times before, the one that taunted me with Ilyan's death, the one I had seen Míra standing in days before. This one was different— a large, open cavern flooded with muddy water. I was convinced I had seen it before, but I couldn't place it.

My heart clenched as the memory embedded itself. The story Dramin had told me so many times smacked me in the face. I knew what this was.

Imdalind.

"Are you watching?" The deathly hollow of my own voice filled my ears as my sight flickered alongside another explosion, the water shimmering as the rocks shifted. Except, when the echo of battle ended, my own image was now standing before the pool. Standing, staring with a bloodied length of ribbon in my hands.

I stood still before another explosion waved amid the sight, wiping me from view and shifting the sight back to the kids, back to Míra who sat, crying in a tent, back to Jaromir who was throwing rocks against a barrier. Each image flashed for a split second before they changed again, replaced by a forest I knew too well, one I had been hunted in for nights on end. Taunted by Cail and his games.

"Are you watching?" the deep voices of a hundred Drak inside me asked again, louder. The death in my voice twisted in my stomach, writhing down to my legs as I fought the need to run. Run past the trees, away from the steps I could already hear coming after me.

With the snap of lightning, with the rumble of thunder, the forest flickered and left, the same trees pulled into a perfect circle, a fire blazing in the center. Wyn, Ryland, and I sat around the pit, sharing the same pie we had so long ago. The sound of our laughter bounced off the trees, bounced in my ears, before it was replaced by the blast of battle, Ryland's scream traveling alongside it.

I cringed at the sound, at the panic, and tried once again to pull myself out of the sight. It stayed, the clearing emptying of people and pie and filling with hundreds of Skříteks, each dressed in clothes more fitted to that of the Elizabethan era. And in the middle of them, a woman stood with hair as blonde as Ilyan's, dressed in white, a handkerchief over her face. Sain stood beside others I didn't recognize with a bright blue Vilỳ I was convinced I had seen before and a Trpaslík on either side of him. The others were crying while

Sain stood still, attempting to hide a smug little smile on his face.

I stared, confused at the scene, before everything rattled again, pulling me into the middle of an ornate hall, large oak doors and marble floors surrounding me.

I knew this hall.

I had grown up in this hall.

But it was not the hall of my childhood. It was the hall of my nightmares.

It was the hall that was full of rot and rats where everything smelled of death and was dripping with water so rusty it looked like blood.

Maybe it was.

My mind said it was.

My mind took me right back to those haunted halls, the explosion that shook the space making everything real.

"Are you watching?" my own voice asked again as the lights in the hall flickered with an explosion.

With each flash of light, a tall woman appeared, shimmering in and out as she had in my nightmares years before.

My mother.

"No."

My heart stopped beating as my mouth went dry, the flickering leaving me staring at her bloodied face. Her feet were twisted on the cracked tiles she stood on, surrounded by the long curls of wallpaper that were pulling away from the walls.

A scream pressed against my chest as I tried to run from her. Run from my mother for the first time in my life.

She looked the same as she had the last day I had seen her, down to the chipped yellow nails that I had watched go limp as a trail of blood trickled from the corner of her mouth.

"NO!" The scream found its way out as my gut tensed and ripped in two. "No."

"Are you watching?" This time, it was my mother who spoke, the words haunted and hollow before an explosion rattled around us, pulling the sight right to the room I had left more than an hour before.

My brother slept curled in his bed, his blanket tucked around him like he was a toddler.

"Are you watching?" a familiar little voice asked.

I turned, expecting to face Míra, only to come face to face with her brother.

Dramin's bedroom fell away to reveal the dark hallway outside of Dramin's room.

Jaromir walked amidst the dark, flinching as an explosion rattled the halls around him. The same explosion rattled my dreams and alerted me to the haunting reality I now faced.

This was *now*.

Another explosion shook both of us. The boy flinched further as tears streamed down his face. Míra followed behind him with a grin so sly it sent shivers down my spine.

"Are you watching?"

The sound of Jaromir's steps was hollow in my ears, an odd squelching noise following each step. He walked as though he were dead, forward, unseeing. Until ...

At once, the vision shifted, the children jerking around and moving forward and back as though they were being pulled by a string, as though the whole sight was being rewound.

"Here, they walk," my voice said, the sudden change in direction pushing a fear against my gut.

"Are you watching?" The depth of my voice came again, pulling me right back to children.

But they were no longer walking in the hall.

Jaromir lay facedown in a pool of crimson, the wet spilling away from him like molasses, seeping into his nightshirt like a sponge, bright red. Míra walked away from him in tears, magic sparking on her fingers as she talked to herself, as she screamed and cried. Cried out to Jaromir. Cursed and yelled at him. But she didn't turn to help her brother. She didn't try to save him. She merely walked past.

"Here, they fall."

Míra walked right toward Dramin's door as everything rattled, stretching her hand across the dark to clasp the knob I myself had closed minutes before. That I had left, foolishly thinking those behind would be safe.

A door I knew at once would never be.

"Are you watching?"

The images faded as the screams of the hall I had left

behind filled my ears. My heart raced in my chest as the panic the prescience had been blocking infected me.

"Are you watching?" I said to myself, sitting straight up as reality returned to me.

Ryland's worried face stared right into mine as he sat next to me, protecting me from the battle that was still rampant.

He was not the only one.

A wall of Skříteks and Chosen surrounded us, their backs to us as they battled.

For a split second, I wondered if we were winning or losing, but I couldn't ask. I didn't have time. I didn't have time for anything.

Right now, she was walking toward the door.

"She is moving," I said to Ryland.

He looked at me in confusion, obviously trying to decide if I was still in sight or not.

"Jos?" he asked, his voice shaking. "Are you okay?"

"Look at me, Ry!" I snapped, not caring about his question. "Míra, she is out. Risha, Jaromir, Dramin, Thom—they are all in danger. You have to move."

His eyes widened for a second, fear turning into anger as he stood, his shoulders square as he muscled his way past the circle of people.

"Ilyan?" I said aloud, hoping he could hear me. "Did you hear that?"

I did.

"Good. Tell Wyn."

With that, I left with a small pop . The booming of my heart moved along with me as I moved to another battle.

One that I would win.

I had to.

12

JOCLYN

THE POP of my return was lost in the screams that echoed inside the dark hall. The only light in the ominous pitch came from the long streams of dawn that permeated the windows in strips of light and dark.

Building shifting and trembling around me, dust and rocks sprinkling over me, the beams shook and shivered from the battle I had left behind. Regardless, I barely noticed anything beyond the heavy galloping of my heart in my throat, beyond the screaming that my magic was already rushing toward. It extended across the hallways and broke through walls, right into the room Míra had already reached. To my brother who had tackled her to the ground.

"No," I gasped aloud, and Ilyan's heart beat rushed into my chest as he felt my panic, as he saw the scene inside my mind.

Hurry, Joclyn! he yelled, his voice filling me as I rushed down the hall, tripping over my own feet in my desperation.

I turned the corner of the wide hall and stoppedɪ in place, everything freezing around me.

Dramin's yell echoed beyond the door to my left, his panic clear, but I barely heard it. I barely heard anything beyond the heaving gasps of my lungs as I tried to take in air.

There, in the middle of the hall before me, was the rigid body of Jaromir, exactly as I had seen in sight. The haunting reality smacked me in the face.

Jaromir lay facedown in the hallway, surrounded by a pool of crimson.

Ilyan, the word was numb in my mind as my heart clenched, magic aching as I felt nothing from Jaromir. No whisper of the power he used to hold. No sound of his breath.

Nothing.

My eyes stung as I stood there, unable to pull myself forward, unable to move toward ... where he was lying there ... just as my mother had.

Just as she had died.

I couldn't breathe.

Joclyn, listen to me, Ilyan soothed into my mind, his magic wrapping around my soul as he felt the desperation gripping me. Even though I could clearly see him fighting at least three Chosen, he was with me. He was with Jaromir. *I'm sending Etma to him. You have to go, Joclyn!*

His voice was a drum beat in my head as Míra screamed, her laugh mixing with Dramin's cries, pulling me out of the hell the sight of Jaromir's body had trapped me in.

Pulling me right back into the hell that was waiting for me.

"I won't let you!" Dramin yelled as I threw open the door.

His emaciated body tackled the girl to the floor, a flash of imagery before her magic exploded in a wave of white. It sped away from her, throwing Dramin across the room and tossing me back across the hall I had left, right into the stone wall behind me.

Dramin's shout mixed with mine as we both impacted with stone and glass and who knew what else.

As I slid down the stone to land on the floor in a heap, my back aching, the strength of her attack rang in my ears like a bell, blocking out the sound of battle with a hollow noise that pressed against my skull. The pain that was already unyielding against my spine increased against the joints in my neck and shoulders. I tried to shake it off, but everything swelled, my heart aching, my panic rising.

"Don't stop me, old man!" Míra screamed amidst the fog.

The numbing buzz fell away with the pain, leaving me heaving as I tried to reach Dramin.

While I gasped from the movement, the pain in my back turned into a live wire, jolting through me. I couldn't stay here and wait for my magic to repair whatever damage Míra had done. I could feel it already trying.

"I have to do this!"

I could have sworn Míra was crying, but I didn't care. I pushed myself up, my magic surging as I stumbled back into the room. My magic ripped the door off its hinges in my desperation to reach Dramin.

Bottles and dishes, plants, and books were scattered over the floor. Thom's bed was upturned, the man who had inhabited it for months nowhere to be seen, hidden behind the straw and feathers that had been ripped out of his mattress, scattered around them in waves of white. I saw nothing. If I hadn't known better, I would have said it was snowing. I would have thought it was ... if it weren't for the red.

It was sprayed over the floors and walls as though someone had taken an ax to a man. The color was so bright, so present that I had no way of knowing who it belonged to ... until I saw Dramin lying on the ground underneath Míra, soaked in it.

"Try to stop me!" Míra screamed at him as she sent another attack into his chest.

His frail, magicless body took the full brunt, his scream ripping through me, pressing my heart into my throat.

I lost it.

"Don't touch him, little girl!" I screamed as I ran toward her, my magic crashing against her as I ripped her off my brother then threw her across the room.

She screamed in surprise, hair and limbs tangling as she flew end over end before freezing as she impacted with the wall.

As though someone had hit the pause button, she froze, and my magic dropped from her as she took control, falling to the ground like a cat.

With a snap, she looked up at me, blood streaked over her face, down her hair, staining her teeth red as she smiled at me. Her eyes were a hard glare before she countered. The snap of her magical attack zapped through the air in a shock wave.

With the tiniest flick, I thwarted her, my magic pressing against her and sending the wave back.

She fell to the ground with a shriek, dodging the attack and letting the magical pulse slam into the wall behind her in a blast that shook the room with a roar.

Dramin's carefully tended bookcases exploded from the impact, sending shards of burning paper, dust, and broken pieces of mugs flying into the air. They showered us in a cascade of flame and smoke, paper and feathers burning against the dim light of dawn like haunted fairy lights. And the air was on fire. The scent was a campfire drenched in the iron smell of blood. The burning embers of paper that fell around us increased that.

"I should have trusted my sight about you." My voice was as hard as her eyes, the anger flowing inside of her glaring back at me. "I should have seen you for what you are and destroyed you when I had the chance!"

"Trusted your sight?" Pain gripped her voice as she pulled herself up to standing, placing herself between me and my brother.

The man moaned as he rolled over in an attempt to push himself into a sitting position, blood spraying from his mouth with a single cough, with a desperate gasp of air.

My heart tensed in a fear beyond what I knew. A desperate need to reach him, to heal him took control, but this girl stood in my way.

She needed to go.

"*Your* sight! I wouldn't even be here if it weren't for your stupid sight!" Míra's magic flared as mine did.

Her power shot from her hand with more strength than I would have assumed her to have. More power than a girl her age should have. Then again, I was reminded when the pain from the blast moved into me, burned me, sending my voice into a scream in the tiny space, that her magic wasn't all her own.

It was Edmund's, too.

The darkness in her magic ripped into me, a weight of familiarity infecting me—infecting my brain. Memories and panic rushed through muscles and nerves, burning and tensing everything as I stumbled back, forcing myself to remain upright as I faced a tiny reincarnation of the man I was supposed to kill. The man I was ready to kill.

Pushing the emotions away, I tightened my jaw, narrowing my eyes as I faced the tiny girl. Her smile was wide, whereas her eyes were sad.

Joclyn! Ilyan's voice rushed into my mind, his concern a warmth against my soul that began to soothe away the agony that was infecting me.

I let him in. I let him fill me, saying nothing. My focus was on Míra, on her rage, my magic bristling, ready for whatever else would come.

"You all said there was good in me. You're liars! There isn't any good in me, not anymore. Edmund saw to that!" Míra screamed as another attack shot through the air, sending feathers and papers flying again.

I deflected it, but not fast enough, not before it pushed against me, sending me stumbling back over the room, against the opposite wall, sliding to the floor beside Thom's upturned bed and Thom, who lay underneath it, blood drizzling from his mouth.

"No," I gasped, my exclamation unheard against Míra's secondary scream of excitement.

With another jolt, she attacked.

I lunged behind Thom's bed in an attempt to dodge it, my heart beating a million miles an hour as my focus shifted to Thom, to the limp and cold man who now lay beside me.

"I'll kill whoever I need to so I can do what Edmund asked of me! That's all that's left for me now. You took everything else away," I heard Míra scream, but my focus was on Thom.

I pressed my hand against his cheek, pushing my magic into him and quickly checking for life, for magic, for anything.

"Your death is all that's left of me!" Dramin's scream rose above the ruckus of the room, taking me by surprise.

I lifted my head in time to see him slam into her like a torpedo, sending them both down to the ground with a *thwack*.

Blood dripped down the back of Dramin's neck as he held her there, his hands moving fast as he grabbed her wrists and pinned them above her head. Little eruptions of magic fired all around them.

"I was told to kill you in order to save Thom. And I will! With my last breath, I will!" Dramin continued to yell as I ducked back down toward Thom, sending my magic into his heart as one little pulse of electricity.

The beat answered back, his magic a whisper.

A whisper more than what it had been for the last few months.

"Thom?" I asked aloud, confused by what I was feeling, by the way his heart rate sped up at the sound his name. That wasn't normal, not for him recently.

"Don't worry, old man; I will gladly take it!"

Míra's scream pulled me from Thom as her magic ricocheted across the room.

Thom's bed was pushed against us as I cowered behind it. The room filled with green light, and my gut twisted, knowing where the attack had landed.

His scream was loud in my ears as he flew into the air before hitting ceiling and wall then finally falling to the floor with a clatter of metal and stone.

"No!" I screamed, my magic flaring as Ilyan's power flooded me. His ability rushed to my heart as the warmth of the air seeped into my skin to warm me. I could feel the power infiltrating me, bolstering me as the bond that connected us began to move closer.

I am coming, mi lasko, he whispered.

The image of the courtyard flashed inside my mind before I swatted it away, jumping over the bed like I was in high school gym class and rushing toward Míra. In two steps, my magic hit her, slamming into her gut and picking her up off the ground, blasting her into the wall across from us, the same as she had done to Dramin.

She deserved it.

Míra screamed, her magic moving to counter in a weak attack that I easily blocked. She stayed pinned there, staring at me, struggling against the bind, but she was stuck. The tears you would expect from a child her age finally replaced the monster the child had become. In that moment, she looked human, but I couldn't trust that.

My heart ached as I walked toward her, forcing myself to remember that she was Edmund's servant and not the child I wanted so much to protect.

"I gave you a chance, and this is what you do to me?" I was angry. I knew it, and I didn't care.

I stretched my magic toward the girl, and Ilyan's intertwined with mine, locking her in place. I was ready to destroy her or restrain her; it didn't much matter which at this point as long as I did it fast. I didn't have much time.

Dramin was in trouble. He was huddled on the floor, repeating three words like a broken record. The needle had stopped right at the end of the song, not knowing how to continue.

"What *I* do to *you*?" she raged, her body shaking as she attempted to fight against me. Her magic was pressed against my barrier like a battering ram, the incessant pressure painful in my chest, but I kept the shield up, holding her place. "You think *I* did something to *you*? I did something *for* you!"

"This is not the way—" I began, but she cut me off with a

snap, her magic slamming into mine so hard that I was forced to take a step back. Everything strained as I kept the barrier against her, barely keeping her in place.

"He wanted me to help you!" she yelled, fully crying now. "I had to do it!"

"You hurt my brother!" I yelled back like I was a child. My heart ached with the need to get to him, to help him, but I was trapped, attempting to battle the tiny assassin. Nevertheless, it was no use. She was too strong. "You were trying to kill him!"

"*Your* brother! I hurt *your* brother?" she screeched, her anger mixing with her magic in a dangerous concoction. "I had to kill mine, all because he wanted me to save you people! And now he's gone! Now you can all burn!"

Her last words erupted with anger as I felt Ilyan rush through the door behind me, Wyn's magic following close behind. Ilyan's magic flared, rushing against the girl. Her eyes flitted between us in renewed horror. Wyn, however, rushed right to Thom, her strangled breaths hissing inside the room as she dropped beside him, her panic and fear clear in the broken sound.

"Míra!" Ilyan raged, his voice shaking the rafters as he took control of the bind I had placed on the child. His magic pressed against mine as he walked toward the girl who was still held against the wall.

Letting him assume control, I sped toward my brother who still lay on the floor, face up, eyes wide, far too much blood covering him as he muttered and trembled.

I had been so focused on the girl I hadn't even realized how quickly Dramin was fading. I hadn't seen how drenched in blood the world had become. Seeing it now, I could barely breathe.

"You have disgraced these halls and our trust. I will not stand for this!" Ilyan yelled, his voice hitting against my back as I clenched Dramin's hand, my magic rushing into him, into his organs that were burned and broken, his bones that were nothing more than splinters. I began to heal him, desperation taut inside of me with the extent of his injuries.

His hand was so cold, so stiff that I feared he was already gone. Ice gripped my heart at the possibility. Then I became thankful when his focus drifted away from the ceiling. The slight movement of his eyes was enough, although I was confident he did not see me.

"I'm here, Dramin," I whispered, my face burning. I didn't think I was getting enough oxygen. "It's okay. Everything is going to be okay."

"Fine, then," Míra hissed from behind me, and Ilyan's panic slapped against my gut. "You won't have to."

"No!" Ilyan yelled, and my magic rushed to my heart as the barrier broke, as the reason for Ilyan's panic became clear.

I turned, expecting a battle, knowing she couldn't win against the two of us. However, there was nothing except the red-tinted grin of her smile and the sound of a faint pop. The girl pulled herself across the worlds, away from us, and into a stutter to who knew where.

As I stared at the now empty room, at Ilyan who stood as confused as I was, at Wyn who sat crying in the corner with Thom's head in her lap, everything felt hollow.

I knew I should be scared about where she had gone. I knew I should care, but I couldn't, not with Dramin's hand still wrapped in mine. Not with the look of hopelessness and sorrow Ilyan was already fixing me with.

I turned back to my brother, my heart rate escalating further. Everything in my stomach beat and swelled and pulsed so much it was starting to hurt.

Healing magic wound throughout him, stitching skin back together and restarting organs, but I already knew it wasn't enough. Even with magic, I doubted he could survive what had been done to him. His magic had been dead for months, just as he would be before the sun fully rose over the red-tinted sky.

"Joclyn," Dramin gasped, his voice a scarce breath from under the blood filling his mouth. It trickled from the crease, and Ilyan wiped it away as he came to sit beside me, his leg pressing against mine.

"Uncle." The word no longer seemed right, so I shook my head as I clung to his hand, leaning closer. "Brother, my brother, I'm here."

The words were as strong as I could make them, knowing it was not enough. It didn't say enough. It wasn't loud enough. I wasn't even sure he could hear me.

He stared past me, into the sky, as though I were nothing more than air between him and wherever he was going.

"You're my brother," I sobbed, trying so hard to get the courage to say what needed to be said. "I'm here ... I'm ... I'm sorry I didn't get here sooner."

I paused, everything closing up in my throat as I felt Ilyan's arms wrapping around me, his head pressed against my shoulder.

I'm here, Jos. I'm right with you. His voice was calm, soothing, filling me from within. The words were simply for me, yet I thought they were meant for Dramin, as well.

"Jos?" Dramin gasped, his voice odd and distorted as he continued to look beyond me.

I squeezed his hand, leaning over him in an attempt to get him to look at me, to get him to see, but it was as though I was invisible. I was gone, just as he was leaving. He didn't even squeeze my hand in return.

"Dramin?" I could barely get the one word out.

"You are the most beautiful queen," Dramin panted, blood trickling down the side of his mouth as he tried to force the words out. Everything came out broken and strangled. "I am so honored to be your brother."

"You are my brother, the best I have had."

He laughed at that, although it was pained.

"Always be what you are. Always be ..." More blood dripped from his lips with each word.

I waited, knowing there was more. But none came.

None ever came.

I had seen death so often in movies. I had been around death so much over the last few years you would think I would be numb to it by now. That I would be used to it.

I wasn't.

I never would be.

Pain ripped through my chest so intensely I couldn't breathe, couldn't speak, couldn't move. I froze, my hand tightening around his as Dramin's eyes drifted away to stare at whatever beautiful thing he had seen, his soul leaving to find it. Leaving us all in the calm silence that ripped me open.

My heart turned to ice as that iron cage I hated so much snapped around it.

"No," I gasped, part of me still not daring to believe. Still expecting a cough, a gasp, a gurgle of blood, and some Miraculous recovery.

There was nothing. Nothing but my tears and Wyn's tears as she rushed over to us.

I was left to wonder for an eternity what he had been about to say, wondering for an eternity what he had been staring at, where he had gone. Left staring at a man whose heart had beaten so long and loved so much and was now quiet. Part of me wondered if I would ever learn to love as much as he could. As much as he had.

The laugh that was always ready, even in the worst situations, was gone forever. Part of me had been swept away alongside him.

Kneeling on that old stone ground, Ilyan's arms around me as he cried with me, his own heartbreak matching mine, our two emotions weaving into a desperate pain, I couldn't move. I sat, clutching a lifeless hand of a brother I didn't get nearly enough time with, of a family I had always wanted and I had so suddenly lost.

Dramin's hand fell from mine as I turned toward Ilyan, his hands warm around mine.

Mid-sob, I stopped, turning toward my brother at the swell of his magic that filled the room. I expected to see him staring, to see him sitting, but he was still. Nothing but the ripple of his power as it drifted from his body in a fog that flowed over the ground away from us, twinkling in the red light of dawn.

All that remained of my brother moved away from us in the faintest line of white in the air, the relics of his magic visual as it glistened and glittered. It seeped inside the walls, moved past the windows and out into the air, the bright red of the sky swallowing him whole as he left to find his wife, to find his children, to find the rest of our family.

"I hope you find your way home, my old friend," Ilyan whispered from beside me, the simple words slamming into my chest, bringing around a fresh round of tears.

I fell forward, over my brother, caught by Wyn. The strength of her arms pulled me into her as she hushed and hummed like the mother she really was.

I lay there, sobbing, thinking of all the people we had lost.

It wasn't fair.

This needed to end.

"I'm going to kill him," I sobbed, my voice seething through the tears.

"Edmund?" Wyn asked, brushing my hair behind my ear.

"No," I said, moving to sit before turning to face the two of them, my pain quickly moving into anger. "Edmund is dead. But Sain ... Sain is going to pay for this, for all of it."

No one said anything. No one had to. They were all stuck in the same paralyzing moment, all in agreement of the proclamation I had made. We had all made the same one at least once. I knew it wasn't my first time.

A million questions ran inside my mind as the agony of loss fueled them. I stayed quiet, for as the sadness tried to take me, another voice was added to the tears of those around us, one that I hadn't heard since we had entered this godforsaken city.

From the voice came questions, and they ended in a panicked yell.

"Wyn? Ilyan? Hello? Help!"

As one, we turned toward the other side of the room, toward the man part of me had already counted for dead, assuming Míra had done away with him, as well.

"Thom?"

13

SAIN

THE THREE MEN shivered before me, their bodies construed on the floor in poor attempts of a bow. They quaked with every step I took before them, the sound of my footfalls loud in the hollow expanse of the hall. The echo of the void made everything louder. I could even hear them breathe in sharp little inhales that accentuated their panic.

"This is a grand hall." My voice was a loud snap as I continued to pace, sidestepping a large pool of still damp blood that remained from the massacre of a few days ago. "I remember when it was carved out. Three skilled Trpaslíks stood in the large cavern we now use as a walkway, their magic pulsing, moving, melting the rock. That was before the fire magic was lost to your kind. That was before any of you were born ..."

I ended with a laugh, the loud, disreputable sound barking inside my chest in a pleasant ripple, echoing against the hollow room with a ridge of danger that was not missed by the three men.

They shivered all the more, curling their spines into themselves as if that could somehow save them.

I laughed harder. Nothing could save them. They would understand the punishment for defying me soon. Then death would find them. I had a job for them first, however.

"I was alive, though," I continued, the laugh ending with a snap, the rough edges of my voice hard against the rocks. The entire room trembled underneath it, underneath my anger. "I saw it all. I was here when they carved the hall, when they protected the deep wells of magic. It was my magic that they cowered beneath, much the same way as you do now."

They shivered more. Georg even shifted his weight, pulling his body back again in a desperate attempt to get away from me. Not that I blamed him. I could feel his magic pulse in fear, the strong barrier I had placed over them still restraining his power.

"It was in this room that I ruled. In this room, I was king. It seems fitting I put my throne in this room. I much prefer this one to the old wooden ones they gave us before," I mused as I left the floor they cowered on, jumping lithely onto the raised stage of the old council room. "They were so bland, so boring. *Wood*," I scoffed. "Nothing more than a chair your grandmother would knit in. They were supposed to show how humble we were, how much like you."

The large metal coffers lining the back of the stage erupted to life as I approached them. Brilliant orange flames jumped to life, igniting the dark stone of the stage in streams of color and casting the massive throne I had made for myself in lines of light and shadow.

Bones.

Hundreds of bones. Ripped from the bodies of those who fought and lost. Many of them still glistened with the blood of their former owners. Glistened with the loyalty they held toward Edmund. The loyalty that had ended in their deaths.

The loyalty had been reduced to a place for the king they should have worshiped to sit.

White and red, it rose out of the black stone in twisted lines, rib cages intertwined with arms and legs, fingers stretching over the arm rests, curling over bones.

And above it all, a blackened skull. The fractured remains of a burned king, his eyes nothing more than hollow sockets, chipped teeth of yellowed ash protruding from a slack jaw, opened in an eternal scream.

"I am not like you," I continued, my back to them as I moved toward the massive structure, a smile stretching over my teeth. "I never have been, and I will no longer pretend to be."

Blood-soaked cloak rippling behind me, I sat, sinking into the oddly comfortable structure.

Running my fingertips over the bones of the throne, I sighed, enjoying the oddly gritty texture of the skeletal remains. The smooth, almost rock-like surface was familiar and pleasant, made even more so by the vibration of magic that always lived deep within the marrow. I could feel it in the long femur that stretched over the armrest. My elongated nails tapped against the knucklebones, the tiny bones placed like studs against a seam of fabric, binding them together in infamous beauty.

"I am sure you have questions," I began, shifting the subject as I continued to drum my fingers over the bones of the chair. "About why you are here, I mean. About why I have called for you."

They continued to tremble as I spoke, their hearts pounding so loudly I could hear their faint echoes in the silence of the dead room. Fingers twitched, backs quivered, yet none of them said anything. They cowered in fear, their panic increasing my joy.

I smiled. How could I not with the way they shivered?

"Yes … yes … my king …" Alojz finally answered when it became obvious I was waiting for a response, his fear-swollen tongue barely able to get the words out.

"It's quite simple. You see, whispers have been floating around Imdalind, whispers about you three."

Allowing the ominous depth of my words to drift into nothing, I sat, listening to their dread of discovery beyond the still hush of the cave. The fear tightened their backs as they began to shift, long glances unhidden as they contemplated if they should fight, if they should run, or if they should face me with bravery that I was positive, until this moment, they'd had no doubt of.

"Whispers about you and your loyalty." The lie left my tongue with rancid honey and vinegar, the disdain masked by a false sense of security I could tell was not enough.

I would have to play their game if I wished to gain their trust.

"Rise."

As one, they stood. My wicked smile faded before they could catch a glimpse, the shrouded truth of what they had walked into hidden by a look of piety.

"We live to serve you," Alojz whispered, his head bowed in reverence, a smile shoddily hidden beneath the long curls of his beard.

"Serve." I repeated the word to myself, the thinly veiled disbelief hidden under my breath.

It was all lies. Lies I was already eager to strip them of. They lived to serve no one but themselves, no one but the man I had already destroyed.

Heavy emotion rippled over me, tensing my muscles and twisting my stomach in eager anticipation. My soul called for the crimson blood of the three to wash the floor now and not to wait.

With their eyes focused on me, I stood, letting the blood-soaked robe fall around me like the cloak it had become.

"Damek has assured me that your skills are beyond compare, that your loyalty toward me has grown beyond what your kind is capable."

Despite my kind words, a hint of danger infected them, poison dripping from each syllable. It was not something that was missed.

As I sprang from my podium, the blood cloak rippled behind me with the sound of a loud *crack*.

"Is this true?" I asked as I circled behind Bronislav, my voice a cool chill in the harshness of the winter we were trapped in.

Bronislav shivered under the pressure. Each of the others glanced at him in fear, the reality of what was happening hitting them.

The wave of my magic smothered them with the deep emotion I was convinced they had thought they had escaped.

Layer by layer, I stripped away their pathetic securities, leaving them bare and exposed. The temporary calm I had given them before was nothing more than a cruel joke now, a joke I was certain they would kill to have returned.

"Yes, my king," the elderly man whispered.

"Good."

Withdrawing my magic enough that the lies of safety and stability could find their way past again, I stopped before them, my spine tingling in exhilaration for the trap I was about to set.

"My sight has shown me the greatness that I am to rule. It has shown me what you will become and what I am to command. It has shown me a death, a single death that will lead to this, and the bravery of the three who will bring it to me." I paused, my smile struggling to remain hidden before I continued on. "I have seen you three within the walls of Prague. I have seen you in battle, and together, I have seen you destroy Ilyan Krul, the usurper who has kept our races controlled for centuries."

The fear they'd had before left in a breath. A gasp escaped Georg whose eyes were so wide I didn't think he would ever be able to close them again.

"I have seen you behead the would-be king of the Skříteks

and deliver the dripping monstrosity to me. I have watched us all indulge in his still beating heart."

Open glances passed between the three as anticipation grew, everything from before forgotten as I handed them their archenemy on a platter.

They had been trained to think of him as such, and that brainwashing ran so deep it even trumped the need for revenge that had fueled them to date.

"In a few days' time, I will be re-opening the pits. I will be recommencing the promotion battles for the Chosen and letting the blood flow again. In the pits, we will present this delicious gift to the masses, and you will be the ones to do it." Perhaps it was wrong to lie, but with the excitement on their faces, it didn't matter. Also, I didn't care. "I need you to make that happen." Glaring at Alojz as I spoke the last few words, I let the possibility of the scene play into his ego.

Feet shuffling in eagerness, eyes wide as glances passed between them, they stood. The awe of having escaped the wrath they were convinced they would meet mixed perfectly with the future I had displayed before them.

The chess pieces moved forward.

"You have seen all this?" Alojz asked, his eyes narrowing at me.

I jerked, not liking the way he questioned me, not liking the depth of his eyes as they bore into me. It was the same as Ovailia, that smug power I had no interest in seeing.

He had no power.

Just as she had no power.

No matter how many fires they put out.

The others looked at him in confusion, obviously not understanding why he would question such a gift as this. Their own need for Ilyan's death drowned out their better logic.

Alojz was wiser than I had assumed, it seemed.

My own silent warning met his dead-on. Eyes narrowing, I took a step forward, my silent threat understood.

"My king."

But obviously not in its entirety.

I wasn't a fool. The well-kempt man wasn't asking if I had seen this; he was asking how deeply I was able to see.

I smiled, careful to keep the wicked gleam out of my eyes. The wide grin portrayed a calm comfort that was almost more perverse than letting the warning glare through my eyes. "Bronislav," I said, still not letting my eyes drift from Alojz's. "Come here."

I could see Bronislav hesitate out of the corner of my eye, his jaw slack as he looked between Alojz and me. The former returned his look in confusion. I still did not look away from the man before me. His own confusion spiraled into fear as the older Trpaslík finally moved to join me.

"I wasn't going to do this," I said with a sigh, removing a small leather pouch from the pocket of my worn and baggy jeans, "but seeing as Alojz needs proof of what is to come ..."

Without warning, I reached forward, grabbing Bronislav's hand and pouring a small amount of the liquid from the pouch over his skin.

On contact, he began to scream, the powerful magic in the water burning through him. Meanwhile, I felt the cool comfort of the liquid, my sigh of contentment lost under the sound of Bronislav's screams.

"Black Water," I announced, my voice distant as I felt my magic begin to connect with it. The powerful wave of sight moved into me as my magic connected with his reality, with his fate. "The true power of the Drak. The power that shows me everything."

Blinking, my eyes drifted to black.

The gasp of shock and fear from Georg and Alojz was a whisper before sight took me completely, before images of Bronislav's life passed before me.

Flashes of children running and playing.

Flashes of his bonding ceremony.

Flashes of his future.

Watching it all, I hoped for some sign of what was to come, for some hint as to what my path could be. However, Bronislav held nothing, merely flashes of their meetings, flashes of each failed attempt to trap me, and finally, of his death. Of his head rolling over the dirt pits of the battlegrounds, blood spraying over the battle that surrounded him.

It was as I had planned, but he would not live to see the culmination of that battle. He knew nothing of the outcome, of my victory.

His sight was useless to me.

"His blood will flow over your hands," I forced the words out with the hollow sounds of the Drak, the sight's ominous roar following the false words. "Your banner will be golden, your future as bright as the glint it brings."

I pulled my hand away from him, leaving him still gasping in pain as the other two watched me, their faces muddled with anticipation and horror.

"You will be one of the greatest of your kind," I said directly to Bronislav as the old man stared at me with tears in his eyes, clutching his hand to his chest. "Go seek out Damek; have him wrap your hand. Your preparation for the accomplishment to come begins now."

My focus drifted back to Alojz, the man's face now a stone mask, the fear clear.

I couldn't stop the smile. I couldn't stop the wicked gleam from moving over my face, the malice so clear he flinched.

Still, I didn't look away. I let the glare seep into the defiant man before me as the echo of the door Bronislav left through reverberated around us.

"Georg," I said, holding my hand out to him in expectation, my fingers waggling like I was going to give him a sweet.

"My king," Georg began, his voice quiet as he took a step away from me, "I do not wish to know my sight ... I believe you ... I do not question your power."

Alojz flinched at Georg's insolence, his own fear clear as my focus snapped away from him, going right to the cowering man beside him.

The man pulled at his long beard in nervousness.

"Georg."

A snap, a steady hand, a glare, and the man stepped forward, shaking from head to toe as he placed his hand in mine.

His scream became a loud echo as I splashed the water over his hand. A large amount covered his palm, drifting up his wrist in a burn that would haunt him until I removed his life.

While I gasped in ecstasy, my magic connected with his soul, feasting on the sights of his past, of his future. Letting them run over me, I watched his youth, watched him lust after a woman I had seen several times before. Watched him kill many Skříteks in battle.

He was a good, useful soldier. I reconsidered sending him to his death, but then I saw the image of his head rolling across the sand right alongside his friends, and I sighed. The image was so beautiful I couldn't possibly part with it.

"Your future is set, your path true, and glory will follow you until your last breath, your days filled with regality, with accomplishments." My eyes snapped back to green as the last of the false words left my lips.

The man still heaved before me as he fought the need to scream.

"Damek. Now." I didn't need to tell him twice before he tore from the room, whimpering in a desperate attempt to keep his cries at bay.

Joy pressed against my skin as he left, my magic vibrating within me in anticipation. I couldn't keep the wicked smile from my face.

The door closed with a snap, and my focus slammed back to Alojz, the once defiant man jerking with power.

I said nothing. I simply lifted my hands in expectation, my request clear, my eyes hard in a warning he could not ignore.

His eyes were hard as he stepped forward, placing his hand in mine without hesitation. Then he hissed in pain as the residual water in my palm pressed against his skin.

"Hurts, doesn't it?" I hissed, clamping my hand around his as my magic began to move into him, twisting inside him and freezing him in place. "It's a beautiful burn ... Black Water. It gives me life, gives me sight, and hurts anyone weaker than me. Burns my enemies."

Tightening my hand around his, I lifted the pouch above his hand, letting it hover as I looked at him, drinking in the fear in his eyes as if it were a fine wine.

"I know what you are asking," I whispered, now so close to him I didn't have to raise my voice to be heard.

"Wh-what ... am I asking? I don't understand." He could barely get the words out past the pain.

I narrowed my eyes at him, the silent warning hitting him square in the chest.

"My ... my king."

At least he was catching on quickly.

"Your perceived cleverness is thinly veiled. Even without my magic, it is as translucent as a windowpane. You have been a curious little beast, asking everyone you can about the magic of a Drak. About what we are, about what I am.

About what I can do. Testing my abilities with pathetic little attacks."

His eyes widened as I smiled, his fear adding to my joy.

With the tiniest flick of my wrist, I let another drop fall onto his palm, the burn hissing beyond the silence before his scream rent the air.

He twisted and contorted his arm in an attempt to move away from my grip around his hand, only to realize I had frozen him in place, his body and magic ice and steel.

"Shall I tell you what I really saw when I peered into your friends' realities? Shall I tell you of the secret meetings held in old closets and the attempts to overthrow me?"

Alojz's eyes widened with each word, his jaw snapping shut in an attempt to keep the scream hidden. His last whisper of pride quickly disappeared.

"Shields, barriers—any magic you throw my way cannot block my sight," I hissed, stepping toward him as saliva sprayed over his face, my anger dripping from me. "I see everything." I paused. "Shall we see what you show me?"

Another shriek ripped from him before the water even hit his hand. This time, I poured a waterfall over his palm, over his arm, dripping it over his face and neck.

The skin smoldered as it burned, the flesh melting away. Sight developed stronger within me, dancing to the sound of his screams. My eyes plunged into sights's ember burn as I took control.

My magic swarmed the room, pressing against every wall,

every bone, every rock. I felt them all. I memorized them. And then I controlled them.

The same way the sight of my kind projected onto Black Water, the magical surface shimmering with sight so those who sought council could see, I projected the sight into the room surrounding us, the true form of my restricted magic flying free.

From smoke and ash, the haunted imagery of the coming opening of the pits began to form. The high seats of the stadium surrounded us, the images distorted like looking through water, but clear enough that, with one strangled gasp from my captive, I was confident he was questioning the reality before him.

Together, we stood in the center of the pits, a few battered Chosen wrestling in the blood-soaked mud as the packed house exploded in screams and cheers. The volume was so loud it pounded within my head like a bass drum.

The black of my eyes stared at him as both the prescience and the room around us played in perfect tandem. Ghostly images of his conspirators walked past us, their eyes full of hope for success as they prepared to begin the coup I had seen again and again.

Alojz watched them, confusion settling in beside his fear as the scene played out.

One move from Georg caused the crowd to rise up as one, the assumed success of the coup seemingly imminent.

"It's beautiful, isn't it?" I sneered as the black drifted from my eyes; albeit, the apparitions surrounding us remained, the scene continuing to play out as the battle rent the stadium apart, blood spilling as those loyal to Edmund began to kill my followers mercilessly, the screams of enjoyment turning to those of fear and death. "Although, it is odd how subjective it all is."

With those few words, the scene that surrounded us froze in place, blood freezing in the air as it fell around us like rain, the wide open scream of a woman stitched into memory as it paused.

Alojz's fear grew as his vision followed mine, the panic in his eyes drowning him.

"Isn't it odd how part of the story can be construed as the whole?" I smiled at him as the vision began to move in reverse, blood rising into the heavens, a scream sucked back into a throat, his friends stalking back toward us, translucent images that moved around us, amongst us, back to where it all had begun. "A reverse usually whispers of warning and certainty. It's a sign of importance within sight."

Once again, the images froze around us, the two Chosen awkwardly posed as they fought; the crowds tarried in cheers. Bronislav and Georg flanked the restrained Alojz, their eyes eager as they spotted the man they were positive they were going to kill before they looked up into the stands toward me.

"But this time, a reverse means something different." I smiled.

Alojz's focus pulled away from the shadowed images of his friends to me, his eyes widening as they began to move.

"It means I lied."

Eyes fading to black, the scene we were trapped in

continued forward. The Trpaslíks stalking to begin the coup, their laugh a hollow sound as my magic brought everything to life, as the battle began again and the blood began to spill.

This time, it was not the blood of my loyalists as Alojz had assumed. It was the blood of the Trpaslíks. It was my laugh that echoed around the stadium.

They were losing. There was no way it could be another way. It was a realization that shone clearly within their expressions.

If only they had not been raised to be the defiant Trpaslíks they were, if only they had a need for self-preservation above that of killing their enemies, their bloodlust making it impossible for them to see.

So they fought, they bled, and they screamed.

Magic flew uselessly around them until, one by one, they fell. Lifeless bodies heaped over rubble and carnage, while my stoic figure still stood in the high box of the stadium, not so much as a scratch covering my body.

I froze the image there, letting it fade away, leaving the three headless corpses on the stone floor and allowing the wide, frightened eyes of the tiny man before me take them in.

"Did you really think you could defeat a Drak? Did you really think that your silly little games would be enough to defeat me?"

Alojz's focus snapped back to me, the dark pupils of his eyes shaking in fear.

"Your friends will be punished for their wrongdoing.

Whether they sense the punishment or not, whether they sense the betrayal, they will fall."

I stepped away from him then, walking across the hall and amidst the shadows of his friends. The magic dissolved back into stone at my touch, leaving us standing in the hall once again. Alojz still stood frozen beneath my ever-present magic.

"As will you. But I don't think you are going to get away so easily ..."

A deep sound ground from the man's throat. The desperate attempt to speak, to plead, to beg ripped from him, blocked by the black water burn that plagued him.

"I'm sorry. What was that?" I asked with a laugh, the sound a gleeful bell that rang over the stone. "It must be something important if you are trying to talk through the pain. Come again?"

"What ...? What ... are you g-going ...?" he asked, his voice barely able to rise above a whisper due to the control I still had over him.

"What am I going to do to you?" I filled in the blanks, another laugh following behind.

I released all of my magic from him, sending him to ground in a heap.

"That's quite simple, really. I am going to rip you apart limb from limb and make you bleed. Then I am going to let everyone scream at the sight of you. I am going to destroy you all."

14

OVAILIA

I DIDN'T HAVE much time. I urged myself on as I rummaged through the drawers of an old bureau in the king's suite. Rolls of socks and T-shirts were thrown in so haphazardly it looked like little more than a laundry hamper.

Sain had gone to trap the traitors and left me here with strict instructions not to leave, something I didn't take to very kindly.

Instructions. Demands. I was used to following orders, yes. My entire life had been spent following orders. I strived to serve, to protect. Not to wait around in dark rooms.

Not to hide, cowering in the shadows like I couldn't hold my own. As if I couldn't kill on command or take down an entire coup single-handedly; or couldn't single-handedly put out a pekelný.

I had days ago while Sain had been trapped in some sight. I had put out the flames that dozens around me couldn't even make a dent in. I had devoured some of the strongest magic.

All while hundreds had watched.

Hundreds of Chosen and Trpaslíks who had approached me in the shadows had passed scraps of parchment bearing the same few words.

You should rule.

Me, not him. Not the filthy man who refused to see what I had accomplished. Refused to use me as the asset, as the strength that I was.

He didn't trust me, and that was what bothered me. After everything I had done for him, after everything I had proved, he continued to treat me like a child, like a liability.

A danger.

Maybe I was. I surely didn't trust him. I hadn't for thousands of years. I had followed him weeks ago because of the power I had seen in him, the strength he had kept hidden from me a devilish secret I couldn't wait to indulge in.

Like chocolate and wine.

However, I hadn't noticed how the chocolate was moldy and the wine was rancid.

I hadn't noticed how the strength I had lusted after, that my magic had trouble controlling itself around, was cracked by madness.

Something he had made clear.

"*Something a child could accomplish,*" I growled to myself, the hatred I felt toward him rotting the words.

I hated him. I had hated him from the moment I had bonded with him. I had hated him when he had died. And I had hated him more when my father had found him very much alive.

"I have to find that blade," I said to myself, my voice crisp. "I have to destroy him."

Looking up from the messy drawer at the old mirror that hung above the bureau, I pursed my lips. The ice in my eyes stared back at me. I was as beautiful as ever.

Smiling at the beauty, at the power in my eyes, I could already see myself plunging that blade into his heart, the same way he had my father. I could already see my magic surging past it as I absorbed his magic and trapped his soul.

"Now, it's my turn." Shuddering in eager pleasure, I pulled myself away from my reflection, my hair falling over the side of my face like a sheet as I turned from the bureau to move toward an old trunk that stood at the foot of our bed.

No, *his* bed.

The bed, the room, the belongings—he had taken them all from my father, from Ilyan. The bloodstains on the carpet were a twisted sign of ownership. Like a dog who pisses on the wall, Sain left trails of blood behind him.

He needed to be fixed.

My shouldered stiffened, my lips pursing in anger as I searched with a deeper desperation, ignoring my hair as it fell over my face.

My heels clicked as I moved to the massive hand-carved wardrobe. I knew it had to be in this room somewhere. There wasn't anywhere else he would hide it. I didn't think there was anywhere else he could. I knew it wasn't on him, and he didn't trust ...

He didn't trust me. So why would he put it somewhere I could find it? Why would he put it somewhere that wasn't secured in some way?

Eyes drifting out of focus, I froze, hovering over the drawer. The smell of my shampoo was strong in the air as my mind took me right back to when we had first moved into this room a few weeks ago, to him hovering in front a wide stretch of stone, stone that wasn't quite right.

His magic hadn't been quite right.

I gasped in shock, the sound of my discovery followed by an intake of another kind, one that wasn't an echo.

I straightened, turning on the spot as I shut the heavy door with my hip, the loud smack of the ancient wood clamping shut, echoing beyond the still of the room.

I had thought I had heard something—some sound, some whisper of magic—but no one was here. No one except me, a prisoner locked in a glass box.

Eyes narrowing, I turned back to the dresser, my magic on high-alert as it infiltrated the room, searching for some sign of magic, of some concealed army.

There was nothing.

I had never been able to sense magic like my brother did, a skill that would have come in handy in times like this.

I let my magic wrap around me, strong ribbons bound around me like a shield. One short glance up at the mirror to verify I was gone from sight and I moved out of the room, toward the large bathroom attached to the suite. My magic lifted me above the ground enough that my heels against the stone could not be heard.

No sound, nothing other than the tiniest flutter of a breeze.

I wasn't foolish enough to think that, because I didn't see anyone, no one was there. You couldn't see me at the moment, either. Just like I couldn't see Sain, but that didn't mean he wasn't watching my every move.

The thought moved up my spine in a slither of ice, a slow snake that shivered within me no matter how hard I tried to stop the disgusting convulsion.

Pathetic, disgusting emotion. I had better things to focus on.

With a roll of my eyes, I escaped into the lavatory in silence. The room was exactly as it had been built centuries before, all except for the addition of the toilet. Even that was archaic, having been installed in the 1920s, a pull string for flushing and all.

Yellow polka dot heels appeared out of nowhere as I slipped them off my feet, letting them sit in the middle of the floor as if I had just stepped out of the tub.

Restraining a hiss, I placed my bare soles against the icy tile of the mosaic floor and then ran past the large inset stone tub, attempting not to think of how many germs were now attaching themselves to my perfectly manicured feet. Moving past the large closet still full of Ilyan's council clothes, I guessed neither my father or Sain could part ways with them. They were as old as both their reigns. Funny, considering they would be the first to go if I took control.

When I did.

I needed to find that blade.

Lips pressed into a hard line, I straightened my back, sweeping unseen amid the museum of clothes, coming face to face with the wall I had seen Sain stand before.

I knew at once the wall was not really there.

My magic jumpstarted with every step I took toward the thing, the shield dropping from around me as my hand drifted into view. Manicured fingers raised before me, shining like drops of blood against the surface of the rock, I hesitated, frightened of what lay behind the stone, of what would happen when I pressed my palm against the rough-hewn edges of stone.

With a gasp and a roar of fear, I pressed my hand against the stone, expecting the chill of the rock, the rough edges of the quarry. Instead, my hand moved through it, my entire arm plunging into ice water as the solid surface I had been expecting swallowed it, my arm disappearing from view.

Gasping from the chill, I stared at the waving line of magic that shimmered around my forearm like a circlet, a delicate embellishment begging me to step into the stone, begging me to find more.

Before I could take a step, the feeling of ice moved up my arm like an infection, a slow slither that crackled in the air in a pressure that pulled me into the void. It was more than the feeling of ice, however; it *was* ice. It glided over my skin in blossoms of crystals that flowered and thickened, holding me in place, freezing right inside of me.

"Sain!" I growled past gritted teeth, shifting as I attempted to pull my arm out of the wall. However, the ice continued to move up my arm, nearing my shoulder.

Each pull that I gave against the ice hold was unyielding, the grip increasing. I was stuck there.

Anger replaced the disgusting fear as I pulled against the ice, my magic building into an immense roar as my anger fanned my blood.

Placing my free hand before the false wall, I let my magic surge, a powerful stream of red light flying through the air to hit against the magical wall with a smack. A bolt of lightning moved over the surface like a web, burning away the façade. For one brief minute, the false wall vanished, revealing the large room behind it and the glistening shard of the Soul's Blade lying on a countertop in plain view.

"Found you," I hissed as the wall rebuilt itself.

My mind was still focused on the spot where the blade lay, even though all it was now was the Mírage of uneven gray stone.

It was right there, inches from me. The soul of my father, his magic, ready for me. All I needed to do was take control, and then Sain would be as good as dead.

A wide grin swept over my face, teeth glistening in the muted light of the closet as I lifted my now thawed arm, spreading my fingers wide in preparation to shatter the pathetic attempt of a barrier into a million fragments of magic and ice.

It was nothing more than the pekelný.

Nothing more than what a child could do.

The smile grew as my magic did, charging through me to drain into nothing as a noise sounded clearly behind me.

I turned, knowing that I was no longer alone, only to come face to face with Damek.

His eyes were wide with the same fear he always had, his body shadowed on the other side of the clothes forest.

"I've been calling you, my lady," he simpered, his voice a shriek as he took a step forward, toward the dim ribbon of light that fell from the mirrored skylight between us. The light fell over him in more shadow than gold, making him look distorted and broken.

"You should have kept calling," I snapped as I turned toward him. The ends of my hair tickled against my back, the sheer fabric of my dark top not enough to completely cover the skin. "What are you doing back here?"

"I have been calling you, my lady," he repeated, his voice shaking even more as he began to writhe his hands one over another.

I laughed loudly, one loud sound of irritation, as I moved away from the wall that, until a second ago, had been my target. Now I moved toward a new one, the man seeming to break down with every step I took.

The light of the skylight washed over me, warming my skin as it reflected off my hair, making everything glisten.

His eyes widened at the illusion of an angel, and I smiled, the nefarious gleam in my eyes taking away the heaven and replacing it with hell.

He took a step back, still writhing his hands.

"And you assumed you could come back here?" My voice was calm, the storm behind it clear.

I almost expected him to turn tail and run, but he stayed his ground. The muscles in my back tensed as those in my stomach began to writhe with as much panicked urgency as his hands.

He looked at me once, and the sensation continued. However, I kept my face strong, my back straight, and my jaw tight. I felt as fearful as he did right then.

"Did Sain send you?" I asked, my voice strong despite everything else in me shaking, a million panicked questions ripping within my mind.

How long had Damek been standing there?

Had he seen?

Did Sain *see*?

Clenching my teeth, I took another step forward, tapping my fingers against my hip bones as I pressed my palms against my lower back. "Spit it out, Damek."

The man nodded furiously, taking another step back, as if he were prepared to make a running escape, his eyes darting away from me.

Darting past the closet.

Darting to the wall behind me.

He knew. Whether he saw me or not, he knew something.

My heart fell, each heavy beat painful inside my chest. Still, I didn't let it show. I smiled, my hands eager to reach out and grab the mongrel before me. To shake the information out of him like one did a dog.

"He's in the main hall, my lady. He's waiting for you." He spit the words out in a torrent, the consonants falling over each other, eager to get out.

Sure enough, the moment they had left him, he turned, stumbling in his desperate escape of me.

He didn't make it more than a few steps before I grabbed him, my magic wrapping around him as I lifted him into the air, swinging him wide before I slammed him against the opposite wall. Hangers and clothes swung from the impact, the soft thud of flesh against stone melodic.

I slammed him again, bringing him back before me.

His eyes were wide as a small trickle of blood began to seep from his nose.

"Silly man," I seethed, my words grinding against my teeth like snakes. "Did you really think it would be that easy?"

His eyes widened, his mouth opening and closing mechanically as he gasped for air, as he tried to find words to fit the panic he was drowning in.

"What do you know about this wall?" I jerked my head behind me in explanation.

His eyes widened farther as his shoulders stiffened. He lifted his previously flailing hands to wrap around his neck, the plea obvious even without the words.

Rolling my eyes, I dropped him, wishing I hadn't left my heels in the bathroom. There was nothing dangerous about walking around a man in bare feet.

"Speak, Damek," I prompted, moving behind him as I blocked his way out. The clothes that were hung on either side shifted a bit from the movement in the tight space. "What do you know? What did you see?"

"I ..." he gasped, his chest heaving as he tried to catch a breath. "I didn't see anything ... but Sain ... Sain coming out."

"When?" I spat, my voice a harsh warning, and the man below me curled into a tight little ball, the fear of a hit evident.

"Just once!" he screamed, his fear making him useless. "Just once. I don't know ... anything. I don't know anything."

I sighed. As much as Damek had irritated me in the past, he had actually begun to prove himself quite useful. I supposed the way Sain broke his servants was good for one thing. He knew nothing, and his loyalty laid in fear, not body. He wasn't sharing anything unless someone squeezed it out of him.

"Don't tell Sain where you found me," I snarled, squatting over him until my body was like a cage over his, my mouth inches from his ear. My hair fell around both of us like a curtain, adding a depth of secrecy to my hissed warning. One he shivered beneath, the weight holding him still. "Do, and I will kill you."

He shivered again, and my smile expanded, the joy of dominion ripping away the last of my anger, even if I did have to find my current slave keeper.

I guessed Damek and I had that in common.

"Do you understand?" I asked.

The sniveling man beneath me nodded in desperation, a whine of fear spewing from him as though he had sprung a leak.

"Good. Now go," I spat as I turned away from him, fully intent on returning to the wall in order to secure the blade before I went to meet Sain, before I would let him meet his fate.

But Damek didn't move. He stood, folded like a beast, writhing his hands, eyes locked on the floor.

"Go, Damek," I repeated, the anger in my voice paramount.

Still, he stayed.

"Damek!" I roared as I took a step toward him.

This time, the man raised his head, all signs of the cowering, sniveling fool Sain had made him gone. His eyes were hard with the same anger I felt running inside me.

"Do not retrieve the blade yet," he whispered, his voice so quiet I barely heard him. "Wait. Meet with Sain and find me in the room where Cail took his last breath."

"What?" I gasped, my voice shaking as much as my body, the conversation no longer making any sense.

"We are playing a game, my queen. I think it is time you joined us." He shuffled away from me before I had even removed myself from over him, slithering like a snake over the floor in an attempt to get away.

I stood frozen, barely able to coax myself to turn toward the door. I remained still, listening to his retreat.

One stress left as another pressed against my shoulders with a weight I knew wouldn't leave.

Roles. Queen.

I was already aware that I wasn't the only one who sought the blood of Sain to be spilled. I wasn't the only one who was playing this dangerous game.

But did I play it on my own or with them and risk being seen?

You couldn't hide from a Drak. That much, I knew.

And if I were to succeed, I would have to hide in the darkest shadows. I would have to find my own blood-soaked cloak before I stole his.

With a sigh, I turned away, my steps quick as I made my way out of the closet and toward the hall where Sain was waiting.

15

OVAILIA

SITUATED on that twisted throne of his, Sain sat with his hand atop the repaired remains of my father's skull. Blood oozed from between his fingers as it ran down the charred bone as though it were weeping blood red tears that dripped onto the floor in long, steady streams.

Looking at him, I expected some injury. But he sat, smiling, the same blood spilling over his face, dripping off his nose and getting tangled in his beard.

He stood then, signaling for me to join him on the stand, something I did in one quick step, no matter how much I was revolted to stand beside him.

"I take it that your plan to destroy the traitors went well?" I asked sweetly, the sound of my heels echoing loudly in the space as he moved right to me, wrapping his blood-soaked skin around me then placing his hand against my jaw.

I tried not to cringe at the contact, at the knowledge that, with that one touch, I would have to throw away the shirt slash short combo I was wearing. I loved this outfit, too.

The blood was cool against my face, the heat of his hand underneath it a stark contrast, one my magic answered to at once. Awakening in a bubble of desperate need I knew I couldn't fight, it roared under my skin, begging me to reach out to him.

I hated it. My magic wanted his, while my heart wanted him dead. I wished I could fight it. I had tried enough and failed every time.

He sensed the rise of my magic, too, and smiled, the wide grin revealing white teeth against the blood that glistened in his beard.

"It went better than expected." His smile grew, and my magic bubbled further at the sound of his voice.

It moved around me like jelly. The warmth fueled by the power and authority that drenched his voice, making me lose control of the hatred that had been feeding me.

"Wonderful," I sighed, the lust seeping into my voice as I leaned closer to him, all thought of saving my outfit forgotten.

"Come, dear," Sain said as he pulled away, wrapping his slick hand around mine as he led me into the shadows behind his throne, the darkness that used to be reserved for the Drak seers centuries before.

I had always known this space as the forbidden shadows where the Drak would stand amongst us during council, but it didn't seem so dark, thanks in part to the golden fireflies that dripped from the ceiling. They were little spots of light that fell from the sky, extinguishing with a small hiss.

"What is it?" I asked, the temporary lust leaving as anticipation began to wind within me.

A dark shape beyond the glistening lights came into focus.

Sain's smile stretched as I dropped his hand, plunging into the dark before him, desperate to see what was before me.

A dark whisper ran over me with each click of my heels against the stone as a warning I didn't want to acknowledge pounded against my skull. A warning as loud as the whimpers that came from somewhere before us.

Painful, panicked moans grew louder as I stopped in place, the final echo of my heels fading into nothing.

As he left me standing in the dark, the painful cries of what used to be a man whispered before me. The dark shape of the creature was visible beyond the soft hiss of the golden embers that fell from the ceiling to the floor.

Punishment was too simple a word for what Sain had done. I had never seen my father be so cruel. I had never seen a warning of obedience played quite so loudly. The warning echoed in my head, telling me leaving the knife beyond the false wall had been a glaring mistake that I hoped had gone unnoticed by the seer who came up right behind me, the soft touch of his hand against my hip as caustic as acid.

"Come and see," he whispered, pushing his hand against my waist as he prompted me forward.

I followed, followed and prayed that he hadn't seen. That this fate would not be my own.

"Beautiful," I forced the word out, pushing my fear down as

the heavy beat of my heels echoed like a bass drum in my head.

Dark masses of stalactites and stalagmites jutted around the dark shape I had seen. The bright embers of flame danced between them like the bars of a cell. A drop of gold, a hiss of steam as it vanished, not fireflies. Molten stone. The unsteady rhythm cast the darkness in an oddly distorted light.

Stepping toward the prison with an unsteady gait, I strangled a gasp in my throat, the huddled mass of a man finally recognizable.

Alojz.

Or rather, what was left of him.

The man huddled behind the stone, his eyes wide in obvious trepidation. The fire and will that had supercharged his soul had been beaten out of him. Not even a whisper remained.

His eyes were sadness and fear now.

Sadness and fear that echoed loudly, right into my soul, echoing a deep warning. A warning of what would happen to me if I defied him.

My heart stopped beating as Alojz attempted to move his broken body into an uncomfortable crouch, a dead arm dragging on the ground beside him.

"Say hello, Alojz," Sain taunted, his voice a dangerous whisper that I jerked at, the movement thankfully missed by Sain.

Alojz looked at me, his eyes wide in an understanding that

terrified me, his bloodshot eyes crying an identical crimson. He opened his swollen jaw with a gasp, his teeth and tongue missing from the void. He gasped and spluttered as he looked at me, his eyes as red as the deep crimson splotches of his own blood that covered his clothes.

"Wonderful," Sain said with a clap of his hands, finally leaving my side to circle around the prison.

I had hoped to calm at the distance, but my anxiety grew. Alojz's mutilated face held me captive.

"What do you think, my darling Ovailia?"

"Beautiful," I repeated.

Sain's sigh of pleasure was loud in my ears as he rushed back to my side. I almost expected him to touch me, to pull me closer, but he stayed an arm's distance away, my magic pulling away from me in an attempt to reach him.

The emotion, along with the lust, was disgusting, but now it was more. It was a disturbing need that was made more twisted as I faced what he could easily create of me.

No, I realized with a start, what he could create of us all.

He was the blood-soaked king, and this was his reign.

"Indeed. If you think this is beautiful, you should have heard his screams as I ripped him apart. As I twisted the bones in his arm and burned his tongue from his mouth."

I shivered, fear rippling up my spine, burning into my bones in a powerful surge that I was having trouble containing. I could still feel the lust for his power, still feel my magic pull toward him, but now, even my magic was afraid.

Afraid of the idea that was cementing itself inside of me.

I had destroyed the pekelný. I could destroy him.

I didn't need to follow power. I had that power within me.

The power to destroy him. The power to take control.

And he knew it if the fear that was clouding his eyes were any indication.

Forcing myself to stand still, I smiled, my focus calm, though my heart rate had picked up on something dangerous. The way he was posturing, his hand strong on my elbow, didn't help.

"After being at the receiving end of such torture for years," Sain began, his voice a dangerous hiss as he pulled me closer, "it was a delight to find I could still have joy in the gift of giving it to another. That I could come up with new and amazing ways to make someone hurt, to make their devotion change." Sain pulled me into him, his lips inches from mine, his eyes the only thing I could see.

I gasped, losing my breath as the warning in his words dripped clearly, his threat tearing through me.

He knew something.

"You will have them all on their knees." I kept my voice low, feigned longing dripping off me in liquid lust as I focused on the deep green of his eyes. Pursing my lips, I ran the side of my finger down his cheek, wiping away some of the still damp blood that was attempting to congeal there. "No one will dare defy you after you reveal what you are capable of."

"Even you, Ovailia." His grip on my waist increased with a violent jolt, shoving me against him as a dangerous flash came to his eyes. The creature beside us whimpered in fear of the monster who had unfurled inches from me. "Would you dare defy me?"

"Never, Sain." My heart beat so fast I could barely hear the words over the thunder, sure the lust I was taunting him with was unrecognizable. "I am not the devil. You are my king."

He didn't move, didn't look away. His eyes remained locked with mine as his hot breath ran over my lips.

My heart pounded against my ribs.

"I will destroy your devil, Ovailia."

"There is no devil to destroy, only hell."

He smiled, content with my flattery. Releasing me, he stepped away, and my chest ached with a sigh of release that I wouldn't give him, not yet.

"A hell that everyone will soon see. Then I will show them the power that lies before them, and no one will dare cross me." Turning toward me, he smiled gently, lifting his hand to press against my jaw, his thumb against my cheek.

I expected the volatile pressure of his anger, but it was simply a gentle flutter of skin against mine.

The disgusting lust increased under my skin, my magic swimming to meet his with eager energy.

"Don't worry." Sain kept his voice low, the deep, sultry notes affecting me like warm milk lulling me into a stupor as I fought the need to melt with the deep need that was threatening to drown me. "You will see this hell. You will help me kill the devils before us. I know it. I have seen it ... my queen."

I started, the similarity in what he had said, in what Damek had said, coating me in panicked fear.

He knew.

He had to know.

The way he smiled. The way he pulled me into him.

This was a warning, a chilling threat.

Sain's eager grin was ripe with the same malicious intent mine was. The look was so clear I wondered which one of us would kill the other first, whose blood would be a brighter stain against our skin.

Stomach twisting, heart pounding, I stepped closer, leaning in as I breathed him in. I breathed in the bright green of his eyes. I breathed in the smell of blood that infected his skin. I breathed in the tickle of beard against the softness of my cheek.

"My king," I whispered, letting the hatred drip from me, blending with the lust so powerfully I was certain he didn't miss either emotion.

He pulled away, his green eyes hungry as his lips twitched. His beard pulled before he leaned into me, pressing his lips to mine with a deep hunger that infected me.

I kissed him back, letting his magic tickle against mine before pulling away with a smile, despite part of me not wanting to. Part of me was dying inside.

Sweeping my hair over my shoulder, I took a step closer, pressing my hip against his. "I live to serve you," I whispered into the dark, my hatred of this man finally taking control with the realization that I could use him. "Tell me what to do."

He opened his mouth, but the words were sucked from his throat as the main doors to the hall were thrown open, and Damek rushed in with a look of awe and fear.

"Damek!" Sain screamed.

The intruder froze in place as Sain rushed into the bright open part of the hall. Sain's shoulders pulled into a tight line of anger as Damek began to wilt beneath his glare.

"I told you not to disturb me, no matter—"

"But, master ..." Damek began before the words faded into the clicking and gasping more akin to a fish out of water.

Sain's hand twitched as his magic closed the man's throat, punishing him.

"Speak, Damek," Sain teased, but the request was unneeded thanks to the girl who rushed through the door, screaming like a banshee, her hair wild as it flew behind her, her skin and clothes streaked with blood.

No. It couldn't be. I had thought she was dead.

"Míra!" Sain yelled gleefully, as if he were a rotund grandfather welcoming home an estranged love one. "I had a feeling I would see you today."

"He's dead! You killed him!" the girl screamed, her magic sparking a second before she attacked. The stream of red fire sparkled across the air toward Sain.

His laugh boomed above the current of her magic a second before it vanished. The red dripped to the ground like wax, the fire dissolving to smoke in the air.

Míra's eyes widened, her anger swept away by fear as she began to tremble.

Sain's laugh grew deeper. His own magic flew across the air with a flick of his wrist, wrapping around the girl and trapping her inside the deep sheath of black smoke.

Stomach tensing, I took a step forward before freezing.

Damek's wide eyes met mine, the hushed conversation we'd had clear in the bloodshot gray. Every coded word and hushed phrase stuck out as the scene before me began to unravel. I froze, my stomach twisting as my magic jerked around inside of me, dying to get out.

However, I was no longer clear on who I would attack or even why.

"I killed who, exactly?" Sain mused, his voice full of false promises as it echoed around the wide cavern. "Your master? That weak man who infected you with a Štít? Yes, I killed—"

"You killed him! I killed my brother because of him – he didn't have to die." Míra interrupted, her voice strangled underneath the malevolence that was as bright as the blood on her face. "You killed my brother! He's dead because of you! Because of both of you!"

With the snap of her anger, Míra's magic broke free of Sain's control, a whip of gray hissing through the air to slam against Sain's chest.

The old man gasped, stumbling back into the dark as the magic moved into him. His blood-soaked cloak fell from his shoulders, waving through the air like a fallen banner.

As my chest heaved with dissidence, my magic prickled against my skin as I waited for the right moment to attack, to know what to do.

"You don't deserve to live!" Míra snapped before another bolt of magic, another attack moved across the air and right into the old man as the child ran toward him, obviously intent on ending him.

Heart thumping in my chest, pressing against me, eager to watch his end, I did nothing.

I stood and watched … waiting.

Míra sent another attack as she screamed, tears streaming down her face and mixing with the blood that caked over her skin to create haunting rivers of red that flowed over her cheeks, dripping against her filthy clothes in a pool of heartbreak.

"If I can't have him, no one ca—"

Her words were cut short by the violent snap of Sain's magic amongst the dark, a brilliant light burning my eyes as Sain fought back, the girl flying through the air at the impact.

She didn't even scream. She soared, falling end over end before landing with a solitary thump of flesh against stone.

I cringed at the sound, jerking as the silence of the battle stretched around me.

Damek's heaving breath was the lone sound. The lone movement … until …

With a slow, haunting chill, Sain began to push himself into a standing position, moving slowly in the dark. The bright spot of red and white fabric was a wad in his fist.

I stepped back in disbelief, my heels clicking once in the silence, and Sain's eyes flashed to mine, the white bright against the dark. Bright with anger.

"Don't think I don't know your true meaning, my dear," he growled, his voice violent as he stepped back into the dark, his eyes again focused on the girl. "And you said there was no devil in you. I will deal with you later."

My heart stuttered painfully, and a lump lodged itself in my throat.

I tried to swallow, but everything was blocked by fear, the sensation so unfamiliar it drove the fear further.

"Your brother ..." Sain mused, his magic lifting the girl into the air, letting her hang there, twisting aloft like a rag doll.

She could be dead.

My muscles seized at the possibility, but her eyes were alive, the wide orbs staring straight at the old man who held her, fear as clear as mine staring back at me.

"I have seen your brother in my sights. I have seen him laid into the ground, dead and cold, head almost ripped from his shoulders," Sain said with a laugh. "If he is dead, you were the one to kill him. Did you kill your brother, little girl?"

Her eyes pulled wider, her jaw moving as she attempted to work the words out.

"You were supposed to die, little girl. But it seems that

Edmund's magic still lives inside of you, which suits me fine. The more power I can absorb, the better."

Damek and I exchanged looks at Sain's admission. His shock seeped across the air so heavily I was in no doubt he was about to attack Sain. I was one step behind him. If Edmund's magic was alive, if it was alive in this little girl …

Sain's malicious laugh pulled me away from my hope as his magic shot like lightning through the air and right into the little girl.

She screamed as the current moved into her body, screamed as the demon of a man stepped toward her, his lips extended into a wide, caustic smile.

His smile bore into me, awakening my own need for his magic, for the magic I had coveted for so long.

It should be mine.

The fear faded as my own smile took its place, my magic bristling under my skin with the need for her blood, for that which should be mine.

Sain had gotten there first, however. His own scream echoed hers as his magic began to move into her, ready to rip Edmund's magic out of the Štít.

Damek fell back, cowering against the stone, pressing himself into it as he tried to move away from the electricity that crackled in the air, everything as bright as day. Even the half-man watched in fear, cowering in his cage.

I, however, stepped forward, my eyes wide in awe as the crackling lights faded, as the screaming stopped and the child fell to the ground in a heap, her skinny limbs twisted awkwardly, unmoving.

"No!" Sain snapped the second she fell. "It's not there …"

"Sain?" I asked hesitantly, my powerful voice shaking with uncertainty. I wasn't even sure if I had heard what he had said. I couldn't look away from the child.

"How could it not be there …"

The admission pulled me from my horror, the tension in my jaw increasing as I turned toward the man who looked at me with unabashed malice.

"Edmund's magic isn't there?" I questioned.

He rounded on me, kicking the girl once before he rushed to my side.

Míra didn't even make a noise at the impact. If she weren't dead before, she was now.

"No!" Sain yelled in my face. "The Štít isn't there. Nothing is there."

I looked at the girl hungrily before Sain's magic wrapped around me, pulling me toward him with a snap.

"I said it's not there," he hissed, saliva spraying over my face. "Don't think that you can go and find it yourself. I can see what you are thinking, Ovailia, I can see your pathetic greed. I can see your weakness. Leaving the child to attack me. I should rip your magic from your heart right now, leave you as dead and useless as that one."

He knocked his head toward what was left of Alojz, my heart speeding up as if the thing could tell what he was talking about, its own fear of being stripped of something so precious ripping me apart.

"You couldn't ..." I began. Although strong, I could feel my words falter inside of me. I didn't dare finish. I knew from the look in his eyes, from what I had seen, that he could.

That he would.

"Don't try me, Ovailia," he snapped, pressing himself so close to me I could smell the rancid fish on his breath. "You are as dead and useless as that one. You only have use as long as I deem it. Don't force me to change my mind."

I cringed, hair waving down my back as I tried to move away, but his fingers clawed around my forearm, pulling me back.

Damek's whimpering increased as he continued his attempt to move into the wall, but I didn't look away from the green eyes of the devil before me.

I didn't care what he said. He was the devil.

A devil I would destroy. I had to.

"Yes, master," I said, emphasizing the word and letting it seep into him and soothe his ego. Although, I was confident he could taste the deceitfulness in it.

He smiled, obviously pleased with himself. "Good." He released my arm, and I teetered on my heels, resisting the urge to rub the pressure out of the skin. "Now take this girl and dispose of her. I have no use for her."

Sain gave me one more look before he turned and exited, leaving Damek and I standing alone in the hall, surrounded by skeletons.

I looked from the girl who lay lifeless on the floor, to the man, the once powerful servant who was now as oppressed as broken as I. The same death in me as clear as it was in him, I would say he was already dead if it wasn't for the fire I saw in his eyes. The same one that was alive in me.

"Are you going to play?" Damek asked, all sign of shake gone from his voice.

I stared at him, eyes glancing at the door, at what was left of the child and knew what faced me- the same fate I would find no matter my path, it seemed.

It was blood either way.

I nodded.

16

RYLAND

FOR MONTHS, the hospital had been full, healing the Chosen and Skříteks who were injured on raids. The air had been filled with the smell of plants and salves and tea. Now the injured had been cleared out to make room for the dead and dying.

The beds were covered with white sheets, the air saturated with the overwhelming scent of blood.

This is a familiar scent for you, isn't it, son?

Blood was everywhere, staining the floor and dripping from sheets. It covered my chest and hands, infecting my clothes and drying the cotton against my skin in a rigid cast. It dripped from my sagging curls and down my face, mixing with the silent tears that wouldn't stop.

I didn't even try to clean the blood, just as I didn't try to stop the tears.

You should.

Are you so weak you would cry like this?

Ignoring the voice, I squeezed the tiny hand that was clutched in mine, expecting to feel the tiny pressure of his.

There was nothing. The fingers were cold and rigid beneath mine. Jaromir was already gone, a gray sheen painted over his skin, his lips and eyelids a haunted shade of blue.

I stood beside him, staring at the bed right beside his, at the Skřítek healers who were rushing to-and-fro in a mad attempt to save a life.

Her life.

Risha's.

I couldn't see her through the wall of activity except for the waves of strawberry curls that fell over the side of the bed. The usually soft curl in her hair was damp and sagging from her blood. The same blood that covered me.

It covers you because you were too weak to do what you needed.

Too weak to do what I asked ...

No. Weakness does not live in this moment, Father. Muscles tightening, I stopped the voice with a snap, not willing to let it take over. Not now, not after everything Risha had taught me.

I needed to take control.

For her.

For me.

"We need a stronger salve," I heard one of the healers say, her voice tense, and the lanky man in front of me turned to the nightstand between us.

"Does anyone have any deadwood bark?" the lanky man asked, his hand moving fast as the smell of lemon grass overtook the smell of blood while he began to grind something in a mortar.

"I need stronger magic to stop this bleeding," said another, their voice panicked. "I can't knit the skin back fast enough."

"Where is the queen?"

"She said she is coming." My voice was as dead as I was, one hollow note of sound that hit against my heart painfully.

A few of them looked up at my response, their lips pressed into the same tight line before they went back to work.

Everything was distorted by my tears, everything except the profile of Risha's face that peeked out from between the quickly working Skříteks. Eyes stinging, I stared, crippled by the sight of blood that seeped from her nose and mouth, as well as her eye socket that was sunken and inflamed.

I swallowed, my throat a painful lump that restricted my breathing. Then I gasped, suddenly uncertain if I would ever get enough air again.

"She's coming," I repeated, willing it to be true, although I knew as all the others did that she might be a while. I knew where she was … who she was with.

Jaromir wasn't the only one who had died.

My heart tensed as my hand tightened around his, his little fingers as stiff and cold as ice.

"Please, Joclyn, hurry. Please," I growled to myself past clenched teeth.

My heart raced inside my chest with the fear that the healers who flittered and fluttered around the girl I had so quickly fallen in love with were right, that they couldn't do much without Joclyn's aid.

But the fear was more than that. It was the fear of what I had said—the terrible admission that I had fallen in love. I had fallen in love with this girl who now lay on a bloodstained sheet, fighting for her life. I was in love with her. And I was about to lose her.

It would figure that I would fall in love, only to lose it again.

No.

I couldn't think like that.

I wouldn't.

Pinching my eyes together in an attempt to block out the sound of the Skřiteks, to block out their panic, I focused on the last time I had seen her, how soft her hand had been against mine. How warm she had been. How much I had wanted to kiss her. How much I wanted to feel her lips against mine.

The precious memory was shattered by the sound of the large wooden door at the other end of the hall. Air rushed past us as Ilyan and Joclyn ran in.

Ilyan's arms were full of a large sheet, the formerly white fabric covered in crimson stains that spread over the fabric like blossoms.

Several of the Skřiteks who were tending to Risha ran toward Ilyan, their hands over their mouths as the panic in the room increased, the agonizing tension pressing against my chest.

I wanted to tell them to stay there, not to leave Risha, that she needed them. However, I couldn't get the words out past the lump in my throat.

Besides, Jos was already bee-lining right for us, her eyes as puffy and swollen as mine; her skin and clothes as blood colored. If I hadn't known better, I would have said the red sky Edmund had covered us with had fallen down upon us and drenched us all.

"Jos," I gasped, my voice coming out in a stutter she didn't even seem to notice.

I finally let go of Jaromir's stiff, curled fingers and ran around the bed to meet her, my tiny best friend whose head was a full foot below mine.

Jos ran right into me, her arms wrapping around me as mine did her. "I'm sorry, Ry."

It was all she said, three words that slammed against my heart and twisted my gut so tightly the tears came again. They rushed from me in loud, obnoxious sobs. The emotional breakdown was made worse by the pressure of her body against mine, by the feeling of sorrow that we both shared.

It ripped through me, tensing every muscle and tightening my lungs. I gasped for breath, desperate to get air but also not caring if I ever breathed again. Everything hurt too much. I didn't want to feel it anymore. And from the way Joclyn sobbed and clung to me, I knew that pain, that desire, was not only mine.

"I'm sorry, too," I gasped out past the tears, the words broken and painful.

Her arms fell away from me as she took a step back, turning toward the girl I could now see clearly. For the first time since I had put her on this cot, I could see every injury: the way her arm twisted the wrong way, the way the skin on her stomach was ripped open, the way part of one of her legs was mostly detached.

I swallowed, willing the bile threatening to come up back down, and pushed my way to her bedside, leaning against the wall as I pressed my hand against her blood-soaked hair, too scared to watch Joclyn as she went to work. Too scared to look at Risha. Too scared to admit that this might be the last time I saw her. That this would be my last memory of her.

This broken, beaten, blood covered girl.

I didn't want this to be my last memory. I didn't want this to be the end.

"Try, Jos," I said more to myself than to her, but she heard me, anyway.

Her silver eyes took one long look at me before she went to work, her voice echoing around me as she began to order the others around.

I barely heard her.

Everything was inaudible over the fearful buzzing in my ears, the sound of my heartbeat rumbling in my throat. I could see Joclyn talking and see the others rush around.

In the overwhelming static, Ilyan ran up to us, wrapping his hand around Risha's wrist as he looked at me, his face intense with something I would never hear.

It was merely buzzing.

Merely heartbeats.

Merely pain.

Say your good-byes, son.

The voice was a taunt. It was wickedness. But for the first time in a year, I listened to it.

Leaning over Risha, I pressed my cheek to hers, feeling the surprising warmth of her skin against mine and the warmth of her blood.

Wiping away the crimson stain, I kissed her for the first time. I pressed my lips to her cheek, letting a tiny spark of my magic flow into her, wishing her magic would respond to it and that I could feel her magic against mine. Nevertheless, there was nothing except the startling heat of her skin, the fever that was ravaging her already broken body.

Not caring who saw, I let my lips linger there before I shifted, whispering in her ear the words I should have said weeks ago. I hoped she would hear.

"I love you, Reesh."

I didn't know if I had expected a Míracle with those words. I didn't know if I expected anything. But with that single admission, the buzzing that had filled my head ceased, and the sounds of the room flooded me as the panic and fear I had tried to escape came back, slamming me in the chest and flattening me against the wall.

What did you expect, you stupid boy?

I said say good-bye.

This isn't a fairy tale.

The words were stuck in my head, no matter how hard I tried to push them out. They were as stuck as I was while I watched Joclyn and Ilyan standing on either side of Risha's bed, their hands wrapped around her, eyes locked, magic locked, tears streaming over their cheeks.

Stuck as Joclyn gasped, her lips pressing into a tight line.

Stuck as Ilyan turned toward me, his wide eyes sad, apologetic.

No.

Not apologetic. It couldn't be. I didn't want it to be. I didn't want to admit I knew what that look meant. I didn't want to admit I knew what was coming.

Yet, I knew.

I knew the second Ilyan let go of Risha's hand, the second he let it fall back to the bed with a thud that rumbled through the air and smacked against my chest.

Ilyan said nothing as he stepped toward me, before hugging me the same as Joclyn had done before. Except this one was different.

It pressed against my heart and soul and held me in a way I had never been held before. A hug so tight I could tell he was trying to hold me together while I tried to fall apart. It was a hug that tried to give me strength, that tried to make everything okay.

But it couldn't.

Nothing was okay anymore.

Nothing would be again.

The emotion twisted out of me, desperate to find something to hit as Joclyn placed Risha's hand over her chest then covered her with her own bloodstained sheet. As she removed her from this world.

I needed to hit something. I needed to hurt. But Ilyan held me there. He held me as I collapsed to the ground, trying to hold me together.

But nothing could hold me together. Not anymore.

"I'm sorry."

I didn't know who said it, and I didn't care. They could say it all they wanted.

It didn't change anything.

It didn't bring back what that little girl had taken away.

It didn't take away the pain.

17

WYN

"I feel like I'm hugging a dead chicken," I said, happy to be in his arms despite missing the usual bulk of his muscles.

"Sorry about that, Wyn. I was too busy not dying to find time to hit a gym." He chuckled, the laugh rippling over me.

The sound was a familiar blanket that wrapped around me, rattling against the wreckage that was still scattered over Thom's room. It attempted to scare away the memory of what had happened hours before, but there was too much.

Ilyan had tried to cover it up, cleaning it the best he could, but the destruction was still scattered over the floor, stained on the floor, smeared on the walls.

For the briefest of moments, however, I forgot all of that. Thom forgot all of that. And the room was happy, familiar. Then the laugh ended, and death enveloped the darkness again, leaving us lying on his bed, wrapped together in our bubble, savoring the last shard of joy that existed in the cathedral.

By some Mracle, Thom was alive. Dramin's magic had freed him from whatever Ovailia had done to him. It was the last act Dramin would ever do—saving his best friend's life.

At least, that was the best guess Ilyan had been able to come up with. Nothing else made sense, which was probably why I was having trouble accepting that all of this was real and not some drug-induced hallucination.

I lived during the 70s, you know.

I mean, not in that way, but I *get* it.

Cuddled together on his bed, we lay in the dark. Our fingers danced above our heads, twisting and tangling over each other as though we weren't certain if we should hold hands or not. I didn't know if I wanted to or if that small movement would kill the dream.

I guess it didn't do to live in fear.

"You can hold my hand, you know," I teased, poking him in the side with my free hand. "It's not going to eat you."

"It might. You don't know," Thom retorted, twisting his fingers through mine again before letting them go. My heart stuttered at the brief pressure. "It looks lethal."

"Thom," I moaned, fully aware that it was something I had picked up from Jos. Thom knew it, too, and he laughed, both of us shaking from his chuckle as it rippled within him.

"Besides, I'm too mesmerized by your new adornment."

"It's a hole, Thom," I sighed, moving my hand up so what little light we had in the room shone through it and over us. "Not an adornment."

"But it could be."

It was my turn to laugh, the sound strained with emotion and slightly out of place. "You sound like Joclyn. She wants me to put a spy glass in the—"

"And you haven't yet?" Thom asked, attempting to shift his weight enough to see me and failing, falling down to the bed with a grunt and a sigh. "What is wrong with you?"

"Something drastic, obviously."

"Obviously." He chuckled, the fluid dance of our hands stopping as his fingers trailed up my arm, the touch soft on my skin, tickling against my neck and jaw bone. "I guess we'll have to fix that."

"I don't see how you plan on doing that." I teased.

"I think I'll find a way," he snickered, moving himself so close to me that I could only see the bright blue of his eyes. I stared at the color, desperate for a breath I couldn't get, for his lips were already locked on mine, his hands already twisted around my waist as he pulled me against him. The light pressure of his fingers made me shiver as they trailed up my spine before fanning over my neck, locking me in place.

My gut twisted from the touch. Regret, want, and guilt wrestled with each other. They twisted together until my heart pushed them away and rejoiced in this moment, in this kiss that one very loud part of my soul had desired for centuries. We hadn't shared a kiss like this since before our daughter had been taken from us.

The kiss was pain and sadness, but it was also beautiful and wanted.

My magic reacted to the touch, flaring and burning inside of me. I could barely breathe as he held me against him, his lips strong as they grabbed at mine, pressed against me. One after another, deeper and deeper, he smothered me with them, moving them over my jaw and down my neck.

The heat of my magic erupted as he continued, the fire burning me as it tried to reach him. The sensation was familiar, one that I had missed for centuries. It was different than with Talon. The magic was different, the feeling different, but I still wanted it.

I didn't care that I could barely breathe. I didn't care that my mind was screaming for oxygen and my magic for escape.

I wanted more of this ... more of him.

I had forgotten how much I had missed and loved this. I had forgotten how good of a kisser Thom was. Forget letting him run his thumb over my hand ... That wasn't enough anymore.

With a sigh, he pulled away, leaving me lying against him, heaving, my lungs finally receiving the air they were so desperate for. Thom's hand was tight against me, keeping me pressed into him as he, too, heaved. The heat of his skin lessened, and the sound of his heartbeat rattled in amped up excitement.

"Either you enjoyed that, or you are going into cardiac arrest," I teased, my voice windswept.

"I was wondering why my arm was numb," he teased back, shaking it above us. "I guess that's why I kissed you—reflex from all the extra blood that's pumping through me."

"Ha! Don't pretend you didn't enjoy it!"

"Oh, I'm not pretending. I did enjoy it." Thom gave me with that same deep, smoldering look he had for so long. His eyes melted me as his magic pressed into me.

Yep. I was forgetting to breathe again, which was fine by me. I didn't need oxygen as long as I was kissing him. So I did, pulling him into me and running my hands over his shoulders and arms.

A deep groan of pleasure came from his throat as I moved to kiss his jaw. His breath was hot on my face as the sound escaped, his body shivering underneath me.

My magic heated, pressing against me in such a desperate need to reach him that Thom gasped and removed his hand from my bare back.

I was that hot.

"I think..." I gasped as I pulled away, but his arms were so tight I couldn't move very far. Fine by me. "I need to amp up my kissing game if I am going to be any kind of match for you in the future." I was so out of breath I was surprised I got the words out or that they were even coherent. I might have said something about spaceman underpants for all I knew.

"What do you mean?"

"Thom ..." I hesitated, clearing my throat dramatically as I sat up to look at him, hoping it would take my butterflies away. Nope. It made them worse. "You are an extraordinarily good kisser." My voice cracked. What was I, twelve? How on earth did my voice crack? "I mean, you were good before ... but you must have been practicing or something."

"No practice, just patiently waiting for you." He smiled,

moving closer.

I knew what was coming.

"You mean..." Everything was tight and twisted in nervousness and excitement, making the snark all that much harder to process. The hard drive in my brain must have been shutting down. "All of that is natural talent?"

"As natural as a poison ivy rash."

"Ew."

"You know you love it," he said with his own sass. "I think we should do that again."

"I'm not saying no," I replied, moving away enough that he got the hint, "but I think we should take a break. That is, of course, unless you want third-degree burns."

My magic was a little too hot, fire sweltering over my skin.

"Hmmm, I think I'll pass on that." He smirked, tucking me under his arm in an attempt to keep me safe or warm or something. I didn't need any of those, but I wasn't about to complain. "We've had enough death and maiming around here. Let's give everyone a rest."

It was a joke, but I still stiffened underneath him. I still felt that sharp, stabbing pain in my chest, the same one I'd had when they had removed Dramin's body from the room. The old man had been such a fixture that I couldn't believe he was now gone.

Maybe I didn't want to.

I wondered how Jos was doing.

The thought hit me like a ton of bricks, my gut twisting into the dance of the butterflies.

I needed to see her.

"I didn't even get to say good-bye," Thom began, his arms still tight around me as he pulled me right back to the consuming sadness, the bitter reality smacking me upside the face.

I hadn't realized that Thom had been deprived of that moment. It was an unfair truth that tickled my nose. Dammit, I didn't want to cry.

"I didn't expect to wake up to this," he choked out with tears.

The longing in his voice burned my eyes with grief.

"To death?"

He nodded, his hand pressing against my spine, holding me close as he moved his thumb over my skin.

"To betrayal," he amended. The word, while harsher, fit a bit more.

I wrinkled my nose at that, knowing how painful the truth in those words must be to him.

Thom had woken up to nothing more than a bad dream. Worse still, he had to hear of everything secondhand and accept that his best friend, Sain, had turned on us all. He had to accept that the man Thom had been hidden away with for hundreds of years, the one who was more of a friend than he would like to admit, was gone.

"We can still say good-bye," I said, trying not to think of what that really meant. I sat there, letting the silence and the pain in my words linger in the air like a vile perfume, infecting us. Then, with an exaggerated exhale, I twisted against Thom's chest, wishing there were anywhere else to look other than at empty beds and bloodstained floors.

"I know," Thom finally said, his voice too soft for him, broken by too much emotion.

Sitting up in surprise, I looked at him lying there all weak and limp, his eyes clearly glistening with foreign tears. "Are you crying?" I asked, my mind running over every possible reason for them, from internal bleeding to possession to memory loss.

My heart beat more loudly with each one before he smiled, the wide grin out of place with the tears.

"Wait. Are you possessed?" I asked, my voice shaking with my own tears as his began to flow. "Because I have seen *The Exorcist*; I am fully schooled in what to do."

"I'm not possessed," Thom said with that gruff voice of his, his still strong chicken arms pulling me back into him, holding me against his chest. "I am allowed to be sad, Wynifred." His voice rumbled through his chest and into me as I lay there, listening to his heart, feeling his magic press against his skin, my own warming within me at the close proximity. "Besides, I have cried before."

I knew that. I had seen him. I had seen him cry and sob when it had happened, when she had been taken from us. Both then and in the months after.

The temporary comfort I felt vanished, the imagery of that moment, of those tears, hitting me hard in the chest. Her cries echoed inside my head, even without the blade, and I jerked.

Thom tightened his arms around me in what I knew he thought was a show of comfort. However, I was suddenly feeling very trapped.

"I saw her, you know," he said, breaking the silence, digging the blade I knew I had been stabbed with a little deeper, carving out my heart bit by bit.

I was sure the bottom of my soul was falling out.

That sounded a bit like an Iron Maiden song. They were not my favorite.

"I saw her while I was stuck ... wherever I was." A seriousness that was unfamiliar to him took control of him, and I tensed, my heart beating so fast now that everything was going numb, the world around Thom and me spinning.

I ignored it, though, keeping my focus on the way his hand felt against my back, on the sound of his heart. Everything around us was going topsy-turvy, but those were constant. Now they needed to stay that way.

"I would hear your voice, feel your magic, feel your hand against mine, and then I would dream of you and Rosy and even Cail. But not psychopath Cail. Cail the way he used to be. Cail when he was my friend—"

"It was the blade," I said, staring at an old brown stain on the sheet that was stretched over Dramin's part of the room, the white cotton splattered with red.

The imagery was too much, and I sat up, hovering over him, swallowing in a desperate attempt to get the lump out. Part of me wished I could stick the information in his head like Jos and Ilyan were able to. This whole show and tell thing was a tad bit painful.

I was covered in badges of survival, covered in reminders of everything I had done.

"You got a piece of the blade?" he asked, and I nodded.

His face lit up as he pushed himself into a sitting position, the bed creaking as he leaned against it.

I wanted to tell him to lie down or even force him to. What I was about to tell him was going to be a sucker punch, not the story of success that I already knew he expected it to be.

From the moment we had watched Rosaline die, from the moment we had watched Edmund create the jagged piece of blood and stone from the purity of her soul and the magic in her blood, it had been our task to retrieve that monstrous thing.

To retrieve it and to free her.

After so long, I had found a piece.

"I don't have it anymore."

Sucker punch! Achievement unlocked.

His face fell, his brow furrowing in what I knew at once was more anger than disappointment.

I sighed. I never really liked facing Thom when he was angry. I would rather charm a cobra.

"I found it inside of Ryland," I plowed on before more rage could explode out of him. "I removed it when we escaped the massacre, right at the beginning. It's probably the only reason he's not such a mess anymore. Edmund was using it to control him."

"Edmund was using it …"

I nodded. My lips were a tight line as his jaw snapped closed, the hollows of his cheeks more pronounced than ever.

"I should have known better, Thom. I was stupid. If Edmund was using it that way, I should have known what was coming for me." I sighed, the sound loud and long as I attempted to expel the extra stress that was building up in my gut.

It didn't help.

"I could hear her voice all the time: during the day, while I slept. But it wasn't some pretty song or memory; it was her death ... always her death. I used to get dreams about it before, but then I didn't know what they were. I didn't know what I was seeing. Talon always told me it was another life ..." I smiled, the honesty in what he had said hitting me. "This was so much worse than that."

Thom was silent. I couldn't even look at him. Admitting that flooded me with far too many memories of that night, of watching my little girl go through that, of Thom running away.

It hurt too much.

Pressing my lips into a tight line, I steeled myself, knowing I needed to continue. "I would put the blade in your hand when everyone was asleep, part of me hoping that maybe you would also hear her, that maybe you could hear the good thing. Maybe it would wake you up." Shaking my head in embarrassment, I leaned against the footboard, the creaking of springs and frame loud in the silence.

"But I saw her, Wyn. Even if I didn't wake up, I saw her. I

talked with her. I held her …" His voice caught as my chest tightened, a heat spreading over my face as I tried not to let the tears force their way past my badass exterior.

I already knew I wouldn't be successful.

Just hearing him say it brought back that moment, that same beautiful and horrifying moment of holding her, of loving her, even if it was one last time.

"So did I," I said, my voice breaking as the tears that began to fall down my face. Chilled rivers of them flowed over my cheeks before splashing against my collarbone, a hiss barely audible as the heat in my skin sent them back into the air in steam and smoke.

Thom's eyes widened as worry overtook his pain. "Running a bit hot, are we?"

"Yeah, I warned you I would burn you," I said without thinking. "It's been an issue ever since Jos and I knocked down that chapel. I should probably try to restrain my magic a bit better, but seeing as Jos isn't around, it's not my first priority."

If I needed to be around her, perhaps I would wear a full body sock.

I laughed at the thought, lost in my head.

Thom, however, was staring at me with changing degrees of confusion and worry.

"Wyn?"

"That blade messed up a lot, Thom. *A lot*. But I also got to see her when Edmund took control of the blade. I *saw* her." Speaking carefully, I lifted the hand he had been so mesmerized with, the hole angry and red, as if it knew I was talking about it. "She saved me. She saved us."

Hand before me, I uncurled my fingers with my palm facing Thom as I smiled at him through the gap before pressing my palm against my eye and looking through the hole like it was the spy glass Joclyn wanted it to be.

"See? You should—"

"He tried to take control of me, Thom. He pushed the blade into my hand, but Rosy saved me. She fought his control. She got me here so I could save you ..."

My stomach fluttered, my words shaking as I retold everything that had happened.

His lips pressed into a tight line as the story unfolded. The fascination faded into horror as he finally understood what the gap in my hand really was.

The look of realization on his face was making me uncomfortable.

Shifting my weight, I started to move away, but before I could get far, Thom grabbed me, pulling my hand toward him. His soft fingers moved over the skin, his touch gentle now, as if the skin of my palm was sacred.

His eyes grew wide with fear before narrowing in the perpetual anger that made him so Thom.

"We have to stop him. We have to stop all of them. We have to make them pay: Edmund for hurting her, Ovailia for helping—"

"What if Edmund is dead?" I interrupted, the same tinge of regret I had been fighting smacking me around. I wanted to kill Edmund. The fact that I might have missed my chance was infuriating.

"It doesn't matter. We will destroy who ever we need to in order to save her," he said with his usual grumble, as if the end goal made it all better. "Besides, if Edmund is dead, and Sain is responsible, he may have had more to do with her death than we thought. Sain let Ovailia poison me, he's been working with her. He's been working with them both for a long time."

"I want to say he's your best friend, and that he wouldn't … But I don't think I can swallow that lie anymore."

"He's not my best friend, not anymore!" he snapped, his anger erupting like the volcano he was. "My best friend would not have told Edmund of our escape and told him how to kill her in order to make the blade."

My gut twisted, the memory of the night rushing back to me, unwanted. "He was in the sight of our escape, Thom. We both saw him."

"He can control it more than he wants anyone to believe." He sighed, slamming his hand into his forehead in a regret I didn't think I understood. "I've seen him do it before. If he had any part in Rosy's death, I will end him."

"You would kill your best friend?" I asked, not believing for a second that it was possible for him to do. "You risked everything for him before …"

I knew he could, but that type of reversal didn't seem like Thom. Then again, Sain's betrayal didn't seem like the man he knew, either.

"I would kill whoever I needed to in order to make this all

stop." Now that sounded like Thom. "No matter how long of a line I have to stand in to get there."

"That line seems to be getting longer every day," I said with a sigh, the tension in my shoulders leaving as his thumb moved over the skin of the hand he still held. "I'm gonna have to fight to be first, aren't I?"

"Not as much as you think. I know that bloodlust in your eyes better than anyone, Wynifred. If you get there first, take the shot. Don't hesitate. Do it for her. Besides, as long as someone destroys him, I'll be happy."

"That, I believe, is a given," I said, unwilling to let my eyes leave his. The gentle flicker of red daylight glinted past the window, making everything a bit more nefarious than it needed to be. "I don't think there is any way this can end without Edmund slash Sain face down in his own blood."

"You say that like you are speaking of the epic ending of a six-year-old's birthday party."

"Maybe I am." I shrugged, my hand finally leaving his as I lay back down next to him.

The deep laugh I loved so much filled the depressing space and sucked the ominous pressure out of the air.

"All we need is a clown," I quipped.

"Or pony rides."

We laughed at that, but it was shallow, full of all the fear and trepidation our world was surrounded by.

Ignoring it, I curled into Thom, letting all the crap pass us by. I wasn't going to move anytime soon. I would stay like this for the rest of my life if he asked me. Of course, that required Thom never leaving the bed and me not beating him in destroying the mysterious Edmund slash Sain combo, both of which were not going to happen.

"You better not go anywhere else," I gasped out, knowing how pathetic the worry sounded in my voice and not really caring.

"Where am I going?" he teased, poking his fingers into my side. "Guam?"

"You know what I mean." My voice was barely above a growl.

"I could say the same thing, Wyn," he said, the grip he had on me increasing as he pulled me closer. "Before Jos saved you, I thought for sure you were a goner."

"Nice to know you were rooting for me to pull through." It was hard to keep the irritation out of my voice. Though I knew he didn't mean it the way I had taken it, I was suddenly on high alert, expecting the dream to turn into a nightmare or some such nonsense.

"I was, Wyn." He sighed, his hand leaving my arm to run down the side of my head, his fingers soft as they glided over my hairline.

I shivered.

"Just as you were, I never left your side—"

"I think," I said, my heart suddenly beating a million miles an hour, "that we have had quite enough of near-death experiences and bedside vigils."

"I can agree with that," he said with a laugh, his fingers tangling in my hair as I rested against him.

The tension in my neck and chest began to release.

"Good, because the less of those this world has, the more it can have of other things."

"Other things?" he asked.

I was walking into a bear trap, and part of me didn't care.

"Yeah ... you know, like monster truck rallies and Styx reunion tours that go on outside of Wendover, Utah, and kisses and terrible books and—"

"Wyn?" Thom said as he pressed his finger against my chin softly, tilting my head enough to look at him.

Instead of the deep, passionate blue of his eyes, I was met by a mischievous glare and a sly smile. It was a look I returned, knowing Thom far too well not to realize something was coming.

"Yes?" I was understandably wary.

"How did you manage to destroy the cathedral and *not* be murdered by my brother?"

"Let's say that Ilyan had more important things on his mind." I snickered, leaning against him again. "That and I saved him from an army of undead corpses; that probably helped, too."

"*Undead corpses*?" Thom gasped, obviously concerned.

"We have much to talk about, young kemosabe."

"Thank God we have a lifetime to do it."

"Indeed."

18

JOCLYN

EVERYTHING WAS STILL in the drenching silence of misery that had taken over the camp, soaking into each of us until we were nothing more than a damp rag.

At least, that's how I felt. And, with the way Ryland slumped against the wall next to me, he was a damp rag, too.

Damp and hollow and empty, like the long hospital corridor we sat in. Like our souls.

I might be mistaken, but I thought mine might have slithered away, off to find a land full of real sunshine.

I told Ryland that, and he tried to smile, but mostly, he cried and slammed his head into the wall we sat against.

"Don't do that, Ry." I moved to lean against him, but thankfully, I stopped myself from resting my head on his shoulder just in time. The familiarity of this position made that movement too easy.

"Don't do what?" he snapped, his anger working hard to mask the crippling pain of loss. "Cry? Yell? Run out and find the little brat who did this to us?" His voice rose with each word as he gestured with his hands toward the large wooden door at the end of the hospital, toward the room that used to be a broom closet and now held the three sheet-covered bodies of our family.

I stared at the door as his fingers began to shake, my heart in pain that I tried arduously to dismiss. But looking at the door and knowing what was behind it hurt.

"No." I felt the need to cry but couldn't make the tears come. It was lost, just like my soul. "Crying is okay, especially right now. Hurting yourself, however ..."

He cast me a sidelong glance. "Point taken." His response was barely above a growl, one that spanned over the still silence of the room, over the soapy floors that some of the healers had desperately tried to clean before being ushered out by Ilyan, who was on his way to another council. The council would decide the fate of those who had chosen to fight against us. The council would also seal our fate for the battle that was coming.

You couldn't win a war if everyone left. And that, if what Ilyan and Ryland had told me about the battle I had missed was true, was exactly what was going to happen.

I didn't know how much more of this I could take.

Sighing, I slammed my head into the wall exactly as Ryland had, regretting the action immediately. That hurt.

"Now who is hurting themselves?" Ryland prompted, the anger still drowning his voice.

"I'm not hurting myself," I retorted, my eyes burning with the ripple of the impact. "I'm trying to dislodge whatever it is in my brain that is causing this mess and get us out of this nightmare and back to reality."

"I don't think it's that easy, Jos."

"Nothing ever is." This time, I did lay my head on his shoulder. I knew I shouldn't, but right then, there was no monster left in him. There was only my best friend.

There were only two broken hearts.

"I loved her, Jos," he admitted after a minute, his shoulders tensing into a rock underneath me.

I hadn't expected that.

I tried to swallow, but it was all dry and prickly. The tension in his muscles moved through me, knotting my stomach.

"No, Ry." I was barely able to get the words past my desert dry-throat. "You still love her. That doesn't have to go anywhere."

"But she does."

His heartbreak echoed my own. It leached into his words and tensed in his chest, pressing against my own heart so heavily I was having trouble breathing again. The flood of tears came shortly after.

Our sobs were the only sound in the long hall, broken and pained and heart-wrenching until the loud slam of the door interrupted us.

All thoughts of tears were forgotten as Wyn began walking toward us, bottle and glasses in one hand, Thom leaning heavily on the other.

"Thom."

The one good thing in all of this. The only good thing left, it seemed. We hadn't lost everything.

Struggling to my feet, I raced toward them.

A wide grin spread over Thom's own tear-streaked face. "Hey, Silnỳ." His voice was soft and weak, his gaunt face pulling oddly under the smile.

I hadn't noticed how much weight he had lost while he had been lying in the bed day after day. Now, seeing him standing, he was little more than skin and bones. His arms were sticks, the muscles and sinews popping out along his joints and neck like the seams of a puppet. Even his eyes seemed sunken.

I realized I was scared to touch him as I stopped mere inches away before I collided into him. It was something he noticed, and he smiled.

"What? No jubilant greeting for me?" Wyn taunted, her smile as strained as the rest of us, although her joke was unsurprisingly pure.

"I see you every day, Wyn, so don't be greedy." I contemplated hitting her then stopped when Ry stepped around me in an attempt to reach his brother, shock on his face.

"Hello again, brother," Thom said, his voice just as weak as his body looked. "We meet again."

Ryland chuckled uncomfortably before stepping forward, embracing Thom as though he had known him longer than the few days before Thom had been plunged into his never-ending sleep.

"As long as you stick around, I'll be glad for it," Ryland gasped out, his voice strained. "What brings you here? I didn't expect to see you—"

"We need to see Dramin," Wyn said, pulling my focus from the men and back to her, back to the bottles she was holding and the door that stood behind us. The door might as well have a spotlight on it.

"We need to say good-bye," Thom continued.

Their words hit me hard in the chest, sending the stationary room into a spin as a sight tried to take control, tried to pull me down.

Pushing it away, I shook my head, willing the people before me to come back into focus. Still, my heart pounded in my chest.

I was not a fan of being in the same room with my brother, of seeing him one last time ... of never hearing what he had been trying to tell me.

I didn't think I could be there when they pulled that sheet down. I didn't know if I could see that without it destroying me. I was positive it would.

I had seen Dramin's funeral far too many times in sight. I knew the moment we all stood on the mountain side and placed that handkerchief on his face was a gateway to something bigger, and now it was here.

I still didn't want to accept it.

Wyn interpreted the horror on my face as any good friend would. Her eyes softened as she placed her arm across my shoulder, the glasses clicking behind my back. "Don't worry, Jos," she whispered low enough that the men who were inches from us couldn't hear. "We'll wait. You don't have to be there."

Mi lasko? Ilyan's voice filled my mind, his soft, soothing words pulling me from the horrors of what Wyn was planning.

Ilyan. I hadn't been certain my stomach could wind itself up in heavier knots. I was wrong.

One word and everything in me was iron and ice.

"Is it done, then?" I asked aloud, forgetting that Wyn was in front of me.

She screwed up her face in confusion, but I waved it off, and her confusion was quickly replaced by an eye roll and a scowl of irritation.

I ignored her. I was getting pretty good at that, especially when I wanted to hit everyone.

Yes, I've just left the council.

I tensed, feeling his trepidation. I could feel the fear that was traveling alongside his magic.

I shivered.

How did it go? I didn't want to ask.

His magic pressed against me, the sound of his steps hollow as they moved across our connection, from his ears to mine. He wasn't far. I didn't know if that made it better or worse that he was running in my direction.

That bad, huh? I tried to put a joke into the words, but it didn't stick. It melted away like the emotional bomb we were surrounded by.

It wasn't good, he finally answered, his voice tense in my head as the door opened with a smack, and everyone turned at the sound, looking at Ilyan as he strode into the room.

"How *not good* was it?" I asked before anyone else had a chance to speak.

The look of joy they'd all had at the sight of Ilyan vanished with my question, their heads bouncing back and forth in confusion that slowly slipped into fear. They all knew where he had been, what he had been doing.

Ilyan walked toward us, his lips pulled into a tight line as flashes of images from the council began to filter into my mind through our connection. The yelling faces and hurled rocks smacked me right in the chest.

"You're not giving me much confidence for what we're going into," I gasped as I pushed the memories away. My voice was broken and strained, so much so that it barely made it past my throat.

"If you don't have much, then I don't have any," Wyn said, her voice hard as she held onto Thom, taking a protective stance in front of the emaciated man. "I was at that bloodbath we tried to pass off as a council. I highly doubt this one could have gone any better."

Ilyan reached us then, his hand firm on Thom's shoulder. The touch was meant to be comforting, but the look he fixed me with fell short of that.

I didn't want any more bad news.

"They aren't giving me much hope for what is coming," he said with a sigh, and my shoulders tensed as the bands of his memory began to loosen, letting the misery that was plain on his face fill me. "Many of them wish to leave."

I could have never expected that.

Neither could anyone else.

Ryland finally took that step back while Wyn took one forward, forgetting about poor Thom who struggled a bit to hold his own weight. Luckily, Ryland was paying enough attention to at least notice and catch him.

It all happened in a matter of a second, a shuffle of movement that fluttered around me while I stood in place, thinking if anything else were to happen today, the barrier would fall, and then we would all be screwed.

Hell, we were already screwed.

Sain really had won. All of his planning, all of his deceiving, had worked. I had never been more ashamed to be his daughter.

The emotion swam toward Ilyan, and he moved his hand to my shoulder, pulling me toward him as if he were afraid I would suddenly take off and try to kill that vexing man. Not that it would be a bad thing.

"How many?" Wyn asked, her question awakening the memory in Ilyan's mind, pushing it back into mine.

My magic flared at the invasion, a sight glistening around me as my magic showed me the same moment.

Beyond the empty hospital, I could see the council in shadows, see the wide majority of people step forward in the hall, their hands raised above their heads. A solitary vote for dissension. For leaving.

"More than half," I answered for him, watching the scene continue as more and more joined them. Only a handful were left on the outskirts, sheepishly standing their ground, although many of them looked unsure of their choice. They wouldn't last long. "No more than two-thirds."

Thom groaned, Wyn swore, and Ryland looked like he was about to throw up. His jaw worked wildly as he tried to find words, his skin turning pale as he twitched a bit, looking at something far over my head with enough anger that I could have sworn the ceiling had offended him somehow.

"I guess it's better for them to leave than to fight," he said to the ceiling, his voice strong despite everything about him looking weak. "We couldn't trust them ... We can't save them anymore."

"Where are they even going to go?" I asked, the sudden ridiculousness of their request hitting me in the gut. My pride bristled at the treachery I was enfolded within.

"Some payback for saving them—walking away. Where are they going to go? Into the infested city with no escape? Dumb," Wyn asked, putting all of my irritation into words. "They'll be lucky if they survive."

"It is their choice," Ilyan said, his voice strong as he straightened himself up to his full height, his anger and frustration clear. "We can't save everyone. If they choose to die, so be it. All we can do is save ourselves and do our best when the time comes to enter Imdalind."

"You mean, kick some trash," Wyn spat, anger radiating off

her. She smashed her fists together before stepping back to Thom, though she didn't offer to take his weight from Ryland. She stared at Ilyan and me so intently I could feel my magic prickle in expectation.

Breathing deeply in an attempt to control my magic, I pushed it away. I really didn't need to bring down the hospital, too.

"I can take down Sain on my own, anyway," Wyn continued, the same anger pulsing within her. "You just need to get me there."

I really didn't need to remind her again that it was my job.

"I'll get you there." As far as I was concerned, she could have it. Although I didn't see many complications with killing my own estranged father, I knew it was wishful thinking.

"How many are left?" Ryland asked as he finally looked away from the ceiling, pulling the conversation away from Wyn's murderous tendencies and back to the new complication.

"Less that twenty," Ilyan answered.

This time, I joined in Wyn's over-exaggerated frown. That was worse than I had thought.

"Did you let them go?" I asked, knowing he had no other choice.

He nodded, his lips a tight line of defeat, of fear, of acceptance. It was a simple move he could not control and one that might have sealed our fate.

"Good riddance, I say." Wyn smiled through the dark cloud that had covered us. The usually joyous expression was full of far too much savagery to be comforting. "If it's only the four or us, we can get in, kill your dad"—she pointed at me —"and all y'all's sister"—she waved toward the boys—"and we'll be set."

"Excuse me. There are five here," Thom interjected, pulling away from Ryland in an attempt to stand on his own.

"Are there?" Wyn asked, her banter loud as she placed one finger against his chest and pushed him back into Ryland. Luckily, his brother was ready for him. "I see four unless you were planning on me pushing your wheelchair into Imdalind ..."

"I will walk on my own, thank you."

"You can barely stand!"

"That doesn't mean I can't fight."

They continued to bicker, Thom's smile deepening as Wyn's exasperation grew.

Poor Ryland was stuck between it all, looking as lost as a child in a theme park.

I was looking at them, but I barely heard. I barely saw. My mind was locked with Ilyan's, running over the map of every possible scenario, running over what Wyn had said.

There were four, possibly five, of us. Not many. Too few to really be noticed if we went in under a shield. Too few for anyone to know what was going on before it was too late.

Just like in Rioseco.

Just like now.

"If what we have heard is true ... Edmund's men don't like

him," I spoke aloud, forgetting that a million other things were happening around me.

The battle of the banterers ceased, everyone looking toward Ilyan and me in confusion.

They are planning something, Ilyan said, his eyes intense as he caught up to where I was.

If only I could see into his camp ... if only my sight would show me something!

"But even if it can't, my love," Ilyan interrupted, "it still shows that he does not have full control. They are fighting him."

"We could slip in and out. We could cause havoc, and no one would know we were there."

"That's it!" Wyn yelled, pulling me from my reverie to look at her. All three of them looked slightly uncomfortable. "No more secret conversations. I'm done. You two are driving me mad."

I was ninety-nine percent certain at this point that was she was about to explode. I could feel the heat coming off her skin.

"Spill."

"You're right, Wyn," I said with a smile, the emotion feeling odd against the painful puffiness of my eyes. "We can all sneak in and destroy him—"

"Take note that the Silnỳ said *all*, Wyn. That's important," Thom interrupted.

I ignored him, plowing forward.

"No one would even know we were there. We could end this."

Wyn smiled before her face fell, the manic bloodlust falling right beside it. "You are forgetting one thing," she said, pointing her finger toward the ceiling. "We are trapped here."

Plan foiled.

Sighing, I squished my face up in frustration. My heart, however, didn't really stop fluttering in my chest. My breathing didn't really slow down. My sight flared with one image of Míra before she vanished in Dramin's, one image of my father underneath the cloak as he vanished from the streets of Prague.

"They got through," I said to myself, grateful for Ilyan's understanding sigh behind me. At least someone was paying attention.

"So can you," he said, his voice the same powerhouse it always was. The power and strength in the man swept over all of us. "Tomorrow, we will have the ceremony of farewells," Ilyan continued.

Ryland's tears came back in full-force, yet I didn't understand why. It was only when Ilyan replaced the words with the more familiar "funeral" that everything began to swim around me uncomfortably.

No.

Before the one word could seep into my mind, my tears had swollen to match Ryland's, Wyn's, and Thom's.

Ilyan stayed strong, the strength of a king shadowing all of us. However, I could feel the tremendous loss that was crippling him.

"Then we will fight," Ilyan continued, his voice breaking. "We will find a way in, and we will destroy them all."

"It's time."

19

JOCLYN

OUR STEPS ECHOED around the empty courtyard like the slow tolls of a bell at midnight: solemn, rhythmic. The tents were gone. Those who had inhabited them had already been removed from underneath Ilyan's barrier. All who remained had been placed in the hospital, both to help the sick and guard the dead before they were laid to rest and their souls returned to Imdalind. All told, there were twenty-three of them. Twenty-three against an army.

My heart tensed painfully, the sounds of our steps growing louder as we turned into the massive stone hallway. They echoed the sadness we felt in their monotone chimes, each beat hitting against my chest.

I tried to ignore it, exactly as I tried to ignore the bloodied footsteps that guided us toward our room, the prints too small for an adult. Too small for what had happened.

My back straightened painfully, and Ilyan's arm tightened around me as he sensed the sudden change in emotion. Sensed the pain.

"How are you holding up?" he whispered into my hair, his voice soft as his own pain seeped into me.

"I should be asking you the same," I joked.

He didn't laugh. I couldn't even force one out from myself.

"Let's look at it this way," I finally said after a moment of silence. "We are both still standing, and we are both still moving forward."

"Are you calling that a success?"

"This time, I am." I sighed, leaning my head against his chest, letting the sound of his heartbeat rumble through me.

He looked at me as we walked, sadness and misery lining his face. There was a spark of joy there, but it was masked, the hopelessness of this day overwhelming it.

His finger was soft as he ran it across my face, over the cemetery of tears trailing down my jaw to the bridge of my nose and finally brushing the hair out of my face in an attempt to see me better.

His touch sent ripples of pleasure over my skin and down my spine. The sensations floated through my stomach in a tickle of want that, for a second, made it hard to keep walking, to keep breathing.

"Beautiful woman," he gasped aloud as he pulled me to a stop right before our door, pressing me against him then leaning down, his movement slow, his touch gentle. With a flutter, his lips barely brushed against mine. The feeling was more breath than contact as he chuckled, his laugh increasing the tangle of knots he had already infected my stomach with.

"Butterflies" was an understatement.

I gasped and tried to pull away, but he came in closer, still not quite kissing me.

I gasped again, not able to find words in the goo of whatever he had left me in.

He didn't miss that and smiled, the bright blue of his eyes glistening in the dim light of the hallway. The love I had seen before was still there, still strong. It was merely clouded by what was coming.

"Do you want to escape with me?" I whispered, knotting my fingers underneath his shirt to touch the skin of his hip, teasing him with my real meaning.

He chuckled, the touch calming him, even with the pain. The sound made me smile, the bittersweet emotion sneaking in whether I wanted it to or not.

"I would love to escape with you," he whispered back, pulling me against him as we escaped into our room, tripping over each other on the few steps before we fell onto the bed, our arms and legs tangling around each other from the fall.

"Come with me, můj kamarád," he whispered, closing his eyes without another word, his magic prodding me. The invitation to enter the Tòuha was clear.

My smile deepened as I, too, closed my eyes, leaning into him and allowing his magic to take me completely. The warmth of him consumed me as his fingers trailed up my arms, over my collarbone, and across the lines on my neck.

I didn't dare open my eyes.

I shivered from the touch, the ripple of pleasure moving down my spine.

"My Joclyn," he whispered the moment his finger connected with the raised brand on my neck.

My magic swelled as his wrapped around me in an equal crescendo, pulling me, mind and body, into the sacred space we shared, the place that was even more of a sanctuary in this moment than I could have ever hoped for.

I heard the waves before I opened my eyes, the hot sand against my skin a comforting blanket that I was eager to be wrapped up in.

Ilyan's hand was a gentle caress against my skin. The soft touch created a powerful trail of desire behind it. It was filled with power as it always was in this space.

Carefully restraining a shiver, I sighed, letting my body collapse into the sand, keeping my eyes closed as I focused on his touch, on the sound of the waves, on the heaven that I had suddenly found myself in.

"Open your eyes," Ilyan said with a laugh.

I smiled. "What if I say no?"

"Open your eyes," Ilyan repeated, his laugh growing into a deeper chuckle as his touch continued making intoxicating trails across my back.

I listened to the sound, getting lost in the rhythm, getting lost in the sensation of his touch against my skin.

The soft tickle of his fingers moved down my back, over my arms, across my cheek, touching all of me. Igniting all of me.

"Open your eyes." This time, he said it softly, and with a soft, little flutter, they opened. Not to the bright sunshine that I had been expecting, but to a beautiful overcast day, like the many that were taken for granted on a beach.

Everyone always wanted the sun; they always wanted the warmth. But warmth could be there even without the blazing rays of the sun. Warmth could be there even if it was hidden. Sometimes, when it was hidden, just knowing it was there could make it all the more pleasurable.

"You should take your own advice." Ilyan laughed, reading my mind. "Warmth, life, happiness, joy, fear—it's all the same, my darling. Joy is still there. It's just hiding behind a cloud right now. Just like Dramin."

"Are you saying Dramin is behind a cloud?"

"No, I'm saying Dramin has found his warmth. Maybe he has moved past the cloud and found a sanctuary in his own Tõuha, lying together with his wife. Together for an eternal life of perfection and bliss."

It was a bittersweet happiness, but one I let overwhelm me. It was a good thought, a beautiful picture, for a man who very much deserved it.

"I can accept that," I said, wiggling myself over the sand, nestling myself against Ilyan's chest.

Lying there, he ran his fingers over my skin while mine traced the deep scars that crisscrossed over his chest. I had followed them so many times before that they were memorized now. Their movements, intersections, and odd imperfections were already a perfect map in my mind.

He gasped, shivering beneath me as the same passion that I was feeling began to affect him.

"Did I ever tell you that that tickles?" Ilyan asked.

"No," I replied with a laugh. "That makes me want to do it more, you know."

"Then maybe I should have told you that long ago."

I sighed, never ceasing in the gentle touch against his chest, letting my mind run free and calm.

We lay like that, forgetting all the troubles and doom and losses of the world we had left behind. But, as always, we both knew that this could not last forever. Not yet.

"Someday, it will," Ilyan said, answering a question that really didn't exist between us. "Someday, this will be our every day, and there will be no wars, no more blood, no more death."

"You say that like it's a daydream."

"To me, it is," he responded, his voice suddenly strained. "I have been lost in this war for hundreds of years, my darling. To me, the future beyond can only be a daydream."

"What if I make it a reality?" I asked, knowing the weight of what that really meant, knowing the impossibility of what was before us.

"What if we do it together?" Ilyan asked, his soft touch leaving, replaced by a strong palm against my back. The weight was pleasant and warm as he pushed me into him, my arms and legs tangling around his in a comfortable pretzel against the sand.

"I would like that." I sighed as his magic swarmed into me with that same unparalleled power you could only find in the Tŏuha. I gasped at the impression and the raw vulnerability that filled me.

"Then perhaps you will finally allow me to show you my house. Your real house, not that one."

I couldn't restrain the laugh. He had been trying to get me to visit the house on the beach for months. I was certain it would be as clear in the Tŏuha as it was in reality, but that didn't matter.

I wanted to see it within the real world. There were too many parallels in my life, sights of the total futures that were unsure, Tŏuhas that let me live in the daydream that Ilyan longed for.

But that moment—walking into that house that Ilyan had built for me, for us, and for our eternity—I wanted it to be real. Not something from the confusing spaces that my life had given me, that my magic had created for me. Not sight, not Tŏuha.

"Yes," I said with a laugh, pulling away to look him in the eye, those bright blue eyes that danced with the love that had been missing lately. "When we create this reality, then you can show me."

He didn't smile, although his eyes were happy.

He held me close, his face glowing with an immense love as he moved his thumb over my back, each swipe of his skin against mine sending the same intense ripple of need over me.

I knew what was coming.

"Kiss me," I begged, knowing it would be more than the tickle of his lips against mine this time.

It was.

It was strong and powerful. It was skin against skin. It was his tongue dragging over my lower lip as his hand tangled in my hair. It was his gasp in my ear as I kissed his neck. It was my giggle as he tickled mine.

"Ilyan," I sighed as I pulled myself away.

A small groan rippled deep inside his throat, the desire clear.

The desire was the same as had filled me.

However, I could already feel the dream shattering. I could already feel reality pressing against my chest. Some invisible clock was ticking down beside us, as if warning me what was coming.

I already knew.

"I love you, Ilyan." I gasped out as I dragged my thumb over his lips. "I love you more than the world. More than life itself."

"I know," he whispered. "I can see it in your eyes, even if you don't think so."

I smiled, and his own grew to match mine as he pulled me back into him. His lips met mine once more before dragging over my cheek and down my neck.

"I have loved you all of my life, and I will love you until the end," he said.

I closed my eyes, letting the warmth of the beach fill me just as the sun peeked out from behind the clouds, and the warmth of this life found us inside of the Tŏuha, if only for a moment.

20

JOCLYN

WIND BLEW THROUGH MY HAIR, pulling at the strands like some demon that was trying to whisk me away. What hair the beast managed to pull from my braid blew around my face in a mêlée of black. The bright gold ribbon moved with them, as if it alone was battling an invisible foe.

I just didn't care.

I walked against the wind, through the chill, holding the thick wool blanket that had been on Dramin's bed around me, wishing it were enough to block the chill. Regardless, it was still biting, moving through me with every step. I didn't even bother to heat my magic to warm me. At least with the cold I didn't feel quite so dead inside.

Normally, this close to the barrier, everything would be hot and stifling, the air so thick and muggy you could feel it press against your skin like mayonnaise. Right now, with the way the wind rushed around us and the snow beat against the barrier feet from us, it was cold. The air was a brittle chill as the outside world found a way in, as the earth itself felt the bitter agony of losing someone so great.

The earth knew why we were here, she knew why we were gathered on a little hill, surrounded by miles of farmland with enough of a rise in the earth that it lifted us above the hell the city had become, looking over it like the rulers we were.

It was the city Dramin had called his home, the city we would bury him in. Up here, I could see why he loved it so much. I could see his home. I could see my home.

"I'm sure it was beautiful," I sighed out, my voice broken as the sobs tried to quiet briefly. "When it was first built ... before all of this ..." I waved my hand over the city, displaying the ruins before us, as though Ilyan hadn't seen them before, as if he didn't know how it had been.

Ilyan pulled me into him as he pulled the thoughts from my mind, his own comforting words drifting to me through our magic. The warmth of his power settled into my bones.

It was. It was his home.

Sobs stuck in my throat, I turned into him, my cold cheek pressing against the warmth of his arm as he held me, tangled awkwardly in the cold. He was the only comforting thing this hilltop had for us, so I held on to him, watching our ribbons dance and tangle in the angry wind.

Ryland stayed back, the wind attempting to devour him as he stood between two fresh dirt mounds, his hands and knees covered with the dark earth. His sobs swept into the wind like the howl of a demon, his mourning knell hitting me in the chest.

Watching him there, watching his heartbreak, knowing what was still to come, ripped open my heart again, and the sobs came. Deeper and louder this time, the pain stifled by Ilyan's arms as he wrapped me up in him.

His sobs increased as Wyn and Thom began to drag Ryland away from the two people he had considered family and toward the last one, following the few of Ilyan's people who had come up here with us.

"I'm not sure I can do this," I said between sobs.

Ilyan's hand was soft as it ran down my spine, the blanket shielding the touch from view. "Do what, mi lasko?" he asked, his tall frame bending over me as he whispered in my ear.

"Step over there. Say good-bye."

Ilyan stiffened with the shake in the words, the reality hitting him as it did me. As wrapped up in him as I was, I could feel him shudder. His magic pressed against my heart as I felt his lips press against my hair. His breath was warm as it flowed with the wind that still tried to move into me, warm breath and cold wind tugging and pulling at my hair.

Good-byes are never easy, he whispered in my mind. *Nor are they final. His magic is all around us, my Joclyn. You saw it as it left him, and you will see it again ... whether it be in this life or the next.*

"Or the next," I echoed, my voice muffled as I pressed my face into the crook of his arm, burrowing into the blanket that was wrapped around us.

I didn't want to watch Ryland as he walked closer to us, all broken again. I didn't want to think of the next life, the life that might be too close thanks to the premonitions and fathers who lie and mess everything up.

At first, it was me, and then it was Ilyan. Now it might be any one of us.

It was already Dramin.

And Risha.

And Jaromir.

"I have told you of how we release our kind, the Skříteks, into the earth, yes?" Ilyan's voice was an accented rumble as he whispered against me, pulling my mind from the flashes of sights.

"Into the underwater river that flows throughout Imdalind," I answered, the imagery clear in my head, just as it had been when we had buried Risha a few moments ago: The large cavern; the quick flow of icy water; the way the body, all wrapped up in white, was placed in the flow, swallowed beneath the surface to return the physical body back into the earth that gave it life and allowing the soul and magic to find their final resting place amidst the rock and sky and air of the world that had created us all.

"Do you think they will get lost?" I asked, knowing Ilyan was tuned in to me. "That they will get stuck in the barrier and never find their way home?"

I knew it was a silly question. I didn't even know where home was after this. I didn't know if there was a heaven or a hell or some combination of the two. I hoped Dramin's soul would find what he was looking for, find his way back to whatever blissful eternity he wanted.

Barrier or no.

"He will," Ilyan whispered as Ryland's loud cries passed by us.

I listened to his sobs before the wind drowned them.

"Skříteks are released into the earth." His voice was calm as he pulled me from him, the blanket falling from one of my shoulders with the slow, mournful steps we took toward the final mound where Ryland and all the others were. "Drak's are released into sight. We release them from their past so they are free to find their futures."

My heart fell to my toes, my gut twisting painfully as Ilyan pulled me back to the horrors of what we were moving toward.

The small group was already making a circle around his body.

The icy air sucked the oxygen from my lungs, my heart twisting and cracking. I didn't want to be here. I didn't want to see this. Nevertheless, I couldn't stop moving forward. I couldn't stop everything from dying inside of me.

Everything from hurting.

Dramin lay in the middle of everyone, the sheet pulling against the icy blast that made it hard to stand, hard to breathe. Everyone was huddled under blankets and ripped coats, gathered around my brother as though we had come to hear him tell a story.

Risha and Jaromir had stayed covered as we had buried them and said good-bye, their bodies wrapped up tightly. In two steps, though, Ilyan went to Dramin and ripped the loose covering off, leaving him lying there, freezing in the winter air.

Freezing.

"He's cold." I didn't think anyone could hear me.

I had been to one funeral before these. I could still vividly see my grandmother lying in a casket, her arms folded against her stomach, against the pretty white dress that my family had chosen for her to wear. Her skin had been strangely pink, a lipstick that was far too red coating her lips. I could see the white satin of the casket and the rose-colored wood of the lid as they had closed it over her.

To me, that was death.

That was the end.

That was good-bye.

I had been wrong.

There was no fancy satin-lined casket. There was no fancy suit or gunk in Dramin's hair to make him look like he was going to a dinner party and had fallen asleep on the way. There was no makeup to cover the death that had taken over his face, his eyes sunken in, his lips shriveled and black, his skin gray and stretched over sallow cheeks, and a jaw that had shrunken.

He looked forgotten.

There was no soul left in him. Seeing him like that, seeing the life stripped from him until he was nothing but a vacant shell, made me wonder why the mortals tried to make their dead look like there was life still in them.

Yes, there was something to seeing a body the way that you remember them, but then, they are just a person in a box.

This man, he was gone.

You could tell he was gone. All that was left was sallow gray skin stretched over bones. The life was already lost.

"Please, if you knew this Drak's past, we ask you to join us, to step forward and help us to send his soul away." Ilyan pulled a large bottle and a handful of white handkerchiefs out of a large burlap bag one of the others had handed him.

They were handkerchiefs I recognized at once, and I tensed, the muscles in my shoulders tightening as my already pained heart began to beat faster.

Thom nodded, his body shaky as he moved away from the support Wyn was giving him in an attempt to reach his friend. Wyn, realizing he couldn't make it on his own, rushed to his side, flinging her arm around his waist in a bolster of support.

"You can be a man later," she scolded, and a small chuckle escaped from the dreadlocked man.

"What am I now, a goldfish?" Thom retorted, reaching toward his brother as Ilyan put the six handkerchiefs in his outstretched hand.

"If you keep acting like that, then yes," Wyn said.

They stood, Ryland joining them, as the handkerchiefs were passed between them, their smiles beginning to fade.

I stood, staring at them, at Dramin, at what was left of life, everything bathed in red.

I didn't know how long I stood there before Ilyan came over, pulling me toward the others ... pulling me toward my brother.

Wyn smiled sadly, her eyes swollen and red as she handed me a handkerchief, and the pace of my heart inside my chest accelerated. I was not quite sure what I was supposed to do with it or even if I wanted to touch it after everything I had seen.

Wyn moved back over beside Thom as, together, the four of them arranged their handkerchiefs in the palm of their left hands, the open palms extended out as though they were handing it to Dramin, yet he didn't see them.

I expected the brutal wind to pick up the light squares of white cotton and send them into the air like a scarf at a train station, but they stayed, still and calm, magic holding them in place while hair, coats, and blankets kept flying.

Without a word, I followed their example, ready to secure the handkerchief with my magic. The moment it hit my palm, however, the white cloth sagged against my skin, any life that was in it, any life the wind would have given it, sucked dry.

It was as dead as everything else.

The parallels were heartbreaking.

My mind did not need the whispered words that Ilyan provided, his words and magic calm and soothing in my mind.

Thank you, I whispered in response, my voice shaking inside of his mind.

His lips twitched before his focus lifted to mine, his bright blue eyes sad as they locked me in place, holding my confusion and heartbreak captive.

I wanted to tell him it was okay to cry, but I knew at once it wouldn't matter. He wasn't trying to avoid crying because of who he was or because of some image he had to portray. He was trying not to cry because he knew Dramin wouldn't want him to.

"Life is frail," Ilyan began in Czech, his voice a lullaby that rang across the icy air.

With those few words, everyone's attention turned to him. Those beside Dramin still stood with our hands outstretched.

"Our lives are strong, but they can be lost within a moment," Ilyan continued, and everyone nodded in agreement of the stark truths Ilyan was presenting.

I was left in the dark, the same dark I had been swimming in for days. The uncertainty put me on edge, made the emotions harder to handle.

"We have lost this life," Ilyan's voice broke, tears beginning to stream down his face.

He wasn't the only one.

Thom and Wyn were huddled against each other, sobbing in silence. The heavy shudder of Thom's breathing echoed around us like the ripple of fabric in the wind, ripping him apart. His pain lingered in the sound, cutting into my chest as my own sobs rose to meet his. Our heartbreak wove together as one painful keen.

"This life will be missed. This life met its end, and we will always remember his past as he goes on without us to find the depth of the future his sight has created for him," Ilyan said over the distressing sounds of our sobs, his own voice continuing to break right alongside ours.

Keeping his palm flat, he shifted his weight, lifting the large bottle as he clamped his teeth around the cork. I could feel his magic surge as he eased it out, and the bright smell of wine swirled through the icy air.

I wrinkled my nose at the scent. While familiar, it reminded me of way too many late nights in the LaRue's kitchen— Edmund's kitchen. It was a reminder I didn't need, not right now.

My stomach twisted uncomfortably as I pushed it away.

After spitting the cork into the dead grass, Ilyan put the opening of the bottle over the handkerchief, letting it hover there, one slight tip away from spilling over. He froze there, his emotions swirling powerfully through me as his magic began to shake, his hand trembling visibly.

"He taught me patience," Ilyan gasped out in pain, his hand tipping as he released the bright red fluid from the bottle, splashing it onto the white handkerchief he held. It landed against the cotton, the red against white abrasive as the droplets ran down the side of the fabric, absorbing into the white as he passed the bottle to Thom.

Thom's hand shook as my face burned and I tried to keep the tears hidden, but they came, anyway, as Thom poured his own amount onto the white cloth. The crimson stain spread over it, seeping into it as it stretched toward the edges until there were only a few spots of white left.

"He taught me how to love after everything was broken," Thom whispered, his eyes still focused on the red wine that was seeping throughout the fabric.

Without a word, he passed the bottle to Wyn. It was like before the battle, during the first night: a drink, a word, a tribute to those you have lost. No, not a tribute. A memory, a piece of his past.

Memories from each of us poured onto fabric like blood, dripping from our souls as we shared the intimacies of not only ourselves, but of the life we were honoring.

"He forgave me," was all Wyn said as she splashed a large amount of wine onto the cloth, the brilliant crimson seeping so fast I knew it wouldn't hold it all. It dripped from the edges onto the ice-coated grass like tears falling to the ground.

Without a word, Wyn handed the bottle to me, and my hand shook as I wrapped it around the neck. Thankfully, I didn't drop it as she let go. It was heavier than I expected it to be and slippery underneath my fingers.

"He reminded me I had a family," I said.

My nose tickled, the tears kept coming, and I could barely get the words out. I let them flow while staring at the white of the handkerchief before I poured the wine onto it. Watching the blood red absorb into it, I gasped, feeling the warmth against my hand, pooling in my palm hidden beneath the surface.

I stared at it for a moment too long before Ryland reached for the bottle, reminding me of what my job was.

He grabbed the bottle without hesitation, splashing some

onto his own, his lips a tight line as he said, "He was the man his father pretended to be."

The words struck home, and I gasped, my tears flowing more freely as Ilyan walked around Dramin's body, grabbing the bottle from Ryland and continuing the process all over.

"He showed me how to laugh."

"He never gave up on me."

"He saved me in more ways than he knew."

On and on, they went until each of our handkerchiefs were soaked with wine and our palms were full of the deep red fluid. Then the bottle was empty and set beside Ilyan's feet, rattling against dying grass and stone as it rocked in the wind that blew past everything. My emotions by now were so raw and open that I was amazed the wind didn't pick me up and carry me away.

Ilyan took a step forward and knelt in the dirt beside where my brother lay. Carefully, he placed the handkerchief over his face exactly as he had in the sight. The wine-soaked cloth covered the gray skin, the sunken eyes, and the jaw that looked so broken it didn't even resemble my brother anymore.

"I will take care of her as you asked," Ilyan said, his wine-soaked hand grasping my brother's dead one. His stiff fingers were like rocks underneath Ilyan's strong grip.

Ilyan did not move as Thom limped forward, Wyn helping him to kneel beside his brother. His hand shook as he, too, placed the cloth over Dramin's face.

"I will never forget what you have done for me," Thom

whispered, his hand replacing Ilyan's against the stiffness of Dramin's.

Without a word, Wyn knelt beside Thom near Dramin's feet and leaned over both of them to place her handkerchief over Dramin's face, on top of all the others.

"I will be worthy of your forgiveness," Wyn whispered, her hand clutching Dramin's before wrapping around Thom's. Her head fell onto his shoulder as the tears flowed freely.

Kneel across from me, můj kamarád, Ilyan prompted inside my mind, his voice quiet as he gave me the needed instruction.

Everything felt weak, numb, and broken. Each step opened up a new agonizing pit in my stomach as I moved toward him then kneeled across from him before I placed my handkerchief over Dramin's face.

"I will always be your sister."

I squished my face together in an attempt not to let the tears find a way past, in an attempt not to sob and cry like a pitiful little girl. Regardless, the sounds came out. The heartbreak bled from me, anyway. All I could do was sit there and cry.

I didn't even hear what Ryland said as he placed his handkerchief over my brother's face. I couldn't hear beyond the wind that roared around us and tried to carry me away. I couldn't hear beyond the sobs that racked my body.

They grew inside of me, swelling and growing into a pain I could no longer hold back, a pain I didn't want to feel anymore. I didn't want to. I let all of the anger, all of the pain, and all of the loss go in a crippling despondency that escaped from me in a scream so loud and feral everyone around me jumped.

I screamed as I clutched Dramin's hand. I screamed as I clawed at his arms. I screamed as I tried my hardest to shake him awake, knowing that it wouldn't work and not caring.

I clutched at his clothes, at his dead, lifeless arms. Everything was cold and stiff and uncomfortable and not him anymore. Not him ever again.

He was gone.

There was nothing left.

I cried so loudly and so hard I could barely move. I held on to Ryland and Wyn as they flanked me, holding me, trying to calm me.

It was no use. The heartbreak grew as I felt Ilyan's magic surge, the earth reacting to it, and the soil before us shifted and moved as it began to swallow Dramin whole.

The tears kept coming, and I tried to reach him, but he was already being swallowed by the dirt. He was already leaving.

He was going, and I couldn't go, too.

I couldn't.

But I wanted to.

I wanted him to come back.

Wyn and Ryland tried to hold me back as I lunged for him, part of me needing to claw him out and part of me needing to follow.

I had done this to him. I needed to make it better.

I could make it better.

It was the only thing that was left, that and tears. I didn't even know what was going on around me anymore. I could feel hands against my arms. I could hear pleadings in the air around me. But the next thing I knew, there was only dirt, and my magic was angry, and I was angry, and my magic surged to the surface as I screamed and Wyn grabbed me, trying to help me.

Our magic reacted, and everything went white.

But not the white of the sight I had pulled everyone into before. It was the white of the explosion I had seen outside of the cathedral, the blast so bright and so hot that everyone's shrieks rose to match mine. Everyone's pain rose to match mine.

Everyone was as trapped in it as I was.

It was then I realized who those two figures I had seen in the explosion of my sight were and why this moment was so cemented within our timeline.

As the explosion began to fade, as the cries of pain began to lessen, as the heat of the blast began to subside, I opened my eyes.

I opened my eyes to a beautiful, blue sky and to snow blowing over us all.

21

SAIN

THE SMELL of dirt and blood mixed with the scent of sweat and desperation in a way that was intoxicating. It lingered in the air and dripped against my skin in tiny pricks of energy, each one infecting me... awakening me.

Of course, I was positive it had more to do with what was coming than the two women below me who were currently pulling at each other's hair, a move that would normally insight cheers of glee in the crowds.

Only a few clapped their hands.

A coup was moments away. I could feel it in the pinpricks of my sight, feel it in the eagerness of the crowd, their attention half-focused on the battling women in the middle of the mud-filled pits. Their eyes constantly darted to me then darted to the large door inset into the floor of the arena.

Even if I hadn't seen what was coming within sight, I would have been able to guess. They gave themselves away.

Foolish Trpaslíks.

Smiling to myself, I sat back on the many velvet pillows that Edmund had used as a throne, sipping Black Water like wine. Wine for the greatest of shows.

One woman clawed at the other before wrapping her teeth around the soft flesh of her neck and pulling. Red sprayed from her neck in a fountain as a large chunk of flesh was pulled from her like overcooked meat.

The comical reaction was enough to pull the audience's attention from what was coming. With a roar, they cheered as the bleeding woman fell to the ground in a heap while the victor turned to me, her eyes dangerous as she smiled.

I laughed at the look, the raw danger she tried so hard to show me. Yes, she would be good in battle; I could see that at once. However, it was the warning behind her eyes that forced the laugh from my chest.

The threat was clear. She might as well have said, "You're next, Sain."

I laughed harder, the sound echoing around the stadium as her face fell.

Even the Chosen who were being forced to fight for their lives knew what was coming. They were ready to try to overthrow me as much as the Trpaslíks who were now looking at me with varying degrees of fear and confusion.

"I am quite ready for this attempted coup to begin," I said underneath the laugh quiet enough that Ovailia could hear from where she sat, nestled against my legs, one tier of bleachers down.

Below me where she belonged, where she would die.

Maybe I would end her in the pits just like all of these fools.

Ovailia didn't turn to look at me. Her hand shifted to rub against my leg, her magic swelling. "Is that why you are laughing?" Her voice was dark molasses, sweet and dangerous. It drifted across the tense anticipation in the air like candy, swirling over everything.

I sighed, pulling long strands of her hair gently before running my fingers over the top of her head.

She shivered, her magic quivering alongside, and my smile grew.

"Among many things." My voice was even lower now, something Ovailia didn't seem to mind. Damek, however, stepped closer to us, away from the door he was supposed to be guarding, his fear unabashed as he tried to pick up as much of the conversation as he could.

With one sharp look, I caught him in the act, sending him scuttling back toward the entrance to our little alcove, his shoulders hunched and shivering.

I would have to punish him for that little trick later. Maybe let him and Ovailia battle it out in a pit of their own.

The women in the pits had given me something to chew on.

"Did you see the look on her face?" I whispered into Ovailia's ear, meeting the glare of the woman below me, the hatred fading a bit due to the look I fixed her with.

"Hers?" Ovailia asked, her voice shaking a bit as I leaned down toward her, pressing my cheek against hers, our conversation hidden from prying ears.

"Yes. Did you see the hatred?"

Ovailia shivered as my magic pressed against her, searching for hers. I let it flow, feeling her unease. The emotion was so strong I could taste it. Delicious.

"I saw the darkness in her eyes," Ovailia answered, her uncertainty fading as she pushed strength into her voice. The stoicism that I loved bled into me as she lifted her hand, brushing it against my forearm, her magic sparking pleasantly against my skin. With that one touch, my magic reacted, attempting to connect with hers as she attempted to connect with me. It took all my will to keep my magic restrained. "She wanted to kill you. Do you want to kill her?"

"I want to kill them all," I answered as a roar encompassed the crowd, the sound loud enough that I jerked.

With my cheek still pressed against Ovailia's, I glanced toward the pit, my heart a thunder of hope that perhaps this would be the start. But no, it was just two scrawny teenage boys dressed in blood-soaked clothes that I knew didn't originally belong to them.

They looked at me with the same defiance the woman had. Their hands pressed against their hearts in a salute before they bowed, the motion rehearsed as they turned, shaking in preparation for death.

"I *will* kill them all," I declared, my voice a snake as I smiled. The eagerness for what was to come flourishing.

"Will you?" Ovailia whispered, turning her head toward me as the words grazed across my cheek in hot breath and soft lips.

Heart racing in both need and disgust, I pulled away from her, looking her full in the face as my temper howled under

347

my skin. "Don't question me," I snapped. She flinched, the reaction fueling my authority more. "I don't need bottom feeders, Ovi. You either follow me, or I dispose of you. Don't you like your spine where it is, inside your pretty little back?" I ran my finger up the appendage in question, tracing over the fine silk of her shirt.

She jerked, attempting to move away from the threat, from the look in my eyes. But I held her against me, letting my magic shoot into the bones of her back in tiny shots of pain.

"I keep telling you not to unleash the hell inside of me, Ovailia. Why must you keep defying me?" I kept my voice low, the deep, sultry notes affecting her the way I knew they would. The woman melted beneath me in fear, in need. "Do you want to see hell?"

"I want to see the end, Sain." She smiled, the grin long and menacing as it stretched over her face.

An end, I could give her. An end of a blood red blade as it intersected with her neck.

My own smile stretched, fueled by the sight my magic had given me which was playing on repeat.

"I want to give that to you, Ovailia. I can end this once and for all. *We* can end this once and for all," I continued. The words were a lie, bitter and gross in my mouth. I knew I didn't mean it, and I was certain she knew it, too. *We* would not do anything.

It didn't matter, however. She smiled, anyway, drowning in the power I taunted her with. The power she had wanted since the very beginning.

"Then let's end this," she said, her voice full of lust and

need, her magic pressing against me again in that disgusting desire. I let it twist over me, my own spreading to join hers, my heart betraying me with the contact.

"Let's." I was drowning in her proximity, desperate to connect to her, to feel her.

I considered slapping myself back to my senses; I would have if it weren't for the roar that went up from the crowd, the noise signaling the end of yet another battle.

I didn't even glance toward the stands to congratulate the winner. I was pretty certain what I would find down there, anyway. I could already smell the blood. And sure enough, the boys were covered in it. But they were both still standing, very much alive. They were both staring at me.

Staring just like everyone else.

"It's time," I announced, a sneer twisting over my lips as excitement invaded me.

My sight wasn't far behind, pushing against me in need, but I thrust it away, letting my deeper magic flare, bringing it to the ready. I had already seen what was about to happen; I didn't need another recap. I did, however, need to be ready for a fight.

"Go get my creature, Ovailia," I hissed.

My anger drenched her pretty blue eyes in a luscious syrup. Watching her was like watching a well-practiced Oscar performance. Anger, seduction, lust, frustration—they all played upon her face in perfect harmony, stirring my own hunger from deep inside of me.

"Make Damek do it," she hissed, her anger growing. "I need to be here. They need to see us sta—"

"They need to see where my power lies. It is not with you!" The snap of my voice smacked her right across the face, and she flinched, cowering away from me.

Ovailia. Cowering. The brief image was beautiful.

I had always been told that the witch couldn't be controlled, that she could never be a true servant. Yet, here she was, beautifully submissive.

"Go. Get. The. Creature." I snapped each word like a whip, each one making her recoil, curling up her spine. "*We* need to show them what we are capable of. You are not *we*, not right now." Pushing a hard edge into my voice, I moved away from her, leaning back against the rich softness of the pillows, the plush red blending perfectly with the bloodstained bathrobe I still wore. "Go," I spoke without even looking at her, my focus on the boys below me as all of us waited for the next step in the show to start.

I knew it was coming.

Ovailia left without another word, her sheet of hair falling down her back against the red silk of her dress. The crimson matched her shoes that tapped over the distant screeches of the crowd. They were a countdown that ended with the smack of a heavy door somewhere in the distance.

Pushing her out of my mind, I forced my focus back to the pits, back to the men who were now walking onto the field, back to the deathly silence that had suddenly taken over the space.

George and Bronislav walked into the center of the pit, the

sound of their steps against the blood-soaked dirt so thunderous I could hear them echo off the metal stands. They ricocheted, the tone of fearful exhilaration so loud now that I could swim in it.

I looked down at the men as they looked up at me. Their faces were filled with gaunt exhilaration. Bronislav's smile was visible from under his beard, the look so out of character for him that I could laugh.

And I did.

I laughed.

I laughed in the silence with a deep belt of humor. I laughed over the tension, and everyone in the stands turned to face me, their previous countenances of eager bloodlust vanishing into confusion and fear.

I didn't stop laughing as I rose from my pillows, and the robe caught in the breeze, sending my magic out from me in a powerful, impenetrable shield. Keeping the magic steady and strong, I stepped forward over the metal bleachers, dancing and jumping until I stood atop the lowermost tier, facing the usurpers and all of their minions, all of whom were ready to rip my head from my shoulders, all of them blissfully unaware of what was coming for them.

"Friends," I yelled, my voice a boom over the nonexistent chatter of the crowd. I lifted my arms in wide vulnerability. "You wonderful friends, I knew I could trust you to put together this wondrous event! You have done it! What an amazing way to celebrate the people we have become! To celebrate the possibilities that are before us."

Keeping the widest smile I could, I plastered on all the

sugar, sharing the feigned gratitude in a slather that they gobbled up. My smile was exuberant.

"You have done such a wonderful job that I would like to give you something," I began, the sugar that had dripped from my words leeching into acid, rancid tones that weren't missed. "A gift if you will."

All signs of the jovial character I had created vanished in a flash. Arms falling, I then lifted a large, red blade from my pocket, the same blade I had used to destroy Edmund, the same one they had all seen protruding from the chest of his corpse.

Visibly, they stiffened. Even Damek jerked from where he stood in the corner. Quick side-glances pulsed between the men below me as Bronislav shifted his feet, debating whether or not to run. I wished he would.

Twisting the blade in my fingers like a parade baton, I took a step down onto the narrow metal rail that separated the stands from the large open pit the two men stood in. It was a sheer drop of at least fifteen feet from where I stood, pacing and dancing on the narrow line. With the shield still tightly pressed against me, I waited for the first attack.

"It's the best kind of gift. Would you like it?" I asked as I jumped along the railing, the red blade reflecting the color of death over the stands as it spun between my fingers.

I expected the scared men to begin whatever pathetic attempt at a rebellion they had planned, knowing the pride of the Trpaslíks. Instead, Bronislav nodded in agreement. The smile was gone from his lips as he narrowed his eyes at me.

Well, that was unexpected. No matter. Slight changes were meaningless. They were still walking into death, and being close enough to see the look on their faces when death met them face to face was an added bonus.

My heart thundering wildly in my chest, I jumped, the wind and magic catching me as I soared down to the pits, landing lightly before the two men. All signs of their fear were gone as they smiled at me, their eyes glistening as though they already thought they had won, something I was content to let them believe for now.

Bronislav held out his hand the moment I landed. When I stepped toward him, the man smiled, the look in his eyes giving him away so obviously I laughed, the sound cutting into them. As close to them as I was, I could see them wilt. I could see their supposed victory slip between their fingers.

"Oh," I said, my voice dark as I let it rattle over the stands, hitting all of them. "You thought this was the gift?"

My laugh continued, pressing against them and wilting their souls as I twirled the blade once in my hand before tucking it into my pocket. The men watched the movement, their eyes widening as their jaws began to open and close in panic and fear.

They thought it would be that easy.

Fools.

"No, no, no, no." I clicked my tongue with each word as I shook my head.

Circling around them, I looked up at the stands, my heart thundering pleasantly due to the mirrored look from all those above me as well as below. Panic, confusion—they all felt them. Now I needed the last piece to fall into place. I needed the fear to come. Then they would be mine. Luckily, that piece was steps away.

"This is not your prize. I have a prize for all of you!" I yelled to the crowd as I stopped in place, the backs of the two Trpaslíks to my left, bare and vulnerable. "Ovailia! Come, my darling. Let us show them!" My voice rang throughout the stadium, my eyes cast toward the large door I had hidden Alojz behind earlier that day. My heart thundered in my ears, excitement ringing as I waited for the doors to swing wide, for my creation to enter.

There was nothing.

Nothing but silence.

"Ovailia!" I yelled, the single word echoing around the silent space, banging against the two men beside me, against everyone in the stands, wiping the panic from their faces, smearing it over my chest in a coating so thick I was having trouble breathing. This is not what happened in the sight.

This was not what I had seen.

"No," I gasped, the word swallowed by the laughter that had begun to pop around the stands, little titters that quickly began to multiply.

"You're right," Bronislav said from behind me, his own laugh clear. "This is a wonderful gift. I'll have to thank Ovailia for abandoning you. We hadn't planned on that."

"What had you planned on?" I snapped, turning toward the man, the robe rippling behind me. I expected them to cower, but they both stood, smiling, looking far too smug and proud.

I would smack that look off their pretty little faces.

"This," Georg said with a smile, his arms folding over his chest as something hit me in the back and pain swept over my ribs and down my spine.

Someone stabbed me in the back.

22

OVAILIA

"Do it now." Damek's whispered words followed me into the underbelly of the stadium, locked inside my head as I was locked out of Sain's little alcove. All with the snap of a door. A snap that ricocheted painfully inside my head, mixing with the angry thunder of my heartbeat and the rapid pulse of my breathing.

As if I needed another reason to go through with our plan. As if I needed another reason to destroy that man.

No matter what pain awaited me on the other side of this choice, I couldn't say no. It was worth it if only for the chance to see him bleed.

I always knew his promises of regality and equality were for the horses. But now, to be treated as nothing more than a servant ...

"No one treats me this way," I hissed, taking one last look at the door before I stepped away, my heels clicking against the cement as my heart pounded in my ears. The sounds were discordant, like in an out of tune marching band that pulled me forward. My anger fueled my magic into a rumble.

"We will show them, will we, Sain?" I said in an irritated jest, my brow furrowing in a deep scowl. The tap of heels grew louder, my gait increasing into a run. "Will we?"

Magic sparked through the air around me with the pulse of my anger. Angry little pops of it swept over the air in snaps, singeing the metal framework of the underside of the bleachers black, sending smoke and ash into the air behind me. The air was burning like everything else in this world. Everything in this life I had chosen.

Let it burn. I would set it on fire.

The sparks of my magic continued, igniting over walls and sky. Ashes fell around me as I came to a stop, color and light dripping through the air and down the concrete steps inches before me.

I stood, watching the color fade into the dark cavern, staring down the long, dark stairwell that Sain had sent me to. The haunted cave would take me down to the pit, down to the cage where Sain had taken Alojz ... where he expected me to release him like a lion into the arena.

That was my job. That was all he wanted of me ... until he killed me. The need for that moment was growing in him, I saw it swell in his eyes every time he spoke of my beauty, every time he spoke of my future. Even though he might mean them, they were words that were based on lust; a bitter falsehood for what he really meant. For what he really wanted. I could see that in the look, in the desire he fixed on me. I had the same in me, the same need to end him. I was just better at concealing it.

"Do it now," I repeated Damek's words aloud, my hair falling around my face as I took one step closer to the stairs, the toes of my heels pressing against the edge of the topmost step, my weight pulling me forward.

My hatred pulled me back.

Damek and I had originally agreed that we would release the mutilated Alojz before going to the girl. That way, Sain wouldn't have any idea anything had changed in our loyalty, that anything was wrong, not until the knife pierced his back.

Quick. Seamless. He would never suspect.

Standing here at the top of the stairs, however, I didn't care. I didn't care if he found out. I didn't care if he knew.

I wanted to kill Sain.

It was all there was: Sain's death and my freedom. I didn't know what would be waiting for me without a master to serve, but this master was not the one I thought I had chosen.

As I stepped back, the single beat of my shoe reverberated, sparking along the cement floors in a bolt of lightning that stretched out from me in a spider's web. It burned the cement in charred design that someone else would have to admire.

I had already turned. I was already running, my heels clacking, breath heaving. I bolted back down the hall, past the outcropping where Sain was nestled against his blood-soaked robe and pillows, past the entry hall that was nothing more than shredded canvas and broken sconces, and into the icy air of the Chosen's camp.

The biting wind smacked against my face and sucked the air from my lungs with the first step outside the warm confines of the tents. It hit against the bare skin of my arms and past the thin fabric of my dress. I gasped, my skin breaking into gooseflesh as I plunged myself into it, dreaming of the heavy fur that still hung on the wall where Damek stood by the door, staring at Sain.

Staring at our target.

I didn't have much time.

Judging by the still quiet of the camp, everyone was in the stadium, and without a peep hissing from the massive structure, nothing had started.

No battle. No bloodshed.

If I was lucky, he wouldn't know of my plot yet. He wouldn't know of my betrayal. It was moments away. I had only moments.

Ice and snow swirled in the air around me as I ran through the tent village. Tiny specks of wetness hit against my already frigid skin and deepened the cold that was now seeping into my bones.

With one flare of my magic, I could warm myself, but it wasn't worth the risk. Once he knew what I had done, he would search for me. He would find my magic. He would find me, but even worse, he would find the girl. I couldn't risk that, not until she got me back into the dome then to Ilyan.

Picking up my pace, I ran faster, dodging between tents, running past them. Canvas rippled behind me as I emerged from another one, stopping in place as shouts of fear lifted from the stadium. I turned toward it, my hair fanning out as it was tossed in the wind. I stared at the stadium, my heart pulsing as more screams joined the first.

He knew.

It had started.

Without waiting, I turned, running faster. My heels sunk into the soft earth, the sharp points of the heels collapsing so fast that, with each step, my legs wobbled and shifted awkwardly beneath me. With a groan, I ditched the heels, bidding a silent good-bye to the bright red beauties. Then I turned another corner, dodging into a large tent.

The icy air evaporated as the canvas fell closed behind me, trapping me inside the hot air that smelled of feces and blood. The aroma twisted my stomach, threatening to boil it over.

Clenching my teeth together, I clapped my hand over my mouth, determined to keep the bile down, desperate to smell the perfume I had spritzed myself with this morning and not the vile aroma I was trapped in.

Suddenly wishing I hadn't been so hasty to leave my shoes, I stepped over the cluttered mess, stepping in something far too moist and far too soft. While I tried not to think of what filth had defiled me, I pursed my lips and continued toward the back corner, toward the moving blankets covering the only living creature in this tent.

Nests of blankets and sleeping bags were spread over the floor. The pattern was so uneven I skipped and jumped in an attempt to get to where I was going. A wide step over a brown and gray blanket, a hop over a pile of blood-colored clothes. Another step and the canvas of the massive tent shifted, the sound a jolt that jerked through me, sending me leaping over a sleeping bag and turning toward the door, my magic flaring between my fingers in expectation of someone being there.

Of Sain having found me.

There was nothing except the canvas of the tent as it shifted in the wind and the piles of who knew what that I had already danced past.

"You're mighty jumpy," a little voice tittered from behind me.

I jumped even farther, twisting in the air to face the little girl I had come to find. The girl who was the key to making this plan work.

Míra.

She stood not far from me, emerged from her blankets in a rat's nest of clothing and hair. Her long locks were cut short and darkened, her eyes bloodshot and desperate. She looked like her brother, or so she had told me, something she wasn't very happy about.

She didn't smile; she glowered at me with that same dead gaze she'd had since the moment she had woken up. Her face was the same except for a long scar that ran from her right eye and down to her neck. The nasty looking thing was still pink and healing.

"I was coming to get you," I retorted, popping my hip as I took a step closer, narrowing my eyes at her.

I hadn't liked this little girl's defiance when Edmund had

chosen her, and I didn't like it now. If we didn't need her so much, I would have disposed of her as Sain had asked.

He was the one who had left the task up to me and Damek. Maybe he was too trusting.

"I know. I remember the plan," she said, obviously irritated. "You seem to be here earlier than I was expecting. Has the coup already started?"

"I don't see how that's any of your concern," I snapped, my irritation bubbling up. I already barely had enough time to get in and out of Prague and to do that before Sain tracked us down.

This girl was trying my patience.

"If you want to find your brother, you tell me." She was defiant, stubborn. It boiled through me, and I gave a dark sneer as I stepped forward.

The effect was lessened without my heels, but she still jerked. I could see her debate whether she should step back.

I wished she would.

"We've been over this, little girl," I taunted, keeping my voice high. "I saved your life, which means I own it."

Her defiance faded, boiling back down into anger as I put her in her place. The death in her eyes twisted even further into the anger and revenge that fueled her.

She narrowed her eyes at me, her lips and nostrils flaring as she fixed me with a glower as deep as the ones I had mastered so long ago.

"Did you deviate from the plan?" she snapped, jumping over the large sleeping nests to get to me, her body moving fast.

"I did what was needed, little girl." My voice swallowed hers as I stepped even closer. I stood over her, looking down at the child who looked up at me, her jaw set and eyes hard as she met my glower match for match, her anger rivaling mine.

"We had a plan, Ovailia," she hissed, stepping so close she had to look straight up to attempt to make eye contact.

The image of her craning her neck to see me was comical. Unable to help it, I laughed, the noise dark and haunting as it filled the large tent. The sound danced with the steady beat of the canvas as it moved with the wind, with the sounds of battle that were slowly filtering through the fabric. I guessed it was in full-force now.

"I didn't break it. It doesn't need fixing. But now we are going to make it better." I grabbed her arm, ready to pull her out of the tent and into a stutter, but she pulled away, jerking her arm from me.

"I am the last piece of your father's magic," she yelled, still looking at me with that same awkward positioning. "I am the magic you need in order to kill that man."

Stiffening, the fear I had felt from the moment I had turned away from the stairwell ramped up, twisting in my gut and soul in an uncomfortable pain that ripped through me.

She was right, and I hated it.

I wanted nothing more than to rip this little girl limb from limb, teach her not to defy me, teach her not to stand up to me. Make her pay for thinking she was better than me. But I couldn't, because she was right. I needed her. And as the smile spread over her face, the blood hungry glare returning to her eyes, I could tell she knew it, too.

"You are to get me to my brother, Míra," I said, my voice strained beneath the iron clench in my teeth.

"Then we can kill Sain?" She smiled, seeming as innocent as a child asking for candy.

Bouncing on the balls of her feet, she stepped away from me, her eyes dancing with a look that banished my fear for the briefest second.

"You can kill anyone you want," I answered, turning back toward the entrance, ready to begin.

One step into the chill, I knew everything had changed, more than the coup.

Panic had gripped the camp. The previously abandoned site was now full of people who were running and screaming. More than that, it was full of fear. I could see it on each of their faces as they sped past the camp, casting glances behind them in wide-eyed horror as though they were being chased.

As though they were being hunted.

Except, no one attacked. No one fought. In this camp of magic, not one spell was cast, yet the fear increased, the running increased. The cries rang in my ears, tensing the muscles in my neck.

"What did you do, Ovailia?" Míra asked as she appeared beside me, the tent flap closing and leaving us standing in the bitter wind. "Do your feet smell that bad?"

Normally, I would smack the girl down to her place for such a comment, but with the fear in their faces ... Something was seriously wrong.

Gingerly, I stepped my bare foot forward, placing my tender sole against the ice-covered ground. A chill swept up my leg, frigid ice that was ignored as I continued forward, the running hordes spreading around me with each step.

Like the breaking of waves, they moved around me, hitting my shoulders and banging against my legs. I should have yelled at them. I should have commanded their allegiance. I almost did ... until I turned toward what they were all running from and saw what they were all afraid of.

The glare that was so familiar to my brow faded, my eyes widening in panic.

"What is it?" Míra asked as she came up beside me, her eyes widening as she, too, saw the city, saw the soldiers who were streaming into the camp, saw the Vilÿs that were not far behind.

The city, the encampment ... It was free. The barrier was down.

The red dome was gone.

But we were also under attack.

"Well, great. What are we going to do now?" Míra asked, the question pulling me out of my stupor and back to the girl. The tiny thing was pressed against me as the wall of people jostled against her.

"I need to find Ilyan," I snapped, everything falling into place as I forced myself to look away from the city and back at the girl, back to the plan that had suddenly become much more of a dire necessity.

"Then let's go." Míra grabbed my wrist, ready to stutter me past the barrier as we had discussed.

"There is no need for that, Míra." I pulled my arm away from her grip with far too much force. "The barrier is down. I can get there myself. I need you to go into Imdalind. Find the blade I told you about. We need to get it before—"

"Go alone? What if Sain senses your magic? What if he 'sees' you?" Míra asked, her eyes wide as someone else ran into her, jostling her around before she came right back to standing. "You said—"

"That barely matters now," I snapped. "There will be much more magic heading right toward him, and I need to find them before they get here. Do you understand?"

She nodded once, grinding her teeth together, her eyes back to the hard death look that was so familiar to her.

"Find Damek if you can. Find the blade, hide it and meet me in the old hall, where the men would meet. Once we have the blade and Ilyan we can end Sain. It's the only way. We need a blade in our possession before we are to face him. Do you understand?" I didn't even look at her. I stared at the city, at the ruins that were alive with light and Vilÿs as they took off into the air, attacking the dozens of helicopters and planes that soared across the now open sky.

Fire erupted from one as the Vilÿs took control, sending the helicopter down toward the city in a ball of fire. The soldiers who were going around the tents, searching for survivors, looked back at the explosion, only to increase their search.

Many of them began to drop to the ground, attacked by the winged monsters my father had created.

This game had suddenly become very dangerous.

"You'll need to stay hidden, Míra," I finished, finally turning back to the girl. "These men will stop you. The Vilỳs will eat you. Everyone will destroy you."

"Don't worry, Ovailia." A smile spread over her face so wide and innocent that it looked out of place, stretching her features the wrong way. "My brother died because of him. I'd rather die before he sees another day." She smiled again, her white teeth glinting in the obstructed light. Then she turned from me, running around the tents and dodging soldiers and Vilỳs before she disappeared completely, shrouded by her magic.

"Ma'am!" a deep voice yelled at me, and I turned to face a large man clad in black armor, a large, unnecessary gun in his hands. "Do you need help? We have a large—"

"You are the ones who will need help," I said, the chill in my voice matching the icy air that swirled around us.

The soldier looked at me in confusion. The look switched to fear as a Vilỳ flew behind me, coming right up, ready to attack.

"Zdechnout," I hissed, and the creature fell to the ground with a thud.

Meanwhile, the soldier had cocked his gun, ready to fire. He stood, staring at me, confused about what had happened, confused about what I was and what side I was on.

"Ma'am," he said, his voice shaking underneath the strength he tried to convey.

I smiled, the power in my look making the gun shake in his hands.

"I'm going to have to ask you to come with me."

"So you can save me?" A deeper grin, a bigger shake.

"Ma'am—"

"You think you saved us from hell?' I asked, lifting my fingers to look at my perfectly manicured red nails. "You and your men have released it. You better hope I can kill him first."

I smiled at the man who stepped back in obvious confusion. His eyes widened as he looked around him, desperate for backup, but before he could find anything, I snapped my fingers, sending a wall of flames up around us, circling the tiny alcove of the campsite in flame.

"Run," I said before I left him, vanishing into thin air and leaving the man standing in the flames, staring at nothing but fire. Facing nothing but death.

For the first time, I actually hoped I could succeed before Sain killed us all.

23

JOCLYN

With a *whoosh* of wind, the barrier fell. It pulled at coats and hair and dirt with such force that I was afraid it would sweep us away, back to the city that was now bathed in bright light.

Cowering against the force, we huddled over the fresh grave of my brother, snow swirling around us and coating everything with a fresh layer of white.

Just as it had in all the sights I'd had of this moment.

The cold air bit against my nose and cheeks as I looked up from the security of Dramin's old blanket. The wind swirled before the gap in fur and skin as, for the first time, I saw the city of ruins that had been my home for the last few months.

Everything looked different in the yellow light of the sun. The hauntingly beautiful frame of this skeletal city glistened in the light. Broken glass twinkled from the twisted stone of the ancient architecture. The beauty of the dilapidation did not last before the wind began to slow and the screams began to fill the air. The howls of the creatures that had hunted us for so long ripped through the silence of the snow, tiny specks of brown and gray emerging from their hiding places within the ruins and exploding into the sky in streams of the undead. They defiled the beauty of the scene in ribbons of mud, the winged rats ready to feast on new meat.

With my heart clenched in fear, an angry agony gripped me as I pushed myself to stand, ready to soar into the air and fight the things, to stop them as they began to swarm the helicopters of the mortals who were already soaring into the city.

I got one foot off the ground, ready to follow Wyn and Ilyan who were already running to the low outcropping on the hill we stood on, but instead I collapsed in a terrifying free fall, my head spinning as my magic pushed through me with a speed that sucked the breath from my chest.

My sight spiked as I fell, the image of everyone running toward the city clear, only to have everything plunge to black with the impact of my head against the frozen earth.

The hollow memory of screams rang in my ears, the sound fading into the same black I looked into, my magic growing and swelling as it taunted me with sight.

However, there was nothing.

The heavy weight of the nothing pressed against my chest, spinning inside my head so fast I wasn't sure what way was up anymore.

Then it stopped. Everything settled as the sound of my own breathing broke past the black in quick and fearful gasps.

"It has broken," my own, older, voice cut through the dark.

The calm settled in my heart before I was plunged into color, my mind swarming with image after image as they flashed past me then slowed as the yell of the woman pulled at them, showing me bits and pieces of what I had missed, of what Sain had blocked.

Sain and Ovailia stood in an unfamiliar room. Sain ran his hand over her skin gently, his words soft when he whispered in her ear. The affection was not returned, however. When Sain was not looking, her face twisted, a hatred I had thought was only reserved for me glinting in her eyes. The hatred infiltrated the sight, the walls around them dripping with it before they faded.

My sight picked up into a sprint as flashes of cathedrals and funerals and tents and caves moved past me, some familiar, some new. Everything was confusing until my focus pulled toward a large stadium, Sain walking across the center of the empty arena.

My heart took off at once, this was something I hadn't seen in weeks, something new.

With a smile and a flourish, Sain opened a large door, and a mournful whimper seeped from the dark in a haunting melody. It cut into my heart, twisting in my stomach, against my ribs. Sain, however, smiled wider, his eyes glinting with delight.

My soul turned to ice at the look, an anger I hadn't known rising up. I would have stuttered right to him and destroyed him if I could, but this was the past, and the twisted man was no longer there. Still, the need remained, following me as I was pushed back into the quick succession of sights.

The images slowed as I caught a glimpse of Cail holding me in the forest, taunting Sain with my existence before his knife moved over my throat. The image immediately shifted to another of the wide pool I had seen before.

The water was still and calm, unmoving. Meanwhile, the ghostly shadow I knew to be me flickered in and out of the scene, appearing and reappearing with each painful beat of my heart.

I disappeared with a thud, watching the pool in expectation of my return. Instead of myself, it was a bright blue reflection against the water, a single dot of light floating above and below the surface. My eyes widened at the sight of it there, something pulling me toward it, needing to be with it. I could feel my magic swell with the need. But before I could act, it all vanished, plunging me through flashes of sight before settling on a something I had seen before.

A little boy ran down an alley, attacking the swollen and poisoned Vilÿs with ease; the power beyond what a child should be able to do.

He turned the corner, running past a stone storefront and into what was unmistakably the cave. It took me a moment to realize the change, to notice the stutter within the sight.

I stared at it, confused as to its meaning. I had seen this before. I knew that child, but he lay buried beneath the snow behind me. This scene could never be, and yet, here it was.

He ran into a darkened room where Ovailia stood, disheveled and broken in the dark, her bare feet bleeding against the stone, obviously waiting for him.

"I got it," the child said in a panic before the door closed behind them.

The voice pulled me from my expectation, hitting me hard against the chest.

It wasn't Jaromir.

It was Míra.

"Wonderful, and my brother?"

"He was in the blue room, the one where the fight broke out..."

"Stay here." Ovailia rose in the dark, standing before the girl in a red dress that was ripped and stained with mud. "I will retrieve my brother, and we will finish this."

Ovailia held out her hand in expectation, Míra stepping toward her as she pulled a jagged shard of red stone from her pocket.

A blade.

Ilyan.

This was it. This was how she was going to kill him. And Míra was going to help.

I had been wrong. I had been wrong from the beginning. The girl wasn't going to save him.

She was responsible for his death.

The thought hit me when the sight shifted again, pulling me back into the large, carved hallways of the cave. Zooming amidst them like a mouse trapped in a maze, the motions pulled at the panic Ovailia had given me.

The emotion grew as the frantic movements continued, growing faster and faster until they stopped, freezing in place at the sight of a little girl standing in the middle of the hall, a child I had seen before, blood dripping over her face.

She stood there, her dark hair hanging limply around her face, blood dripping from her hair and hands into pools of red and black. Rosy looked at me with eyes as dead and black as her mother's, made it clear she could see me, even in sight.

"This is where I died."

The pain in her voice pulled at me, ripping me away from the child and dragging me back down the halls I had traveled, right into the room I had seen time and time again.

But this time, it was not the little girl who stopped the movement. It was Ilyan standing with the same death in his eyes, standing with the same blood dripping over him.

"This is where I die," he said, his voice as dead and lifeless as hers.

"No!" I bellowed, the word ripping through me again and again as the sight began to move, down more halls, deep into the dark and to that same pool I had seen time and time again, the older version of me standing at the banks.

"This is where we change the world." She said, her voice the same hollow that had been present in my sights since the cathedral came done.

She left in a flash as a roulette of moments sped over my mind before stopping on the static-filled images of the past: to Edmund who stood in a white robe before Sain, the vile man cowering before Edmund, his laugh booming inside my mind. Slowly, Sain stood, Edmund's eyes widening as the pathetic man grew before him. A bright red blade glinted in his hand before he plunged it into Edmund's chest, Edmund's scream following as the sight shifted, fading to a dimly lit hall and Edmund's corpse walking along a stage.

Edmund's call of death faded, the sound overrun by shouts of fear. The sight shifted to his people, to their fear, before the images faded. The shouts increased as the images grew from the black into the same stadium I had seen before. This time, it was full of people. It was full of destruction.

Everyone fought against each other while Sain stood in the middle, laughing. He laughed as the people he was supposed to rule fell to their deaths. He laughed as he forced Chosen to step before him, wastefully ending their lives in an attempt to save his.

The stadium rumbled with an explosion then, and my sight flashed alongside the blast with a single image of the pool, of the blue light. My heart and magic reacted with the same desperation as before.

Sain's laugh echoed through the still silence of the space, banging inside of my head before the black returned. Everything came back into focus, leaving me staring at the blue sky from where I lay, snow dusting over me.

Ilyan, Wyn, Thom, and Ryland looked over me with concerned expressions. Ilyan was angry rather than upset. He knew I was okay, and from the anger clear on his face, he knew what I had seen.

"Are you okay, Jos?" Wyn asked, her voice uncharacteristically freaked. The panic she stared at me with made it seem like I was dead.

But I wasn't, not yet.

Without a word, I scuttled away from them, gasping for breath in an attempt to regain my bearings, desperate to put the onslaught of information I had received together in my head.

The icy air bit at my lungs as I heaved, my chest burning with each breath. I focused on the pain as everything fell into place, knowing exactly what we were heading into and not liking it.

Ilyan! I yelled into his mind.

The man scuttled after me, wrapping the fur I had left behind around my shoulders. It was something I was instantly grateful for. The chill of winter was too much for me.

Mi lasko. His concern was obvious. His touch was soft as he reached for me, but his eyes were hard, his jaw set.

I could feel the strength of his fear and anger through our connection, the replay of the sight consuming him.

"You saw?" I gasped, desperate not to have to replay it all for him yet panicked he might have seen too much.

I didn't need him to see his own blood-covered visage. I hadn't needed to see it, either.

"I saw enough," Ilyan said, the source of his emotions becoming clear. "My father is dead."

I nodded in acknowledgment, letting my memories of the sight flicker through him until he landed on the one I couldn't shake: of Ovailia and Míra in that dark room, plotting his death.

We messed up. It was hard to keep the tears at bay. It was hard to admit what that choice really meant for us.

For him.

It will be all right, my love, he whispered into my mind, running his hand over my hair as he held me.

His body was tense and fearful against mine. His heartbeat plunged inside of me in a quick staccato beat, fueled by his fear and anger. The power in this man twisted through me, igniting my magic in a heat that burned the air.

"It will be," I said to myself, my voice swept away by the wind as I leaned against Ilyan. The two of us, bundled together, sitting on the cold ground.

The others came to us in a rush. Ryland and Thom looking troubled. Wyn, however, wasn't even looking at us. Her focus was passed us, over the small outcropping of hills, toward the broken city that was alive with screams.

"Guys," she whispered, her voice dead, "I think we might have a problem."

Heart lodged in my toes, I turned, the wind blowing my hair over my face, over the ruins that were now a battlefield.

Smoke rose from the city in long tendrils, the gray plumes masking the Vilỳs that swarmed from place to place, heading right for us.

"We are shielded," Ilyan announced as he stood, his magic emanating from his skin with a powerful pressure. The strength hit against me, pulling me in. "They cannot see us."

"Thanks, bro," Thom said with a grunt. "I'd rather not go through that again."

"Mortals are idiots," I growled as I jumped to my feet, glowering at the city as if it had offended me. They kind of deserved it. "We ripped apart the only thing that was keeping them safe. They should be running away."

They had started a battle as we were about to go into another one.

"No, no, no," Wyn moaned, breaking past Ilyan and me to get to Thom as a Vilỳ-laden helicopter nose-dived into the city.

A ball of fire erupted from between the two buildings with the impact, causing one of the few tall buildings in the city to collapse with a crash that rumbled the ground underneath us.

"They need to get away from them if they are going to do anything," Ryland said from somewhere to my left. He stared over the city as the rest of us did. "Those rats are going to kill them all."

"Those rats are going to kill them no matter what they do," Ilyan's voice was hard as he stood, his hair blowing in the wind, his gaze jumping from location to location. I could already hear him planning our battle inside his head. "We barely survived those things the first time. How do you think the rest of the world is going to do?"

"They'll be fine," Wyn snapped, her lips turning up into a

smile. "They need to nuke the crap out of them. They thought it was a good idea to use it on the city before. Obviously, it's going to work without a giant barrier to absorb the impact."

"Yeah, I'm sure we will be fine. Nukes always end well," Thom egged her on, the joke clear in his voice, although neither of them smiled.

None of us could.

"We cannot worry about them now. We need to move," Ilyan announced, his voice the hard edge of regality I had come to expect in these situations. "My shield cannot last for long, not against the Vilỳ's. Now is our time to strike. Joclyn has seen that Sain killed Edmund as we had assumed. He has taken control of the Chosen, and we need to act now."

The other Skříteks on the hill began to gather around us, the power of his voice pulling them in.

"The city is in ruins, and the camp of Edmund's Chosen is in battle. From what Joclyn could see, they are attempting to dethrone Sain. If we go in under the cover of this disaster, we will be able to find the man and destroy him."

"If the Trpaslíks haven't already," Wyn said with a smile. An out of place pride for her race was smeared over her face, the light in her eyes far more frightening than I had ever seen. I didn't think I had ever seen her quite so quick to claim her heritage before. It would have been awesome if she didn't look so dangerous.

I fought the need to step away from her, to step away from the power that was radiating off her. Ry and Thom's exchanged glances pulled me right back into the battle that was steps away.

"There," Ilyan continued as he turned, pointing his long finger toward a camp on the other side of Prague.

The large plot of Edmund's tent city lay beyond where the barrier had been, just as I had seen in sight so many months before. The tents were as destroyed as the city, smoke rising up from flames that were quickly spreading. And in the middle, there was a large ring of canvas and metal. The structure was so large I couldn't understand how Edmund had hidden it.

"The stadium," I gasped. The image from my sight flashed again and again as I stared at the massive structure, watching a swarm of Vilỳs move into it.

"What is it?" Wyn asked, coming up beside us as she looked over the city, her jaw dropping as mine had.

"It's where Sain is," I said, knowing it wasn't nearly enough of an answer, but she didn't seem to care in that moment.

She kept her eyes forward, glowering at the offending building alongside the rest of us, glaring at the city that was covered in a sea of brown.

"Maybe a nuke isn't such a bad idea," Ryland whispered, standing on the other side of Ilyan, his face as angry and upset as both of his brothers'.

This time, Wyn laughed, the sound a devilish growl that cut through me. "I think I know where I can get one."

"Our battle begins today," I announced, cutting Wyn off before she got any more ideas and then turning toward the other three. My golden ribbon spun through the wild snow with the snap of my movement. "Sain will be dead by nightfall. I don't care who does it or how, but we need to work together. We need to save as many lives as possible."

Wyn was silent as she stood in the snow, wearing nothing except her worn jeans and a band T-shirt I had seen way too much of since we had been trapped here. The heavy fur she had covered herself with lay in a drift of white by her feet. The snow that landed on her skin evaporated back into the air with a hiss, the sound barely heard over the wind.

"Our queen is right," Ilyan said with a nod, moving between us all as he began to issue orders.

The few Skříteks who were still with us broke away as he ordered them into the city, into the Vilýs in an attempt to save as many mortal lives as possible.

His words washed over me as my focus was already pulling back into the recall of the sight once again, the blue light hovering above the pool just out of reach. I needed to get there; I could feel it. The need to get there was ripped away from me as the recall shifted, taking me right back to that night in the forest and to Sain who had seemed more than willing to watch me die. To fight beside me. Now I had a disgusting feeling that he might have enjoyed that moment. He might have enjoyed watching Cail slit my throat.

The thought twisted my stomach into angry, little knots.

Two years ago, I wanted nothing more than to have my father back. Now I wanted nothing more than to have him dead. I didn't know what kind of person that made me—to think of killing my own father so callously.

If he was a good father and a decent man, then I might say you are evil. But he is not this man, and removing what he is from our kind will save us, not harm us, Ilyan said, his voice a calm warmth as he turned from the last of the Skříteks, a man and woman who took off into the sky on an unknown task.

Ilyan stepped toward me, his eyes smoldering as he wrapped his arms around my waist. His lips hot against my forehead, he pulled me into him.

I know, Ilyan. I shouldn't be questioning this.

"The barrier is down; nothing is stopping us," Wyn said, pulling me from my worries as she came right up to Ilyan and me, dragging Thom with her. Poor Ryland looked irritated as he followed behind. "What's the plan?"

"We need to find Sain," Ilyan began, his magic surging inside of me from the exhilaration of the moment. "I have a feeling that, based on what Joclyn saw, we need to find and secure Ovailia, as well—"

"Secure her?" Ryland interrupted, his green tint increasing as his anger boiled over.

"That better be a fancy word for *kill her,*" Thom snapped.

At least I knew his volatile anger hadn't been affected by his three-month long coma sabbatical.

"Agreed." Ryland glanced toward Thom appreciatively. Both seemed happy to have an ally.

I wasn't really looking forward to this. I had seen Thom and Ilyan duke it out over Ovailia already, and adding Ryland to the mix seemed far too unpredictable.

"She doesn't deserve to live, not after what she has done," Ryland stated.

"I do not disagree with you, but she is our sister," Ilyan announced as if the simple statement was enough to put the debate to rest.

Ryland and Thom fumed more, and I took a step back on habit. This was not my fight, and I was not interested in joining in. Besides, I wanted her dead, too. Dead before she could reach Ilyan. I knew Ilyan would not approve of that.

"Edmund was our father," Ryland said, his voice shaking. "And Sain is Joclyn's. That doesn't change anything."

"Killing nine people instead of ten does not give her reason to live, Ilyan," Thom retorted, his chest puffing out in irritation.

"Hey!" Wyn interrupted with a snap, her magic fuming as her eyes grew darker than night. "Watch who you are judging about 'the number of kills.' "

Thom wilted underneath her retort, his mouth opening wide and his will to fight disappearing with a snap and a grunt. His nostrils flared in an attempt to conceal his anger.

Ryland looked between them in confusion, his anger rising due to the sudden abandonment of his partner in crime.

"Wynifred is correct." Ilyan nodded once toward her before stepping back into the center of all of us. "I am not saying she will not meet her end. But she has done good for us in the past—"

"For her benefit," I interrupted him without thinking, tension moving within my chest in sudden regret.

Ilyan gave me a sidelong glance, his irritation at my outburst clear.

Rolling my eyes, I looked away, feeling even worse because of the supportive looks from Thom and Ryland gave me.

"Capture Ovailia if possible. Kill her if you must. We have had enough death, and it would do well for us to limit it," Ilyan continued, his voice a hard line of authority.

I suddenly wished I could melt right then and there.

Ryland said nothing more than a grumble. Thom's lips were a tight line as his eyes met their brother's head-on. Ilyan was a good head taller than them both, but it didn't seem to faze them. I, however, stood silently to the side, carefully blocking my mind from Ilyan, grateful he was focused on something else for the moment.

I knew he meant well. I knew the fear of losing his sister, of losing his family. Hell, I had just buried my brother. However, I couldn't stand by and watch her kill him. If it meant saving his life, I would gladly end hers.

"Once again," Ilyan continued, the power in his voice deflating the two men before him. "We need to find Sain and apprehend Ovailia and possibly Míra—"

"Wait. Míra's alive!" Ryland interrupted with a snap.

This time, he was silenced with one look, Ry's jaw snapping closed. I had a feeling, judging by the anger that was moving within Ilyan, the motion wasn't entirely his choice.

"Yes, and we are running out of time. People are dying, Ryland. We can't argue this anymore. We need to move."

"Let Thom and me find Sain," Wyn interjected, obviously

willing the conversation forward. "We will find him, Ilyan. You know we will defeat him."

Ilyan smiled, a wicked gleam of power clear in his eyes. The altercations of before seemed forgotten as the two of them stood there, grinning like fools at the possibilities.

Wyn's magic mounted into a flame that heated the air, melting the snow from the sky and burning the grass around us into shriveled black points.

"Watch it, Wyn," I said, stepping away from the ring of energy before it hit me. "We've already destroyed a barrier today; I'm uncertain how much more we can do or if we want anyone finding us up here."

"Point taken," Wyn concurred, withdrawing her magic with a snap, her bracelets jangling with the movement.

"You and Thom will have your chance, Wyn. I need you and Jos to stutter into the camp on the other side of Prague." Ilyan turned back to the still smoldering tents, the power in his eyes matching the flames that licked the air. "Then I will fly in with Thom and Ryland. When you find him, Joclyn will guide us to you." He was alive with the idea, exhilarated for what was to come.

Wyn's face, however, fell as soon as he said *stutter*.

"As fun as that sounds, I'd really rather not be ripped into a million pieces and rearranged. There wasn't any teleportation in *Firefly*, and I think there is a reason for that. I stand with Captain Mal." Wyn's face was as pale as the snow that surrounded us.

"Actually," Thom said, his voice the deep grouch that I knew from him, "there is quite a lot of teleportation in *Firefly*. Both in the battle—"

"Come on, Wyn," I said with a smile, stopping that argument in its place. We really didn't have time for it. "It wasn't that bad."

Wyn glared in response, the look split between Thom and me. Obviously, she didn't agree with me nor him.

Thom glowered deeper, shrugging his shoulders and shaking his head, his long dreads clumping awkwardly.

"Do you really think that's wise, Ilyan?" Ryland asked, his eyes wide with a fear I didn't quite understand. "That involves touching, right?"

Oh, yeah, that.

"Don't worry, we've done this. And all without destroying the alley we were in. I'm pretty sure we will be explosion free, Ry."

Ilyan's lips twitched into a smile, his eyes moving between the two of us, humor clear on his face. "Well then I guess we shouldn't worry then. And seeing as Sain was terrified when he saw Wyn, alive, in Prague two weeks ago; there is something there. If you two can restrain your magic for a second of time, then I am sure you will have the best chance of keeping him at bay until the rest of us get there, if not defeating him altogether. I know Wyn considers herself first in line to destroy him."

"If all I have to do is restrain myself for a minute in order to kill Sain," Wyn said, the fire coming back into her eyes, "then I can do that ... for Rosy."

"And Ovailia?" Thom asked, the growl in his voice making it clear that he wanted no one connected to his father's murder to survive.

"She will find us, Thom," Ilyan said, the irritation swinging right back into his voice. "She will be allowed to live until a trial can be held."

Thom glowered, clearly hoping for a different outcome, one he was not going to get.

"You better find him fast, Joclyn," Thom warned, his eyes still focused on Ilyan. "Someone needs to pay."

I knew he was talking to me, but I barely heard. My mind was too focused on the sight, on that moment in the cave that had haunted me for so long.

My recall slammed into my head, putting pieces together where they didn't belong.

Ovailia disheveled in Imdalind.

Ovailia killing Ilyan.

Ovailia searching for Imdalind.

Ovailia needing a blade.

Everything flashed before me, each piece out of place, not quite fitting together.

I knew there was something I was missing, but I didn't know what.

It will be fine, Ilyan interjected, his voice strong, although I could sense the worry in his soul. *Even if she tries to destroy me, I can face her. I have before.*

I looked at him, wishing desperately that it was enough. It wouldn't be, not really. Not with the way his blood-soaked body kept replaying in my mind.

Ilyan smiled, anyway, running his finger down the side of my cheek. The touch that was meant to be comforting filled me with more fear, instead.

I couldn't lose this.

I couldn't. I had to do something.

"Ready?" Wyn asked, slipping her shoes and socks off, leaving the bright red Converse sitting alone on the ice-covered grass, the kitten socks balled up on top. "I can't say I'm eager to be massacred by your teleportation magic, but if it gets me closer to Sain ..."

"Be safe," Ilyan said, bending down for one quick kiss against my jaw bone. "Don't go ripping a hole in time and space."

"Why do I have a feeling this is going to end very badly?" Thom asked, his voice lost to me due to the fear and the focused look I was giving Ilyan.

"Be safe," I said to him, knowing he would take it seriously, knowing he knew what I meant.

Without looking away from him, I grabbed Wyn's arm, my magic flaring against hers as I pulled her into the stutter. The sound of her screams followed us into the camp on the other side of the city, a million more joining hers.

"Yep, I still hate that," Wyn gasped as she tripped over her own feet, doing her best to stay upright, something that was very needed right now.

I had stuttered us right into a battle. Everything around us was chaos. From on top of the hill, I hadn't realized it was so bad. Being down here ... Everything was exploding.

Tents were on fire; Vilỳs were ripped apart bodies left and right; mortals and Chosen ran past tents to get away from the creatures that would stop at nothing to destroy them.

"Here." I pulled Wyn into one of the few remaining tents, the canvas ripped and burned in places. I knew it wouldn't last long, but it would last long enough for me to find out where Sain was, and that was all I needed.

The canvas closed behind us, trapping us in the chill of the tiny space. The smell of filth smacked against us, making my head spin. I tried to breathe past it, but it got worse. My magic flared as it pulled at me, stretched away from me, soaring beyond tents and farmland, leading me right to where I needed to be, as if it knew what I was looking for.

As if it wanted me to be there.

"He's north of here ... miles away ... in the cave." The words came out choppy and broken as my sight began to clear, a faded image planting itself over the vile tent we stood in. I saw a shadow of my father sitting on a blood-covered throne.

"He's in Imdalind." Wyn put the few clues together as the faded image of Sain vanished from my view. "I know where he is. Come on," she said.

Wyn didn't wait for an answer before she pulled me from the tent and into the air, soaring through the Vilỳs and toward the man she was so intent on killing.

I let her drag me, already looking for someone else; already looking for *her* magic.

For Ovailia.

I needed to find her.

I needed to destroy her before she had a chance to take Ilyan.

I needed to get there first.

24

SAIN

Pain spread over my back, the ends of my nerves erupting in pricks of fire that encompassed my muscles, pressing against me until I screamed. Warm fluid poured over my skin.

My scream was lost in the sound of the crowd, lost in their jeers. It echoed in my ears as I fell to the ground, my magic rushing inside of me as it tried to find out what had happened, as it tried to heal me.

Except, there was nothing to heal. Nothing but the heat of my magic as my shield protected me. Nothing but the bruise from the knife that the man behind me had attempted to stab me with.

They were superficial wounds that would heal in seconds. The man behind me, however, would not survive.

It took the crowd a second too long to realize the blood that poured down my back was not mine. That the knife of assassination was firmly planted in the chest of my assailant and not inside of me.

My pain-filled cry turned into a laugh as I whirled toward my attacker, shocked to see one of the poor boys from the pits behind me, his eyes wide. The child stared in horror at the hole in his chest. The gaping space was still raw and bleeding from where the knife had moved straight through. His eyes trembled as he looked from his hand to his chest and the blade that had embedded itself there.

He gasped, his breathing strained as his lungs began to collapse. Blood drizzled from his slack jaw before he fell to the ground, face first in the mud that was already soaked with his blood.

The cheers of the crowd silenced with his fall. The hollow thud of his collapse was the only sound.

The silence stretched before I laughed, one loud guffaw that drenched the stadium before they began to scream. Many of the weaker ones rushed to the exits, while many more jumped into the pits, anger fueling their rash and possibly foolish decision.

They circled around me, Chosen and Trpaslík alike, magic sparking off their skin in electric shocks that heated the cool air of winter that had found its way in.

Warning seen.

Challenge accepted.

The Chosen who surrounded me far outnumbered the Trpaslík, the dirty servants following orders as they had been trained. Good. I needed that obedience. This was going to be bloody.

The thought made my grin widen.

"Did you really think that would work, Bronislav?" I asked, finally turning toward the man in question.

Joy swept over me at the sight of the horror that encompassed his features. The usually strong Trpaslík wilted before me.

"One stab wound and you would be rid of me. After all you have tried, after all of your secret meetings and magical *tests* you have given me ... That was your end game? To stab me?" The final words gushed out with a laugh.

Turning from him to look at all the people who had jumped into the pits, the angry horde that was slowly moving closer, I made eye contact with each of them. I laughed at their anger as though they were in on the joke.

"Does it matter?" Bronislav finally answered, his voice shaking. I knew he was trying to put on a show for the people who had led him into this disaster. "You are still outnumbered. Even with all the power in the world, you cannot win against all of us. Ovailia has left you. Even your bodyguard is cowering in the corner. There is no escape, Sain, so you might as well surrender." He ended that with a smile.

Georg stood beside him with the same jeer on his face as many of the others in the stands. Their confidence in their win was disgusting.

"You think I am alone?" I asked, my magic prickling up my spine in irritation of Ovailia's betrayal, tensing my muscles in an anger I wouldn't be able to restrain much longer.

In a rush, it left me, spreading over them all like a silent disease, an infection that they could not escape. One by one, my magic found the Chosen. It wrapped around them, leeching into them. It connected with them. *I* connected with them.

Completely unknown to them, I had cast out my strings. I had set my trap. Now all I had to do was reel them in.

"You think I would go into this day, knowing what you had planned if it was as easy as '*we have you outnumbered*'?" I clicked my tongue, the sound a stab as the pride on their faces began to fade. "I already have you surrounded."

Fear crept into them as they looked from door to door in expectation of some hidden army.

A woman near me jumped, ready for some unseen foe to barge through when a moan was issued from behind the wooden door. The fear in her was comical. They really did have tiny, unoriginal minds.

"Oh!" I said, pulling them along by the strings I had already wrapped around them. "Not there. No, no, they aren't there." My leer grew, a grin that made one of the Chosen closest to me jerk, the man ready to run.

Perfect.

He would do nicely.

I looked right at him as my magic, the deep magic that was already wound into him, connected with his. It connected with the Drak magic that each of the Chosen had. The Dark magic that I could so easily control.

His eyes widened as he felt it, as he felt his arms go numb and his body disconnect from his mind, his body connect to me.

"Here they are," I said to the frightened chosen as he began to move forward step by step, unable to stop himself. Of course, I could tell by the look in his eyes that he was trying to fight it.

He couldn't fight it.

He continued forward until he stood beside me, looking at Bronislav and George. The panic of the two Trpaslíks over what they were witnessing was clear.

"Kill them," I said to the man beside me.

"No," the poor man gasped, his hand beginning to rise, his magic rolling through him, his fingers sparking.

I laughed as the man began to plead for surrender, began to cry for mercy. His desperation turned into panic as Bronislav and Georg stood, convinced it was a joke.

"Kill them now!"

The Chosen man's magic erupted at my command, ripping from his hand without consent as he yelled for a relief that never came.

The attack spanned away from the man, hitting Bronislav in the chest. Another attack followed the first, smacking against Georg's back after he finally had the good sense to turn tail and run just like the coward he was.

Laughing, I stepped toward the two traitors, the two men who were now spread out over the dirt, blood seeping from their wounds. The blood flowered over the dirt under them as Bronislav pushed himself up, ready to attack, ready to face me. He was barely able to hold his own weight before he collapsed again, one last breath erupting from the stupid man in a puff of dirt.

It was a beautiful sight. It beat against my heart and supercharged my magic as I pushed it outward, continuing to take control of each of the Chosen in the stands. I wrapped my magic around theirs without their knowledge.

After what they had seen, I was positive they knew. How could they not? A few had even tried to escape, but too late. They were already under my control. Their cries of fear were lost in the growing yells now filling the stadium.

"You are fools," I hissed. "No one can defeat me. No one."

It was then that the stadium erupted. A million eruptions exploded around me. Everything filled with smoke and color as attacks flew toward me, hitting against my barrier with a resounding thud before I sent them back toward their owners like I had the knife.

Some dodged, many countered, and a few watched in horror as their supposed death knells smacked against them, sending them into whatever fate death had for them. All the while, the Chosen stood, trapped underneath my magic, trapped underneath my control. Terror was painted clear on their faces, their eyes watching me in fear of the hell I had dragged them into.

A hell I was ready to deliver.

"Attack them!" I yelled, and the Chosen turned toward the Trpaslíks, cries and pleas for mercy and death ringing clearly. "Kill them all!"

The stadium erupted in color, fire, and smoke as the Chosen

attacked the Trpaslíks. The battle ripped them apart in an eruption of color and smoke. My magic controlled the power of the Chosen as they fought, leaving them as they died.

A Trpaslík jumped from the top of the stadium with a scream that cut through the air, sending my heart into a panic as he landed right before me, a giant uncoiling with a grimace wicked enough to match mine. His grew taller at the thought of his supposed success, only to fade as the attack hit him in the back. The Chosen I controlled had attempted to warn him of his actions before his hand was forced.

The large bear of a man fell to the ground, dust wafting into the air around him and trapping us in a fog of dirt and smoke. It cleared in a rush of icy wind, revealing the Chosen before me.

A young boy had tears running down his cheeks, his hand still outstretched from the attack he did not want to deliver, his eyes wide as he stared at the bulk of a man he had not wanted to kill.

"Tsk, tsk," I said, wagging my finger before me like a primary school teacher. "Trying to warn him. What a fool you must think me." The boy flinched as I stepped over the corpse, dodging another well-placed attack in the process. His eyes widened further. "I suppose you will have to guard me, then. You will have to protect me."

"No," he gasped, more tears streaming down his cheeks as I prodded him forward. My magic guided him step by step as I brought him up to stand by my side.

"Oh, yes," I sneered, throwing my arm around him, feeling

the boy shake beneath me. "You'll love this because I don't even need a shield anymore, not if I have you."

The battle that surrounded us became a graveyard as I twisted him before me. The powerful shield dropped from me as I held the boy in place while his hand fluttered underneath my palm like a misfiring engine.

He shrieked in fear as another attack streamed toward me, the child directly in the line of fire. The magic hit him right in the chest.

"Whoops," I said, trying to hide the laugh from my voice unsuccessfully. "I suppose I forgot to let you fight back. We'll do better next time, won't we?"

The boy's sobs rang clearly as I forced him back up, moving him into place as I pulled several other Chosen along with him. Five little puppets were all pulled into a circle around me.

"Stay still and quiet, and I might let you live," I said to them all, my voice loud as I competed with the noise of battle. "You are lucky enough to guard me," I said with a smile, and each of them looked back at me with varying levels of fear and disgust. The looks fueled my magic more.

They were a sorry lot, and their magic was woefully subpar, but they would do, if only as a physical shield. They were disposable and better than that dratted Damek would have been, if he would live through this.

If he did I would make sure he would find death soon.

He and Ovailia. Just the thought of their blood running over my hands ignited my magic. The power rumbled over the air in a flash of white that fell on those closest to me, their bodies flung away from the force of the blast.

"Whoops." I chortled, enjoying the show as a few stumbled back to their feet, many of them unable to.

"You deserve to die," a tall Chosen woman spat, her words more comical than venom.

"Do I?" I asked, coming up behind her and running my hand over the small of her back. "Or do you deserve to die for me?"

Her eyes widened for a second before I threw her away from me, right into the line of another attack coming my way. I heard her scream and saw wetness spread over her pants in fear. The smell of urine hit me as I blocked the attack. My power evaporated the magic a second before it would have hit. The attack was so close her ripped and torn sweatshirt was singed from the power, black char covering her belly. A shadow of pain ran over her, the narrow miss making her heave as she stared in panic.

"We'll have to do better next time, won't we?" I sneered, forcing her and the others to move closer to me, shielding me as I pulled up the recall of my sight, only to freeze in place as a small, wrinkled body fell from the sky, landing at my feet in what looked like little more than a paper bag. But I knew at once what it was and what it meant.

The calm of sight vanished, leaving my heart twisting and pulling against me, desperate to get out. Desperate to run.

It couldn't be.

Kicking it with my toe, the poisoned Vilỳ flopped over. His eyes were dead as he stared at the sky that he had come from. The sky, I realized with one look, was full of many more of his kind.

Thousands of them.

A swarm was right over our heads.

A swarm was descending on us.

And it could have only come from one place: Prague.

"No," I gasped, watching the Vilỳs join the fray, falling on the Trpaslíks and the Chosen, ripping flesh from bone before anyone had a chance to stop them.

A new assailant to the battle, one that no one could stop.

This couldn't be. I hadn't seen this. I hadn't seen any of this. I was never wrong!

Anger blurred my vision as the coup fell apart. The screams of battle deteriorated into fear as more and more of the wicked things descended on us and helicopters began to soar overhead.

"This can't be."

My anger was so deep I could barely move. I could barely control the Chosen. I just stared at the sky, my magic ready to explode out of me.

"This can't be!"

But it was. The barrier was down.

Prague was free.

And that meant Joclyn was on her way to me. She was on

her way to kill me. And here, among my enemies, she would win.

I needed to get out of here. I needed to use my sight and find out what she had changed. What Ovailia had done. What Joclyn had done. They had done something!

"I am never wrong!"

Joclyn must have changed something. Blocking her from my sights had blocked the real future. It had blocked me from what was true.

I had only seen the future without her in it.

She had done something to change it, something I couldn't see. I would destroy her. She had ruined this, and she would pay for her mistake.

Releasing the Chosen from my magic, I vanished from the arena with a tiny pop. The sound was unheard over the battle as they fought the Vilỳs, dying under their claws.

In a flash of color, the space under time sped by me. Ribbons of red and gold wrapping around as I moved past them and back into the caves of Imdalind, back into the throne room and my high seat.

The slight pop of my return was the only sound in the silence of the cave. The battle was far behind now ... with my enemies.

I would return to it once I knew what had happened. Once I found out where she was.

Once I destroyed her. She was my first priority.

"Foolish child, I should have never given you life!" I cursed to the emptiness.

Breathing deeply, I absorbed the silence, savoring the smell of blood and water that lived in the walls of this sacred space, the fire and smoke of the battle left far behind.

It smelled like home.

Breathing it in, I savored the silence before dashing to my throne, desperate to jump into sight, to plunge into a future that was now ahead of me and find her before she found me.

Settling onto the rigid throne, I placed a hand over Edmund's skull and sighed as I let my magic flood into me. My eyes drifted to black as a sight took me.

I braced myself, expecting the usual flash of images, expecting the barrage of what had been kept from me thanks to the Zámek. Instead, I stared into the vast white nothing I had seen in the barrage of sight Joclyn had pulled me into before, staring at the same girl, the freckled, green-eyed child I knew too well.

"Hello, Sain," she said, her voice tugging at my heart as my memories pulled me somewhere I did not want to go. "It's been a while."

"Joclyn." My voice caught as I greeted her.

The tiny girl smiled so widely the bridge of freckles on her nose wrinkled together into a strip of brown, just as they had when she had been a child.

"You didn't listen to my previous warning, I see." She stepped toward me, the dark swing of her hair against the glaring backdrop pulling my focus. "You killed him, anyway."

"Oh, I didn't kill just him," I taunted, my irritation at the way she spoke to me rising. Irritating child. "I killed as many as I could. I did it for you."

The words ground my teeth as the apparition approached, her eyes darkening angrily with each step she took. My shoulders knit together, pulling with a white-hot rage that cut into my anger.

"You will suffer for that choice, Father."

"Suffer?" I laughed, the sound cracking against the white. "I made the choice that was required for the sight that was given. I will suffer for nothing!" My voice rose as my fists beat against my thighs. The pain was enjoyable against my agitation.

I fought the need to rush her, knowing I wouldn't be able to hurt her here. I had tried before. I was close to trying again.

Joclyn read my mind, smiling before she began to laugh. The sound was the same high-pitched giggle that Jeffery used to love in his child. Now it grated on me, the positive association to a life I had never wanted infuriating me.

"You will suffer for more than you know. You were warned—"

"*You were warned*," I mocked, flipping my hand through the air in irritation, the lack of a magic spark obvious. "I was shown a future, and I have done all in my power to guide the world toward that beautiful bliss!"

"Is that what you think?" Joclyn asked, stopping her forward progression as she cocked her head to the side. "That you are guiding them toward what you saw? Or what you have created?"

"I know what I saw. I know what needs to be done. My people have suffered from the moment I was removed from their lead," I hissed past clenched teeth, my jaw grinding together as I glowered at the girl. "It is only with me, a true Drak, at their head that they can be saved from the evil I have seen."

"The evil you saw was created by you. Are you so blind you have not seen that? Father—"

"I am not your father," I interrupted her with a growl.

She just stared at me with that knowing smile that had always irritated me.

"You say that, but that is because you do not realize what I truly am."

"You are nothing," I hissed, my magic attempting to bubble from me.

"I am more than the *hell* you claim to be. You have told many people that before. Hell does not work for others. Hell devours them for its own." Her anger rose to meet mine, her eyes flashing red in a warning I did not heed. I did not attempt to hide the twitch of my lips, the truth of her words causing my chest to swell in glorious pride.

"Yes," I hissed, a smile finally breaking free. "I am hell, but only because I have to be. To stop the destruction I have seen, I have to be."

"You are foolish to think they are one in the same. You

cannot lie to me, Father. I will see through it. I see everything. I am—"

"You. Are. A. Child," I snapped, rushing toward the girl, happy when she jerked back in an attempt to escape me. The subtle movement prodded me on, anger and magic rising into a comfortable heat against my bones. "You are nothing, and you see nothing. How could you ever understand such things?"

"If I am nothing but a child to you, if Joclyn is nothing but a girl to you, then you are more foolish than I assumed," the girl scoffed. The youthfulness of her voice faded into the terror I had seen in her before, into the maturity that had haunted my sights for so long. "How could I be here if I was nothing but a child?"

"I am the first and hold more magic than anyone below me. My magic showed me all I need to know." I threw my hands up in the air as I stepped closer to her.

Again, the girl did not budge.

"I taught you to use your magic. The magic that showed you Edmund's purpose, how he would unite our kind with the mortals. It showed you Ovailia's true mate, the man who would help her bring a great ruler into the world. It showed you of—"

"Enough!" I roared, the single word soaring through the air with such force that it ripped past the white space I was trapped in. A dark line cut over us, zagging across the sky in a bolt of lightning.

The little girl didn't even jump at the sound. She stared with that same ridiculous grin, her face squashed together awkwardly.

"Enough?" she asked in her ridiculously high voice, a giggle following. "What have you had enough of? Truth? Or have you finally grown tired of the lies you shove down your own throat?"

"Enough of you!" I shouted.

The crack above us enlarged. The dark line opened to reveal a flash of light, color and shapes moving in a strobe beyond the white space.

I stared at it, heart pulsing in confusion as eyes looked down at us, followed quickly by a hand and the white of someone's eye.

"Not possible," Joclyn said from beside me.

I didn't look at her. I stared above me at the flash of a Vilỳ moving beyond the white that trapped us.

"When you have truly had enough of me, you will have moved on from this world."

"It's sight," I stated, my heart beating eagerly at the realization.

"Yes?" the girl asked, her query confusing.

I waved her off. I didn't need any more riddles or threats, not with what I was staring at just there, just beyond us. I could get at it if I tried. I had to destroy a little girl first.

"I wouldn't do that if I were you," Joclyn said, pulling my focus back to her as she read me, clearly understanding what I had been thinking.

The thought irritated me, as it did her. Her smile was gone, a deep scowl replacing it, digging into me with a clear warning.

I didn't care.

"I will do whatever is needed to get me to what I have seen. Haven't you noticed?" My voice was low as I leaned over her, my face inches from hers as I hissed in anger. Little droplets of spit flung over her, but she didn't even flinch. "I need that sight, and I will destroy you in order to get there. You mean nothing."

"I am everything." The tiniest bit of a whine filled her voice. It dribbled over the air and twisted against my spine. I flinched, tasting the ugly desperation of the child, letting it heat my power.

"You are a mistake."

I expected her to flinch, to cower and cry, run away. The Joclyn who Jeffery had raised would have, but this girl simply stared at me with a death that was more frightening than the smile she had previously held.

"Oh, Sain." She clicked her tongue like an adult ashamed of a child. The role reversal might have been funny to anyone else, but it grated on me. My irritation was reaching a point I didn't think it ever had before. "You are a fool. By the time you remember what I am, what your daughter is, it will be too late for you. Let's hope it is not too late for the rest of us."

I opened my mouth to retort, ready to scream and yell, but the white space collapsed around us, and the girl vanished with the crack of the collapse.

Sight poured around me. The larger than life image

drowned me until I was left staring at the jarring image of my own death. Of my own blood seeping over my throne and pooling at my feet while everything around me was wrapped in fire.

Wyn's fire.

I had seen it before, but it could not be. I would not let it be!

"No!" I screamed at the imagery, screamed at the sight as it left, fading to black before the large cave came back into focus.

My breath was heaving, and I desperately tried to catch it, but I couldn't. I could barely calm down from what I had seen. The cruel reality hit me in the chest as the very woman whose fire had devoured me walked through the door with my daughter right behind her, wide smiles on both their faces.

"See? I told you he would be here." Wyn laughed as she stepped into the middle of the hall as though she had been invited.

She hadn't.

"Of course it would be you." I smirked, rising from my throne as my magic erupted, ready to fight the two powerhouses before me. I already knew I could not face them. "Both of you. You just won't die."

"Really? Because I think I could say the same about you," Jos said, her smile fading as her attack flew toward me.

Wyn smiled from beside her. "Let's see if we can fix that."

25

WYN

JOCLYN'S ATTACK cut through the pitch of the hall in a bolt of white light that shimmered in the dark, heading right for the wicked man who sat on his ugly throne with an equally ugly smile on his face.

Watching the liquid lightning soar, I waited for it to hit, for it to impact with the shield I knew surrounded him.

He was a coward. Cowards always hid behind people and walls. He had killed all the people he had hidden behind. Now it was just walls.

Walls, I could tear down.

The idea was far too exciting.

The lightning of her attack encompassed the massive hall in ferocious bolts, ripping through the air to rebound off his barricade.

Shielding my eyes as best I could, I refused to look away. The thunderous impact banged through my skull as I stared, wide-eyed, at the blast. The same lightning that spread through the air also spanned over his barrier, cutting into it, weakening it, showing me every flaw. The ground swelled under my bare feet with the impact. The power of the shield rippled past the stone, reacting with my magic in a sting.

He was hidden behind a wide shield that spanned from floor to ceiling and across both walls in one solid mass.

Even if I used the fire magic to its full potential, I would have trouble getting past. A shield of that strength had a major flaw, however. It was impenetrable from either direction, so unless he weakened it, he wouldn't be able to attack us.

I was fairly certain his ego wouldn't allow him such pacifism, especially against "little girls" who should "already be dead."

He was really getting on my nerves.

Sure enough, Sain laughed at Jos's failed attempt. The sound was forced as he tried to posture to us, tried to scare us. Neither worked.

Joclyn rolled her eyes, while I met him with a stare that I had used for centuries. My lips curled as my magic reverberated under my skin, hot and violent in preparation for what was coming.

I knew Joclyn could feel the power. The small sidestep away from me was not enough to protect her from the heat I was emanating.

"I am beginning to think I misinterpreted the sight," he sneered, rising from his throne. An ugly, dirty robe fell from his shoulders and unfurled behind him like a child's cape. "From what I have seen, I know now that in order to succeed in what the sight would have me do, I am the one who is supposed to kill you."

His magic sparked as he moved to attack, thrusting his hand in front of him as a wave of deathly gray sped toward us. The sticky magic was meant to infect us with a slow torture. Too bad I was faster.

Just as he attacked, so did I. A needle of flame sped from my good hand, soaring through the air with a pace his couldn't hope to match. Only a bullet of fire was visible thanks to the smoke that followed, a trail that gave me away.

A trail Sain stared at with wide eyes.

His attack moved past his barrier, my knife of fire hitting against it simultaneously. A razor point of flame pricked against the powerful wall, intersecting right where his magic had created an opening to attack us. The fire blade used the same opening to move past it.

It hit against his magic with a blast of flame, an explosion that pushed beyond the protective wall Sain hid behind, burning it to the ground in heavy drops of molten glass that spread over the stone floor in rivers of muck.

"That was easier than I thought," I jeered, making sure to keep my magic strong and hot under my skin. "Here I was, thinking you were going to destroy us."

"At least with that wall gone, he can try," Joclyn added with a sidelong glance, not quite willing to let her father out of her sights. "No more hiding, Sain. It's time to end this."

Sain's focus snapped to us, his anger clearly boiling in his eyes. The warning in the dark of his glare thrilled me.

"You want to end this, child?" he hissed, his fingers continuing to spark and smoke. "Are you prepared to fight me? To fight true power? Or would you rather die by it?"

"Stop being so melodramatic," Joclyn groaned, stepping in front of me to face her father. The muscles in her neck tensed and pulsed. "We don't need your monologue. We just want to stop you."

"Or kill you," I amended, jumping around Jos like a Jack-in-the-box, my attack already speeding toward him. Color exploded from my hand in an array of lights, speeding across the air toward the irritating little man.

His eyes widened in surprise before he countered, his own attack exploding through the dark. The shards of light soared past mine, sending them spinning against the wall. Another assault followed a bright stream of yellow that snapped and hissed before it was intercepted by Joclyn. Her hands moved fast as her counterattack gobbled up his. Her magic devoured it into nothing but a puff of smoke.

"Nice," I commended her, attacking again as I sidestepped another blast from his arsenal. The powerful discharge hit a wall, leaving a crater in its wake.

He was a much more aggressive fighter than I had assumed. This was going to be fun.

Maybe I would even get another scar.

Continuing to watch his movements, I tried to find a weakness big enough that I could take him down ... or at least capture him.

Jos might want a quick and clean death, but that was not what I had in mind. Sain didn't deserve an easy death. I was going to make certain it was slow and painful. I needed the truth about his part in Rosy's death from his blood-soaked lips.

The imagery of that moment, of gaining that absolution, fueled me. It ignited my power into a greater wave that sped from me, mixing with Joclyn's attacks in color and fire that danced around the air together, smothering the large hall in a fog of black smoke. It covered us, sticking in my eyes and nose as it pressed against me.

"No," I heard Joclyn gasp from beside me.

The sudden blindness tensed my muscles. My mind moved into hyperactivity due to the unfamiliar vulnerability. I suddenly felt very weak. I never felt weak.

"Watch out!" Joclyn tackled me from the side, throwing us both down to the ground as a wide attack sparked overhead … right where I had been.

My shoulder impacted the hard stone with a jolt. The contact of skin against stone sent my magic through the earth in lines of fire that cut across the floor, melting the stone into rivers of lava.

Joclyn hissed as she scuttled off me, holding her hand where my skin had burned her, where my magic had tried to attack her.

"Dude! Are you okay?" I asked, pulling my fire from the earth, attempting to control it again, to keep it tucked inside of me and away from the girl who would make me go off like a bomb. Better safe than buried under a mountain of molten rock.

"Probably not the right question to ask right now," Joclyn hissed, glancing around the room like a lion waiting for a kill. "But I'm okay."

"Fine. What is the right question?" I amended, sitting up as she was. There was nothing around us but smoke. "Who won the battle of Serenity Valley? Because if this ends anything like that, I'm out of here."

Unsurprisingly, she ignored me.

The fog pressed against us, blocking everything from view. Even Joclyn was shadowed a mere two feet away.

Everything was too similar to a horror story for my liking. All we needed was a blood-curdling scream from somewhere in the room.

"I can't find him, Wyn," Joclyn hissed from beside me.

Or that. I thought that might have been worse than a shriek.

Ice ran down my spine in a slow drip as I placed my hand against the ground, letting my magic stream away from me, through the stone in search of him. It flowed over the massive room, peeking through the smoke in ways I could not. She was right; there was nothing.

"Do you think he left?" I couldn't dare hope.

"No, he's still here."

I looked at Joclyn. Her green eyes were wide as they faded to black, staring at me while she looked into something beyond us.

I shivered. I had seen that look before. It didn't make it any less creepy.

"Oh, my gosh. He can't!" she hissed, pressing her hand against the torn sleeve of my T-shirt in an attempt to shove me back down to the ground, a move that I resisted. "Stay in the smoke as much as you can. You cannot fight this one, Wyn."

I was about to retort, to give some loud explanation of why she couldn't keep me away, when she turned, and Sain appeared behind her with a sudden pop, an attack already forming in the palm of his hand.

She had obviously seen his arrival before he came, because her attack was already speeding toward him. It never made contact, though. It sped through the air where he used to be, slamming against the far wall with a force that made the whole cave rumble and shake.

"Hide," she told me, disappearing as she stuttered, appearing across the hall with a pop right before Sain did.

Her attack hit him in the back with a thud, and he cried out in pain, shuffling over the floor as he turned to face her. She was already gone, her attack meaningless as he, too, vanished.

The two reappeared again, fighting in a flurry of spells. They appeared and reappeared, spells and attacks flying through the air as they fought, moving past the large hall in a confusing mass. Everything moved so fast I couldn't keep up. I didn't know where to look. Jos was right; this was a battle I could not face.

Once again, Sain disappeared, and Joclyn popped out of

existence behind him. But not before she sent an attack toward me, the red electricity crackling above my head.

Watching it with wide eyes, I tensed, expecting it to hit me. Instead, it hit Sain as the man appeared over me with a smile. His eyes flashed from black to green as he held a red knife above my heart.

I saw the image, the glint of the knife clear in my eyes before his yell overtook me.

The man stumbled before he disappeared again, and then the sound of the battle continued as the two of them danced through those terrible stutters, their precognition anticipating everything.

The blur of noise and color continued, but I didn't see it. I stared straight ahead, the red knife clear in my mind. The sharp point of my daughter's soul glinted in the light right before me. I could reach out and grab it.

It was the other piece. I needed to get it.

Shuffling to my feet, I spun around, my magic ready as I attempted to find some pattern, to find a place to attack. There was nothing but the flashes of bodies and sparks of magic. Everything was a blur.

Sain would have to attack me again if I wanted to get a good hold on him.

I wished he would.

Perhaps I could make him.

Forcing out a shout, I sent a line of fire directly into the ceiling just as they appeared again. The room lit up with the bang, but they didn't seem to notice.

Their fight continued with magic and fire, knives, and who knew what else speeding through the air.

Then, with a bang, they halted. Sain stopped in place, a smile on his face.

I didn't care that he had stopped, that he was smiling. All I could see was the knife.

I took my chance, an attack speeding through the air, ready to immobilize him, ready to destroy him.

He didn't even seem to see it coming, but he stepped out of the way, anyway. His focus was intent on the smoke in front of him as he began to laugh, slow and demonic.

The nefarious sound plunged into my heart, ice moving beyond the fire of my soul and extinguishing it as I saw what he was so focused on. My best friend on her knees, hand over her chest, blood pouring from between her fingers.

"No!" I yelled, this one real, agonizing.

Sain heard this one. The sound had broken through the spell that had been over him, and his focus snapped to me.

His eyes glinted as he once again vanished. This time, however, with the anger that had taken control of me, with the power of my magic that was roaring inside of me, I was ready for him.

As fast as he had disappeared, I extended the fire magic into the ground, letting it ignite the earth I stood on.

With a pop, Sain reappeared before me, unaware of the landmine I had set in the ground beneath him.

His feet had barely made contact with the stone floor of the cavern when it went off like a bomb, rock and fire exploding around us, sending Sain into the air. His blood sprayed over my face in a line of damp that sizzled against my skin, boiling from the heat there.

Watching him soar, I let the smoke swallow him before I ran past the fire that still burned against the stone. The heat licked against my skin, comfortable and soothing. The feeling did not last. It vanished in a splash of cold water against my skin, the scene on the other side smacking me in the face.

Joclyn knelt, ash falling over her like the snow we had left. Gasping for air, she stared at the blood that dripped from her chest, the same bright red color that drizzled from her lips.

"Jos!" I ran toward her as Ilyan appeared between us, his body snapping into place with a pop as he ran toward his mate, his scream ripping my heart in two.

"No!" he yelled, the pain in his voice making it clear he knew something I did not.

"Ilyan," she gasped as she looked up at him. Her blood-soaked hand extended toward him before she collapsed, Ilyan barely catching her.

"No! No, no, no!" Ilyan cried, his panic cut apart by a dark laugh that I had been expecting before.

The haunting sound whispered over the last of the smoke as it finally cleared, revealing Sain sitting upon his throne.

He had survived my attack, although not very well. Blood seeped from his hairline and a large gash that ran down his arm, so deep I could see the bone. The bone was a stark white contrast against the dark horrors he sat on, the burned and bloodied bones that surrounded him.

I could tell he was weak. It was only his pride that kept him laughing, his pride that kept him here.

He was a fool. I would have run and hidden from the monster he had unveiled in me.

I was going to kill him for what he had done.

Ilyan didn't even look at the monster as he unveiled himself. His focus was on Joclyn as he held her, pressing his hand against her cheek as he sang to her, rocking her in his arms.

"You're wasting your time, Ilyan," Sain said, the taunt clear even though his voice was weak. "I think that one is a lost cause."

I spun to face him, the man sitting calmly as he bounced a ball of light from his hands. The gash in his arm was almost healed. The magical orb refracted light over the dark cave as he played with it. The violent attack that it restrained was waiting to be thrown.

Magic boiled under my skin, the fire desperate to escape. I knew I couldn't restrain it. I couldn't stop it. Not anymore.

I didn't want to.

"Proud of yourself, are you?" I asked, my voice seductive as I stepped toward him, fully aware my hips had begun to sway. I didn't even try to restrain the seductress I had been raised to be, even if I didn't look the part in a band shirt and bare feet. "Felling accomplished?"

"Accomplished would be an understatement, my dear," he sneered as he spun the ball over his fingers, letting the light reflect over his haunted face. His eyes glossed over as he watched my hips sway. "She was supposed to be the greatest power. She was supposed to end your greatest threat. Instead, I ended her."

I tried not to flinch at the amount of pride in his voice, her possible death giving him joy.

Tears pressed against my eyes, hot and painful, as I stared at him. Ilyan's sobs echoed around the large cavern as he lifted Joclyn into his arms, running from the room.

I turned, my magic at the ready in case Sain attempted to stop them, but he waved good-bye with his bottom lip jutted out. The false sympathy was disgusting.

I watched them go, wishing to help, wishing to say good-bye to my friend. I didn't move except to turn back toward Sain, my magic thundering into the ground again, unseen by the man who sat, smiling from his throne, his barrier firmly between us.

"But, yes, Wyn," he continued as he leaned toward me, his eyes wrinkling together. "I would have to say that ending my daughter's life is one of my greatest accomplishments. Right up there with helping Edmund take Rosaline's."

I stopped in place.

Thom was right. He couldn't be, but...

The magic in his hands popped in white light over his head in a harmless explosion. I didn't even notice. My world was ice and fire.

My fire screamed, desperate to explode out of me, but it was frozen underneath the shock, against the sound of his laugh. Frozen behind my tears.

I stared at him, unseeing, my hair whipping around my face as an attack sped past me. The colors pulled me from my shock as they spread over Sain's wide barrier.

"Why, Thom!" Sain yelled, the name jerking me as long, dirty dreads swung into my peripheral vision. "It's been ages! How are you, my friend?"

"Do not use that word for me!" he vented, his hand wrapping around mine and pulling me out of my emotional swamp. "I am not your friend and will never be. You killed our daughter!"

"Oh! You heard that," Sain called, clapping his hands together in enjoyment. "Wonderful! No secrets between us, right, old friend?"

If it weren't for Thom's hand wrapped around mine, his grip a vice against my fingers, I would have attacked Sain right then. Barrier or no, I was pretty positive I could reach him and rip his head off.

I didn't think anything could stop me.

"I am not your friend," Thom growled, stepping toward Sain.

I didn't stop him.

"I know what you are, Thom."

The joy in Sain's face vanished, his hands slamming together in another clap. This time, the sound rippled through the air, the sound a hundred decibels above what I had expected. It flowed, hitting against the massive doors of the hall, closing them with a jolt.

I jumped, looking at Sain as he stepped toward us, his eyes black and dangerous.

"I created you. I molded you into what you are. It will make it all the easier to destroy you."

26

RYLAND

A SHAKY INHALE rattled through my chest. The desperate gasps for air were the only sound I could hear, the only sound that made it past my panic. The world was only comprised of breathing.

Breathing rattled off the stone hallways as we ran past antique side tables and towering wooden doors. Breathing matched the impact of my rubber soles against the cold stone in a perfect rhythm. Breathing smothered Ilyan's desperate sobs, drowned out the whimpers from the girl he held, devouring the sound of his own steps.

Only breathing.

I let it smother me, smother the world, desperate for it to cover the already pained pressure that was taking over my chest. A pressure that had been there for days, a pressure that only kept increasing.

I wasn't sure how much more I could take.

You can't.

You will rip yourself apart with these foolish emotions.

You should have followed me from the beginning.

Shaking my head, I dismissed the words before the truth in them took hold, before that desperation that was moments from devouring me won out. The words left, allowing the world around me to return.

Sound flooded my mind with the agonizing pain of Ilyan's cries, the soft whimpers from Joclyn as she fought for her life. They hit my heart with even more pain, my chest tightening as everything began to turn to ice, the agony so great it couldn't be contained.

Better not to feel than to hurt.

I quite agree.

The cave shook as we ran, and the sound of some distant explosion rumbled through the stone, knocking an old vase off a small table that was inset into the stone. The blast shivered around us, sending rubble over our heads like rain. I jerked, suddenly not so sure the cave wasn't going to come down on top of us.

"Keep moving," Ilyan barked from in front of me.

"But the cave ..." I returned with a heave, my eyes drifting up to the ceiling that continued to tremble above us, and one of the many clusters of mirrors rattled dangerously.

"It'll be fine. There is magic stronger than us in this stone. It would take the end of magic to bring it down."

At any other time, I would have been inspired by that answer, awed by the space that I had waited my whole life to enter. But I couldn't. Not now.

"Keep up," Ilyan said, his focus steady as he turned a corner and Joclyn's feet hit the wall, sending a wave of iron and salt over me, the air infused with the smell of her blood.

The ice in my heart stabbed painfully at the smell, at the way her feet shifted like rags against the stone: lifeless, dead. Just like my heart that was slowly turning to ice and stone that would never feel again. How could it after everything? It had only just survived Risha; I didn't think it could survive this.

It can't. I will make sure it does not.

Another stab, this one more painful.

I cringed and sped up, running past an overstuffed chair that had been ripped and pulled apart. I kept Joclyn's long hair in my line of sight, the strands falling over Ilyan's arm, the braid she had worn earlier all but gone now. It was a tangle of curls now, the long golden ribbon dragging along the ground, the beautiful color stained with the same crimson as everything else.

I swallowed as Ilyan turned again, and Joclyn's face came into view for a split second. Her beautiful diamond eyes were cast in the black that had become so normal for her, staring into nothing. Her mouth moved in silence, the singular word she had been repeating from the moment Ilyan had burst through the doors still playing on her lips, her body limp in his arms.

"Imdalind."

Imdalind. The caves we were running through, the caves I had heard legends about for my whole life. More than that, the pool of water deep underneath where the first four had come from, where magic came from, and where Ilyan was taking us.

"Ilyan," I gasped out as I pushed my legs harder to catch up. They were stiffening in my attempt to keep the speed Ilyan was moving at. He didn't seem fazed by it, though. He only soared farther, his magic moving behind us as it prodded us forward. "How much farther?"

"Not far," he gasped, the pain in his voice making it clear he was speaking to Joclyn, not to me. I didn't care. It was still the answer I needed.

"We can make it," I whispered, determined for the statement to be true.

I had barely gotten the words out before Ilyan's breakneck pace slowed, the magic that was prodding us forward falling from the air. For the first time since he had commanded I follow him, he looked at me.

"Someone is ahead. I'll need you take them out before we continue. No one can see the entrance. I can't risk Sain finding it."

Don't worry; you are going to take me right to it.

Nodding once, I ignored the voice, looking away from Ilyan's icy stare and toward the dark turn in the cave ahead of us, toward the unknown attacker who stood somewhere ahead.

Madness pressed against me, fueled by the need to save my friend, the heat of my magic not far behind. The two opposing strengths pressed against each other, both threatening to attack, to devour me.

It was a familiar sensation, but one I could control. I already had at the battle during the council just days before. I would here.

Can you?

I had to.

Do you really think you won't kill her, instead?

I would do anything to get Ilyan where he needed to go.

My legs moved faster as I controlled my magic, pulling ahead of Ilyan as we began to round the next bend in the corridor. The dark stone swallowed us before a bright blue light flooded the hallway, spreading over the dark stone from an oversized passageway just ahead.

The narrow, dark stone hallway opened up into a massive commons room with high ceilings that reached far above us, covered in glass and mirrors. The mirror work tinkled with another distant explosion, twisting in the air as they reflected the blue light, the ethereal glow turning to ocean waves against the stone.

Water lapped against stone, against several large tapestries that were hung on the walls, against the ancient furniture that was littered throughout the space. Many couches and chairs were upturned and ripped apart. I was sure it had been beautiful months ago, but now it looked haunted and forgotten.

The mirrors shivered with another explosion, sending the light into a dance, everything quaking except for ten spots of dark that circled the space, spreading out from the larger room like spokes on a wheel.

I looked at the cavern in awe before my heart was ripped

from my chest when a young boy emerged from one of the oversized entryways, running across the wide space with a wide look of panic on his face. The image slammed into me, taking me back to just a few hours ago when I stood on that dratted mountaintop, pushing his hair back from his grey face.

"Jaromir," I gasped, the word swallowed by the knot in my chest.

"No," I heard Ilyan gasp as he came up behind me.

I didn't turn toward him. I stared at the child, my heart rate increasing as I took a step forward, ready to tackle the boy, ready to grab him and run out of this mess. For a moment, it didn't matter that I had buried him, that he was gone. It was him. It had to be. It was him, and everything was fine. I almost expected Risha to run in right behind him. I expected their laughs. I expected life to rewind and be what it was, what it was going to be.

Don't get too excited, son.

How many times do I have to tell you that life isn't a fairy tale?

I know it's not—

You are a fool.

I am not a fool.

Look again.

I had taken two steps toward Jaromir before I stopped short, the haunted words of my father hitting far too clearly as my heart seized, and my eyes saw for the first time what I had missed: hair that was far too blonde; a face that, while similar, was missing the mark on his face. The kiss that had irritated him so before he had found out that it had given him magic wasn't there.

It wasn't him.

But I knew who it was. Only one other person looked so much like him.

"Míra!" I erupted, realization smacking me across the face, stinging my eyes as my already unstable magic roared to life. The voice inside of me laughed in excitement.

Maybe it is a fairy tale.

The girl stopped short as she turned toward me. A large pink scar stretched over her face, distorting her features as her jaw dropped into a wide "oh." She wasn't looking at me, however. She was looking at the man next to me, the surprise meant for him.

"Ilyan! There you are! I need you!" The fear I had expected in her was lost in a kind of relief she shouldn't have felt. A relief she shouldn't be allowed to feel. Not after what she had done. Not after what she had taken from me.

Then why don't you make her pay?

Why don't you make her hurt?

Make her cry ...

Maybe I will.

Fury rushed within me, erupting in a feral shriek that resonated through the hall, slapping against her face and wiping the relief from it. The fear she should have felt from the beginning took its place.

"Ryland."

"You killed him!" The words broke free as any restraint I had snapped in half. Wild anger ripped out of me as my father's laugh grew into a raucous growl. Magic rumbled underneath my skin, boiling inside my muscles in a desperate attempt to reach her.

To do to her what she had done to me.

Make her pay.

Watch the regret on her face.

It's beautiful. You need this.

"You killed her!"

"Ryland, no!" Ilyan screamed from beside me, his panicked counsel falling to nothing as a blast exploded from my hand.

An attack that was meant to kill streamed from me, dyeing the bright blue light of the room into a deep green as it sped right at the child. Right at her chest, ready to do to her what she had done to me.

Míra screamed as Ilyan ran past me, her frightened howl a comforting lullaby as she jumped to the side, behind a large destroyed davenport in a desperate attempt to escape my attacks. Attacks kept coming, one after another, ready to destroy her, to end her.

Tables exploded; glass tinkled against the stone. Everything around us began to explode as I attacked her, each assault chasing her down in an attempt to reach her. My anger grew as the once fine furnishings of the room got in my way. No matter. I would destroy it all to get to her.

"Ryland! No!" Ilyan repeated his plea as his body impacted with mine, a heavy shoulder slamming into my back, the lanky weight of my brother pinning me to the ground. "Stop! We talked—"

"I'm not going to take her alive!" I writhed underneath him as I yelled, twisting, slamming a free hand into his shoulder. A single spark of magic moved into him, erupting inside of him and ripping the muscle and flesh.

His blood showered over me, raining over my face and arm as he was thrown back through the air in a blur of blond hair and gold ribbons. His yell of pain and anger faded as my scream followed his flight.

"She doesn't deserve to live!"

Neither does he.

Don't hesitate, Ryland.

Kill them all, son.

The glass and mirrors above us shook and rattled from the impact of his body against the wall, the blue light quivering around him as his body peeled from the stone and fell to the ground with a *thwack*.

"Only her, Father. She's going to pay," I said quietly, more to myself than to him.

Turning from Ilyan, I looked at the girl in question as she glanced at me from behind the large couch that she seemed to think would be some kind of safety.

I smiled at the imagery, sending the couch flying with one little flick, but not before she had sent her own counterattack speeding toward me in a ribbon of violet that sparked and crackled. The blue air filled with electricity, and the oxygen around us ignited with the heat of her attack.

The wild spark of her spell sped closer as I took a step toward the girl. The dangerous warning in my eyes caused her to step back, grinding her teeth together. I swiped my hand once through the air, and a steady stream of magic shot from my fingers and right toward her. Her own attack was only inches from me.

The electric air around us made the hair on my neck and arms stand on end, my magic prickling in response. It was an odd sensation, one that flowed through my magic, charging it as I prepared my attack.

The air around me continued to explode as her attack was about to make contact, my own countering at the last minute. The line of electric violet sizzled to nothing, and the stream of energy fell to the ground with a simple flick of my finger. The air was now full of nothing except a little bit of grey smoke.

"I would just give up if I were you," I taunted, shoving a large chair to the side without touching it.

Taking a step toward her, I moved another chair, this one slamming aggressively against the wall just as she waved my own counterattack away, the power from it strong enough that she burned her hand.

She hissed, waving her fingers through the air in an attempt to dispel the pain, but her eyes never left mine, even as I began to step closer to her, my eyes lowered in clear warning.

"You are just like your father, Ryland," she hissed, narrowing her eyes in an anger I didn't expect. Not from her. Not about him.

Yes, you are.

It's a beautiful thing.

Her words cut deeply as the laugh in my head grew into a wall of sound I couldn't escape. The sound was so loud it drowned out the words the little girl continued to yell at me, her anger clear.

I heard none of it.

Even she sees it.

When are you just going to accept who you are?

When are you just going to become like me?

Stop stalling.

Do it now.

"No!" I erupted, the reaction not expected by the girl.

She jumped, jerking into the air as her eyes widened, the same fear I had seen when she had spoken of my father now directed at me.

"I won't let you say such things!"

Again, I attacked her, a heavy spell soaring through the air with the speed of a bullet. She threw a table at it in an attempt to deflect, but her weaker magic just bounced off. The little girl squeaked in fear before jumping into the air in a desperate move to escape, one I had anticipated. An identical strip of magic was already ready for her.

"What do you take me for?" I snapped with a laugh. "A fool?"

Her face fell as the attack hit her in the chest, freezing her magic in place and sending her back down to the ground, an impact she escaped, thanks in part to Ilyan, whose magic shoved one of the few remaining couches below her just in time.

His face was pure anger as he came to stand beside me, blood seeping down his arm and over his face from somewhere in his hair line.

"Calm down," he hissed while he wrapped his strong hand around my forearm, shaking me in his anger. "Fight her if you must, but she is a child. Whatever death she finds should not be this way. It cannot be this way."

"This is the only way!" I yelled back, breaking free of him and turning to face him as his anger began to lessen. "Get Joclyn to the pool. Let me handle this, Ilyan!"

I had barely gotten the words out before a wave of ice water splashed over my back, freezing my nerve endings and holding me in place once again, this time by magic.

"Ilyan!" Míra shouted from somewhere behind me. The beautiful fear I had painted on her face was all but gone now. "I need you to—"

Her plea was lost when, with a snarl, I broke free from her spell. My magic rushed through my muscles, and a wave of blue and white shivered through the air away from me. The wave shifted the rubble of the room toward her as the once powerful magic the girl had bound me with left.

"Don't listen to her!" I yelled as I began throwing attack after attack in her direction. "Get Joclyn to the pool! You don't have time for this! I can handle it!"

Ilyan stared at me, his jaw a tight line as he looked from me to Míra, obviously torn about what he should do.

"Don't do anything stupid, brother," he finally growled, the look on his face making it clear he did not like this decision.

"No promises!" I yelled as I turned away from him, ready to fight Míra, only to see her running away from us, down one of the many dark hallways we were surrounded by. "After all, she doesn't deserve to live."

No, she doesn't.

End this now.

The words were a powerful chant that reverberated within me, energizing me in a comforting lull that sent me forward, amidst the dark, after her.

The magic that was already pulsing at my fingertips was ready to destroy her.

27

JOCLYN

BLOOD WAS EVERYWHERE. It stuck to my skin in patches that pulled and stung. It poured from me, dripping from my fingers in rivers of red, long lines that trickled my life away.

I leaned against the uneven stone wall, folded on the floor where Ilyan had left me, hands clamped against my chest. My magic was attempting to heal me, to knit me back together, but it couldn't. Sain's attack was still there inside of me, infecting me, keeping my magic from the injury, slowly killing me.

Even Ilyan's magic wasn't enough to stop it, to heal me, but I could hardly feel that, anyway. The warmth of his magic was leaving, seeping from me as our connection began to close.

I looked toward him, toward where I thought he was, as if seeing him would force the bond to return. Yet I couldn't see anything other than the smears of color that swam in the blue ocean of the room I was trapped within.

Smudges whirled in slow spirals as a battle raged before me, wobbly bodies moving slowly, sparks of color blasting through the waves in bubbles of sound.

Rough rock pushed painfully into my head as I tried to shift my weight in an attempt to reach Ilyan. Nothing happened other than me falling forward, my body giving way as my face impacted with the hard stone of the ocean floor.

The broken gasps of my breaths echoed against the stone I was awkwardly pressed into, the sound louder than the blasts, louder than the painful stutter of my heart.

Neither were working right.

My heart faltered and started again, the sound slamming against my bones. My breaths were desperate puffs, my lungs unable to fill with air. I was left gasping, my head swimming.

My vision was blurred and broken as I tried to make sense of the slow moving ocean that I was drowning in, grateful for the reprieve as my sight kept blinding me in waves of black, the same image playing over and over.

The pool of black water and comforting blue light flitted through the dark. I needed to go there. My sight wanted me to go there.

Ilyan knew where it was, but every time he tried to tell me, I couldn't hear. His mind was cut off from mine, everything but his fear.

I could feel it rushing through me, crippling me, although that emotion might be my own.

I couldn't tell anymore.

"Ilyan," I gasped into the stone as more distorted colors

erupted around me, one blast rumbling through the stone. "Ilyan," I said again, trying to force the word out with the limited air in my chest.

I wasn't sure it worked. He didn't seem to hear me.

The battle continued to explode, pops of color fading to the silvery blue light of the ocean and then again to the cave, to the solitary orb of blue that floated above the black waves.

The light shimmered in my mind, pulling me toward it before a spark of yellow pulled me back to the battle. The wall rattled, a blast exploding above my head with a low, shallow beat, the deep sound stretched out.

Sparks of color fell over me like feathers, soft and hot against my skin. I knew they should hurt. I could feel them burn, but it was only another pain. Another pain didn't matter.

All that mattered was that blue light and that pool. I could see it now, just in front of me. I needed to get there.

With a slow blink, Ilyan's face appeared before me, his hands hot against my shoulders as he placed me back against the wall. Everything was fuzzy as I stared at him, at his mouth moving in some desperate message I couldn't hear.

I couldn't hear anything.

Only the running of water, water so fast and so cold.

I wondered where it was coming from. Maybe I could use it to wash off all this blood.

Ilyan faded from my sight as the ache in my chest grew. I

gasped for air, more blood pouring over my fingers, everything aching as Sain's magic devoured me.

My vision faded again into the black of the pool and that comforting blue light. The clear, undistorted image faded in an out with the slow beat of my heart, the blue light growing brighter and brighter each time I saw it.

"I am waiting," a deep, familiar voice said, the sound rattling inside my head as it faded again, leaving me staring at the Vaseline smear of the battle, colors popping and sticking in the air like paint.

"It's time," my own voice echoed within me, pulling my focus from the colors as they dripped to the woman I had seen before, myself, but from years before.

The older me stood as clear as day near an outcropping of the hallway, wearing the same clothes I did, the bloodstain wide across her chest.

"It's time for what?" I asked, amazed I could get my own voice to work with the amount of pain I was in.

"It's time for the end," she said, a coy smile crossing her face as she took a step closer to me, her hand outstretched.

"No end." The words were distorted as I tried to push them out with so little air, my chest aching again as I took another breath. "I have to save Ilyan."

I turned toward him then, toward the battle that was still echoing in my head with blasts and bangs, but everything was color now, drips of it everywhere.

"You will," the other me said, pulling my focus so fast my

head hurt. Her image began to fade and spin just like everything else. "But you must come with me."

She stood there, her hand outstretched, her eyes desperate as she looked from me to the battle.

I stared at her, struggling to take a breath, blood pouring from my hand as my vision began to fade, the same pool coming into focus, the same blue light calling to me.

"I need to get to the pool." I wasn't even sure the words came out the right way.

"I can take you there. Let's go," she said, her voice hard as her hand wrapped around my blood-soaked one, pulling it away from my chest and toward her.

Her hand was warm, comforting, and familiar. And not just because it was my own, but there was something else there, something I had felt before. It was her magic; it wasn't mine.

Stumbling to my feet, I followed her, letting the strength of her magic pull me forward, my legs tripping and faltering as I attempted to stay upright.

Her magic moved into me in a surge that reacted with my own just as the magic from the earth did. Just like when I heard Dramin and Wyn and all those Chosen. It was the earth's magic. That's what she was. She wasn't me. She was earth.

"I am you," she said in a clear response to my thoughts, her pace increasing as she led me around another corner and down another hall, this one filled with frightened Trpaslíks. Each of their faces was turned toward something I couldn't see, as though I was nothing more than an apparition among them. Perhaps I was dead already. "We are the same."

Her words were a confusing mess as we turned again, the hallway sloping down. The sound of the rushing water I had heard before echoed from somewhere below us, somewhere in the dark.

"It's time," she said again, her focus forward as she finally came to a stop in a dark, narrow room where the sound of water was overwhelming. "We must end this now."

Unable to hold my weight any longer, I fell to my knees, glancing around the room that was suffocating in a smooth oil, lines and features indistinguishable, although I was sure there was a large door somewhere on the other side. All I could see clearly was the shadow of my other self and the rushing underground river she stood next to.

Against the far wall, water rushed over the stones in a torrent, swirling into a bright white foam before that was swallowed by a wide open mouth of stone, the tiniest hint of bright blue light glowing somewhere beyond it.

The same light I had seen. The same light I was drawn to.

"Imdalind," I gasped, my voice strangled.

"He's waiting for you," the other me said, pulling my attention from the glow to her. She was sadly smiling before she faded into nothing, leaving me staring at the dark stone and the sound of rushing water loud in my ears.

I stayed there, crouched on the stone as I tried to keep myself upright, my desperate breaths growing farther apart, my magic pulling me forward. Pulling me toward the light, toward the river that I was sure was the one Ilyan had told me about.

The one where the dead are sent back to the depths of the earth.

"Ilyan," I gasped as I struggled over the stone, praying that he could hear me, that I could feel his magic one last time before I went in there. Before I, too, went back to the earth, back to the magic that was already pulling at me, calling to me.

"You are running out of time, Joclyn!" my own voice yelled at me, echoing over the dark pit of earth and back to me. "You have to go now."

"Ilyan!" I gasped again, pulling myself over the stone. I tried to force as much sound into my voice as I could but couldn't get much above a whisper. "Ilyan, I'm sorry."

Stone scratched against my arms and legs as I dragged myself toward the river, toward the light, desperate to reach it, my body numb against the smothering pain. Slime covered the ground the closer the end came.

"Ilyan," I breathed out on a sigh as my hand slipped, sending me face first into the freezing water.

Skin burning and stinging from the chill, I felt my magic spark from the power inside of it. But it wasn't enough.

Water smothered me as the current pulled me under, filling my nose and mouth as I tried to take a desperate breath. My insides burned from the cold, the icy fire consuming me while I thrashed along the stream, thrown against walls and floors.

I fought against it, pointlessly battling the current in a battle that was far too familiar. A battle I was sure I had fought before.

Breathing in the burn of water, I opened my eyes to the bubbles of the stream and to Sain's face. His laughing, smiling face. Clean shaven, scar-less, younger.

It took me a moment to recognize him as a sight, to recognize the image as past ... as a past that seemed more like memory.

He laughed while he held me beneath the waves, my body thrashing against him, against the current, against the water that filled my lungs.

I gulped again, my head smashing against stone as the vision of Sain departed, leaving me staring into dark bubbles and stone, everything fading as my already water-filled lungs gave up, as my oxygen-deprived brain began fading into death.

I tried to fight it, to rip myself from the water, but my strength was gone.

I was gone, sinking into the icy water. I was swept under the current and into the mouth of the earth, its depths swallowing me.

I love you, Ilyan.

28

ILYAN

"DON'T LISTEN TO HER!" Ryland screamed as he continued to fight the frightened child at the other end of the blue room, the once beautiful gathering space now in shambles.

I attempted to stop him again, knowing he was moments away from killing the girl, but Ryland just shrugged me off, pushing me away from him with a glare so deep I momentarily saw our father in him, all signs of Ryland lost.

My temper bristled at his inappropriate command, at his lack of respect. He had already attacked me. He was lucky I hadn't ripped his head from his shoulders.

"Get Joclyn to the pool!" he continued, the anger vanishing as he pulled me right back to where I needed to be, to my mate, to the woman I had left propped up against the stone wall, moments from death. My heart sagged, everything throbbing in pain. "You don't have time for this!" Ryland screamed again, "I can handle it!"

He was right. I needed to let this go. I could punish him for his subordination later, but right now, I needed to save her.

Looking from Ryland to Míra, I swallowed my pride, my jaw tight as I forced the anger back down.

"Don't do anything stupid, brother," I said, fixing him with as much warning as I could.

He met the look dead-on before throwing himself back into the fight, leaving me to Joclyn as his half-hearted promise fell on deaf ears, my focus already on something far more frightening: the smear of blood that lined the floor right where I had left Joclyn.

Right where Joclyn had vanished from.

"Jos," I gasped, my stomach twisting in agony as I turned, trying to find some sign of her, trying to understand where she could have gone so quickly. Nothing was there, nothing except a bright smear of blood that led off into the dark, down the long hallway to the dungeons, to the river of farewell.

"No," I gasped, the already twisted fear that gripped me tightening until I could barely breathe. I knew what was down there. It was the end ... the end of this life.

The tunnels of Imdalind shook around me as the dark opening of the tunnel grew in my mind. The dread of what I was facing transformed into a monster as my fear screamed of the death I would find.

Turning back toward Ryland in a panic, my heart fell further when I found him already gone, following the girl to some new battle. I was the only soul left in the derelict space.

"Joclyn!" I yelled as I turned back to the smear of crimson, pushing myself forward as I followed the sinister path that she had left behind, right toward the dark hallway of dungeon and death.

Running down the hall, I let my magic roll out of me, the power that was so used to being restrained truly free for the first time in centuries. I was ready to fight, ready to rip whoever had taken her limb from limb.

Ready to save her.

"Joclyn!" My voice was an echo as it stretched down the dark hallway before me, the empty corridor swallowing me as the ominous pressure of what I was approaching hit me.

I let my magic stretch away from me in a desperate attempt to find her, knowing our connection should pull me right toward her. I should be able to feel her, to hear her inside my mind.

But there was only a low buzzing as faint as if the wires between us were snapping, one after another.

Joclyn! I screamed again, keeping my voice in my mind as I forced it through the last of our magic, the fragile fibers stretching and cracking under the pressure. *Joclyn, answer me, please! I'm coming!*

Pushing myself further, I ran down the halls, my heart stuttering painfully as the answer to my plea came, not from my magic, not from my mind as I had grown so used to, but from the shadows ahead of me.

"Ilyan!" A single word echoed back from the dark, the sound distorted as a single cry hit me in the chest, pulling my heart into a broken abyss. "Ilyan, I'm sorry."

The break in my soul shattered into a ravine of pain, the already fragile wires between us snapping one by one.

"No!" I cried, letting my voice carry over the stone and to the small room that was only steps from me where the sound of the river that carried the dead roared in my ears. "Joclyn! I'm coming! Hold on!"

Pushing my legs faster, I soared over the last few feet, terrified about what I would find in the hall ... about whether I would be too late.

Magic roaring to life, I prepared for a fight as I soared into the tiny room, expecting Trpaslíks to swarm the space, to be throwing Joclyn into the depths of the world.

But it was only her, only her frail body at the river's edge, her body shaking as she fell headfirst into the roaring waters, the current grabbing her and pulling her under.

"No!" I screamed as I rushed toward her, my magic reaching for her, unable to grip her, unable to pull her back.

It was only the desperate grip of my fingers as I reached for her, the slick ribbon from her hair as I wound it between my fingers in a desperate attempt to hold on to her, to pull her back from the undertow.

"Joclyn, no." My voice was broken as I tried to hold on to the ribbon, to stop it from sliding between my fingers, to stop her from leaving me. Before one beat of my broken heart could stutter into existence, however, it was gone.

The ribbon slipped from my fingers as she was sucked into the dark. She was ripped from me, and the last fragile string of our bond snapped, leaving me alone. Alone as I always had been. Alone as I had been told I would always be.

My throat was ripped into pieces as I screamed, falling to my hands and knees in a desperate reach for the water, ready to throw myself into the foam, to follow her to whatever life followed after this. Ready to die alongside her.

But, with one touch, the water shot through me with a blast that burned and snapped against my bones, pressing against me like a boulder in my gut. Joclyn's familiar magic threw me back with a protective spell that sent me soaring over the stone of the tiny room.

With a whack, I landed against the stone, my hands and knees stinging and burning from the impact. I felt the burn. I felt my own blood pooling against my skin. But it didn't matter. Nothing mattered. She was gone.

Falling back, I sat on the ground, her blood covering me, my hands stretched toward the swirling water, toward the only thing I wanted in this life, and I screamed. I screamed with the pain of loss I had never hoped to feel, the pain of a thousand years of waiting, the pain of a thousand years with her I would never get, the pain of a life I didn't wish to continue without her.

I didn't want to.

The screams continued to rip from inside of me, rattling in the air. I screamed my anger at the milky foam of the river, the last haunted echo of her voice rippling through the room.

I love you, Ilyan.

29

JOCLYN

"Oh, yes, hit her harder because that worked so well last time."

A sharp pain moved over my cheek as a slap reverberated in my ears. The impact pulled me out of the dark bubbles that had surrounded me and right back to the pain that splintered my bones and twisted my chest. Except, now the pain was full of a cold so penetrating it burned my skin. Every inch of me was covered in the burn of frost from the icy water I had thrown myself into.

Long icicles were frozen in my hair, the fragile points cracking as I gasped for breath. My chest arched in desperation. I writhed, blossoms of color and sight sparking through the black behind my eyes. My lungs burned with the inhale, the taste of blood strong against my tongue as I coughed and heaved, water gushing from my air-starved lungs as it was expelled along with other vile things.

Lungs and throat burning, I was rolled onto my side by strong hands, giving the water and vomit somewhere else to go besides all over me. A flash of a hundred swords cracked within the black of my sight as I hurled, each one strapped to the hip of an army. I watched them march, each fall of their feet ripping through my body, tensing my chest as the agonizing pain from Sain's attack ripped me from the sight and back to the blurred swirls of stomach acid over rocks.

"See? Told you it would work," a tiny, high-pitched voice answered the other one.

Cold air moved over my face as someone moved my hair out of the way of the mess that kept coming, the acid making my throat burn more.

"Hitting someone back to consciousness does not qualify as *working*," the first voice, a woman, said in irritation.

"And yet she is awake," the tiny voice snapped from somewhere in the dark above me.

I attempted to turn, to see who was there, but there was nothing but black as my sight took me somewhere far away, to Ilyan as he sat, sobbing in the dark cave I had just left. Heart tensing, I watched the image, the moment gone a second later and replaced by Wyn. A mania in her I hadn't seen before took over as she screamed into the dark.

The moment with Wyn was just as important, but it was Ilyan who stayed with me. It was only Ilyan I saw.

Ilyan, I gasped in desperation, unable to make the words come. I just kept throwing up, knowing someone was around me yet not caring who they were or what they were talking about.

Ilyan! I'm here!

I needed to get back to Ilyan and save him. There was still time. I knew it.

He was all that mattered.

Ilyan.

Attempting to focus past the oppressive darkness, I screamed for him, but there was only silence. No response, no whisper of him, of his magic, of our bond.

It was all gone. He was gone.

No.

Ilyan! I screamed, attempting to push myself up and find a way out of the dark I was trapped in. However, I barely moved. What little movement I could muster was immediately squashed by the hands that seemed to be everywhere. Hands that pushed and prodded and shoved me back down to the stone.

Head rattling against the impact, I gasped, pain flowering from my mark in a spider web that cracked across my skull, breaking into smacks of color and flashes of sight, everything blending together in a deeper pain that pressed against my skull.

I tried to scream, but no sound came other than a splutter of water and a gasp. The sights continued to flash, an image I had never seen but remembered very clearly coming into focus: Me dancing on my back porch, my parents hanging the decorations for my party, and a bright blue Vilỳ fluttering right behind me.

The image was pristine before pain wiped it away, sending

me back into the icy chill of black. One thing was very clear. I had felt this pain before.

I waited for the scream to rip from me as I shook and writhed. One of the warm hands pressed against my neck, the slight pressure numbing the fire.

"Shhh, child," a calm female voice whispered. "It's okay. You're okay."

Ilyan. Desperate to hear from him, I pled, the single word on repeat as I was rolled onto my back with a groan. The cold of the stone was welcome against the racking pain of my body as it attempted to turn itself inside out. *Where are you?*

"Where ...?" I forced out through the burn, desperation churning in my gut as my panic mounted.

I needed to know where I was, where Ilyan was, what had happened. My plea was an unheard gasp of air, however; the single word question fell to nothing.

"We have been waiting for this moment for centuries, Rinax. Be kind," another woman said, different from the first. This one's voice was an odd gruff of irritation.

Soft hands continued to move over my face, a comforting heat sinking into me with each touch. It filled me, flowing over my muscles and bones as pain leached from my skin with each stroke, with each pulse of the stranger's magic that coursed through me.

Groaning, I focused on the calm, letting it fill me as the confusing flashes of sight left. A haunting blue glow pulled me past the black. It floated above me, hovering in the air the same as it had in my sights.

"Imdalind," I gasped, my throat burning in agony.

My sight flashed back and forth between the glow above me and the orb I had seen beside the wide black pool of water.

"And she can talk, too," the squeak said, sounding just as irritated as he had been before. "You two need to stop doubting me."

The squeak was met by a grunt, and the warm hand left my cheek as a blurry outline of a face moved in front of the glow, brown and orange smeared together in a confusing streak that solidified into a face.

"Joclyn?" the deep voice said. The wobbles of color shifted with the single word, making me sure this was the one who was talking. "You are here with us. We pulled you from the river that runs through this cave before taking the dead to the center of the earth. We felt your magic before it faded completely and revived it. You are here, right where you need to be, Imdalind is feet away. You are almost there. Can you hear me, Joclyn?"

I lay there, listening to the voices, feeling the deep reverberation of magic flow from the hand that was once again pressed against my jaw.

"Ilyan," I gasped, panic rising as my sight flickered into a single image of Ilyan, his eyes hard as he faced his sister, clenching his teeth in preparation.

I knew that face, and it was terrifying.

The image was distorted enough that I could tell I was peeking into the future. It was coming, and I needed to get there before it did.

Before she killed him.

"I need to go. I have to save him." My stuttered words broke past the burn in my throat as the sight disappeared, leaving me staring at the people above me, their faces doubling and tripling as my vision slowly came into focus.

"You cannot, child," the calm woman whispered down to me familiarly, her visage finally ceasing its dance, and I saw her for the first time: hair bright in the dark, so pale it looked to be woven from pure light. "There is only one way to help him now. He will understand. He was created to understand. I raised him to understand."

"*Raised him*?" I asked as I stared at her. Her bright blue eyes cut into me with a dark familiarity that made my magic pulse and pull.

It was then that the familiarity of the voice made sense. The comfort of her magic and touch, it all made sense. As impossible as it seemed.

"Frain?" I asked. The story I had heard only a few times smashed into my head.

Her name was a stutter on my lips, but her smile was wide as she nodded. I barely saw the movement before my sight obscured her. The same woman who sat before me was now kneeling in an ornate courtyard, dressed in an elegant gown from many centuries before, and standing before her was a little boy I recognized at once, even though he couldn't be more than eight.

She smiled at the young Ilyan before the sight faded, leaving me staring at the same woman, shrouded this time in the dark that surrounded us.

"No," I gasped as everything broke in two, death and failure hitting me hard in the chest.

Right then, the pain didn't matter. The way my head was splitting in two didn't matter. My heartbreak, however, mattered. My failure mattered.

"Joclyn?" she whispered as she pressed her hand against my cheek, and what I was sure was her magic moved into me. "Silnỳ? Are you all right?"

"I failed. I didn't save him. I didn't save any of them," I said, the china plate of my soul cracking into slivers.

"What are you talking about, child?" the gruff voice of the second woman asked as she came up beside the first, her annoyance reflected in the dark of her eyes. The rich color glistened through the black that obscured most of them. They were the same as Wyn's, the same as every other Trpaslík I knew.

"Chyline," I sobbed, my voice broken by the tears that were flowing freely now.

The woman only smiled, her deep mahogany skin crinkling.

"It's true, then? I died. I failed."

The tears fell faster. The pain from the knowledge hit me hard. No wonder I couldn't feel my connection with Ilyan. No wonder I could scarcely feel my magic.

"Oh, what are you on about, *I died*?" the squeaky voice mocked. The same blue glow from before joined the women, hovering above me. I turned my head, staring at the face of a tiny blue sphinx. "You have got to be kidding me. Are you really that daft?"

The creature lingered in the air above me, his upturned nose squished up in irritation. Fast moving bright blue wings pushed cold air over me as the Vilỳ fluttered.

"A Vilỳ," I gaped at him, at his beauty, at the familiarity to the being I had seen in sight moments before. The same one I had seen drawn on the walls of Ryland's mind. The same Vilỳ who had bitten me.

"Really? Where?" He mocked me further, his irritation mounting. "I thought you said you were dead, not hallucinating."

"But you are here," I said, my voice strangely monotone in shock. "And you passed centuries before—"

"You *can't* die, foolish child," Rinax spat as he landed on my chest, perched like a misshapen dog on my still blood-streaked shirt. "Just as we cannot. Your life is the earth's, and you cannot die until she does. How many times do people have to tell you what's going on before you believe them?"

The damp fabric of my shirt made odd squelching sounds as he pranced over my ribcage, leaving me staring.

"What do you mean I can't die?" I asked, my mind stuck on the statement, something that only irritated Rinax more. "Everyone dies—"

"I will not repeat that again," the Vilỳ interrupted with a growl. "If I could not taste your magic when I bit you, if I could not sense it in the air around you, I would question if you were the right one. You do not seem like the Silnỳ that raised me."

"Do not worry, Rinax; she is the right one," Frain said. "I can feel the earth magic in her, as well. Even the part she gave to Timothy's daughter is there, barely hidden."

"So, I'm somehow *magically* unable to die?" I asked, my mind still stuck on the conversation of a moment ago.

"You see the future and conjure spells, and this is the magic you doubt?" Rinax hissed with a roll of his eyes, his wings smothering me in cold as he hovered inches from my face, the close proximity causing me to flinch. "I have never known someone so ridiculous."

The pit in my stomach grew with each word he spoke, falling farther and farther to my toes as his truth became clear.

I swallowed, my magic flashing again as sight blossomed before me, image after image of magic and Miracles rotating inside my mind: Dramin's healing; Wyn's revival; Ilyan's impossible stutter, his connection fusing with mine. They came one after another until they ended with the image of Ilyan and Ovailia locked in battle. I felt the desperation to help, that knot of need twisting in my stomach.

With a flash, the images left as I looked back up at the stubborn Vilỳ, his eyes glistening with smugness.

I bit my lips together in a tight line, staring at him dead-on. He was right. I knew he was. Still, something about the way he looked at me was making me very stubborn to admit it.

"See?" he shot, his attitude bristling more. "We are not dead … just as you aren't."

"Not yet in this life," Frain added, her smile a calm shadow that soothed away my pride.

"But we are. The first four ... We have all passed from the world long ago."

I looked from Frain to Chyline as the two women moved closer to me, a haunted sorrow painted on both their faces. I stared at them, my mind spinning on its axis because of what she had just said, refusing to comprehend.

"How can that be?" I asked, still trying to understand. My heart stuttered painfully, the organ encompassed in the dread that had filled the air.

I knew magic could do something so crazy, yet I was lost as to how it could be.

"Perhaps the better word is not dead, but passed. We cannot die because, as the first of our kind, our magic is bound to the earth, just as you are. We have been here for centuries, waiting for you," Frain said, smiling gently.

"*For me*?" I asked, yet more confusion rising up.

Rinax took flight with a grunt of disappointment, a trail of light speeding from him as he soared away from us, a string of complaint and what I was sure were profanities following behind him.

"Don't mind him," Frain said with a smile. "Vilỳs are not known for patience."

Rinax huffed angrily from where he hovered somewhere in the distance. The only thing that remained of him was a solitary blue light suspended elegantly in the dark.

The ceiling and walls were indistinguishable. For all I knew, the cavern went on forever, stretched throughout the core of the earth in an abyss. Only Rinax's light gave me some idea of the space, thanks to the massive black pool his light reflected off of. Exactly as I had seen in my sight.

"It was him," I gasped as my magic shook inside my bones, placing the clear image from my sight, from this moment, into a perfect overlay. "That is where my sight wanted me to be."

"What do you mean?" Frain asked, pulling my attention back to her.

With a hiss of pain, I pulled myself into a fully sitting position, my hands pressing against the rough stone floor of what I now recognized as a cave. "My sight showed me this. It wanted me to be here," I gasped, each word tightening my chest painfully. "It wanted me dead."

"No, child." Ilyan's grandmother smiled, her hair shimmering as though it were made from light. "It wanted you home."

Home.

Something about the word pulled at me, tugged at my heart and pulled me right into sight. My pained chest gasped for air as the same cave reemerged before me, only brighter. Everything was clear and crisp, as all sights of the past were. The clarity in the sight was as alarming as what was in it.

Myself, the same self I had seen in that haunting white sight. The same who had prompted me to the underground river, standing on the edge of the massive pool.

Gasping in shock, I watched myself, my heart plunging to the ground, terror gripping me as I stared at the water's edge, the two of us breathing in deep synchronization. The water below her began to bubble, swirling around her calves as she waded in. Her own gasp of shock rippled across the silence as the surface broke with a torrent of bubbles, four small bodies appearing just below the dark water: two boys and two girls, one of the boys blue and wrinkled.

"The four," I gasped to myself in recognition, my mind still reeling as I tried to understand what I was looking at and why I was there.

My heart tensing, I watched myself rush deeper into the waters, pulling the blue boy out in desperation.

"No, no," her frightened voice echoed around the cave as she worked to revive him. "You can't die on me, boy. We need you."

The other four, just children, made their way to the banks and circled around her as the older me worked in a panic.

She compressed his chest once more before she turned her head, placing her ear against his chest as she listened for a heartbeat, her eyes looking straight at me.

Straight into me.

She could see me.

"Do you understand now?" she asked as she lifted her head to look at me, everything freezing around her as she stepped toward me. My own feet moved back with terrified confusion. "Do you understand what you are?"

I stepped back again, my breath caught in my chest as I was backed into a wall.

"I am Drak," I was finally able to answer, forcing the words out through my panic. "That is what you said before."

"It's true. You are. You are the first of the Drak. The first of the Skřítek. The first of the Vilỳ. The first of the Trpaslík. You are the first and the last of magic. I am. We are all." She smiled, the grin a wide span across her face in an odd wickedness.

"Why are you here?" I asked.

"Why are we here, you mean," she corrected, her smile widening. "You see yourself in this life that you assume is not yours, but it is yours. It is your life, a life before this one, a life that was taken from you."

"Wh-what are you talking about?" I stuttered, my heart beating faster as my magic ignited, pulsing and pulling at me, trying to show me something. But I couldn't let it. I was stuck looking at this other me who merely smiled.

"You will see," she answered, her voice dark and frightening as my sight vanished, leaving me staring at black. Black faded back into the cave and the two woman who sat before me in awe, the adult counterparts to the sight I had just had.

They stared in amazement, obviously having not missed the black sheen of my eyes. I, on the other hand, could only look back at them in horror, my heart beating too fast and my muscles too tight.

"What did you see?" Chyline asked, the hunger in her voice further igniting the panic and confusion I already felt.

"I saw myself," I spat, barely able to control my emotions. "I saw myself ... in the water. I saw you coming out ... out of Imdalind. But ... But you were children." My panic had increased far too much.

I jerked away from them just as I had in sight, my gaze

flickering in desperation to find some kind of escape from whatever hell I had wandered into.

"So you know, then," Frain said, her calm smile out of place.

"Know what!" I yelled, my resolve snapping as I jerked toward them.

The two woman hardly flinched, and Frain's smile still remained firmly in place.

"You know what you are." The voice was different, but the words were the same, Chyline echoing exactly what I had said to myself.

"Don't give me that. That's what she ... what I ..." I stuttered to a stop, my frustration continuing to boil over. "I don't know. I don't even know what I saw!"

"You saw the beginning of magic," Chyline finished for me, her smile so wide any hope of falsehood in the sight was forgotten. "You saw your true self begin it."

"You saw yourself as you brought us from the mud," Frain finished for her, the few simple words twisting inside my gut.

"I don't ..." I gasped, desperate to refute it yet knowing I could not. "But that is not me. It can't be. Don't you see?"

"I do," Chyline interrupted. "I see the same woman who raised me. I feel your magic. I know it is a jumble to you. But that life is your life, just as this life is your life. They are one in the same."

"Does anyone speak English around here?" I mumbled under my breath, hardly able to control another outburst.

"Calm down, Silnỳ," Frain said, her hand soft against my arm. I still flinched.

I knew what I had seen. I knew what it meant.

I knew it was true.

I didn't want to admit it.

"You said I wasn't dead."

"Not in this life," Chyline answered. "You are the same as us. No, even above us. The magic of the earth is tied to you. Even when Sain thought he had killed you after Edmund's ascension, you came back. And, I must say, coming back as Sain's daughter was quite the trick. I would expect nothing less from you."

If I was confused before, it was nothing compared to now. The cave around us moaned, shaking the floor I still sat on, sending the pool splashing over the bank. But I didn't even turn. I scarcely registered it.

"Sain killed me?" I asked, my voice quivering as I watched Chyline. Her Cheshire smile was all that was visible as she moved into the depths of the cave we sat in.

"In a past life," she answered.

"It's not possible."

"It is," she said from the dark.

"You are the Silnỳ," Frain added, the words I heard so many times before causing a fresh wave of panic to cascade against my soul.

"Powerful." I tried not to sound frustrated, but it sneaked out, anyway.

"It means so much more than *powerful*, so much more than what was shown in sight. It means you are the first—*the very first*," she continued, her voice echoing hauntingly as sight pulled at me, a single flash of myself reviving the blue-tinted boy breaking through.

"It is me, then," I said as my magic roared a bit, flashes of sight still fueling my confusion.

"She is not stupid, this one," Frain said with a wide smile, her eyes shining just as Ilyan's did.

"She never was." Chyline smiled as Rinax came back, landing beside her, a smile still devoid from his face.

The two woman continued smiling at me while Rinax stared at me in expectation as my magic swelled, the pain that had been slowly deserting my head returning with a roar.

I yelled in pain as I slapped my hand against my head, hoping desperately that the pressure would disperse the pain. However, it grew as my vision left again, plunging me into the golden glow of sight.

I saw myself with the same children I had pulled from the dark water of Imdalind. The blue child transformed into the Vilỳ who had been fluttering before us. I watched the five of us laugh as I taught them how to use their magic, as Chyline transformed a rock into liquid gold, a young Sain screaming in terror.

That image faded and another replaced it, the same cave surrounding me as Sain approached, his eyes sad with each step forward.

"I'm tired of waiting, Silnỳ," he said as he fell down at my feet. "All of my siblings have found their love, and I am alone."

I looked at him before turning toward the pool, my eyes sad as I led him toward it, as I showed him how to drop a single droplet of blood below the surface, to let it blend with my magic and create a new life.

Dramin.

The sight shifted to the four as they ruled, to cities as they were built, to the large pools of sight that Sain and Dramin built.

Sight after sight came of a life I didn't know before it stopped on the cave surrounding me as I lay in the pool of dark water, floating there before Sain entered. He was the same Sain I had seen in premonition moments ago when I had been flushed down the river and into the center of the earth.

With a gasp, I pulled myself from the sight, the other three coming back into focus as my heart thundered heavily in my chest. The vision I had seen became a nightmare.

"This is not your first life, child," Frain continued as Chyline patted my knee sympathetically, both women oblivious to the real reason for my panic.

I wished her touch could bring relief. I only had confusion.

My eyes were wide as I looked between one and the other.

"What did you see?" Rinax asked, his irritation finally fading. He folded his arms, pursing his lips as he waited for an answer. "I can see it on your face. You saw something."

"She saw our birth, Rinax," Chyline whispered, her voice

sounding far away as my sight pulled at me once again, a single flash of Sain's face as he laughed from below the dark water.

No, not below.

I was below.

It was the same sight I had seen as the water pulled me under, and now I knew why.

"I saw more than that," I said as I pushed the sight away, looking at the three again, the fear of the admission pulling at my heart. "I saw Sain."

My shoulders pulled in as the sight came again, shifting and moving to that same version of me I had seen before. This time, I was held under the water as Sain wrapped his hands around my neck.

"He drowned me, didn't he?" I couldn't even look at them as I said it. "Before ... when he killed—" I still couldn't make myself say it. "He drowned me."

The three stared at me, their eyes becoming very sad as Frain nodded. My heart fell to my toes in a devastated confusion.

"In Imdalind. He drowned you in the well," Frain said, her calm voice seeming very far away. "Your body was lost. It's why you didn't linger like we do. It's why you had to come back and why you don't remember anything."

"But why would he do that?" I asked. "If I really did create everything—"

"He did it for the same reason he has tried to destroy your life." Chyline's voice was soft as she shifted closer to me, as though she was suddenly worried someone else would overhear. "The same obsession has haunted him for centuries. After Edmund was kissed and the Chosen Children were discovered, you decreed that the four of us were no longer to rule. Ruling is all he desires."

"That retribution has consumed him," Frain continued, the timbre of her voice continuing the haunting quality of the story. "The emotion, the need, was so strong that, even after his passing, after his death, he thought of nothing else. His focus was so singular even your existence was lost to him."

Whatever beating my tense heart was able to muster was forced to a stop, the ironclad evil pressing against my chest in a painful weight. "Sain ...? What do you mean by *after his passing*?"

I really didn't want to know, but I had no choice.

"He has passed from this earth, just as we have, child."

"But he's my father. He walks around and performs magic and ..." I gasped, staring between them, desperate for an answer, desperate for some explanation of what they were talking about, for some calm.

All I got, however, was the overly calm blue-eyed stare from Frain, the look so sympathetic it almost made it worse. My stomach sunk to my toes as I tried to swallow the panic away, but it only mounted, drowning me.

"As we could have if we had chosen to," Frain explained, the words seeming hollow. "But that was not to be, not after what Sain has done."

"What has he done?" This time, I wanted to know.

My blood boiled in anger at the possibility of what else he could have done, at what secrets these three could hold. The anger seemed to be reciprocated for the first time, however. Rinax's skin sprouted into tiny spikes in his irritation.

"He was the last of us to pass from this life," Chyline suddenly interrupted. "He killed the three of us first."

I hadn't expected that.

Muscles tense, I looked between the three of them, not knowing what to say, so I just waited, knowing more was coming.

"He stabbed me through the heart when I challenged him," Frain said, her eyes sad. "We were in the forest, and I would have escaped, lived on as he has, if he hadn't taken me back to the castle and claimed one of the mortals had attacked us. From that point on, everyone thought me dead and my life as they knew it was over. It was imperative I remain hidden. It was safer anyway, what with what my death began."

"It started a civil war," Rinax whispered, the irritation that had lined his voice up until that moment gone, "one that I am sure still graces your textbooks. Thousands died, and magic was pushed into secrecy."

"I was the last death in the war," Chyline interrupted, my brain buzzing with the information I was being inundated by. "The last of the magic, or so the mortals were told by Sain. They tortured me in the bellows of a castle, beheaded me before a crowd of thousands. Sain had convinced them that the war was my fault, my bid for control." She shook her head, her eyes narrowing as my sight flashed.

Eyes black, I saw that moment, saw the beautiful woman

before me folded over a blood-soaked pedestal, the large ax glistening in the sun above her. The ax cut the air, hitting against her skin as the sight vanished, leaving me gasping in the dark as I stared at the woman before me, her head very much attached to her shoulders.

"But why would he kill you if you can't die?" I asked, still trying to put the pieces of this fantasy together.

Chyline smiled as I stared at her, obviously understanding what I had seen. She wrapped her hand around her neck to illustrate the point I was having a hard time making.

"He didn't know. He killed us all, assuming our lives would end as our entire lineage does. But we are tied to it, controlling our magic forever," Rinax said simply, reiterating what was said before; only, now it made sense. "He probably doesn't even realize that he himself is dead."

"Then how do you know he is?"

"I know because I watched him die," Rinax finally announced, the pride in his voice unsurprising, especially with what I knew of Sain. "When Edmund was torturing him to get the sight about you, Edmund slit his throat. I watched him bleed out until there was nothing left to spill from him. I watched Ovailia collapse in pain as the bond between them broke. I listened to his heart stop."

"But ... but ..." I stuttered, desperate for some piece of information that would wipe away his confusion.

"He gasped for air minutes later," Rinax went on, ignoring my stuttering interruption. "No blood in him, and he gasped for air. No life in him, and he stood up. No magic in him, and he still saw into the future. He is the first of his kind. We all are. You can't kill us unless all of our magic is gone from the earth. The Drak magic that was still on the earth brought him back, blood pumping through his veins ... just as our magic brought us all back ... just as yours has."

"But if he can't die—no," I corrected myself, "if he is already dead, how is anyone to destroy him? How am I to kill him?"

"You are the only one who can," Chyline said as she came to sit beside me, her hand gentle as she patted my knee. "He can only die when all of the Drak magic is gone from the earth, and even then, it would take a powerful attack to end his life."

"All the Draks ..." I gasped, my heart tensing in pain as the last piece fell into place. "But Dramin is gone. I am all that is left."

Rinax nodded his head, Chyline's eyes grew darker. "You must die before Sain's life can be truly ended."

I didn't even need Frain's response to know what it meant.

"You must die," Frain said. "To end all of this, you must die."

"It is only *for* Ilyan that you will be able to accomplish all that you must," the three of them began to recite together, their voices the same dull void that I thought was only for the Draks in sight. Yet, here it was, winding down my spine with a chill that made me shiver. "It is Ilyan's place to protect you until the day that you pass from this world and into the next."

"No," I gasped, knowing what they were reciting and not wanting to hear any more.

"This child is power, power that is strong enough for *the*

world," they continued, causing my bones to twist further with the sound of their voices. "The one bred to change the world of magic. The one bred to die."

Silence followed, a numbing low that wound around the cave until all I could hear was the distant rumble of a battle I had all but forgotten and the sound of water loud in my ears, calling for me.

I turned toward the large dark space, feeling the magic move over my skin, melting the last of the ice and warming me, heating me.

"No," I sobbed, tears falling over my cheeks as I stared into the dark toward the water.

"I know you wish to save your love, Silnỳ. I could see your desperation to reach him earlier," Frain whispered, running her hand over the hair on the crown of my head, pulling at the ribbon there. "You would give your life to save him."

"I would." The tears had begun to slow as a familiar magic began to swell inside of me, the smooth surface of the water calling to me.

"It is not by your side that you will accomplish your task, it is for him." Frain whispered, her voice lost somewhere to the side of me. "It is for all of us."

Frain was right. I had spent the last few months preparing to destroy Edmund and then Sain, preparing to save Ilyan. And now it was here, the possibility to do it all. I had just never assumed it would have come in this way, in a willing death ... in myself walking into Imdalind.

Yet it was here, and I couldn't turn my back on it.

I stood slowly, my legs shaking underneath me, and the two women moved to support me on either side, weaving their arms through mine.

"You are very brave," Frain whispered, pushing the dark tangles of my hair behind my ear with her free hand. "My grandson is very lucky to have you."

My heart throbbed painfully, the reality sitting on me heavily, the weight compounding with each step I took toward the pool.

The water lapped against the bank, the waves increasing the closer I moved. The magic in the air rose as the water reacted to me.

To what I was.

It was something I still didn't want to admit, but I knew I couldn't run away from it. I couldn't deny it. Not with the way my magic reacted to the pool, my sight flashing as a perfect overlay moved over my vision.

The older me stood in the middle of the water, the dark liquid swirling around her as her magic swelled. She moved like a dance, the peek into the past haunting.

And then, just like before, everything around her stopped. The water froze in the air as she turned toward me, her eyes dark with sight as she looked at me exactly as I looked at her.

"The end is here," we said together. "The time for magic is over. The time for life has begun."

Our voices faded, but she did not. She stayed heavy in my

gaze, beckoning me into the water as my magic continued to throb and pull.

"Tell Ilyan I love him," I said to no one in particular. "I'll always love him."

Without another word, I walked away from them, following Rinax's light as I waded into the pool and toward the end.

With one step into the water, the world around me seemed to scream in response. The cave shook as dust fell around me, sprinkling over my head. However, I barely noticed, my focus forward, on the woman who was waiting for me.

The cave rumbled again as I stepped farther into the pool, the heat of the Black Water that filled the pool swirling around me. The formerly calm surface was suddenly alive as my magic reacted to it.

Swirls of color twirled like oil over the surface, moving from my skin as I waded in deeper, as if the color was my magic, leaching from me in its own quest to reach home, to be a part of what I was. No, of what I had created I realized with a start. My magic was reacting with a single flash of memory, with a life I had never lived.

Sight flashed bright in my eyes, an image of myself standing before the pool of Black Water I was now swimming in clear. I watched as I filled the depth with my own magic, creating it. The image left in a flash, the black cave rumbling as my consciousness returned to it, my legs pumping wildly as I attempted to tread water in the center of the pool.

The same woman from my sight, however, that haunted apparition of myself, stood still, as though the bottom wasn't leagues away. She faced me, face hollow and sad as I reached her, her dark eyes meeting mine.

With one intense look, the cave rumbled again with so much force I flinched. Several rocks dislodged themselves from the heights of the cave, falling into the water around us without so much as a splash, the Black Water swallowing them willingly.

"This is not the end," the other me said.

The rumble of the cave increased as she placed her hands on my shoulders, my magic reacting with a jolt of electricity.

I gasped from the power it filled me with, and I lost the rhythm of my tread, sinking beneath the surface before she pulled me back up.

"Listen to me, child," she said as I attempted to cough out the water, real fear filling me now over what I was about to do. "This is not the end. This is no ones end."

I opened my mouth to ask more, but the cave rumbled, and more rocks fell around us.

With the screams of the other three filling my ears, I was pushed under the surface, my open mouth filling with water as I was held there, just under the water.

Panic filled me as I began to fight against the strong hands of myself, fight for air my lungs were desperate for. I grabbed at her hands, reached for her face, frantic to claw at her. However, I couldn't reach, and she didn't move. She only stayed above me, the same sadness on her face as my fight slowly left, my arms falling beneath the surface.

I floated there, watching her as she held me, listening to the rumble of the water in my ears. It was just like before, when Wyn and Ilyan were healing my back. Except that this one wouldn't end with healing. My mind barely registered the thunderous splashes that moved over me, the boulders falling around me.

I turned toward the waves, toward the massive boulders as they broke through the water. One after another, they came as everything slowly faded to black.

"You created me?" I laughed, finally pulling Sain's focus from his best friend to me, his eyes widening slightly. "You created Thom? Manipulation and lies are not creation, Sain. You don't really think you can destroy me, do you? That you are stronger than the fire magic?"

Pulling my hand away from Thom, I finally felt the sizzle that was raging over my skin, the heat moving into the air in a radiant pressure.

A devious grin spread across my lips as my anger thundered, my magic moving from my feet and into the stone, ready to swallow him in fire.

Sain's own twisted smirk met mine as he jumped from his throne, that ridiculous cape flowing behind him as he stepped off the platform. He walked to meet us, his eyes unwavering from where we stood, looking from me to Thom, deciding who to attack first.

I was ready, ready to step into battle, when he suddenly

vanished. My heart dropped at the reminder of what we were now trapped with.

With a *pop*, he reappeared steps away from where we stood, his smile wider as he walked toward us, only to vanish back into the nothing. With another *pop*, he reappeared near the rear of the hall, taking another step before vanishing again.

With each step, he moved through the hall, disappearing and reappearing with *pops* that echoed within the open space.

Tensing against Thom, I wrapped a shield around us, the danger we were trapped with horrifying. Sain moved so sporadically I had no chance to attack him, but that didn't stop him from attacking us.

His eyes never left us with all the movement, his focus a hard glare that pushed fear into my chest, rattling the already thunderous beat of my heart. With one last *pop*, he stopped only feet away from where we stood with our arms around each other. He shimmered underneath the heat of my magic, the barrier that he held between us distorting him into a fuzzy mass of madness.

"Don't you see, Wyn? I am stronger than the *most powerful*. I defeated the Silnỳ. You are nothing more than an irritating flare-up needing to be extinguished." A wicked gleam sparked in his eyes, his own power vibrating through the air with enough force that I could feel it against my skin.

"Then I will make you burn." My voice dripped with sugar. It swam across the heat in the air and slapped against Sain who only looked at me more hungrily than before.

I didn't want to think about what he was hungry for.

"Why don't we see who wins, then? Fire or hell?" he said, his hand sparking as he lifted it toward us, an attack building there.

"Aren't you forgetting someone?" Thom yelled from beside me, his motions quick as he slammed his fist into the barrier, the bright red shard of the blade I had pulled from Ryland clenched between his fingers.

The Souls Blade hit against the barrier with a terrible clatter that echoed inside the cave. The eruption, the blade, the terrified look that covered Sain's face—it all converged with my magic in an explosion of color. It erupted from my hands, spraying wide as fire swirled through them in a kaleidoscope. The fiery prism collapsed the last of the barrier, running through it and right into Sain's chest.

He gasped at the impact, stumbling back as he attempted to send a counterattack, his wide movements sending it into the ceiling. Rocks and dirt showered down on us from the blast, the cave shivering.

Thom took his chance, rushing toward him with the blade, ready to plunge the sharp point into his chest. I attacked Sain again, hoping to distract him from Thom's movement, but it was in vain.

He looked at me with black eyes as he blocked my attack with one tiny flick of his fingers. His eyes darkened as his other hand swung up to block Thom, his own blade firmly in his fist.

With a *pop* of red light, the blades met in the air, showing us with a firework of color. The two men stood, struggling against each other in an attempt to make contact, their jaws taut from the effort.

"Nice try," Sain sneered before he slammed his free hand toward Thom's abdomen, his fingers flickering with light as he moved.

With a flick of my wrist, I flung a long chain of fire toward him, the weapon ready to wrap around him and pull him to the ground. It never made contact. It only soared past where Sain had been, my trail of fire uselessly fading into the dark.

Thom stumbled forward as the tension disappeared, my attack narrowly missing him.

Turning wide, I searched for Sain, magic moving into the stone of the floor in an attempt to find him. There was nothing there. Not even the smoke he had used to conceal himself before. Just a wide expanse of cold stone.

"Where is he?" Thom snapped as pushed himself to stand, pressing his back to mine while he began to search for the man.

"I don't trust this," I whispered, pressing against him as we scanned the room the way we had so any times before.

"It wouldn't be the first time he ran away," Thom whispered back, his feet dancing around mine as we rotated on the spot, our hands forward, at the ready.

"Well, aren't you two cute?" Sain's voice cut through the silence, hard and angry.

We jumped, turning toward the sound just as his attack made contact, a stream of violet light hitting me hard in the chest.

I flew through the air as the attack moved inside of me, numbing my arm as Sain's well-placed magic crippled me.

The fire in my blood devoured it as I soared away from Thom and Sain, bright strips of color surrounding them as their own battle began.

My fingers tingled as feeling came back, my magic rushing to the source, wrapping around me just in time to stop my impact with the high wall of the cave, holding me in the air like a rag doll as everything came back online.

I jerked, my muscles and nerves becoming responsive as the attack left. One surge plunged me forward, through the air and back to them in a strip of black. Magic shot from my hand and right into Sain, his barrier blocking it before it made contact.

"Great," I complained as I landed behind Thom. "You're hiding again. Fight like a man, you coward."

"Not a coward and not a man," Sain said, another attack from him easily blocked by Thom. "I am a king, and the last one there will be."

"Fine!" I roared, letting the fire build. "If we don't have kings after we end you, that's fine with me."

I shrugged my shoulders, the power exploding from me, and the blast hit in the chest. The force of it threw him into the air, sending him across the room and against the wall where the old man slid down the stone in a crumpled heap.

Chest heaving, I froze, staring at him, not foolish enough to think it had been that easy.

"Is that it?" Thom asked under his breath, the shard of red blade still clenched in his fist.

I held up my hand, watching Sain where he lay slumped

against the wall. He was breathing, but his eyes weren't open.

It wasn't a guarantee of anything.

"No way," I answered, my magic speeding into the ground toward him.

Thom took that as good enough and jumped into the air, a wide attack flung from his hand in a shower of sparks that soared toward the revolting rag doll.

As Thom attacked, so did I, my magic already spreading throughout the ground around him, shifting rocks, melting them. Stones bubbled and boiled as they began to swallow him. The slight movement jerked into him, his black eyes meeting mine, anger clear on his face.

"Thom! Watch out!" I screamed as, with a flick of Sain's fingers, Thom was sent hurtling through the air, his course spun into a free fall.

Thom's shout of fear erupted through the hall, his magic sparking as he tried to ignite it, to bring the wind back to him.

But there was only air and a stone floor below him.

"No!" I screamed, my magic rushing to catch him, moving across the air as it did through the ground.

Before I could reach him, Sain glanced at me with his dark eyes, and then his attack impacted against my chest, sending me stumbling back and right into the hard rock of Sain's chest, the tiny *pop* of his stutter a ghost in my ears.

Sain's arms wrapped around me, holding me tightly as I fought against him, desperate to reach Thom. But I couldn't.

Sain's laugh was loud in my ears as Thom hit the hard ground, the blade in his hand bouncing away from him with a clatter.

Sain's laugh deepened as his grip on me tightened, pressing his fingers into me as the rough chill of a blade pressed against my neck, cutting into my skin.

The pressure made me stop fighting, a wet heat flowing down my skin.

"Well, that was easy," Sain said, the heat of his breath a breeze past my hair. "I thought you two were going to give me a challenge."

Mommy!

Her voice rippled across my mind with the touch of her soul against mine. I recoiled, shifting my weight as I continued to fight Sain's hold, desperate to move away from the blade. But Sain's arms shifted, his hand pressing against my bare hip as his magic flooded me.

The foreign power swam inside of me, thick and rancid. It stuck against my soul in a heavy weight that made it difficult to move. I squirmed against the pressure, but it grew, his smothering magic trapping me in place.

"No, no, no," he soothed, the false comfort in his voice grating. "It's not going to be that easy for you, not anymore. You get to stay with me for a while. I have some use for you. There are a few people I need you to kill."

Fight him, Mommy! Rosaline's scream echoed in my head, flaring my magic into a white heat that burned against my skin.

I couldn't control it. It was just a rage underneath me, desperate to fight. Desperate to be unleashed.

Tears burned my eyes as I looked at Thom, his body crumpled on the ground, as unmoving as I was. My heart caught as I stared, looking for blood, for some kind of injury. I saw nothing, only the bright blue of his eyes as he stared at me from behind the thick dreads that fell over his face, the light in them fading. The look in them scared.

"Wyn," he breathed, his voice so weak it barely made it to me.

My heart tensed, the heat in my magic mounting as Rosaline's voice came again, banging inside my head.

Mommy! You have to save us!

It was enough.

Enough for one last time.

I looked at Thom, praying he could understand the look in my eyes, that he could understand the warning, see the apology. I hoped he could understand the good-bye. I didn't know if he would survive what I was about to do.

Mommy! I pressed my eyes shut, focusing on her voice as it reacted with my magic, as the blade against my neck heated alongside it, the strength of her presence strong enough that I was sure I could feel her tiny hand wrap around mine.

"Perhaps I will have you start with him. Would you like to kill Thom, Wynifred? Would you like to bring me his head as Edmund commanded you to so long ago?" Sain's voice was wet and uncomfortable in my ear as he pressed his lips against it.

A shiver rippled down my spine with the heat of my magic.

"No!" The word ripped from me as I turned my head, his magic slipping as mine ignited. "No, I won't."

His eyes widened when they met my glare, his jaw tightening as he began to breathe in dark inhales of pain, the agony clear on his face.

The dark scent of burning flesh flowed around us as his hand began to sizzle against my skin. The pain in his eyes turned into a scream when he couldn't take it anymore and tried to rip his hand away, only to find it stuck.

"Did you really think you could win?" I asked, stepping toward him as I took control, my magic so strong now that I couldn't stop the burn from swelling.

It was going to erupt exactly as I had thought.

For the first time since I had learned to control it, I was going to let it free.

Pity, I really liked this shirt.

"Do you want to face me as I am?"

Sain looked at me, true horror painting his face as I finally released him, leaving him to stumble away from me. My skin smoked as the fire took over.

Sain began to run as I caught fire, horror snaking into his eyes as he looked back at me, making it clear I had already started to change. The clothes were burned from my body, and my skin began to follow suit, dripping to the ground in large drops of molten gold. Each drop splattered over the floor, boiling into the rock as I rose into the air. I was nothing but fire and bone as the inferno consumed me.

Sain's skin began to boil as the air in the room became so hot it devoured him ... just as it was me.

I knew he would not survive it.

"Did you really think you would not burn?" My voice was a haunted echo as it flowed around the room.

The man before me screamed and clawed as the last of him was devoured, bursting into flames as the power in me consumed him. As my fire exploded.

With a scream, the last of the fire ripped from me, exploding in a blast that shook the room. It bellowed through me like thunder, dropping me down to the ground in a heap, the skin already knitting back over my bones.

The crackle of flames was loud, echoing over the charred stone as I lay in a heap, crying in pain as my body attempted to put itself back together.

I hated crying. I hated that I felt weak, especially with what I had just done. Powerful magic, a gift from the earth. That's what they said, but all it did was destroy. There wasn't strength in this.

Human bones were scattered around me, charred and brittle as they smoked, the scent of burned flesh overwhelming.

Tucking my head into my chest, I forced them from my sight. I didn't want to think about who they might belong to. I didn't want to think about what I had done, that Sain might have survived. That Thom did not. I didn't want any of it.

Not yet.

"Not yet. Not ever!" I sobbed, the words exploding from me as I stared at the floor, skin rebuilding over my bones as I clawed at the ground.

"I'm sorry," I gasped, the word broken by tears. "I'm so sorry."

Huddled into a ball, I pinched my eyes shut, crying as the flames died around me, their crackle leaving as silence overtook the room. Only the sounds of my sobs were left.

Then even those died, just like everything else.

Just like everyone else.

Just like me.

I could feel death grip me as I lay there, new skin stretched over my body, my heart shattering over and over again until the tiniest voice broke me out of my sorrow, her warm hand on my back.

"Mommy," she whispered, tugging at my shoulder with her other hand in an attempt to get my attention. "Don't be sad, Mommy."

"Rosaline?" I asked, my voice hoarse and broken as I lifted my head to look at her. The little girl I loved so much was standing amongst smoldering rock and char with a massive smile on her face.

"Mommy!" she squealed, wrapping her arms around me as she fell over me, her long, dark hair swimming around us and the smell of her white cotton nightgown clean in my nose. Like the lavender soap I used to use to wash all her things. Clean. Perfect.

"Rosaline!" My voice was a sob as I wrapped my arms

around her, pulling her into me exactly as I had when she and I were in the blade together. The thought seemed to wipe away my joy.

"Oh, no," I groaned, holding her securely against me and pressing my face into her hair, hoping to get lost in the smell of her. "I failed."

"Is that why you're sad?" Rosaline asked, sitting up to cup my hands with hers, pressing my hands against her skin.

Her skin. It was so warm.

She was so warm.

"Because you think you died?" She giggled, the sound out of place with the subject matter, but it didn't matter. The joy in the sound soothed me, the riot of my heartbeat slowing. "You didn't die."

"Then how are you here?"

"Because you saved me." Her smile widened as she squealed, throwing her hands up in the air like it was a party. "Your fire! You freed me, Mommy! You saved me!"

Everything heated and burned, my jaw dropping as I stared at her, the little girl who had jumped up to dance, swirling amidst the dark cave as she giggled, her white nightgown flowing around her.

"I saved you." It wasn't a question, even though it felt like it should be.

"Correction." A voice even more familiar than hers pulled me from my shock, right to my brother, the lanky boy standing next to me, looking at something far off with a cigarette in his mouth. The unlit thing made him look just as he had before the Zámek curse had split his mind. "You saved us—all of us. Everyone Edmund had trapped in that thing, every piece of every soul, you set us all free." Cail looked at me then, the corner of his mouth twitching like it used to, his jaw moving as he chewed the cigarette. "Remind me to thank you sometime," he said, a true smile breaking free as he threw some overly singed clothes at me, the shards of fabric scarcely enough to cover me, let alone put on. But they would have to do.

Cail ran from me to dance with Rosaline as I gingerly pulled the clothes on. Then the little girl ran back to me, a wide smile on her face.

"Come look what I did, Mommy!" she said, grabbing my hand as she pulled me away, tugging in an attempt to get me to follow her.

"Look what Uncle Cail did, you mean," my brother said, the joy on his face unfamiliar. He smiled wide before throwing the cigarette away from him, nodding his head toward something behind me. "Go see, sis."

"I helped, too, Uncle Cail," I heard a pout in her voice, which seemed very far away as I turned, my heart beating in my throat. "Hurry, Mommy!"

Rosaline ran past me into the dark of the cave just as a body came into view, a squat, muscular man groaning and complaining about something as he pushed himself into a sitting position, the long dreads hanging around his face.

Thom.

He was alive.

"See! Mommy! Look what I did!" Rosaline squealed,

running right to her daddy, tackling him back down to the ground. His own astonishment washed over the hall.

I stared at them—Thom's astonishment, Rosaline's loud giggles—before it clicked inside of me.

Tears streamed over my new skin as I ran toward them, my still healing body stumbling over the uneven rocks in my mad attempt to reach them. Luckily, Cail came to my rescue, holding my arm as I made it over to them, only to collapse back down.

Thom and Rosaline wrapped me up in their embrace, laughter and tears and unbreakable joy cementing themselves in this moment.

In me.

"Mommy!" Rosaline yelled joyfully, planting a big wet kiss on my cheek. "Daddy!" she yelled even more loudly, giving Thom a kiss just as large.

Thom's eyes met mine for the first time, tears spilling down his cheeks as his joy seeped into me.

I felt it, too.

The happiness.

But it couldn't last.

Rosaline pulled us back into a hug, her arms tight as she pulled our heads together, another laugh tickling in my ears.

"We're all free, Daddy!" she announced, her voice quick as she plunged into the usual titter that was so familiar, something that had been so missed. "Mommy killed Sain and released us! Cail saved you because he says he likes you, and he thinks you need to be with Mommy. I quite agree, although I am still not sure I like your hair like that. It looks silly."

Thom laughed at that, a deep rumble that moved inside his chest and exploded into the hall in a sound of pure joy that I hadn't heard for centuries. The sound smacked against me, jumpstarting my heart in a flurry of butterflies that I hadn't felt for quite some time.

"I like his hair," I said, and Rosaline turned toward me, her lip jutting out in a pout. "It's better than that stupid hat."

Thom's laugh deepened, and Cail joined in. Rosaline looked between us all in confusion.

"I'll explain when you're older."

I said the words without thinking, the impossibility of that hitting me as the laughter stopped, as the joy in Rosy's face fell and Cail sat down beside us with a look just as grim on his face.

"This isn't forever," I provided, the joy in my heart turning to lead as I suddenly had far too much trouble breathing.

"It's for good-bye," Rosy said, her voice breaking as her own tears dripped from her eyes, staining the ash that had fallen on her face. "It's for now. I'm not gone forever—"

"Just for now," Cail finished for her, wrapping his hand around mine as he held on tightly, his eyes glistening.

"Just for now," I repeated.

Thom wrapped his arms around me as he pulled me into him, Rosy curling up in our laps as she began to cry, pulling and gripping my hip. Her tears fell in my lap as Thom's dripped onto my shoulders.

"I love you, Mommy," Rosaline cried, holding onto us more tightly. "I love you, Daddy."

"We love you, princess," Thom gasped. I was surprised he could get the words out, while I could only cry, the words broken and mutilated by my sobs.

"We love you." Cail gripped my hand more firmly as I tried to speak, looking at him once more, the pressure from his hand leaving as he faded into nothing and the weight of my daughter on my lap leaving also.

The tears flowed, Thom holding me tightly against him as we cried together, the sound of our sobs increasing into a roar that seemed to move into the stone around us, into the cave, shaking it.

It took me a moment to realize it was not the pain of our breaking hearts that was causing it. It was from something deep inside the cave, something that was ripping apart.

"Thom," I gasped, my magic reactivating into the familiar heat as it, too, began to sense what was happening.

Thom looked up at me, the same look of panicked realization clear.

The cave was coming down.

"Run."

31

RYLAND

HER PANICKED breaths echoed inside the long corridors I soared through, rumbling over the stone as they bounced back to me. The panic and fear in the sound were a delectable prompting. She wasn't far ahead, only steps, only one dark turn.

I was almost to her.

Don't let her get away.

Staying as quiet as I could, I floated above the stone floor as I tracked her, careful not to alert her to my presence. I was sure she knew I was following her, but if I could convince her I had lost her, I might still have a chance ... as long as she didn't stutter. I couldn't follow that.

I couldn't risk losing her, not when I was so close.

Keeping my own eager pants masked, I listened to her ragged ones, to the uneven stomps of her feet against stone. My eyes narrowed as we moved deeper into the unfamiliar space, the doors on either side increasing as a deep rumble I was not familiar with boiled my veins.

It's the earth's magic, son.

If you can feel it, I am sure you can use it.

I wasn't lying when I said you were powerful.

Use it to destroy her.

The words brought a smile to my face and prompted me forward, the sound of her steps getting louder and louder until they stopped, the sound of an old, rusty hinge replacing them.

A door.

I sped forward, quickly shielding myself from view. If she shut it, I could lose her. The forest of doors I was surrounded by would make it impossible to know which one she had disappeared behind.

The slam of wood against stone never came, however. Instead, there were only low and angry voices that hissed through the dark.

My chest tightened painfully at the scratch of their voices against my mind, everything buzzing as I moved closer, careful to keep my shield tight but knowing it might not be enough.

Then move up.

With one glance, I looked up at the high stone ceiling of the cave. The height of it was masked in a shadow so dark even I couldn't see past it.

A perfect cover. This time, it was my voice, my eagerness that whispered back to me, the sound of my father's laugh drowning it as my magic pulsed.

The already powerful wind I had conjured pushed me higher, letting me soar into the dark shadows of the high ceiling until, through a narrow ribbon of light and a dimly lit room, I could see her.

I could see them.

Míra and Ovailia.

Their shadowed figures paced before the crack Míra left in the door, blocking the light in spurts of light and dark that, from high above the cave, felt like a child playing with a flashlight.

"I got it, *and* I found him. I'm not totally incapable, Ovailia …" Míra pled, her words drowned as the light left the hall again, blocked by Ovailia this time as she came to stand right before the door.

She stared down the corridor with the same plastered disgust she always had. Her nose was turned up, an ugly sneer spread over her chapped and cracked lips.

I held my breath, sure she could sense me if not see me.

"You are sure you were not followed?" she sneered, a slow-moving ribbon of light slithering down the hallway from her, her magic checking the dark for some sign of me.

"Would it matter if I was?" Míra said, coming up beside her and pushing the door open so that she, too, could have a look. "We need him."

The disgust on Ovailia's face deepened, her focus shifting

from the hall to the girl who stood next to her with a look just as smug.

"We do. Don't look at me like that. You know we do, Ovailia."

Seeing them both together, standing there as though nothing had happened, as though they hadn't killed and murdered so many people, made me want to kill them even more.

My magic flared dangerously, my teeth grinding together in a desperate attempt to keep everything under control. To keep myself hidden. But then …

Why do you need to hide?

I know.

They are both right there.

Ready to pay.

You can take them.

I know I can.

Words bounced around inside of my head as I watched them turn from the door, back into the room that was now bright enough to illuminate the entire hallway, leaving my formerly perfect hiding place exposed. Not that it mattered.

I dropped to the floor without so much as a sound, my magic catching me and placing me gently on the cold stone floor, still shrouded by my magic.

"You have done well, Míra," Ovailia began, her voice muddled as I began to creep toward them. "We need to get Ilyan to us. Sain must have already left the stadium by now. If we can find him before he finds Damek—"

"What are you saying?" Míra asked, her scared face pressing against the opening in the door for a moment.

"I need you to go back."

"Go back!" Míra exclaimed, the panic in her voice causing me to jump a bit, my already accelerated heart rate bounding through the roof. "You can't be serious."

"I am. And what did I warn you ..."

I stepped again, my foot catching on a tiny rock on the ground, sending it flying across the hall and against the door.

I stared at the stone, cursing the luck I had, that after all my stealth, it came down to a tiny stone with a sound so soft that, at any other time, it might have gone unnoticed. But Ovailia had heard, the simple sound stopping her short while I froze in place.

Now! Take them now!

My father's voice beat inside my head, rattling inside of me as it tried to prod me forward, my magic raising in temperature as it, too, answered the call.

"Are you sure you weren't followed?" Ovailia's voice was the last to seep past the gap in the door before a flurry of hushed whispers, a gasp, and tiny *pop* all came in quick succession.

The pop, one I had heard many times before, spun in my stomach. My magic flew to my fingertips, ready to attack, but before I could move, a wall of ice pressed against my back, freezing my magic in place and pulling my shield from me.

"Oh," a tiny voice came from behind. "I guess I was followed."

Míra's attack came before my magic recovered, hitting me hard in the chest and sending me scuttling across the floor and into the room Míra had just stuttered from.

My feet flew out from under me, and I fell into a threadbare high-back chair. The wooden feet creaked loudly as my impact sent us sliding across the stone floor, forgotten articles of clothes and belongings scattering, as well.

The remains of a bedroom surrounded me. A bed leaned up against the wall, and a dresser was torn apart, its contents scattered around us. Just like every other part of these ancient caves I had seen, this room was in shambles. Everything looked as though it had been forgotten long ago.

"Hello, Ryland," Ovailia said, her voice a silky taunt that twisted up my spine, taking me right back to the prison she had created for me. My muscles tensed, agitation rising as my head twitched to the side on its own. "I haven't seen you in a while. How's your head?" Ovailia stepped toward me slowly, running her hands through my hair. The simple touch gave rise to the panic and madness I had already been fighting.

I fought it, desperate to keep control, but just seeing her again brought it all back. The crazy she and our father had infected me with controlled my magic. Controlled me.

She was always the strong one.

You are nothing compared to her.

Ovailia noticed the change in me, and her smile spread. Her magic sparked at her fingertips as she raised them to attack.

I stared at the electric warning, feeling my magic bubble and boil, but I couldn't move. I sat, glued to the chair Míra had thrown me into, my mind screaming while I tried to fight the dragon she had raised inside of me.

One flash of light and she attacked, light streaming toward me, and a scream broke free, erupting through the room in a painful howl.

I pushed past the pain and let my magic explode, soaring right toward her as hers did mine. Mine was faster, though, cutting through her attack like smoke, speeding past and slamming into her, sending her off balance as she wobbled around on her ridiculous heels.

Or maybe not.

Now's your chance.

Take it.

"I'm just fine, thanks," I spat as I jumped up, magic rumbling, ready to face them both head-on. "You seem to be doing well. Of course, being surrounded by soulless demons like yourself seems to suit both of you."

"You speak as though you know either of us," Ovailia said with a demonic laugh, flipping her hair behind her.

"You have tortured me, Ovailia, helped our father rip my mind apart. My family has died by your hands. Yours and that beast of a child!" My voice was darkening as my anger rose, my head twitching painfully with the memory, with the need for retribution. "You think I don't know you, but I know what you've done, and that is enough."

"You foolish boy," Ovailia hissed, her eyes narrowing gravely as she leaned toward me. "You see with your heart. You would do better if I ripped it from you. You know nothing of what life truly is."

"How could I? You have taken away my only chance." I attacked again.

Her smile was as wide as mine as she deflected my assault and jumped into the air, soaring around the wide room while Míra pushed her own attack toward me. The new flash of magic pulled my attention to my sister.

Blocking it easily, I turned, ready to face Ovailia, but I was sent stumbling as a second attack impacted against my side, instead.

Warmth spread over me as blood began to pour down my side, the agonizing sting of ripping flesh tearing me in two.

Screaming in pain, I was thrown to the ground by the impact, the pain spreading throughout me as the blood continued to flow. I could feel it pool against the floor where I lay, soaking into a pile of torn clothing I had fallen into. The agony of the gash left as my magic quickly began to heal it, something I shouldn't be able to do if Ovailia was fighting me with her full potential.

She was playing with me.

Like the fool you are.

Are you going to let her get away with that?

No.

No, I was not.

Looking back toward her, I was met with her bright smile

and the smug look of the little girl who stood right beside her. The haunting warnings on their faces tensed my spine and sent a fresh stab of pain against my gut like the sharp point of a knife.

"Come on, Ovailia," I said with a grunt, my muscles straining as I pushed myself back to standing, my legs shaking underneath me. "Don't go easy on me. Attack me!"

Attempting to control the shake, I hoped I looked like the powerhouse I felt. My magic still buzzed angrily inside of me.

Ovailia only laughed at my attempt, shaking her hair over her shoulder with a flip of her head, her focus shifting to her nails in the usual dismissal.

"Attack me!" I screamed in irritation as my father began to laugh, the sound cutting through my mind angrily.

She simply smiled, her focus never leaving her nails.

Make her pay.

Shoulders jerking with recoil as light and electricity sparked from my hands with the bang of a gun, I stepped toward her, ready to bring the fight to me.

Míra jerked at the sound, but Ovailia stood there as though nothing had happened, the same irksome smile on her face.

"You don't know how much I want that, baby brother," she said casually, her focus on me as she easily deflected the attack that had been seconds away from impact. I swallowed, my eyes hardening at the hatred in her voice. "But now is not the time."

It was then that she truly attacked, her smile dangerous as she unleashed her magic. Now she wasn't holding back.

Perfect.

My heart stuttered with angry excitement, every muscle tensing in fear of what was heading my way as I sent another attack right toward her, determined to meet her head-on.

I sent her attack into the wall with a bang that shook the stone, and she sent mine into the ceiling, the mess of metal and mirrors they used to reflect the light in the room crashing to the floor. Glass sparkled over the floor as everything exploded. What little light remained glittered over everything like a mutated disco ball.

She attacked again, Míra's following right behind as the girl began to run toward the door, blocking me from the exit by quickly sealing the door.

Hands moving fast, I attempted to deflect and felt the heat of Míra's magic brush against my skin when I didn't quite move fast enough, a large headboard behind me making the movement difficult.

Ovailia's incessant attacks ceased for a moment as I took a step back, her smile glinting as she saw the realization spread over my face, the power I was trying so hard to display fading into shock. They had successfully backed me into a corner.

Then fight your way out.

You wanted to kill them, so do it.

The words supercharged my anger, bringing it right back to

the forefront of my mind. I took a quick glance toward Míra, the fickle child fueling me more.

"Fine," I snapped to no one in particular.

The single word confused Ovailia enough that she didn't notice the smoky attack I sent toward her, the strand of magic singeing the hem of her shirt.

She stared at it in disgust before turning back to me, an orb of magic already forming in her hands. Electric yellow crackled over the surface a split second before she released it, letting it stream toward me dangerously.

I knew orb attacks well, and if I didn't stop it, I would be in trouble.

Swallowing down my doubt, I let my anger fuel me, my magic buzzing as I released a powerful wave toward it, ready to stop her in her tracks.

The defense had hardly moved before the one she had already sent toward me devoured it, absorbing the energy as it began to shift and mutate into a wall.

Pathetic.

My father's voice was a growl as my heart fell to my toes, my muscles tensing in painful fear.

Her smile was barely visible from behind the thick wall of magic that was now heading toward me, her smug smile fueling me as I once again countered.

That's it, son.

Destroy her.

Letting my magic flow the way my father had trained me, I

unleashed a powerful jolt that I knew would rip past the wall, break through it in its journey to injure her. To hurt her. To hurt Míra. I needed it to. I needed the chance to take them down completely. To make them pay.

Magic crackled dangerously across the air, slamming into her wall with a jolt that shook the room, a rebound of energy moving back through the room and smacking against me, sending me stumbling back as my magic was zapped into smoke and air like a bug against a blue light.

The air around me was buzzing, the irritating sound rattling in my head as I stepped back to where I had been, watching her wall continue to swell as it absorbed the power from my spell.

You can do better than that.

Destroy her!

You are weak!

No, I'm not.

Then prove me wrong.

The magical wall was inches from me, pinning me against the wall with no escape as I tried to counter, swinging my hand through the air in a desperate last attempt. But her spell was too strong. It moved past mine as though it was nothing but air, slamming into my gut, moving into me with burning ice that twisted and writhed into my muscles, sparking against my nerves in tiny, agonizing jolts.

The buzzing in the room swallowed me whole as I screamed, the sound echoing again and again as the pain spread through me, splitting my skull until I could hardly hear. I could hardly see. Even my own scream faded into a lost depth, my pain swallowing it whole.

I was once again thrown backward. I could feel the air blow past my hair, over my skin, but I couldn't comprehend what was happening over the pain that cleaved my bones and nerves. My vision shifted from the spinning world I was thrown through to an encompassing black, everything fluctuating back and forth in a strobe of light and dark.

The wheel of color faded to nothing as my spine and shoulders slammed against the wall with a thud, the impact mixing with my own scream, with my father's laugh, in a cavalcade that echoed inside my bones, twisting them further. Yet another pain adding to the agonizing burn that ripped through me.

My scream of pain turned into a whimper as I sat, sagging against the wall and floor. The sound was pitiful as the world continued to shift and fade around me. The spell was still working its way through me as my own magic, my own attacks, were turned against me.

I tried to move, but everything was paralyzed under the pain, a new jolt of torture moving through me every time I tried. So, I sat there, trapped in pain, the sound of my father's laughter filling my head before everything around me began to mutate again. Ovailia's and Míra's voices drifted inside the rotating darkness as though they were from another world.

"Keep him here. He shouldn't be much of a hassle like that," Ovailia said, her voice sounding strange with the tiny bit of emotion that had seeped its way into it.

The pain must have been making me delusional to even think that. Ovailia had no emotion.

"Or I could kill him if you'd prefer," Míra sneered at Ovailia's suggestion.

Ovailia, however, seemed proud of herself, her ridiculously forced laugh echoing painfully inside my head.

"Whatever you do, just don't let him get away or hurt himself, or you for that matter," Ovailia continued.

The vision of the two of them standing together was clear for a moment before it faded back to the black pool that I seemed to be swimming in, pain shooting down my arms as I tried to move them.

"You say that like it's easy," Míra hissed, her voice cutting in and out. "I'm too young to babysit."

"I need to find my brother before Sain does. Perhaps even locate Damek if I'm lucky." Ovailia's voice faded away as Edmund's laugh became louder, the sound swelling in my head as the pain shot through me again. It seemed I was doomed to be trapped in one prison or another. "Keep the blade with you. We will be back to retrieve it and the baby. Then, together, we will end this."

I caught a brief glimpse of Ovailia leaving the room, of Míra glaring at me, before a black fog drowned me, leaving me sitting against the wall in a stubborn stillness. It was my only option until the pain began to subside.

I didn't know how long I sat there, refusing to move, forcing my panicked breaths into a calm. I was frozen, listening to the *booms* of explosions that shook the cave, to Míra's uneven steps. I sat, keeping my eyes trained forward as I waited for just a glimpse of her as she paced before me, her eyes wide while she glared at me, just as angry as she always was.

The heavy tension that had twisted my body faded as the black did, dissolving until only the edges of my vision were shivering and twisting with darkness, only the tips of my nerves and the joints of my bones stinging.

If I were smart, I would have sat there for as long as I needed to recover, leaving the girl oblivious to my strength as I formulated a proper counterattack. But I didn't, and part of me didn't care. I was too desperate to see pain on her face, to feel the sweet relief of revenge that my father had always told me about.

It's there, son.

Let it fuel you.

I sighed at the odd calm in his voice, the sound loud in the silence as Míra turned toward me, her eyes narrowing as she took a step in my direction.

"I'm guessing you can see me now," she said, all sign of fear gone from her voice. Only the angry, smug, little brat I had met in Prague remained. "Wonder if you can hear me, though." She stepped toward me slowly, cocking her head to the side as the corner of her mouth turned up, the wickedness shining right through. "I wonder what nasty things I can say—"

"Didn't your mother ever teach you manners?" The growl of my voice ripped past my anger as everything else bubbled underneath, still paralyzed by Ovailia's attack. "Or did she just wash your mouth out with soap?"

The shock at what I had said slammed into the girl, her emotions bristling inside her eyes before it was all replaced with a scowl so similar to Ovailia's I was sure the two had been spending too much time together.

"She did," Míra snapped. "Not sure yours did, though."

"She didn't. My father made me kill her. He made people kill a lot of people who didn't deserve to die. Like Jaromir."

All emotion was wiped from her face. The gaunt horror that replaced it was something I didn't expect. I expected her usual anger, the usual sneer, but she just stared, the look haunting as she looked beyond me to something dark, something that was twisting inside her.

The look sped into me, my pulse increasing as my vengefulness did. Everything pumped and moved in perfect harmony as my magic began to ignite, the last of Ovailia's counterattack leaving.

"He didn't have to die," I hissed, letting my malice press against the little girl, letting it dig into her. Letting it hurt. "You didn't have to kill him. But I do have to kill you."

She opened her mouth, ready to say something, but I attacked, moving my hand fast, as an assault spread through the air toward her. The little girl threw herself to the side just in time.

She screeched in fear as I hissed in pain, the sudden movement sending fire and ice back inside my nerves and bones. I guessed I hadn't recovered as much as I had thought.

Míra saw the opportunity and reacted, her counterattack hitting me straight in the gut as I was trying to shuffle away.

The energy that spread from her hand crackled in the air as she held me in place, the power strong. I forced my head to turn toward her, using all of my strength to fight for that one simple movement.

She smiled as I glowered at her, her teeth tinted red as she pulled a tiny shard of a blood red stone from her pocket, brandishing it at me threateningly.

My eyes widened as it drew closer, blood boiling in fear of the Souls Blade in her hand.

"Where did you get that?"

"Ovailia told me where to find it. Don't think I won't kill you," she hissed, placing the shard below my nose, the smell of acid and blood strong. "Don't think I don't want to."

The darkness that was so common in her took the forefront. I knew I should see it as the warning it was, but I didn't care.

I had the same darkness in me, after all.

"Like you killed Jaromir?" I spat, the words garbled from the forced tension in my jaw, her attack still wringing bones and tendons together painfully. "And Risha! And—"

"You think I wanted to kill them?" she suddenly yelled, the intensity of the spell she held against me increasing with the anger. I screamed, several bones in my chest and arms cracking under the pressure. "You think I wanted to kill my brother? You think I want to carry around this poisoned magic in me? You're an idiot, Ryland! I don't know why my brother ever looked up to you. You didn't deserve him."

Her words caught me off guard, my eyes widening as I tried

to control my breathing, the pain and shock making the action difficult.

"I know you wanted to." I forced the words out, determined to slap them against her despite the pain. "You split his skull in two. He died in my arms, gasping for his mother. *Your* mother."

"Stop!" she yelled again, throwing the blade away as her magic snapped.

Another scream ripped from me as yet more bones began to splinter and crack.

My magic rushed to heal them, but even that was restrained under her hold, leaving me heaving in pain as the broken bones pushed against tendons, skin, and muscles in ways they were not meant to. Given the pain and the way my forearm seemed to be arching unnaturally, I was sure that one broken fragment was about to break through. I screamed in agony, but Míra only looked at me, her jaw tight and eyes wide as she, too, slowly lost control.

"I had to kill Thom to save all of you ... to *stop* Edmund."

"Some good it did you," I interrupted, my words strained and broken through the pain. "You saved no one. And now Edmund is dead."

"Am I?"

Míra's eyes widened as mine did. Her magic fell away as her own fear gripped her, the identical emotion wringing my heart.

Slowly, Míra turned toward the man I was now looking at, the man I had never hoped to see again.

"Father?" I could scarcely get the word out.

Edmund stood in the middle of the room behind Míra, his normally slicked hair disheveled and out of place. The curls that were so much like mine fell over his blood-ringed eyes. He glared, his eyes red and swollen, jaw slightly knocked out of place as he stood, wearing a bloodstained robe. A crimson stain spread over his chest and dripped from the hem of his shirt.

"Edmund!" Míra shouted, her anger redirected to the man who stood before us so blood-soaked I was sure he was an apparition, although he seemed so solid I didn't see how that was possible.

"Oh, look," Edmund hissed, his voice so clear I almost expected it to be inside of me rather than out. "My failure of a son and my failure of a slave. Perfect. If my last act is to dispose of the two of you, then so be it. And all it took was the destruction of the blade to bring me back, to give me one last chance."

"No!" Míra screamed just as Edmund attacked, his palm twitching as a wide, glowing orb of white appeared on his fingertips. The ball sped toward us with one flick of his wrist as fast and as accurate as a well-aimed baseball.

It did not make it far, for as Míra screamed, she also countered, an attack of almost identical weight and speed moving toward him, perfectly intersecting with my father's in a shower of sparks that exploded across the room, catching the bed on fire.

Feathers showered us with the impact, the white blossoms smoking and burning as they fell around the room. I looked at them for a moment before Edmund began to laugh, the sound the same I had been haunted with for so long, the laugh that had been ripping through my head until a moment ago. Now it was before me, separated by only a few feet and some burning feathers.

Now I could destroy it.

I could be free.

"Planning on fighting until the end, are we?" Edmund said with a laugh, cracking his knuckles as the fire began to spread, catching a pile of what seemed to be sheets on fire.

The room was trapped in a crackle of light and dark, the smell of smoke becoming overwhelming as the bright flames threatened to swallow us whole.

"Good. That will make things more entertaining." Edmund stepped toward us as Míra began to move.

Any hope of a quick escape was dashed as Edmund snapped his fingers, the still burning mattress soaring through the air and slamming into the only exit. A shower of sparks and fire covered the room as it flew, bits of paper and fabric that were littered over the ground catching aflame.

I hissed and shuffled away from where I leaned against the wall, my body screaming from the simple movement. I attempted to kick a burning ember back toward my father, but my leg was barely able to move with the broken bones that were still crippling me. Not that it mattered. The fire that engulfed the mattress had already spread to a chair and a davenport that were both now smoking and flickering with flames on either side of the room.

The smoke in the air was smothering, making it impossible to breathe and leaving a weight on my chest.

Coughing, I grit my teeth against the pain and attempted to stand, but nothing responded. Even though my magic could now heal me, it wasn't fast enough. I would have to fight from here.

"I don't know what your idea of entertaining is, Father," I hissed as I carefully shimmied my weight, freeing my limp hand from where my leg had trapped it. "But it's your definition of *end* that I am more interested in."

Edmund raised his eyebrow in derision as his lip twitched, the laugh a second from breaking back into my nightmares. That was before Míra attacked, her magic strong as it hit him square in the chest, catching him totally off guard. The two of us began to work together in an unexpected partnership.

He roared like the animal he was, gripping the air with his hands as he countered without looking, a ribbon of flame soaring toward the two of us.

I dodged as Míra did, his pointless attack streaming through the smoke-filled air and right into the fire that was already engulfing the room. It impacted with an explosion that sent sparks over us, fire dripping from the air as it, too, began to burn.

"You should be dead!" Míra suddenly screamed as she rushed the man who looked like a giant compared to the child. "You deserve to die!"

Edmund moved to attack, but I was faster. His focus was so

intent on Míra that he didn't even see me send a single spark toward him.

His attack froze as his hand was covered in an ice that quickly spread up his arm.

"I killed my brother because of what you did to me!" she continued to scream, attack after attack ripping into the man in her anger. "He was all I had left! And now he's gone. It was all for nothing!"

"You think I made you do that?" He laughed as he finally fought back, sending Míra away from him, her magic barely catching her before she slammed into the inflamed wall.

"I didn't *make* you do anything. I don't make anyone do anything. You *chose* to do it. You failed," he said, throwing his head back as his twisted laugh cut through the damning smoke that danced around us.

"I didn't fail!" she screamed, tears seeping from her eyes as I saw the first real emotion from the girl.

A child.

Just like I once was, forced to do things I never wanted to. Forced to destroy my own heart, just as she had. I wasn't the only one who had lost with Jaromir's demise, with Risha's murder.

I saw myself in her as she screamed, as she cried, as she confronted him in a way I never thought I could.

"Don't listen to him, Míra." The anger that had fueled me redirected itself onto the despot. "It's all lies. He may not force your hand, but you know as well as I do that you had no choice."

Míra looked at me in shock, her eyes wide as tears continued to pour from them. A silent exchange moved between us before she turned back to the towering man, blood still pouring from his chest as he stepped back, an odd fear I had never seen in him clouding his eyes.

"Jaromir was my brother!"

"And you killed him!" Edmund shouted back at her, the fear leaving briefly as he stepped toward Míra, posturing to her.

Míra began to cower, her shoulders hunching as I started to push myself up, my bones cracking painfully as the newly healed breaks threatened to snap. I ignored them. A few broken bones could heal.

This, I needed to end.

"Just like I killed my mother, and Ovailia killed Rosaline. Just like Cail killed Talon, and Wyn killed the Drak," I growled out the painful truth as I limped toward my father.

The bulk of a man I had always feared did not seem quite so frightening anymore.

"I should have killed you, instead," Míra added as she came to stand beside me, the two of us facing the man who had destroyed our lives in such similar ways, who had destroyed our hopes of a future.

"You still can," I said while, as one, we attacked with two powerful jolts of magic that slammed into my father's chest, pushing him through the air and right into the burning rubble that surrounded us.

Wood and flame smothered him, his scream swallowed by

the crackle of the blaze as ash from the impact plumed throughout the room, covering us in a layer of grey.

And then there was nothing.

No screams.

No haunted laugh echoing inside of my head.

No tortured voice.

Just the sound of the sizzling fire and the silent tears of the girl standing next to me.

"I didn't want to kill him," she sobbed out, her tiny body falling to the ground beside me. "I didn't want to kill Risha. I didn't want to kill any of you. But I had to. I had to kill that man with the dreads and go back to Edmund, tell him I succeeded. It would keep you all safe. It's all I wanted. I wanted to keep him safe. I didn't want to kill him. I didn't mean to. I wanted you to—"

"Stop," I whispered as I fell down beside her, my bones twisting from the impact.

Sitting there beside her as she cried, I hovered my hand above her back as I fought the need to comfort her with the need to toss her around a bit.

In the end, I pushed my anger out through my magic, a stream of ice pouring from me as I quickly extinguished the fire that surrounded us, leaving us sitting in a cloud of smoke and soot that fell to the ground like snow.

"Can you forgive me?" Míra asked after the silence became too much.

Focused on the pile of rubble we had pushed Edmund into, I only vaguely noticed that no remains were there.

Normally, I would worry that he had somehow survived. But I knew better. He was gone. He had been for some time. I wasn't even sure if it was him we had fought, anyway.

"I can try," I finally said, my voice breaking as my heart attempted to cleave itself in two again. "He was my family, too, after all."

Her sobs increased at that, her wide eyes staring at me with all the plea and want of a lost dog before she threw herself into my lap, her hands tight around my waist as I sat there, hands in the air, unsure of what to do.

"He was all I had," she sobbed as she clung to me, pulling my shirt.

I finally lowered my arms, an odd emotion twisting within me as I pulled her against me. It wasn't revenge. It was something better, something I hadn't expected. This weird release of forgiveness. I didn't think I could have expected it.

I couldn't have expected the calm.

Expected my own tears to join hers.

Expected my magic to swell in a calmness I had never felt before.

For the first time, I was finally free.

I was finally safe.

32

OVAILIA

I COULD HEAR his pathetic cries long before I found him. The vile sound echoed down the stone halls, roaring over the *boom* of explosions that had increased in number. The cavernous collection of tunnels shifted and groaned in a deep threat of collapse, the explosions slowly ripping them to shreds.

In my need to reach him, I ignored the way the cave was rattling, knowing I was dangerously short on time.

Ilyan's pained sobs grew louder as my heels clicked loudly down the long, dark hallway, the sound of the river hidden by his cries. His pain tightened my heart, pulling it in fear of what I would find. From what I recalled of the image of him in the sight I had stolen from Sain, I expected to find him holding her broken body on his lap as he screamed.

I had only seen the sight a handful of times, the image force fed to me by Edmund after I had accidentally peeked into Sain's mind. But right now, hearing my brother's heartbreak bellow over the stone, it was all I could think about.

The long hall rattled with another explosion, this one so strong I was forced to stop in place, my hand against the wall in an attempt to combat the shift of stone. To keep myself standing, something that was painfully difficult with the sliver of heel I stood on.

This was going to be more difficult than I had expected. If I didn't need him, I would probably just leave him down in the dungeon to rot.

Just like everyone else.

The shift of stone passed, and I lifted my eyes to the large fissures that were slowly forming overhead, the lightning ripping the stone apart.

There was still time to leave him.

I guessed Ryland was wrong. I wasn't that heartless.

Fixing a tight scowl on my face, I broke into a run, sprinting into the small guards' hall my brother sat in, his body folded just as I had seen in sight, his hands pulled forward in that same desperate prayer for mercy.

The image was just as I had seen in sight, the moment just as I had feared. Except, there was no limp body drawn out on his lap, no black hair spread over stone. No death.

Only my brother, covered in blood, his heart broken and shattered over the room.

Days before, I might have rejoiced at the image. I could still feel the vein of pleasure from seeing his pain, from seeing Sain's success, but it was short-lived, causing an unfamiliar queasiness in my gut.

I felt sorry for him.

I hurt for him.

It was something I hadn't felt since the child's, Thom's child, my tiny niece, soul had been ripped from her body. My chest tensed the same way, and I shuddered, gingerly stepping forward as the room quaked around us, the motion lost in the sound of his cries.

"Ilyan," I said, trying to keep the acid out of my voice as I reached out for him. "Ilyan, I'm so sorry."

Ilyan's sobs lessened as he turned toward me, the tragic pain I had expected clear before it changed, warped into dire anger, an anger that was directed right at me.

"You," he spat, his voice a dangerous growl as he glowered at me, bits of rock falling from the ceiling behind him and splashing into the frigid water of the river.

In one swift motion, he rose, a mist of icy water spraying over us both as he towered over me. He was covered in a deep vermillion, damp patches glistening over his body, the color frightening against the dark of the cave.

"Ilyan?" I asked, the pain of his loss smothered by the icy rock of my heart. I shivered under the look he had fixed me with, everything within me screaming at me to run.

In a million battles with him, I had never had the full force of his anger directed at me, never seen a glower with the same intensity that was now bearing down on me.

It was frightening.

My eyes widened in fear as the last drop of my sympathy

left. My anger rose as Ilyan's did, magic flaring at the enemy that had appeared before me.

Ilyan's eyes glinted red as he stepped toward me, magic sparking from his fingers in bursts of yellow flame. His power dripped to the floor of the cave in a hot oil that boiled against the stone with a hiss, melting the rock into a pool of the brightest red.

The cave shook as Ilyan stepped toward me, stones falling around us as the magical charge in the room escalated, mine charging as his did. Even if I didn't really want to fight him.

"Ilyan," I said again, my voice shaking dangerously as I stepped away from him, right into the high stone wall that was shivering from the battle it could no longer contain. "I need you to come with me. I have a blade—"

"You helped him," Ilyan hissed as he took another step toward me, his temper an out of control torrent as he attacked without warning.

"No!" I yelled while the liquid death that dripped from his skin spun through the air toward me. The power mutated into a needle point that, if I hadn't been ready, would have shot right through my heart.

When I clapped my hands, my magic sped out, forcing the weapon off balance and away from me. The sharp point spun through the air. With a powerful blast, the long spear embedded itself a foot into the stone. The rock around it melted as it began to pour from the wall in a river of gold, the heat mutating the stone.

"Helped who?" I asked, my voice hard as my desperation fell away and my irritation came on full force. I tapped my heel against the stone as I popped my hip out, the movement usually enough to disguise the surge of magic before an attack.

My brother, however, saw right through it. His nostrils flared as he screamed, a blast of air knocking me backward, a wall of green following right behind.

I barely caught it, letting my magic absorb the wave, dispelling it into harmless energy that fell from the air. The counter spell twisted my gut uncomfortably, making it hard to stand and face him, my energy depleted.

Ilyan smiled at my exhaustion, his hysteria growing as I prepared for the attack that would come next, knowing it would.

"Who did I help?" I spat, not bothering to hide my irritation. He was really getting on my nerves.

"Take your pick!" he screamed as he attacked again, my counterattack scarcely able to deflect his assault, sending it into the high ceiling where it smashed against the stone, littering us with small stones from the already weakened structure.

I would have to be careful. He could crush me under the stone if I wasn't careful, if it didn't come down on its own.

"Our father, you mean?" I barked, feeling my own anger rise dangerously, everything boiling inside of me painfully. "Or are you speaking of Timothy? Or Sain?"

Ilyan glowered deeper, his eyes shaking with the madness that had already taken control of him.

"That's who you should be fighting, Ilyan!" I screamed as

the cave heaved around us once again. "That's whose heart you should be plunging spikes into."

Ilyan said nothing in reply beyond a growl. He only attacked with a ripple of magic that I sent aside with a wave of my hand, the powerful spell twisting away from me, through the dark and into the stone near the dungeons.

The cave around us heaved more. Sending his attacks into the cave was quickly turning dangerous. I was going to have to find another way to deal with his temper tantrum.

"Oh, I didn't plan on stopping with you!" Ilyan roared, the words hitting me in the chest as he put the force of his magic behind them. The wall of energy shoved me back, slamming me into the uneven wall behind me. "You all have to pay."

Rocks continued to fall from the ceiling as Ilyan attacked again, one assault after another raining down on me. Eruptions of light and fire filled the room, his magic mutating into sharp points and violent ends.

With a scream, I pushed myself from the wall, magic working fast to dodge him, sending his attacks away as I fired back. My useless assaults were only meant to immobilize him if any of them could reach him.

"Ilyan!" I pleaded as I realized what I had walked into, realized the true danger of what I was facing.

All signs of my loyal and compassionate brother were gone. All of his control was gone. He was gone, as gone as Joclyn was. His humanity had left as she had. There was only a monster left behind.

For the first time in my life, I truly feared my brother. I feared for my life.

"Ilyan, I need you to listen to me. I am trying to help you!" I yelled angrily, dodging another of his attacks as my face began to burn. Tears I hadn't felt in centuries threatened to pour over, to stream down my face in a million lines of broken life.

The life I had created for me.

It truly was too late to fix anything.

"You are trying to help me?" he screamed, the vein in his neck popping out in warning as he sent one last attack toward me. This one was captured by a simple spell, the orbs of black spinning through the air between us in a dangerous globe, lightning and thunder spitting from its surface. "Help me how? Betraying me? Killing Thom? Ripping our sister Gielle's head from her shoulders? Spying on all of us? Torturing Ryland? How! How did you help us!"

I cringed with each accusation, my shoulders pulling into my ears as the truth of each charge stabbed into me.

I glowered at him as the reason I was here, the reason I had sought his help, became a further memory. A memory that didn't matter anymore.

"You helped Edmund, Ovailia. You bowed down to Sain. You are as much the enemy as they are! I don't know why I tried to save you, why I tried to help you. You are no better than any of them. You are my biggest regret!"

It was then I attacked.

I didn't hold back.

Magic shot from my fingers in sharp points of energy that ripped through the air as Ilyan began to laugh, the sound the same broken mania our father had made his own.

Ilyan blocked the attack easily, fixing me with a look of pure madness as he returned fire. The stream of color shifted into fire as I dodged it, my own attack zooming back toward him, only to intersect his magic with a blast that showered us in sparks of color and flame.

Ilyan laughed again and stuttered, dodging with the seamless movement of his magic, his body disappearing from before me and appearing right beside me. His laugh echoed through me the second before his attack hit. The powerful blast met with my hip and sent me right into the open stairwell to the dungeon.

Landing with a smack, I hit the stairs, falling down them in a tumble of hair and limbs. Unsuccessfully, I tried to stop myself, my magic frantically attempting to heal the quick muscle deterioration that Ilyan had hit me with.

Continually tumbling down the stairs, I clawed at the wall, my nails chipping until I finally came to a halt, one of my now scuffed and ripped heels continuing down.

Glaring at the loss, I turned, glowering toward the tiny spot of light above me that Ilyan still stood in, laughing.

"I would say I missed sparring with you," I taunted up at him, carefully removing the other shoe and throwing it down toward the dungeon after its mate, "but it's been hardly fair until now."

"You can't possibly think you are as powerful as me," Ilyan goaded as he stepped into the stairwell, blocking the light as he moved down the staircase toward me, "because you're not."

"It has nothing to do with power, Ilyan," I told him as I stood before him, meeting him eye to eye. "Now, now you fight as dirty as me."

With a smile, I slammed my palm into his stomach, twisting my magic inside of him as I hit him with the same spell he had debilitated me with. But instead of blasting him away, I held him close, shoving my free hand against his shoulder as I sent him down the same staircase, tumbling end of over end, down the rough-hewn stairs.

I did not wait as he had. I followed him, soaring into the air and diving down the stairs, ready to attack him on the landing before he had a chance to recover.

A second before I reached him, however, he was gone, leaving only a *pop* and a puff of smoke behind.

"See?" I said with a laugh, looking past the dark prisons around me for some sign of him. "You can fight dirty."

The cave roared around me, stone shifting dangerously as I walked toward the far cell that had once housed Talon, sure I had seen some shadow there. Instead, it was only a pile of bones and Ilyan's malicious laugh.

All of the old metal cell doors closed at once, the loud snap of metal on metal echoing around the dark, hiding the blast of Ilyan's assault.

But not well enough.

I side-stepped, my magic lifting me against the stone wall.

The smell of burning hair and fabric was strong from what little of the attack that could reach.

"Nice try," I provoked as I jumped down, my own assaults already speeding toward him, one after another to match his, my hands moving fast as I both attacked and deflected.

Again and again, I attacked, ignoring the dangerous sounds of collapse that the cave was warning me with. I could have sworn something around me had fallen, but I didn't care. Only the fight mattered. Only ending it.

I sent another quick spurt of blasts, desperate to gain the upper hand. However, I merely found myself losing more ground.

I supposed there was a downfall to Ilyan's change. Before now, my ruthlessness was the only thing that paired me equally with my brother. Now I had nothing. My magic was no match for him, for a man desperate for retaliation, for revenge. Especially with me standing in the way of that.

Grinding my teeth, I attacked in repetition, backing up toward the stairwell, only to find the long tunnel caved in.

The imminent collapse was beginning. This low in the caverns, we would be trapped. If I couldn't run, I would have to fight.

Desperate man or not, I knew I could beat him.

The caves shifted underneath our feet as Ilyan attacked again, his barrage of magic coming as fast as mine, rushing around me while I battled him, my own attacks beginning to make contact.

I could do this.

I attacked again, my magic straining in exertion as he stuttered once again. The shield I placed around me the second he had disappeared was just enough to render his attack useless.

Turning toward him with a fling of my hair, I smiled, knowing just what I was going to do.

"Two can play this game," I taunted, magic surging as I pushed myself into the black of a stutter.

His yell of surprise followed me into the void as I appeared behind him with a *pop*, a smile spreading wide as my magic surged. I slammed my hand into his back, right behind his heart. One sharp point of magic moved into him before he could stop me, the dagger of my energy cutting into bones and lungs to reach his heart, to rip into it.

I could feel his blood pulse against my magic as it invaded him, his own power attempting to retaliate as he gasped in pain. The sound of his desperate inhale was beautiful, but as useless as any chance of retaliation.

"You end now," I whispered into his ear, wrapping my free arm around his waist as I held him still, his body shaking with pain as I held him against me.

With one tap of my fingers on his back, the magic that had already stabbed into him erupted. The tiny sliver of my power turned into a bomb, a powerful blast that ripped into muscles and flesh, tearing his once proud organ to shreds in a detonation that shot through his chest, heart, and bones.

Blood sprayed from him in a fan of red and white that painted the stone wall before us as though it was a canvas. Bits of him dripped from the stone as another *boom* shook the cave. Everything began to give way, boulders falling around us as everything started to collapse.

When I released him, Ilyan fell to the ground, his body a lifeless heap of bones and flesh, all that was left of his life covering the stone he would be buried under.

"Take your own advice, Ilyan: regret nothing," I hissed as I stared at him, feeling the icy water of the river spray over my back as yet another piece of the cave fell into it. "We both should have learned that long ago."

I turned from him, ready to stutter out of this graveyard and into freedom. A freedom I have never had. A freedom I never thought I could obtain.

But nothing felt right anymore now that he wasn't here. Nothing felt like the freedom I was searching for was supposed to.

It felt dead, my soul as lifeless as his, my muscles a tense pain as the weight of what had just happened, of what I had just done, hit me.

Of what I had lost.

Ilyan had been the only one to believe in me, to shelter me in my misery... in my loss. And when he had needed me, I had destroyed him.

I already knew. This action I would regret.

"Regret nothing," I whispered again, willing the words to be true as I turned back toward him right as another stone fell around him, so close it almost crushed him.

"Regret nothing!" I practically screamed, running toward

my brother as the ceiling began to come down on top of us, burying us both.

The sound of the stone was a reverberation in my soul as the world turned to nothing but blackness, my vision only stone, my skin covered in the icy cold of water.

I wasn't even sure if I had made it.

33

JOCLYN

"WE SHOULD STARGAZE," I whispered, nestling into Ilyan's collarbone as the water splashed against my toes. "Should we come back tonight when it's not so hot and see what we can find?"

"You mean the constellations?" Ilyan asked in his deep Czech accent, running his hand over the bare skin on my shoulder.

"Yes," I gasped, my voice shaking under the gentle tickle of his touch.

"I believe, if I am not mistaken," he whispered, "that our constellations are different than yours."

"No Orion?" I asked in shock as I sat up and leaned over him, his long hair spread out around him.

"We have an angry Trpaslík by the name of Brunard."

"Close enough," I sighed as I sunk back down next to him, the sand suddenly feeling cold against my skin, the air like ice.

I gasped at the change, an outburst that went unnoticed by Ilyan. He only sighed and held me closer, the dream shattering.

I lay there, nestled against him, everything growing tighter and more uncomfortable as the chill departed, leaving me again in the warm sun. Although, this time, I was aware of where I was and what was happening.

"Do you think we will ever find each other again?" he asked, wiggling his hand through the sand to find mine.

"I hate when you ask that," I told him, turning away from the boiling heat of the sand to face him, his blue eyes already bright as he stared into mine. "It's not like you. And it normally means that I'm going to wake up soon, and the dream will be over."

Ilyan smiled sadly at me, but he did not respond. He only wiggled closer over the sand, moving until his body was flush with mine, his skin cold against the sunbaked heat I was plagued by. I tried to ignore the way my heart pulsed painfully at that, at the way my magic didn't react to his proximity. It was a reminder that he wasn't really there, and this wasn't really a Tôuha.

"I think you'll find me again," he said, his voice soft as he pressed his lips against my forehead.

My stomach swooped pleasurably from the contact, before the pain came. I closed my eyes against it, focusing on the touch, on the moisture of his lips, on the warmth, only to have it all disappear.

The weight of him, the scent of him—it all left as something pulled me out of my dream, leaving me lying on the beach as always, surrounded by the blanket of warmth that this part of France held at this time of year.

Everything was too warm. The sun was too warm. The sand was too warm. The heat was everywhere, surrounding me on all sides. Regardless, I didn't dare move. I didn't dare open my eyes and let reality wipe away the last of the dream. And part of me didn't care. It was a good dream, the best I'd had in a while, and I was content to let it linger. Besides, lying here in the sand with the sun beating down on me and the sound of the waves and the birds was too comforting.

It was probably why I had fallen asleep.

Not that I minded.

That was why I was out here every day, sleeping, dreaming, refusing to move on, or so Wyn said.

I just wished it was as easy as that. I couldn't move on. My soul wouldn't let me.

Groaning, I rolled over onto my stomach, cringing as the sun-boiled sand pressed against the bare skin on my arms and legs.

"Ouch," I groaned, letting my magic flare just enough to cool the sand, but not too much. Cold sand and warm sun weren't a great combination, either. Trust me; I had tried it before.

"Aunt Joclyn!" a tiny voice screamed through the calm, shattering the illusion I had created and scaring one of the little seabirds that had parked himself in the reeds. The little red-breasted thing took off with a disgruntled tweet.

Still, I lay in place, my eyes closed as I listened to the quick, running feet joining the desperate pants of the child. I wasn't foolish enough to open my eyes just yet. I had gotten a face full of sand before.

"Aunt Joclyn," the tiny little boy said again, his feet carrying him right to me. As expected, he showered me in sand.

I wished there was a way to keep the darn stuff out of my nose.

Desperately huffing in an attempt to expel the sand, I sat up, wiping granules out of my face, facing the towheaded boy who was now laughing hysterically, his arms clutched around his middle.

"I got you!" he said in hysterics, stomping his feet in the sand.

"Oh! You think you got me, did you?" I teased, moving to my hands and feet as I faced him, seeing his humor fade almost immediately. "We'll see about that."

With a squeal from my adorable nephew, I tackled him to the ground, pinning him in the hot sand and tickling him. The boy squealed for mercy between his adorable, squeaky laughs.

"Aunt Jos," he panted, barely able to get the words out between giggles. "Please!" More laughs. "Stop!"

"Stop?" I teased, only tickling him more. "You want me to stop, Cail? What is this nonsense?"

Cail giggled further, now desperate to wiggle away from me, his continued pleas only becoming more jumbled from his laughter.

"Aunt Jos!" he practically screamed between laughs. "Please!"

"Okay, okay," I said, moving back to a sitting position, finally freeing the kid from the torture of tickling. "If you insist."

Cail only rolled his eyes, his lips twitching into a smile as his dark eyes twinkled mischievously. I knew that look. At five years old, he was already hungry for more. He was too much like his father.

"Do you really want to go again?" I asked, leaning forward and wiggling my fingers toward him menacingly. "Because I can go all day."

"No!" Cail cried, wiggling across the sand away from me.

"Okay, I guess I'll let you off the hook ... this time." I smiled at him, moving to lie down, but Cail jumped back to his feet, grabbing my arm and pulling.

"You can't keep being a mopey loner, Aunt Joclyn!"

"Did you hear that from your mom?" I asked, affronted.

He ignored me.

"You have to come with me."

"And why would I? I like being a mopey loner." Ignoring his violent pulls against my shoulder, I lay back down, closing my eyes, content to stay here for the rest of the day.

"But you can't," Cail continued, whining now like the true five-year-old he was. "The king is here."

Now my eyes snapped open—well, just one of them—as I peered at the kid from where I lay, his tiny frame all shadowed black from the sun behind him.

"You mean *Uncle Ryland*?" I asked, trying to retain the laugh at hearing Cail refer to his favorite uncle as "the king." Even though he was, that was far too out of character for this kid.

"No, the king. Daddy says I have to call him king now, and that, if I don't, Uncle Ryland … I mean … The king will get really mad and might even order his guard to cut off my head."

This time, I couldn't help laughing.

"First," I said, standing to face Cail as I wiped the sand off my T-shirt and jeans, "your dad is just messing with you, as he does," I added under my breath. "If you call Ryland the king, he might not be too happy." I smiled at him before turning toward the large estate that was now home while Cail stood still, looking affronted for a moment before he ran to catch up to me.

"But he is the king …" he protested, obviously scared of what Ryland would do. I just ruffled his hair and kept walking, glad he was keeping up.

"He is, but his brother didn't like being called king, either." My heart tensed . I had said the sentence so simply I hadn't even realized what I was saying until it was too late.

"The great Ilyan?" he asked.

I could only nod.

I hated that title. I had a feeling he would, too.

Cue more chest palpitations.

"Second," I began, desperate to move the conversation away from that topic, "Míra isn't going to cut off your head. And you better be nice to her ..." I had a feeling she was going to become more than his guard before the end of the year. I never could have seen that coming.

"So ..." Cail started to ask as we approached the towering manor, the old home set atop a stone ledge, just as Ilyan had built it, "if I call him Uncle Ryland, I won't die?"

"You won't die," I promised, crossing a finger over my heart for good measure.

Cail looked up at me, pressing his lips into a tight line as he contemplated that before coming to a very stoic and difficult, judging by the look on his face, decision. A single nod of agreement was his lone sign of understanding.

After I returned his nod, we both turned toward the house to see Frain and Chyline, who stood near the base of the stone steps that led up it, the pair happily chatting with Míra. The beautiful woman stood in shorts, combat boots, and a tank top, looking more like a punk teenager than the badass guard she was. She laughed at something the Firsts said, her sheet of blonde hair shimmering with the movement.

"See?" I said, smiling at Míra as she turned and waved at us enthusiastically. The beautiful woman she had grown into certainly was one I was proud of. "Míra is not scary. Now get. And go bug your grandmothers. I am sure they have presents for you."

Cail made a face at me before he took off to where the two older women welcomed him eagerly. They were always spoiling him a bit more than they should. Sometimes, I was worried he was too pampered. I guessed it was a good thing he had Thom as a dad.

That ought to keep him grounded.

"Hey, Míra," I greeted as she walked up to me, her large boots slipping awkwardly in the sand. "Ryland's already inside, I take it?"

"Yeah," she answered, greeting me with her trademark hug and dual kisses, something I had never gotten used to, even after living in Prague for over ten years before we had found Ilyan's house. "Something came up, and he needed Rinax's opinion."

"Oh?" I asked, surprised. "Is that the best excuse he could come up with for a visit? No one really needs Rinax's opinion, you know."

That man was far too grumpy for his own good, something Míra understood. She chuckled in agreement before looking sharply toward the inland, her eyes narrowing.

"It's probably just a gull, Míra," I said, knowing her protective tendencies, not just for Ryland, but for all of us. She had burned down one of the outhouses before, and I really didn't need to repair anything else. It always got the villagers talking.

She didn't seem to hear. She had already gone into full guard mode.

With a shrug, I left her, something she didn't seem to even notice, and started up the stairs, following the clear pull of Ryland's magic inside the house.

I had only made it halfway up the stairs before Wyn and Thom appeared at the door. Thom looked thoroughly entertained as he and Wyn laughed over something. I was already sure what it was.

"You need to stop pestering him, Thomas," Wyn said with a barely concealed laugh, putting her hands on her hips and making her already protruding belly that much more noticeable. "If you teach him to be scared of every—"

"I'm not teaching him to be scared, Wynifred," Thom retorted, shoving his hands in his leather jacket. "I'm teaching him to be a man." He pounded his chest.

The whole thing was so ape-like that Wyn broke out into laughter, something that only seemed to upset her more.

Her laughter turned into quite a few spluttering sounds, her hands flailing like crazy before she half-screamed and stomped away, right down the stairs toward me.

I looked up at her then at Thom behind her. He was now making wild gestures of pregnant bellies and crazy ears. I would like to say his charades were a warning, but he looked so ridiculous I laughed, which Wyn did not miss.

She looked between Thom and me in increased anger before turning on me, wagging a finger in the air like an old man. "Don't you dare tell me you had some part in this," she scolded.

"No," I said, not even trying to restrain the laugh anymore. "I told Cail his dad was full of it. That being said, you've gotta let those two figure stuff out. You keep shielding him, and they are gonna have issues. He's got to figure out his dad is a loon."

Wyn stopped two steps above me, her hands still on her hips, belly sticking out toward me. She stared at me, the angry pregnant woman slowly fading until a smile started to peek out.

"His dad is a loon," she said, the smile taking full control now.

"Biggest one I know." I took the last two steps as one, letting my arm drape over Wyn's shoulders as I turned her back toward the house. "And you love him for it."

"I do," she sighed, love dripping from her voice as it usually did when she talked about Thom.

"Good," I sighed, too, my stomach tensing from what I was about to say. "So, now let's calm down, shall we? Let those pregnancy hormones take a break."

"Joclyn," she snapped.

I ignored her, plowing ahead as we moved through the large wooden double doors and into the grand tiled entry hall where Thom, who stood with a very dapper Ryland at the back of the room, looked up at the sound of our approach. Ryland smiled before going back to whatever conversation the two brothers were wrapped up in.

"If you don't, I'm going to make you watch Firefly again," I continued, keeping my voice down, although not by much. "I'll even watch it with you."

Now she laughed loudly and obnoxiously, her own arm winding around my waist. "Wait. Are you meaning to say that you are going to stop sleeping on the beach all day and living in the past?"

I probably deserved that dig after bringing up pregnancy hormones.

"I'm not living in the past," I groaned, still foolishly trying to stay quiet. It *was* foolish, especially considering Wyn wasn't even trying. She was going to drive this home. I wasn't going to get away from this conversation that easily. "I'm following my soul."

"Uh-huh," Wyn said with a laugh. "You keep telling yourself that, and I'll keep pretending that Styx isn't considered classical music now."

"Speaking of that ..." I began.

"Of Styx?"

Ignoring her, I asked, "Why did you tell Cail I was being a 'mopey loner'?"

"Because you *are* being a mopey loner!"

I opened my mouth to retort, but between Wyn's wide smile and the deep burly laughs that echoed over the tiles, I was silenced. Ryland and Thom had left their conversation to join us. Thom smiled smugly, walking next to his much taller and much burlier little brother. The muscular man was dressed in a grey pinstriped suit, something that had become more common on him in the last few years. Always dapper. It would be a good look if he didn't have that mischievous "kid in a candy store" look.

"On, no," I groaned, the words clearly heard by Ryland, who only laughed more loudly.

"Hey, mopey loner," he said with a smile, his curls bouncing as he stepped up to us.

"Don't you dare start," I warned.

He didn't seem to care. He just smiled more brightly, pulling me into him as he held me.

"Hey, Jos," he whispered inside the cave he had created with our bodies.

"Hey, Ry," I said back as I pulled away. "Or, should I say, *Your Majesty.*"

His face wrinkled while Thom began to laugh hysterically, folding over as his laughter crippled him.

"It's been years, Thom, years," Ryland grumbled, running his hands through his hair as he glared at his brother. "Is this ever going to stop?"

"You are obviously underestimating your brother," Wyn said, her own laugh finally joining in.

"Even I know better, Ry."

"This is unfair—"

"Because you are king?" Thom interrupted Ryland.

Ry's chest puffed out in irritation as Thom smacked his brother on the forearm.

"I am beginning to regret being related to you," Ryland said with a laugh.

Thom pretended to look affronted before he stepped away, replacing the farce with his signature scowl. "Sorry, bud. You are stuck with me."

The four of us burst out into laughter, Wyn's ending with a gasp as her hands went to her abdomen. All eyes went to her as Thom became all business, rushing to his mate, his hands on her belly.

I watched them, a calm moving over the room as I felt their magic swell between them. I was sure Ryland could also feel it with the way he smiled and looked toward the door, knowing Míra was there.

"Do I need to ask if you have a date set yet?" I asked him, pulling his focus from the door and to me, his eyes instantly plunging into guilt.

"Ask what?" He couldn't make the words sound guiltier if he tried.

The failure of forced innocence made me laugh more, but it was a sound that was silenced when the large entry doors opened with a snap, pulling us from the conversation as Míra rushed into the entry hall, fear on her face.

All four of us turned toward her, the joy sapping from the room due to the urgency that she brought with her.

"Sir," Míra said directly to Ryland, her voice rattling, "there is a reporter here—"

"A reporter!" Wyn shrieked excitedly, bouncing on the balls of her feet. "Oooo ... We can have some fun with this one. Come on, Thom!"

Thom eagerly followed his bride toward the door, only to be stopped by one uplifted hand from Míra, her eyes still focused on Ryland in some desperate, silent conversation.

The man himself stepped right up to his guard, leaning toward her as she whispered some instruction that sent his eyes into a wide-eyed shock. Then the shock stayed as he turned back toward us, his wide blue eyes focused right on me.

I stared at him, my heart thundering in my chest as I waited for him to say something, for him to end the stress-filled knot that had suddenly taken control of my gut.

"What?" I asked when I couldn't take it any longer, finally drifting my eyes from Ryland to Míra, who was grinning like a loon.

That was a bad combo.

"It must be something really traumatizing if Míra is smiling like that," I continued, hoping to prod Ryland out of his stupor.

His expression remained, and I really started to freak out.

"Come on, Ry; don't do this to me."

"How's your French?" he asked before he turned, opening the door to welcome a lanky man in whose chin was covered with greying stubble, wearing a shabby suit and carrying a very large leather satchel slung over his shoulder. The man was the epitome of a reporter.

"Bonjour!" Ryland announced, guiding the man in as he rattled off in the language I hadn't quite mastered yet. I supposed, if they spoke slowly, I would be okay. "... This is her," was all I caught, possibly because he said it while pointing at me.

My stomach sunk more.

The man's eyes widened as he looked at me as if he recognized me. The look was unnerving.

Without thinking, I took a step back.

"Madame," he said politely as he nodded once, something I hadn't seen since I had walked away from Imdalind and left

Ryland to rule in my stead almost fifteen years ago now. "You are Joclyn Krul, formerly Despain, of the United States?" he finished in broken English.

"Yes." I was understandably wary, especially when his face lit up in excitement.

"I can't believe it," he began in French as rummaged through the large satchel he carried. "Everyone said I was crazy. No one at the office is going to believe me ..."

The rambling continued until the rummaging stopped. A piece of computer paper clutched in his shaking hand, he held it out to me, his eyes wide as he stared.

In one step, Ryland moved beside me, his hand light on my back as if he were trying to support me.

I tried to wiggle away from him, only to freeze at the sight of the paper that was now waving before me. What I had mistaken for a plain white piece of paper was actually a picture. A picture of a man in a hospital bed, his blond hair cut short, blue eyes oddly vacant.

"Ilyan!" I gasped, my legs shifting under me in shock.

Ryland held me in place as I heard Wyn and Thom's gasp somewhere in the distance. I couldn't look away from the photo, away from the man I had spent more than a decade mourning.

"It can't ..." I began, all words lost as I stepped toward the man and ripped the photo from his hands in desperation to know for sure if it was him.

"He says his name is Ilyan Krul," the reporter began, his voice as distanced as Wyn's soft sobs. "He was first admitted to Hospital Isidia in the Ukraine about fifteen years ago. From what I know, he was in a coma for over thirteen years. It's only been recently that he has awoken, and he speaks of nothing but a woman by the name of Joclyn Krul and this house. I have never met the man before; I only heard of him because of the oddities in the story."

"What oddities?" Wyn asked as she wrapped her arm around the other side of me, looking at the picture. The protective best friend vibe was coming on strong.

I knew what she was thinking.

That it was a trick.

A trap.

Something.

That this couldn't be.

But it had to be.

It just *had* to be.

"His heart, for one," the man continued. "It is not his own. It had been transplanted when he arrived at the hospital, although we know not how because he had no scar. For the other, he does not age."

I could barely stand now. Luckily, Ryland and Thom held me up as the picture drifted from my fingers, falling to the floor where Ilyan's face continued to stare up at me.

"Where is he?" I asked the reporter, my voice hard as I narrowed my eyes at him. "Do you have a map?"

The man looked at me in shock before he turned once again to his satchel, rummaging through papers.

545

"Jos, you can't," Ryland said in Czech, obviously intent on keeping his voice low.

"Can't what?" I returned as I turned back to the man, who now held out a map to me with shaking hands. "I'm going. You can come if you like."

"The hospital is there," the reporter said as I took the map, his finger pointing to a large intersection of roads in Kiev.

"Can you clean up the mess?" I asked Wyn, who was already giggling in excitement as I felt her magic surge.

"Tell Ilyan I say hi," she answered, smiling at the reporter who was now looking between us all in differing stages of confusion and horror.

"Ryland?" I asked, holding out my hand.

Ry sighed, knowing he couldn't stop me, and ran his hands through his hair, taking one glance at Míra before he picked up the picture of Ilyan and gripped my hand. One nod was all the answer I needed.

With a surge of my magic, I pulled both of us through the world beneath ours and right to the hospital in Kiev, a shield already wrapped around us.

The lobby of the massive building was a flurry of activity, shoulders already running into us, confused faces glancing back as they tried to understand what they had hit. Normally, I would care. Right now, I ignored them, grabbing Ryland's hand and pulling him into an alcove, leaving a line of confused people behind us, many beginning to snap at each other over their clumsiness.

"Jos," Ry hissed in a panic as I dropped the shield, "have you thought this through?"

"Do I think anything through?" I asked, my heart thundering in my chest as I walked away from him and right toward the large information desk. Well, I hoped that was what it was. The language written below it was kind of similar to Czech.

"Jos," Ryland moaned as he caught up to me, grabbing my arm and pulling me to a stop, "slow down."

"That's not going to happen," I said sarcastically, turning myself back toward the desk and trying to pull Ry with me. He was too muscular for that to happen, though.

"Do you even speak Ukrainian?" he asked, causing the eager thunder of my heart to drop.

He smiled smugly at my obvious answer and, with a deep breath, pulled me toward the desk, sliding his hand down to wrap around my own.

Normally, I would pull away, but I couldn't. I was too jittery, too scared, too nervous, and having that hand to hold on to was calming me down somehow. Well, it was at least making it feel like I wasn't going to suddenly explode.

"Is there a language you don't know?" I asked caustically, my nerves making me snappy.

"No," he retorted, his jaw hard, "because I don't spend all my time on a beach, dreaming of—"

"Someone who might be alive." The words felt oddly foreign.

My heart thundered as we finally reached the desk. Ryland

held the photo out to the kind-looking lady, and she said something in a deep, smooth voice. The woman took the picture and looked from me to the image, her eyes growing wider with each pass.

I looked at Ryland, desperate for some update, but his focus was only on the woman before us, his lips pressed into a tight line.

Silence passed. So much silence. And with each tick of the clock and each frantic look between us, I was growing more irritated. Finally, I couldn't hold it in anymore.

"Ilyan Krul," I finally said, pointing at the picture, shaking it at the woman. "Joclyn Krul." I pointed at me. "Ryland Krul." To Ryland.

With each word, her eyes grew wider until she shot to her feet, saying something quickly to us before she scuttled away from the desk, taking the picture with her.

"What did she say?" I hissed desperately to Ryland, my hand shaking in his.

"To wait here."

"Well, that's not promising," I grumbled, leaning over the desk and slamming my head into it, causing a few people around us to look at us in alarm.

"Just breathe, Jos," Ryland whispered, leaning over me. "Focus on something else. Try to find his magic—"

"If he had his magic, do you think he would still be here?"

"Just do it, Jos. It'll help to keep your mind focused," Ryland said as the woman began to scuttle back to the counter with a large, mahogany-skinned man behind her, dressed just as nicely as Ryland.

I stretched my magic out as Ryland had commanded as he and the nice man began to chatter in the quick beats of the unfamiliar language.

I tried not to focus on it, to let my mind relax as I moved through hallways, my mind open as I watched people walking calmly, nurses running madly, and people huddled together in panicked sobs.

The busy images I was moving through mixed with the loud noises of the lobby. Everything became a buzzing lull in my head as I continued through them. One hallway after another passed by me as I searched, looking for his magic, looking for anything that would lead me to him.

It wasn't until Ryland started yelling when I had reached the fifth floor and a heavily guarded room that I felt something. But it wasn't at all what I would have expected.

A spark so faint I almost missed it of Ovailia's magic.

It couldn't be.

I pushed my magic further, past the guards and right into the room where he sat on a bed, propped up on pillows, talking to a doctor, and just as upset as Ryland was now.

Ilyan.

It was him. Even without the magic, even without his hair, it was him.

My heart almost stopped at the sight of him there. Everything in me exploded, desperate to reach him.

I pulled my magic back into me, my vision returning to the lobby just as two guards walked right up to us, their hands already on their guns.

The sight was comical, and I almost laughed at it, but I had something more important pushing into me.

"I found him," I said to Ryland, pulling his focus from the man who was just as upset as he was.

"Good. Let's go."

I turned away from him, ready to run, but he just grabbed my hand, his need clear.

"We don't have time for that, Jos," he hissed, his magic surging alongside mine. "We have to go. Screw the repercussions."

"Okay, boss," I said as I stuttered, pulling us from the deteriorating situation in the lobby and right into the room I had seen Ilyan in.

I moved fast, freezing the doctor Ilyan had been talking to in place as Ryland blocked the door.

Chest heaving, I turned toward the bed, my heart thundering in my chest as I faced the man I had dreamed about every day and every night for fifteen years.

His eyes full of tears, his face broke out in a smile.

"Mi lasko."

ALSO BY REBECCA ETHINGTON

THE WORLD OF IMDALIND

The Imdalind Series

Kiss of Fire, Imdalind #1

Eyes of Ember, Imdalind #2

Scorched Treachery, Imdalind #3

Soul of Flame, Imdalind #4

Burnt Devotion, Imdalind #5

Brand of Betrayal, Imdalind #6

Dawn of Ash, Imdalind #7

Crown of Cinders, Imdalind #8

Ilyan, Imdalind #9

The King of Imdalind Series

Spark of Vengeance, Book 1

Flare of Villainy, Book 2 (Coming 2019)

Books 3-6 TBA

THE CIRCUS OF SHIFTERS

The Phoenix's Ashes Series

Rise of the Witch, Book One

Fall of the Dragon, Book Two

Flight of the King, Book Three

Flame of the Phoenix, Book Four

The Dragon Queen Series

Rising Flame (coming March 2019)

Books 2-4 TBA

THE OTHER WORLDS

The Through Glass Series

Book One: The Dark

Book Two: The Blue

Book Three: The Rose

Book Four: The Cut

Book Five: The Light (Coming 2019)

Book Six: The Ascended (Coming 2019)

Of River and Raynn, The Series

The Catalyst: Act One (Rereleases 2019)

The Requisite: Act Two (Coming 2019)

ABOUT THE AUTHOR

Rebecca Ethington is an internationally bestselling author with almost 700,000 books sold. Her breakout debut, The Imdalind Series, has been featured on bestseller lists since its debut in 2012, reaching thousands of adoring fans worldwide and cited as "Interesting and Intense" by *USA Today's Happily Ever After Blog*.

From writing horror to romance and creating every sort of magical creature in between, Rebecca's imagination weaves vibrant worlds that transport readers into the pages of her books. Her writing has been described as fresh, original, and groundbreaking, with stories that bend genres and create fantastical worlds.

Born and raised under the lights of a stage, Rebecca has written stories by the ghost light, told them in whispers in dark corridors, and never stopped creating within the pages of a notebook.

Find me online
www.rebeccaethington.com
contact@rebeccaethington.com

ACKNOWLEDGMENTS

Thank you for sticking with me through this journey – for supporting me when life made it impossible to write, and each word hurt.
For cheering me on when everything felt like it was falling apart.

I wish I had words to thank you, for letting you know what each and every one of you meant. But I don't – they'll come soon.

So, for now, thank you for reading, for loving and for sharing.

I simply have the best friends, the best family and the best fans!

JOCLYN AND ILYAN'S STORY IS NOW COMPLETE

AVAILABLE FOR PURCHASE NOW!

See How It All Ended